# LANTERN ACROSS THE SEA:

## The Genoese Arbalester

Michael A. Ponzio

This is a work of historical fiction, although most places and historically documented incidents are real. Except for actual historical figures, the names and characters are either the products of the author's imagination or are used fictitiously. Any resemblance to actual persons, living or dead, businesses, companies, events, or locales is entirely coincidental.

Copyright © 2022   Michael A. Ponzio
Trinacria Publishing Company
BISAC: Fiction / Historical / General
All rights reserved.
ISBN: 978-1-7349723-1-3

## ACKNOWLEDGMENTS

This novel is dedicated to the late Egidio Ponzio of Linguaglossa, Sicily.

*Grazie mille* to:

Proofreader and editor: Nancy Soesbee

Developmental Editor: Pamela Sourelis

This novel was enhanced by my wife, Anne Davis Ponzio.

## ATTRIBUTIONS

Attribution 1. The sailboat image above is used to indicate a scene or time change in this novel. It is a representation of Esmeray's fishing boat. From Wikimedia Commons, the free media repository. Attribution: Jadvinia at Polish Wikipedia. Changes made from the original: one of two images used. Jadvinia at Polish Wikipedia, the copyright holder of this work, hereby publishes it under the following licenses:
https://creativecommons.org/licenses/by-sa/2.5/deed.en.
Permission is granted to copy, distribute, and/or modify this document under the terms of the GNU Free Documentation License.

Attribution 2. Illustration of Harbor of Genoa, Chapter XXI: View of Genoa by Christoforo de Grassi (after a drawing of 1481); Galata Museo del Mare, Genoa - Artist: Christoforo de Grassi. File: Genova 1481 (copy 1597).jpg - Wikimedia Commons.

This work is in the public domain in its country of origin and other countries and areas where the copyright term is the author's life plus 100 years or fewer.

Attribution 3. Chapter II - The illustration of a Genoese nave is used to represent the actual ship The *Paradisio*. Used by permission of the artist, David Bocquelet, from his Naval Encyclopedia. MedievalShipsnaval-encyclopedia.com)https://naval-encyclopedia.com/about.php.

## HISTORICAL BASIS

Before the internet, I studied history from books and papers written by scholars. So, it surprised me to find a rare bit of history as I glanced through my mother's Italian cookbook. The author dismissed the popular legend that pasta was introduced to Italy by Marco Polo from China. "Thirteen years before Marco Polo returned from China, a will dated 1279, bestowing a basketful of dry macaroni, was recorded in the city archives of Genoa. The will was written by Ponzio Bastone, a military man and a sailor, and indicated the great worth of pasta. From the 13th to the 16th centuries, dried pasta was the [Mediterranean] sailor's sustenance while at sea. It was cooked with lard and vegetables if they were available." [1]

Other sources stated that "The Genoese notary, Ugolino Scarpa, compiled a list of the effects of a Genoese soldier, an *arbalester*, a crossbower (sic), Ponzio Bastone. Included in the inventory of possessions was *Una bariscela plena de macaroni* (a barrel full of macaroni)." [2]

This example from the sailor's will was to document that Italians had pasta before Marco Polo returned to Venice. However, over a thousand years before Polo went to China, the ancient Etruscans and Romans made a pasta called *lagane*, which evolved into lasagna.

The quote from my mother's cookbook was all the inspiration I needed to envision the adventures of Ponzio Bastone, an arbalester, a marine, a sailor, during the exciting period of the maritime Republic of Genoa in the thirteenth century.

---

[1] https://www.thejournalnj.com/columns/lets-dish-lets-talk-about-pasta/ August 17, 2020.

[2] https://growinfallinfoyo.home.blog/2019/07/17/you-never-feed-the-badderz-pasta-shirt/August17, 2020.

## AUTHOR's NOTE

To provide a richer experience, the reader may want to "pronounce" as they read the Italian words using the phonetics as follows:

Amilcare is pronounced as: Ah-meel-ka-ray.

Ciciri, chickpeas, is pronounced as: Che-che-ree.

Ponzio Bastone is pronounced as: Pone-zee-o Bah-sto'-nay.

Esmeray is pronounced as: Ez-mer-ay.

Esmeray's nickname Esme is pronounced as: Ez-may.

Genoese, people of Genoa, is pronounced as: Jen-oh-ee-say.

Lucianu is pronounced as: Loo-chee-ah-noo.

Nave, a type of sailing ship, is pronounced as: Na'-vay.

Michael A. Ponzio

## Table of Contents

| | | |
|---|---|---|
| CHAPTER I | ISLAND of CHIOS 1277 AD | 9 |
| CHAPTER II | EMPERIOS | 21 |
| CHAPTER III | NAVE PARADISIO | 27 |
| CHAPTER IV | CAPTAIN'S DINNER | 35 |
| CHAPTER V | MOUNT ETNA, SICILY | 39 |
| CHAPTER VI | CORSAIRS | 49 |
| CHAPTER VII | CONSTANTINOPLE 1277 AD | 57 |
| CHAPTER VIII | THE ASSASSIN | 69 |
| CHAPTER IX | THE SEA OF MARMARA | 73 |
| CHAPTER X | CRETE | 83 |
| CHAPTER XI | CATANIA, SICILY | 93 |
| CHAPTER XII | RIPOSTO, SICILY | 103 |
| CHAPTER XIII | ISLAND of VULCANO | 117 |
| CHAPTER XIV | MALLORCA | 129 |
| CHAPTER XV | THE SILK MERCHANT | 139 |
| CHAPTER XVI | ALMERIA | 151 |
| CHAPTER XVII | HAMPSHIRE, ENGLAND | 161 |
| CHAPTER XVIII | RETURN TO MALLORCA | 167 |
| CHAPTER XIX | LA LANTERNA | 177 |
| CHAPTER XX | GENOA | 187 |
| CHAPTER XXI | PALACE OF THE SEA | 197 |
| CHAPTER XXII | THE BLOCKADE | 205 |
| CHAPTER XXIII | THE ENCOUNTER | 215 |
| CHAPTER XXIV | FAVIGNANA | 225 |
| CHAPTER XXV | PALERMO | 231 |
| CHAPTER XXVI | MESSINA | 247 |
| CHAPTER XXVII | RIPOSTO | 259 |
| CHAPTER XXVIII | SICILIAN FIRE | 271 |
| CHAPTER XXIX | RETURN TO FAVIGNANA | 283 |
| CHAPTER XXX | SIEGE OF MESSINA | 289 |

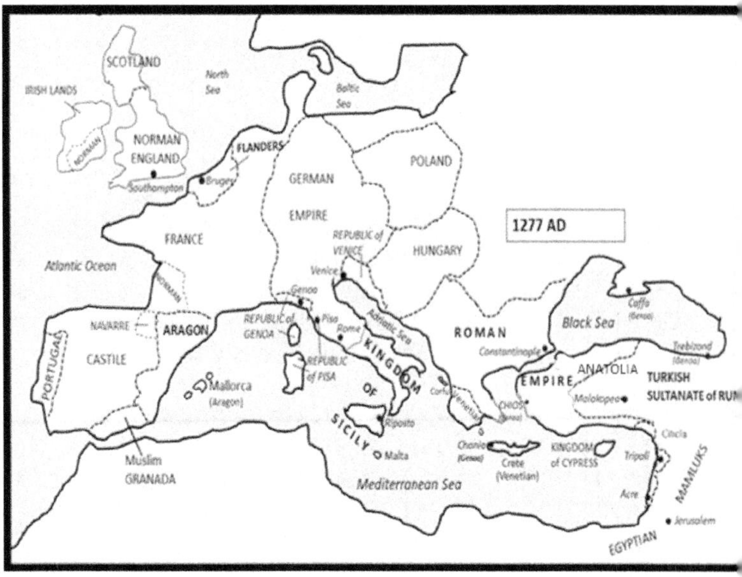


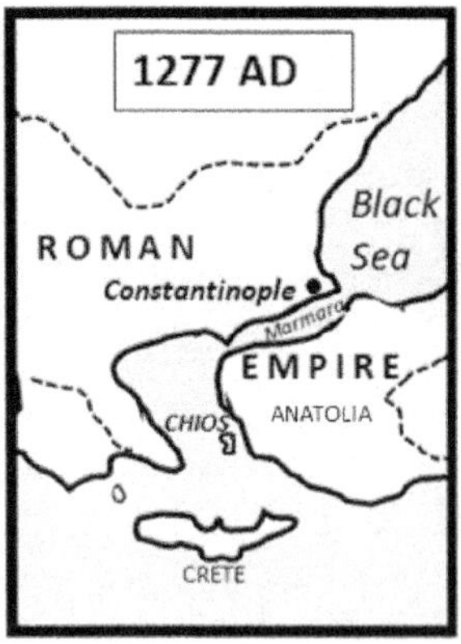


Island of Chios and Genoese Alum Mines

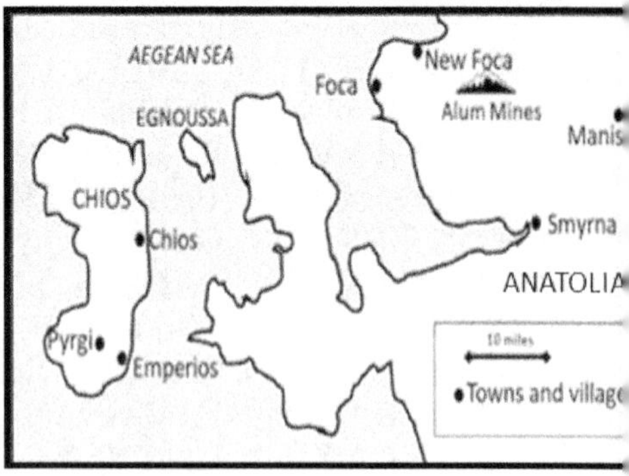

## CHAPTER I  ISLAND of CHIOS 1277 AD

Esmeray waited for her father as the sailboat beckoned, the vessel appearing suspended in pure air as it floated atop the clear Aegean waters. The sun was a glorious companion, rising above the Anatolian mainland, her birthplace far to the east. A cool breeze lifted Esmeray's chestnut hair as she gazed across the small harbor, her dark brown eyes taking in the crystal waters lapping the black pebble beach.

Her passion for the sea was deep-rooted, as was her love for her father and mother. It had been six years since Esmeray had fled the village of Malakopea with her father, when during a raid, the Seljuk Turks had killed her mother and brother. Now it was only Esmeray, her father, and their single-masted fishing boat christened the *Aspasia*, after Esmeray's mother.

Suddenly, her attention was pulled from the sea by the crunch of footsteps on the volcanic stone beach, accompanied by a steady grinding. A *chorikos*, a village peasant, approached, leading a donkey hauling a two-wheeled cart full of large cloth sacks. Escorting him were her father and two Genoese soldiers. Her father laughed, "Esme, my beauty. I thought you would have raised the sail already. You are always so eager to be on the sea!"

The entourage arrived at the fishing boat, a *trohantiras,* the archetypical sailboat used in the Aegean islands for fishing and littoral travel. Beached on the pebble shore, the stern floated on the perfectly transparent water. The chorikos halted the cart with its cargo of mastica gum, the profitable export of the island that was "worth its weight in gold." Most of the gum, its flavor and properties unique to the resin of the mastic trees on the island of Chios, was exported to the wealthy citizens of Constantinople and Alexandria to whiten teeth and freshen breath. Mastica was also used as a flavoring for wine and food and was consumed to cure stomach ailments and to help digestion.

The Genoese soldiers escorting the cart were crossbowmen, arbalesters, each equipped with a crossbow, a rectangular shield, and a quiver. Preparing to unload the cart, they slung off their equipment and placed it on the ground, still wearing shirts of chain mail. The small quivers held arrows only half the length of those used in longbows. The arrows, fixed with vanes of wood instead of feathers, the sharp ends sheathed with iron, were commonly called crossbow bolts.

Esmeray's previous contacts with Genoese soldiers had always been unpleasant. They had teased her with vulgar names and gestures, and she found them disgusting. The people of Chios considered the Genoese pirates because they took over their mastic plantations and forced them to work without fair compensation.

"We have a special job, daughter. The Genoese have hired me to transport the mastica to their ship, docked at Chios town."

Esmeray hastily gathered her hair behind and slipped on her woad blue headband, which partially covered her head, although she despised wearing a head covering, as custom dictated. As a chorikos, it was acceptable for her to wear only a headband, more practical for working women than wearing a coif.

She would rather be sailing with her hair flying in the wind, but today Esmeray and her father would miss the morning fish run. If time allowed, they could reach the traps before nightfall. Esmeray looked out to sea to study the gulls gliding on the drafts. Their paths clued her in the wind direction and confirmed, like most summer days, the Etesian wind was blowing from the northwest. Keenly aware of every turn of the coastline as well as the reefs and bars that might ground them, she envisioned their course, tacking with the northwesterly, then rounding two capes where the winds shifted to northerly. It would take three hours to sail to Chios town.

The arrival of the strangers intimidated Esmeray. She had rarely talked to any of the Latin foreigners, but she had overheard a few speaking Greek. When she had worked in the inland village of Pyrgi, the handful of Genoese soldiers she had encountered had accosted her with bawdy comments and lewd stares. She had always looked away, their brashness making her furious. Ignoring them, she had focused on the tedious work of cleaning the mastica by hand, comforted that she was among her work group of women. The foreign men's accents made them difficult to understand, but she assumed what little Genoese she had learned perhaps sounded just as incoherent to them.

She stepped back a few paces to a comfortable distance to watch the men, busy with their tasks. One of the Genoese removed a leather tube from inside his tunic. He slipped out a rolled parchment, a quill, and a small vial of ink, which he uncorked. As the other arbalester and her father transferred the sacks into their fishing boat, she observed the scribe counting and recording the inventory.

Esmeray studied the scribe. He had a prominent nose, which lent him a robust look. She was pleased by his trimmed dark beard and mustache; many of the foreigners had unkempt, shaggy facial hair. In Malakopea, the village of her youth, the people's eyes were brown or gray. The blue of his eyes mesmerized her, and she delighted in the color's transformation from woad to the aquamarine of the sea as he tallied and recorded the sacks of mastica.

Although her father had made no arrangements to match her, at sixteen, Esmeray was of the age for marriage. She was pretty, although as a working fisherman's daughter, today especially, her clothes did not add to her femininity. A loose tunic that fell above her knees hid her fit, slim figure. Under the tunic she wore pants, cut off to reach halfway down her shins. Esmeray was passionate about the sea, preferring sailing or tending their fish traps over thinking of men. She did not want to leave her father, and she sensed his wishes matched hers, but she was attracted to this stranger.

Her father had not told her of today's special task. When they brought the fish in to sell at the market, she usually wore shoes and dressed in a long tunica that hid her ankles. But now, in a fisherman's short tunic, cut off pants and with bare feet, she felt exposed. He leaned close and whispered, "I am sorry. Just now they asked me to do this, but it will bring us needed coin." He handed her a pair of sandals. "Do these help?"

Esmeray loved her father too much to show her anger. She slipped on her sandals. "Thank you, Father."

He added, "Do you want to run down to the cottage and put on your tunica?"

She shook her head. The soldiers finished loading the sacks of mastic gum into the trohantiras. As the blued-eyed scribe tucked his parchment and writing kit inside his tunic, his partner waded to the side of the boat and hollered, "*Bastone, qui!*" Still putting away his parchment and pen, the marine grew impatient and shouted again, "*Bastone, qui!*" The scribe then tossed their shields, crossbows, and helmets to him, which the marine stored amidship in the open compartment next to the rowers' seats.

Her father had worked for a boatwright for over a year and after learning the craft, with Esmeray as his assistant, he had built his own trohantiras. Father and daughter had drawn closer during the long hours spent constructing the boat, and the years they partnered in fishing reinforced those bonds.

"Esme, you have the tiller," said her father. "Let's push out."

Esmeray hesitated as she stood at the bow. She was used to launching the boat herself, but the craft was now heavier with its load. As the three men gave the boat a shove, she jumped on board. The pebbles crunched under the bow as Esmeray nimbly moved along the boat to the stern. Her father grasped the top of the port side wale and hurdled aboard, as the crossbowmen pushed the boat further into the water and climbed in. The *Aspasia* was a wooden fishing boat eighteen *podes*, Greek feet, long. It was equipped with two oars, a rudder at the stern, and a single mast near the bow, and rigged with two lateen sails, one the mainsail and the other, a smaller jib.

The Genoese marines each manned an oar, and Esmeray steered as they rowed out of the small harbor. As the two men rowed facing Esmeray at the stern, she directed her gaze over their heads, avoiding eye contact with either of them. The boat glided into the sea, leaving the protected waters of the harbor, where Esmeray glanced at the red telltale fluttering from the top of the mast. She called out in Genoese, "Stow oars!"

The rowers paused, their oars suspended above the water. Her father was standing near the bow, holding a lanyard, waiting for her call to raise the sails. The men had never taken an order from a woman, so they lingered. Esmeray forced herself to breathe, hoping her anger wasn't obvious. She continued to avoid eye contact but could detect them in her peripheral vision. The soldier on the port side leered at her feet, legs, and every fold in her tunic. His grin was obscene, but the other mariner, the scribe—was not acting rudely—he smiled as if he was just amused, not trying to see through her clothes.

The man on her left continued to stare at her. Esmeray looked at her father, preparing to raise the jib. She repeated louder, "Stow oars!"

This time, they complied. The scribe uttered something unintelligible to Esmeray, causing both men to laugh.

Esmeray was furious as she assumed they were sharing a lewd remark about her. She stopped trying to hide her anger and reddened in displeasure. The marine leaned forward, insulting her in Genoese. Esmeray flashed a hard face at him, then quickly averted her eyes.

This time, instead of joking with the marine, the scribe yelled at him, as he moved his palms up and down, appearing to be weighing an object in each hand, "*Basta!* Enough!"

The marine's gaze didn't move from Esmeray, so the scribe added, "Amilcare. Amilcare! Stop it!"

The marine turned toward the scribe, snorted, then pointed his fist in the air, slapping his bicep with his other hand. He glanced toward the bow, receiving an angry look from Esmeray's father, who was raising the jib sheet.

Esmeray now knew the marine's name, Amilcare, but she really wanted to know the scribe's name. She recalled she had heard the marine call the scribe "Bastone" earlier. She had always found it disgusting how these foreign sailors hurled profanities at her and other chorikos women, so the first Genoese words they had learned were crude. In the past, the sailors had boasted about what they were going to do to her with their bastone as they gestured at their privates. Had the marine earlier called the scribe the slang word for penis used by the Genoese sailors? And now, Esmeray was curious why the scribe had reprimanded the marine.

The scribe caught her eye and said, "You are at the helm . . . Captain. I am sorry we did not follow your command."

Esmeray nodded without expression, not detecting any sarcasm. She hid her surprise he had spoken Greek, and with very little accent. Perhaps without Amilcare's stares, she could enjoy the fine sun and the salt air, although the strangers on board still dampened her usual joy in sailing. The seas were just turbulent enough to be a pleasant challenge.

She nodded to her father, who raised the mainsail. With both sails unfurled, using the northwesterly Etesian wind, Esmeray steered the boat northeast on a beam reach heading along the coast. Esmeray was skilled at sailing and knew the capabilities of their boat. The trohantiras's steering was less responsive, not because of the sacks of mastic. They weighed less than a haul of fish. The listlessness was because of the two extra passengers with their armor and weapons. After several minutes tacking along the coast, she adjusted and regained confidence in her craft.

Several miles northeast, they passed a cape where the wind shifted from nor'westerly to northerly. Esmeray hollered in Greek, "Bear to port!"

The boat came about and the mainsail boom swung. The scribe leaned back, but Amilcare ducked late, receiving a glancing blow to his head. He gave Esmeray a nasty look as she shared a laugh with the scribe.

Esmeray turned the boat to the northwest, using the northerly wind to beat on a port tack. Sailing on a course parallel to the shore, she tacked to follow the zig-zag direction of the island's coastline. The strait was an excellent location to set fish traps because schools of fish tracked the currents between Chios and the mainland. Esmeray could see gourds floating near the shore, marking where she and her father had located their wicker fish traps.

Her father glanced at her from the bow. "Esme, we will check them on the way back this evening. This morning, we will have an adventure. It's hard to remember the last time we were in Chios town."

Esmeray changed her tack to the northeast, sailing parallel to the shore to head for another cape. The two Genoese marines didn't carry on a conversation, which pleased Esmeray. She relaxed as they sailed on, with only the sound of the wind, waves, and seabirds. After another hour, Esmeray's father passed back a skin of diluted wine to share. Amilcare drank, then passed the skin to the scribe and said, "*Bastone, qui.*"

So, earlier, the marine had not called him a vulgar name. Bastone was the scribe's name. The marine had been saying, "Here, Bastone," to get him to toss the equipment they were loading onto the boat. Esmeray now knew the scribe's name.

Bastone smiled at Esmeray as he handed her the skin, appearing friendly, without hidden intent. Except for her father's loving smiles, she realized it was the first pleasant smile from a man she'd received since they had left Anatolia. After she made sure her father wasn't watching, she returned the smile, then said one of the few Genoese words she knew: "*Grazie!*"

He responded in Greek. "This drink . . . it has the mastica . . . the resin in it?"

Her cheer faded. "Um . . . no . . . I mean . . ." Esmeray became unnerved and clenched the tiller. Looking away, she turned her attention to steering the boat.

Esmeray feared he would think she had pilfered the mastica, although her father had traded fish for the resin. Stealing the valuable commodity, strictly regulated by the Genoese overlords, was a crime punishable by death. The Genoese had built fortifications around the villages, including the mastic groves because the resin was extremely valuable. The process of making small amounts of gum was labor intensive. Workers made special cuts in the bark of the mastic trees, then the harvesters patiently waited weeks before the crystal-clear drops of resin, the "tears of Chios," fell to the ground. The chorikos collected the milky white gum, meticulously cleaning off the dirt and leaves using tiny knives. The people of the island called the drops the tears of Chios because they did the painstaking work, but the Genoese gained the wealth from the mastica trade.

Although she didn't respond, his smile remained. He pulled a small lump of mastic gum from his tunic and started chewing it. He placed the tip of his index finger on his cheek, rotating the digit back and forth, and said in Genoese, "*Delizioso!*" Then in her native Greek, "*Nostimo!*" He handed her a piece.

She glanced toward the bow, saw her father looking away, so she took the gum.

"Do not worry," he said, "you are of Chios, mastica is your heritage. You may have a little here and a little there."

Esmeray chewed, releasing just a hint of the familiar pine and a salty-sweet flavor, which turned into a cool sensation. Her smile returned and her gaze matched his.

"It is wonderful, no?" He waved his hand over the sacks of mastic. "Did you know the nobles in Constantinople and Italy add it to their perfumes and face powders?"

Esmeray again made sure her father was not aware of their conversation, then shook her head.

"We're taking this mastica to our ship anchored at Chios town," said the scribe. "Its main cargo is alum, loaded in Foca on the mainland. On the voyage to deliver the alum, we will sell the mastica in ports of call across the Mediterranean." He patted a sack behind him. "The mastica is very profitable."

Esmeray wanted to explore Bastone's blue eyes, but she was preoccupied with navigating the sailboat as well as making sure her father didn't notice their conversation.

"I have called at the port of Chios town a few times," said Bastone, "but this was my first visit to the south part of the island, where the mastic trees grow. When I arrived here a few days ago, I detected a sweet aroma. It must be the trees?"

Esmeray's father glanced back. She waited for him to look ahead, then nodded. "Yes, the trees are in blossom."

"I see you like to chew the mastica gum, as do I. Do the people of Chios add mastica to food?" asked Bastone.

She paused, then said, "Yes, to make mastica bread."

"Have you eaten this kind of bread? Is it good?"

"No . . . I mean, I have not tasted the bread. They make it especially for the wedding couple to eat after their vows."

"Oh, I don't believe it. A young woman as beautiful as you, who has not tasted the mastica bread."

She blushed, and suddenly her father shouted, "Esme!"

Ahead, a long narrow boat rowed by six men darted out of a hidden cove on a course to intercept them. The Genoese grabbed their crossbows. Still seated, each arbalester inserted his foot in the stirrup at the end of the weapon, fastened the bowstring to the hook on his belt and then straightened his legs, pulling the string up to lock the trigger. Their adversaries were a hundred feet away, easy targets for crossbows.

"Don't kill them!" cried Esmeray.

"They are after the mastica," said Bastone. "Thieves!"

"But they will take revenge on us after you are gone!" screamed Esmeray. "I can outrun them. Please!"

She kept her bearing as the rowboat moved to intercept them. A man stood at the front with a long gaff. With the boat heavily laden, it would take all her skills as a helmsman to elude them. They were almost within range for him to hook their sailboat and Esmeray yelled, "Bear starboard!"

The trohantiras came about. All hands avoided the boom, then shifted their weight against the roll of the craft as they darted out of reach. Staying ahead of their pursuers, they neared another cape. A second boat filled with men appeared around the rocky promontory. As Esmeray had expected, the wind shifted again to the northwest, so she tacked hard to the starboard, leaving behind the rowing pursuers.

"One more!" shouted her father.

Another trohantiras was running with the wind toward them.

When the arbalesters inserted cross bolts, Esmeray yelled, "No! Don't shoot them!"

Reaching under the mainsail, Bastone removed Amilcare's crossbow bolt from his weapon, aimed his own bow, and loosed a menacing, iron tipped bolt. There was a thunk and crack of wood as his bolt lodged in the other boat's rudder, diverting the thieves from their intercept course. The helmsman struggled with the tiller, but the rudder would not answer his efforts. Esmeray urged the trohantiras forward, distancing the steerless boat, leaving the thieves in their wake. Suddenly, there was the clack of a crossbow trigger, accompanied by a shout from Bastone, followed by a scream from the pursuing boat. The bandits continued chasing them but gave up after they fell further behind the *Aspasia.*

They completed the rest of their trip in silence and arrived at the port of Chios. Esmeray worried about the retaliation that could occur when they returned to Emperios. At the mouth of the harbor, Esmeray's father furled the sails. The marines rowed the Aspasia to a three-masted *nave,* a large cargo ship, at anchor. Genoese sailors aboard recognized Bastone, hollering for him to tie up alongside. The crew hoisted the sacks of mastic gum to the ship, then pulled up Amilcare. Bastone waited for his partner to reach the nave's deck, offering several coins to Esmeray's father. "As we agreed, here are three silver *dinari.*" He glanced from Esmeray to her father. "I am very sorry. Perhaps the shot only wounded one of them."

The crew of the *Paradisio* lowered the rope, and Bastone placed his foot in the endloop. "Your daughter is quite a helmsman. I was hoping to show you my uncle's nave, but there is no time." As they hoisted him up, he found Esmeray's eyes. "What is your name?" She glanced at her father without answering. At the top, Bastone looked over the siderail. Esmeray knew her father had delayed arranging her marriage because he could not suffer to lose her. It would break her heart to leave him as well. She wondered if he sensed her intrigue with the Genoese scribe.

Her father yelled, "Esmeray! Her name is Esmeray!"

Lantern Across the Sea

*Trohantiras Aspasia*  *Nave Paradisio*

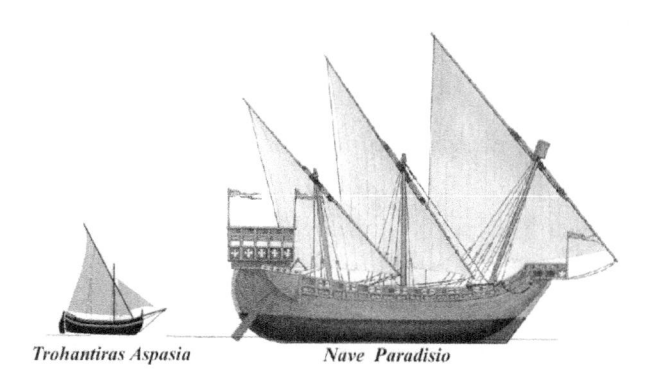

## CHAPTER II   EMPERIOS

Esmeray and her father rowed out of Chios harbor without conversation. She moved to the bow as he took the tiller, nodding for her to raise the sails. As Esmeray pulled on the line, she imagined what it would be like to sail on the magnificent Genoese nave.

They got under way, but her father was not cheerful as usual. Perhaps he was thinking about the men that had tried to rob them, and like Esmeray, feared the Genoese marine had killed one of them. Her father guided the trohantiras to run with the northwesterly wind on a broad reach, only a hundred feet from shore. "Esme, my dear, I want you to tie some gourds together and be ready to go overboard to swim ashore if we see the thieves again."

She obeyed him but said, "I'm not leaving you!" Tears filled her eyes as she relived the past when she had lost her mother. "We can outrun them."

In a few hours, they reached their fish traps without incident, pulling in a meager catch. After beaching the trohantiras on the south shore of the harbor, a quarter mile from the village of Emperios, they retrieved several fish, leaving the rest in a basket hanging in the water at the stern. They would sell them at the *agora*, the marketplace, in Pyrgi the next morning. Her father disconnected the tiller as Esmeray removed the oars to hinder theft of their boat. They climbed the dune to their home, shouldering the equipment.

As on most evenings, they ate in front of their stone cottage on a small hill outside the village. From the slight rise above the harbor, they overlooked the *Aspasia* hauled up on the black pebble beach. It was a pleasant and beautiful evening, with the waxing half-moon at the zenith. The gentle land breeze abated as the sun set. With the darkening sky, the pair said their goodnights.

As Esmeray drifted off to sleep, her mind was busy with worry. Perhaps the arbalester had missed? Or maybe he just wounded one of them? They hadn't seen the thieves on the trip returning from Chios town, but Esmeray recalled she had frequently seen a few of them around Emperios harbor or on the road to Pyrgi. Her concern erupted into a hot flash, bringing her wide awake. She realized that one bandit had made obscene remarks to her once at the agora and again at the harbor front, when her father had been out of earshot. Esmeray was unsettled, fearing he could have recognized her, thus knowing where she lived. It took her an hour to calm down before she could sleep.

Esmeray woke up feeling the chill of night. She searched for her linen covering, the light blanket she used on the summer nights. Her blanket was gone, and her sleeping tunic had been pulled up to her waist. She was half naked. In the dim light from the moon, two men were arguing as they stood above her. She detected a heavy scent of wine.

"I am first!"

"No, she is mine!"

One man held a bloody knife loosely at his side. Esmeray recognized him from among the men who attacked them on their way to Chios town.

Esmeray cried out, "Father!"

"I killed him for murdering my brother!" He glanced at the other man. "Go ahead, then."

The man untied the drawstring on his braies, dropping them to the floor. Esmeray tried to get up, but he shoved her back down. She tried to rake his eyes with her fingernails, but he turned his face away, then pushed her out of range with his longer arms. She squeezed her knees together as he fought to separate her legs. The second man leaned in and held his knife in Esmeray's face.

"Stop resisting!"

When Esmeray ceased struggling, he drew the knife away then slashed it across the neck of the man on top of her, who screamed in pain. Blood splattered on her face as the man groaned, clutched his neck, then fell to the side. A wet, gurgling sound replaced the groans. The other man ignored him, talking over the sounds.

"You will marry me. See. I have saved you from him! Tomorrow, we will start a new life. You will forget all of this."

Pulling down her tunic to cover herself, his crazed stare froze her in place. He was the man who had insulted her around the village. Motioning with his knife, he said, "You're covered with blood. Let's go down to the water to clean up."

It was too much for Esmeray, but she tried clearing her head to convince herself it was not a dream. She raised onto an elbow, the bloody stranger adding to her shock. Esmeray wavered as she stood, folding her arms to warm herself, chilled from the clamminess of her skin. Staggering to the next room, the sight of her father lying in a pool of blood, motionless, horrified her, triggering the sensation she was falling into a bottomless pit.

She stumbled out of the cottage. The killer followed her down to the water's edge where the trohantiras was beached, waiting as Esmeray waded into the water, leaned over, and splashed her face. The cool sea water diminished her shock and brought her back to reality. She burst out crying. But the next splash of water sharpened her thoughts. Likely, she could not outrun him, but perhaps with a head start . . .

Esmeray turned to face him, crossed her arms in front, grasping at her waist, and pulled her tunic up to remove it. The night chill, the water, her fear, all made it difficult to keep her voice steady enough to be convincing.

"We don't have to wait until tomorrow. Come in."

His eyes wide, he stood, took a step toward her, then hesitated, glancing around as if trying to determine where to put the knife. He kicked off his sandals and dropped the weapon next to them. He reached behind his neck with both hands and pulled his tunic over his head. When he regained his view, Esmeray was vaulting onto the bow of the sailboat. Running along the length of the boat, she grabbed the end of a rope on the deck and continued to the stern. There, the young woman slipped her bunched tunic over her neck, tied the rope round her waist, dove into the water, and resurfaced, swimming away. As she receded, a pair of gourds popped overboard, floating behind her into the dark.

Her father's murderer recovered from his surprise, not appearing to be in a hurry as he pushed the trohantiras into the water. The boat slowly floated from the shore as he climbed onto the deck, soon finding there were no oars and no tiller. When he moved to the stern, Esmeray had swum a few boat lengths distant and was steadily propelling herself toward the mouth of the harbor in the fading moonlight, melting into the sea.

With her disappearance, her father's killer snapped out of his rage looking confused, then realized he was standing there naked. Now suddenly fearing he would be implicated with his murderous assault if someone saw him on their trohantiras, he hurriedly swam to the beach, recovered his sandals, threw the knife far into the harbor, then ran toward Emperios.

The moon sank below the horizon as Esmeray continued to swim in the safety of the dark sea. She paused, looking back every few minutes. After ensuring she wasn't being followed, she used the gourds to float and rest. With the moon down, the sky was brilliant with stars. Using Polaris as her guide, she swam south parallel to the shore, its silhouette visible as the land blocked the stars on the western horizon. After exiting the harbor, she let the northerly current carry her further south, then swam to shore. She hiked up a low ridge, crossing the narrowest part of the small peninsula that formed the south side of the harbor.

When Esmeray reached the highest point, she saw among the faint starlight reflections on the water, the *Aspasia* slowly drifting in the harbor. The sight of the trohantiras encouraged her as a sign her mother was watching over her. Excited to reclaim her boat, she hurried down the slope. She arrived at the shore only to lose sight of the boat, finding instead the black silhouette of the mountainous island. The sighting of the *Aspasia* must have been her imagination. She couldn't return to the house. The scene of her murdered father flashed in her mind. She sank to her knees adding salty tears to the sea.

Esmeray fell asleep and woke a few hours later, interrupting a dream that she was walking along the beach, the black pebbles crunching beneath her feet. She was disoriented, unaware of how long she had been asleep. It was pitch dark, hours after the moon had set.

Crunch, crunch . . .

The noise of someone walking across the pebble beach.

Crunch, crunch . . .

The footfalls started, halted, then resumed, as if someone was trying to be stealthy. Were the sounds getting louder?

As Esmeray's head cleared, her alarm subsided. She was sure the crunching was a boat hull shifting with the motion of the sea, scraping the rocks on the beach shore.

She peered into the dark, wading into the water. The skyline was blacked out in all directions except the harbor mouth, where the silhouette of the *Aspasia* was visible among the stars. Her father's murderer, after pushing the boat into the water from its mooring, had found that the tiller and oars had been removed. He had then abandoned the boat, freeing it to drift across the harbor.

Even with the feeble puffs of wind, Esmeray knew she could sail the trohantiras out of the harbor. She grounded the bow on the beach, stumbled over a length of driftwood, lashing it in place for a tiller. With the sails unfurled, she used the mild nocturnal breeze to coax her boat toward the harbor exit, using the stars on the horizon to guide her.

It took all her skills and most of an hour to nudge the boat to within a hundred feet of the open sea. Esmeray made use of all her senses. She trailed her hand in the water, keeping aware of how the mainsail responded to the gentle breeze, and intently listened for sail flutter in case she needed to adjust the tiller. To steel her patience, she knew once out of the harbor she could catch a brisk wind and sail to Chios town, away from the terrors of the night.

The gentle wind decreased, then stopped completely. The oars had been removed for the night. She pushed and pulled the driftwood tiller side to side, stern sculling, using the rudder's motion to fishtail the *Aspasia* to the harbor mouth. The moon had set, turning the night pitch black, but Esmeray continued heading toward the stars visible near the horizon.

Within several hours she reached Chios town and entered the harbor. Even if she found help, if she stayed on the island the man would eventually try to kill her. Esmeray knew she had to leave the Island of Chios, but it would have to wait until tomorrow. After beaching her boat, exhausted, she promptly fell to sleep under folds of sailcloth.

## CHAPTER III   NAVE PARADISIO

Bastone woke up thinking of Esmeray. She was so young, but so confident and he envisioned the freedom in her eyes as her hair flew in the wind. As the ship's scribe and the officer in charge of the arbalesters, he had the privilege to share a cabin in the forecastle with the *Paradisio's* first mate, Ottolino di Negro. A breeze passed through the cramped quarters from one porthole to the open door. Next to Bastone's quarters was another two-man cabin for officers.

Sensing the aroma of macaroni, he dressed, heading to midship where sailors were boiling the dried pasta in an iron pot of water. The container held a mixture of half sea water and half fresh water, according to the sailors' custom and preference, although plenty of fresh water was available in port. A large slate covered with a layer of sand protected the wooden deck from the small cook fire.

Ottolino, the first mate, soon handed him a bowl of cooked macaroni and vegetables, drizzled with olive oil. "Bastone, enjoy the oleo and fresh vegetables. We'll go back to lard, dried lentils, and chickpeas when we are on the high seas."

Bastone loved his pasta any way it was served. He tried a spoonful of the steaming mixture, savoring the flavor of tangy capers mixed with a faint sweet taste. There were basil leaves, beans, and wrinkled black olives in the bowl. He picked out one of the olives, chewed carefully around the pit; it was sweet. Bastone finished, thanking the sailors for the food.

A door opened at the first level of the guests' quarters, the three-story stern castle of the ship where the wealthy passengers quartered on the one hundred foot long, three-deck vessel. The ship was primarily a cargo vessel but was named the *Paradisio* after its two suites of luxury quarters. The captain's quarters occupied the upper level of the stern castle.

Benedetto Zaccaria, the captain, ducking as he exited his cabin through a low door, climbed down to the deck. The sailors perked up but carried on as usual. Benedetto had bought out three of the four owners of the *Paradisio*. Bastone's uncle, Riccio, owned a quarter of the ship. The Genoese trading vessel was one of the hundreds that crisscrossed the Mediterranean carrying goods, such as wine and cloth from the Italian maritime republics to the east and returning with spices and luxury goods.

The captain approached Bastone at midship.

"Captain Zaccaria, do we cast off today?" asked Bastone.

"No, no . . . my sister-in-law, Eudoxia, is in a fit. Her maid got seasick on our sail from Foca and doesn't want to go to Constantinople with her."

A sailor handed Benedetto a cup of wine and he sipped. "I told her that I would delay just one more day before we sail. We are loaded with alum and now we have the mastic for Constantinople. In addition, I must talk with her uncle, the emperor, on trading matters."

He finished the wine, handed Bastone his empty cup, and headed to his cabin. As the scribe glanced at the departing captain, a sailor filled the cup. He sipped and watched a gull suspended on a breeze, recalling how unfortunate it was that Eudoxia's maid had become sick, now delaying their departure. The maid, being about Esmeray's age, reminded him of the fisherwoman. Esmeray was pretty, not a dazzling beauty, but Bastone found her alluring, due to her confident demeanor and skills as a sailor. He wondered if Esmeray and her father had made it back to Emperios safely.

Within the hour, Bastone knocked on the captain's door and Zaccaria said, "Enter."

"Captain, since we are delayed, I can make another run to Emperios for more mastica," said Bastone. "I have found a fisherman who will take me there and return."

"Hmm. So we pay for a round trip, instead of you going overland to Pyrgi as before?" said Zaccaria. He paused, figuring the costs. "Yes, with the limited time, it will still be profitable. You are certain you can return before dark?" added the captain. Bastone nodded, turning to leave, as the captain said, "Take two of your marines."

"Yes, sir," said Bastone.

Benedetto, a shrewd merchant, did nothing for free, so he agreed to Bastone's unusual request. But also, he was wise to people's behaviors. "There is another reason?" said Zaccaria.

"Sir, the young woman. I want to make sure she is safe after the attack," said Bastone.

"I also was foolish when I was young," said Zaccaria. "But make sure you bring back the mastica."

With the Etesian wind at their back, the hired boat reached Emperios harbor before noon. Bastone sent the two guards to the inland village of Pyrgi to buy several bags of mastica. He queried a fisherman at the waterside who said he knew both Esmeray and her father but had not seen them that day. Concerned as well, the man led Bastone along the beach several hundred feet, where he noted that their trohantiras was gone. They entered a two-room cottage.

"Mother Mary!" the fisherman burst out. He took off his cap, kneeling next to the cold body of Esmeray's father. "Why would anyone do this? He was a good man!"

Bastone examined the room. The fisherman made the sign of the cross with his right hand, touching the center of his forehead, then bringing his hand to his sternum, raising his hand to the right shoulder and crossing it over to the left shoulder. Bastone rarely attended Mass, but he also crossed himself, ending the ritual blessing left to right, opposite of the fisherman's motion. Rushing into the next room, he found the blood-caked body of a younger, unfamiliar man. He then hurried outside, circling the cottage as he shouted, "Esmeray! Esmeray!"

His search futile, he returned to the fisherman still on his knees. "Does the village have a priest?" asked Bastone.

"Yes, I will get him and I will bring shovels."

Bastone searched again inside the cottage for clues, discovering the boat's oars and tiller. He went outside to make sure he hadn't overlooked the fishing boat. It was not in sight, which added to the puzzle of Esmeray's disappearance.

He helped dig the grave of Esmeray's father, which bewildered the villagers. Why would a Genoese overlord dig a grave? Bastone learned from the fishermen that the stranger had belonged to a clan of thieves. The priest had to convince the villagers to help him bury the body of the despised man. They reluctantly did so, but in a grave a respectful distance from their friend.

In Chios town, Esmeray woke, hot from the sun under the piece of spare sailcloth where she had slept. She planned to sell the fish and buy clothes but couldn't go to the agora in only her night tunic. After rummaging through the storage box, she found a knife, needle, and thread. She found a remnant of the band of red cloth from which the telltale flying from the mast had been fashioned. Esmeray quickly made a skirt from the sailcloth to hide her ankles and a headband from the red leftovers. To hold up the skirt, she used more of the remnant as a belt, hoping the bright colors would attract the fish customers.

Esmeray collected the fish, still alive in the basket hanging from the side of the boat, and took her catch to the agora, the market in a plaza at the city's waterfront. At the entrance to the harbor stood a large castle. A Greek Orthodox church bordered the west side of the cobbled marketplace and a Roman Catholic church had been erected on the opposite side to serve the Genoese colonists. Chios town had become a major transfer point for goods shipped by the Genoese merchants.

Esmeray placed her bucket on the pavement and shouted, "*Psari!* Fish for sale!" She gazed at the ships at anchor, contemplating the largest one, the *Paradisio,* yearning to sail on the three-masted ship. The young woman envisioned being one of the sailors, coordinating with other crew members to hoist the tall sails. Esmeray was suddenly filled with regret that she had not grown up to become a sailor, but then quickly rejected the notion. Then she would have had to be a man.

Gonfalons flew from both poles and masts of the *Paradisio*, emblazoned with the red cross of Saint George on a white field. At first, Esmeray noted it an interesting coincidence that she was dressed in red and white as well, the colors of the Genoese gonfalons, but the vision of the arbalester's shield with the same emblem reminded her of the Genoese who had caused the death of her father. A lump formed in her throat, she shed the tendency to cry, and instead exhaled sharply and shouted, "*Psari!*"

Among the throngs of shoppers, she watched two young women, both only a few years older than she was. One wore a wimple, a linen headdress covering the head, neck, and the sides of her face, held in place by a woad blue fillet, a headband. Her long-sleeved tunica ended at her ankles, with the cuffs and collar matching the blue fillet. The second woman was dressed less extravagantly, with a wide headband that covered only part of her hair. Both wore pointed blue shoes.

The blue colors of the women's clothes pleased Esmeray, reminding her of her favorite blue headband which was left at the cottage. The memory brought on a sinking feeling as she recalled her father's dead body. She shook off the image by forcing herself to yell, "Fish. Fish for sale!"

Genoese mariners escorted the women as they perused the wares at the nearby stalls. One of the women became unsteady on her feet and appeared close to fainting. The other woman steadied her, exclaiming, "You are still seasick? We are on firm land! How are you going to go with me to Constantinople?"

"I can't go! I'd die first! It felt like I was dying, vomiting all the time. Then dry heaves."

Esmeray hollered, "*Psari!* Fish for sale!"

The woman flashed Esmeray a displeasing look, then addressed her companion, "Mistress, I want to go back to Foca." She peered at Esmeray, "Any *chorikos* can be a maid, emptying chamber pots."

"You ungrateful spoiled brat," said her companion, "I educated you, I taught you how to be a lady . . . which you have forgotten. Go! Leave! I don't want you. You are on your own, here in Chios!"

The maid grasped the noble woman's sleeve, "Mistress Eudoxia, I am sorry. I am just sick."

Eudoxia jerked her arm away, the girl ran off sobbing. Eudoxia approached Esmeray, who suddenly felt small and foolish, now embarrassed of her clothes.

Eudoxia paused to face Esmeray, smiling. Esmeray's prior hawking came out as a weak, "*Psari*? Would you like some fish?"

Eudoxia looked about as she said, "You are alone? No, brother, no father, no companion?"

"Yes, I am alone," said Esmeray.

"Your clothes. You are resourceful and creative."

Esmeray thought the woman was mocking her. Her face reddened and she was about to tell the woman she was too busy for her insults.

Eudoxia continued with a serious face, "It's true. Dear, you have made gold out of mud!"

Esmeray calmed, feeling the heat subside. "I used to spin—flax, cotton, wool . . . now I fish."

"That's obvious, young lady. And your Greek is beautiful! Do you speak Genoese?"

"I am learning," said Esmeray. "Are you from Constantinople?"

"Originally. Now I live in New Foca most of the year. I am married to Manuele Zaccaria."

Eudoxia paused as if expecting a comment, then added, "My uncle is Michael *Palaiologos.*"

Esmeray's eyes opened wide.

"Yes, the Romaioi Emperor," said Eudoxia. "Do you want a job as my maid? And what is your name, young lady?"

Esmeray glanced over Eudoxia's shoulder, just then noticing that one of her guards was Amilcare, the arbalester who had shot the thief. She became unnerved at his sight, nodding as she answered, "Esmeray."

"A lovely name. You are not afraid of men harassing you?" said Eudoxia. "A pretty girl like yourself, dressed in such colorful garb?"

Esmeray found Amilcare's eyes, quickly looked away, steadied herself, her voice hardening, "No, I am not afraid."

"Well, I will need a reference."

"Mistress, a reference?"

"You are a Christian?" asked Eudoxia.

She nodded.

Eudoxia tilted her head toward the church. "The priest will vouch for you?"

Esmeray shook her head. "I am from Emperios."

Eudoxia's face was blank.

"It's a village several hours south by sail. The priest in Chios town doesn't know me."

"Hm. That's a shame. You seem like a sweet girl. Hmm. Well, I wish you luck."

She turned, then paused. "How much are the fish?"

"Five *folle*."

She handed Esmeray a silver *denaro*. "I will take the whole bucket. Is that enough?"

"I do not have change, Lady; you gave me too much," said Esmeray.

"It's fine, Esmeray."

Eudoxia said something to Amilcare, who picked up the bucket, peering without emotion at Esmeray as he leaned over. She molded the sternest face she could muster. Their eyes met. It took all her self-control to keep herself from spitting in his face. After he departed, Esmeray's shoulders slumped. She would be noticed, word reaching the dead thief's family in the south, sooner or later. She must find a way to leave the island.

## CHAPTER IV    CAPTAIN'S DINNER

In the afternoon Eudoxia suggested that she and her brother-in-law, Captain Zaccaria, have dinner together. Her husband, Manuele, had remained in New Foca managing the alum mines, as usual, when she visited her family each year in Constantinople. She asked the captain to bring his officers, hoping for interesting conversation. She supplied the fish.

Bastone had returned from Emperios with more mastica, which pleased the captain, including him as a dinner guest along with the first mate, Ottolino.

Eudoxia had brought her own dinner utensils, its kind rarely used outside of her native city, Constantinople, and paused between bites, holding a fork dangling a piece of mackerel. "Ottolino, I understand you supervised your men to cook the fish. Thank you." She took a bite. "Mmm!"

"And Lady Eudoxia, you selected delicious fish," said Zaccaria.

"Yet you still had a side bowl of pasta served to each of us," she said with a laugh. "You'd think sailors would tire of that hard macaroni."

"It preserves well on the long sea voyages, yes, a good substitute for hard biscuits," said the captain.

"No, I am alluding to how you cook it—it's um, chewy."

"Of course, we Genoese prefer our pasta *al dente*. The fish, you found them at the agora?"

"Yes, I bought it from a sweet fisherm, er, . . . fisher girl?" she laughed.

Benedetto chuckled, then said, "I am sorry you didn't find a new maid."

"I am perplexed that my maid . . . um, abandoned me. Though with her seasickness she wasn't capable. That girl who sold me the fish would have been perfect. She said she was alone . . . no family. but she was skilled. She certainly would not have gotten seasick. But she said she was not from Chios town . . . I could not hire her without a reference, which she could not provide . . . she is a chorikos."

Bastone blurted out, "What was her name?"

Benedetto and the other officers looked at him with raised eyebrows. Bastone was fixated on Eudoxia's answer, "Well, it's odd you ask, but her name was Esmeray."

Bastone's interest in the young woman was renewed. "Captain, you are familiar with our problem with thieves on the way back from Emperios. The woman Mistress Eudoxia met, Esmeray, was the daughter of the fisherman who was murdered."

"Murdered!" exclaimed Eudoxia.

Bastone recounted his findings at Emperios.

"That poor girl!" cried Eudoxia.

Bastone could not forget Esmeray. "I would vouch for the young woman—if you hired her," added Bastone.

There was a knock. The captain nodded to Ottolino, who ducked as he exited the suite.

The dinner party members returned to their meal. After the interruption, Eudoxia changed the topic of conversation. She asked the captain about the voyage to Constantinople.

"I think the Etesian will remain steady northwesterly," said Benedetto, "so we will tack past the island of Lesbos, then make a straight course north-northeast sailing on a close or beam reach."

"I have made this trip five or six times and I still need help with your sailing language, captain," said Eudoxia. "How long will it take to get to Constantinople?"

"Excuse me, yes, three or four days, Lady."

The first mate returned, ducking through the door, "There is a trohantiras alongside with a girl onboard. Arbalesters have the boat in their sights in case it is a ruse."

Bastone stood, glancing at the captain who flicked his eyes at the door. "Excuse me, Princess Eudoxia." He wasn't going to miss a second chance with the young woman, almost hitting his head as he hurried out onto the deck. Bastone saw several crossbowmen leaning over the stern side-rail, the taffrail, who had their weapons trained on Esmeray peering up from the boat.

He ordered the arbalesters to lower their bows. They complied, except for Amilcare, who continued to aim the weapon at Esmeray as he said, "She may be with those thieves. Remember, she didn't want us to shoot them!"

"Point the crossbow away, Amilcare. Now!"

The dinner guests emerged from the guest suite, the commotion distracting Amilcare who joggled his weapon. In a blink the cross bolt zipped away, Esmeray screamed.

They rushed to look over the rail. "Teeth of Jesus! No!" said Bastone.

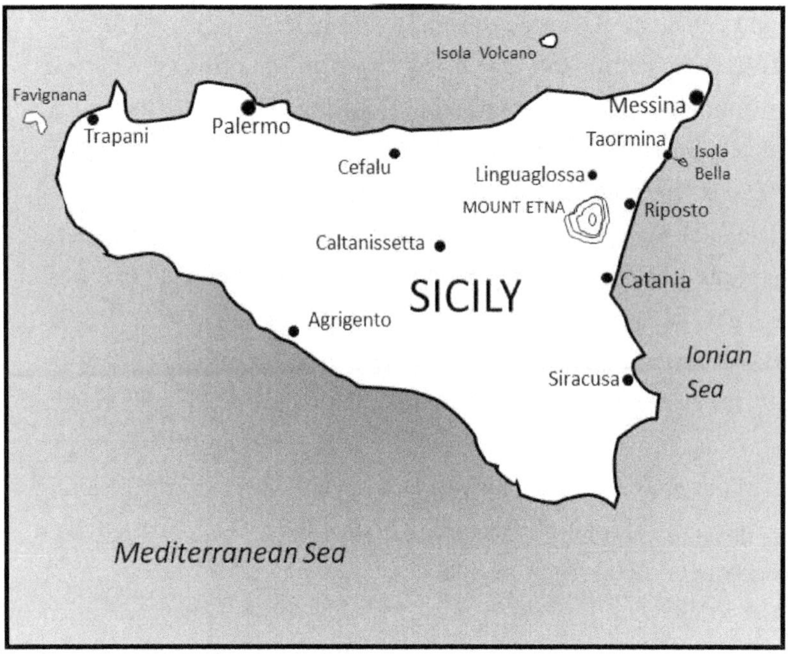
Isola Volcano
Favignana
Trapani
Palermo
Messina
Taormina
Isola
Bella
Cefalu
Linguaglossa
MOUNT ETNA
Riposto
Caltanissetta
Catania
SICILY
Agrigento
Ionian
Sea
Siracusa
Mediterranean Sea

## CHAPTER V     MOUNT ETNA, SICILY

Although huge masses of solidified lava covered most of volcano Etna, spreading along the lower slopes of the mountain was the *Pineta di Linguaglossa*, a forest of black pines, with clusters of birch trees, beech trees, and scattered chestnut trees. Amid the forest, the baron observed the woodsman Marianu, slashing a herringbone pattern in the bark of yet another black pine. He tapped a nail into the trunk at the bottom of the V-shaped incisions. The woodsman hung a clay pot on the spike to collect the dripping pine resin.

"You see, Lord Geoffroi, the cuts to draw the resin are in the shape of fish bones."

"I see the pots are fashioned with a pour spout, which you inserted in the hole you bored in the tree," Geoffroi said. He noted the other pots that hung on nearby trees, "And these were crafted specially with the loop to hang on the nail? Did you make these clay jugs?"

"Yes, Lord, we made the drip pots as well as the melting pots at the works. Both are fired clay."

"The clay is an unusual color, gray with a tinge of blue," added the baron.

Marianu was at ease with Geoffroi, although he was a French Angevin lord appointed by the king, Charles of Anjou. Geoffroi treated the Sicilians in his fief with respect. Most parts of Sicily were not so fortunate. The French lords of nearby Messina and Catania abused their citizens with excessive taxes, hard labor, and by appropriating their property for royal purposes.

Geoffroi, the Baron of Taormina, had been awarded a fief for his service to Charles of Anjou in the French Angevin army during the conquest of Sicily. The baron's lands included the ancient Greek towns of Taormina and Castiglione, as well as the village of Linguaglossa, founded in 1145 by Genoese merchants. Nearby on the slopes of Etna, they exploited the pines to develop an industry producing resin and pitch. The products were primarily used for waterproofing the hulls of ships. Warehouses and docks at the nearby port of Riposto had been built to export the products.

The baron now looked on with interest, as Marianu harvested the resin. The noble's escorts, French soldiers from Anjou, Angevins, stood by, holding the reins of his horse, appearing bored. The woodsman never tired of working among the *pinetas*, the pines, which bestowed the valuable resin.

Marianu finished showing Geoffroi his craft and they headed toward Linguaglossa to the naval works where pine resin was processed into pitch. He mounted his mule, following the troop of French Angevin soldiers led by Geoffroi, their steeds culled from the herds of Sanfratellano horses, a breed raised in the Nebrodi Mountains north of Etna.

They entered the village, riding past the church of Sant'Egidiu, dedicated to the patron saint of the village. At the stables they were received by the blacksmith, Lucianu, Marianu's brother.

As Geoffroi and Marianu dismounted, Baron Roberto Alaimo arrived from Messina, with his wife, Macalda. Geoffroi's wife, Anastasia, a lady of Linguaglossa, accompanied them. Both women rode side saddle, dressed in coarsely spun traveling clothes. Neither had full wimples as was usual in public, wearing casual headbands instead. They dismounted, Marianu helping Lucianu with the mounts. Lucianu smiled, "I will take great care of your *cavaddi*."

Geoffroi laughed, "I lived in Naples and then in Abruzzi. In both places, they called steeds *cavalli*. Now I'm learning a new dialect." He gestured to the group. "It is but a short walk to the resin works, Lord and ladies."

The brothers' gaze followed the entourage as they departed the stables. "The lady from Messina with the blonde hair," said Marianu, "she must be Norman."

Geoffroi escorted the nobles to a roofed structure without walls, a few score paces from the blacksmith shop. Lucianu and his brother continued to watch as Geoffroi showed the group into the production shed.

Marianu slapped his forehead. "Anastasia! Was that *the* Anastasia! According to the tale, she was traveling and sought protection during a thunderstorm under 'the One Hundred Horse Chestnut tree,' an immense and ancient chestnut. The huge tree on the road to Riposto. That's how it got its name, because the tree's branches were so widespread, they sheltered her along with an escort of a hundred mounted soldiers!"

"I've heard that story, yes, but . . ." said Lucianu, "the chestnut tree *is* gigantic, but a hundred knights? Maybe twenty or thirty?"

"Does it matter? The tree deserves a name to match its magnificence, no?"

"Yes, I agree."

The nobles arrived at the resin processing shed, met Concettu, the foreman, who nodded politely describing the works. "The drip pots are collected from the trees, brought to the shed, *carefully* melting the resin over small fires," said Concettu, "then we pour the resin into these larger melting pots."

"You emphasized the word carefully," said Macalda.

"Yes, mistress, the resin will flash into a vigorous fire if we apply too much heat."

The women flinched and backed away a pace.

They moved to the next step in the process. "Here, charcoal and ashes from the wood fires are crushed."

A worker held a wooden mortar with both hands, pounding it on chunks of burnt wood in a stone pestle. He then shoveled the resulting charcoal powder into a pot full of the molten resin, as another man stirred the carbonized wood into the liquid.

Concettu stopped next to a pile of wooden rods, forearm-length and as thick as his thumb. As he brandished one, he said, "I will show you how to make a pitch bastone." He rotated one end of the rod in the melted charcoal-resin mix. After he coated the end, he pulled it out of the molten liquid and the black pitch hardened. "The pitch has cooled to a solid." He repeated the procedure several more times, allowing another layer to harden, before adding the next, until the pitch sheathed the tip, forming a bulbous mass at one end.

Concettu held up the stick. "At the shipyards, the wrights will light these coated rods, then drip and smear the pitch on the seams to waterproof the hulls of the ships."

"Amazing!" exclaimed Anastasia. "It is so complicated."

"Years ago a simpler way was used—they just burned the pine wood and the tar dripped out and was collected," said Concettu. "But you must chop down the trees, which is so wasteful. Instead, we tap the resin from the trees and they live on to give us more resin the next year."

Baron Alaimo asked, "Where do you find the clay for the melting pots? And why are the pots gray and blue, not red as are most clay-fired roof tiles?"

"The clay is unique. Just north of the village," said Concettu, "we found light blue clay in an area where rainwater pools."

With the tour of the naval works over, the nobles collected their mounts from the stables and rode to Linguaglossa. They sat at a dinner in the modest villa inherited by Anastasia from her late parents.

Anastasia and Macalda had changed into simple, short-sleeved gowns, wearing light shawls to cover their shoulders. The linen material fell provocatively upon their figures, but had they been in public they would have added a waistcoat.

A delicious aroma entered the room as a servant carried out a plate of fried eggplant, sliced into bite-size pieces. The eggplant was seasoned with olive oil and sprinkled with chopped olives and pine nuts. "I am confident you will enjoy our local *caponata*," said Anastasia, "it has a unique sauce."

They each speared a piece with their eating knife and savored the antipasto.

"Mm . . . mm," purred Alaimo. "We have caponata in Messina but it tastes different."

"Perhaps because we use pine nuts instead of capers," said Anastasia.

"Ah! Of course, Pineta di Linguaglossa," said Alaimo. "The fabulous trees produce the fine resin, also providing tasty ingredients for the antipasto!"

He tilted his head and stared across the room in thought. "Today during our tour of the resin shop, your workers were busy and productive. Geoffroi, my friend, have the profits fallen off lately? The taxes for Charles sent through Messina have decreased."

"Uh . . . well . . . I have, um, diverted a few men to develop a new industry, Lord Alaimo," said Geoffroi. "The clay deposits just north of Linguaglossa are extensive, and I plan to use the material to produce roof tiles."

Alaimo's eyebrows raised. "Hmm . . . excellent! But . . ."

Anastasia interposed, "Macalda, dear, what do you think of the *caponata*?"

"It is both sweet and sour, a marvelous combination. Anastasia, I want the recipe! It's interesting, just two days' ride from Messina and the dishes are so varied."

As they finished the *antipasti*, a wooden bowl of soup was placed before each of the four diners. The spoon also was wood.

Macalda's frown divulged that she felt slighted at the unrefined tableware. Anastasia noticed and commented, "Dear, we are celebrating San Giuseppi's Day by sharing the *maccu*, the peasant soup of fava beans and fennel. According to tradition, the food is enjoyed using the peasants' wooden tableware. I find it very delicious!"

Macalda eased, and along with the others, slurped from her spoon, nodding to show her approval.

They stuffed themselves through a course of pasta, followed by sausage and bread, and finally dessert. As a tray of puffy, white cream filled pastry disks called genovesi were placed on the table, Anastasia put her hand on her stomach and said, "I feel like a stuffed pig!" They laughed and none of them thought it crude, as they had also consumed ample wine throughout the dinner.

"We can thank the Saracens for these delicious sweets," said Anastasia. "They brought the sugar cane to Sicily centuries ago."

Alaimo took a bite and talked as he chewed, "In Messina these are called nun's breasts."

Wine imbued laughter followed.

The men remained at the table sipping wine as Alaimo asked Geoffroi of his venture to produce the Roman terracotta tiles. The two ladies retreated to a sitting room.

Anastasia and Macalda sipped on limoncello from tiny ceramic cups. "You have such beautiful hair, dear. I have seen a few women who inherited red hair from the Normans, but your blonde color is rare."

Macalda looked away as she wiped tears. "What is the matter?" said Anastasia.

"I . . ." she looked around, then leaned forward and whispered, "I have worms in my hair!"

"No! Let me look." She stood and examined the woman's scalp. "It's just flaky skin."

"Yes, but it itches and I can't wear any dark clothes. You can see white flakes on my shoulders."

Anastasia put her arm around the woman's shoulder. "I can help you. I had the same problem and used a special blend of salves to get rid of it."

Macalda sniffled but appeared hopeful. "We must be discreet!"

"Yes, that can be arranged, and what better place than far from Messina."

The next morning after breakfast the village barber arrived, leading a donkey. He tied the reins of the pack-animal at the front of Geoffroi's villa, pulling a book out of the saddlebags.

Alaimo and Geoffroi met him in the anteroom. "Lord Alaimo, my friend and barber surgeon, Egidiu."

Egidui nodded, and asked in Sicilian, "*Comu sta,* Lord Alaimo?"

"*Bonu,*" said Alaimo, "You must not tell anyone that you treated my wife. Tell them she had a sore tooth. Understood?"

"Yes, Lord." He placed a hand on the thick book and smiled, revealing a tiny space between his front teeth, "I swear to you, Lord."

Alaimo was assured and Geoffroi coughed, suppressing a comment. Anastasia appeared. "Please come with me, Signore Ponziu."

The barber accompanied the women as they left the room. "Can we trust him?" said Alaimo.

"His hard-working family is well regarded; you met his uncle and father at the stables," said Geoffroi. Besides, he will provide a cure for your wife's affliction."

Alaimo's face softened, "Yes, yes . . . you are right. And he did swear on the Bible to be discrete."

Geoffroi smiled.

In the sitting room, Egidiu opened the book entitled, *De Ornatu Mulierum*, "Recipes for Cosmetics," to show the women the ingredients for his planned treatment. He read aloud:

"To remove the scales from the scalp, we must wash the hair with vinegar mixed with rosemary water containing nettles, mint, and thyme."

"That will get rid of the worms?" asked Macalda.

"Worms?" said Egidiu. "There are no . . . worms. Your scalp is merely dry, I suspect."

Lady Macalda, may I examine your crown?" said the barber.

"Uh, yes, go ahead."

Macalda was not born with blonde hair, but she dyed her hair, and the roots were darkening. He finished peering at her roots and scalp. "Yes, your scalp just needs treatment. It will work."

Macalda looked anxious. He glanced at Anastasia.

"Macalda, dear," said Anastasia, "I also had the scales. Egidiu got rid of them."

"Anastasia will do the hair washing for me?" said Macalda.

Anastasia glanced at Egidiu who nodded. "Yes, of course."

Macalda remained unconvinced.

"Lady Macalda," said Egidiu, "I found this hair treatment in this wonderful book along with many other cosmetic procedures. It was written by a woman, a famous physician."

The women's eyes raised, their heads tilting.

"Her name was Trotula di Ruggiero of La Scuola Medica Salernitana, the Medical School at Salerno, where she practiced and taught medicine over a century ago." Seeing Macalda relax, he said, "I have the supplies in my saddlebags."

Macalda nodded. Anastasia called in a servant. "Go with Egidiu to get his ingredients and meet us in the kitchen."

An hour later Macalda sat, her hair wrapped in a towel, the washing completed. Anastasia retrieved her only mirror, an expensive wedding gift from Geoffroi. It was polished silver, the size of her palm. Macalda let her hair fall to her shoulders, holding up the small mirror examining her tresses. She discovered her roots had lightened.

"Your hair is beautiful, Macalda," said Anastasia.

"Your barber is a genius chemist! And my toothache is gone, too."

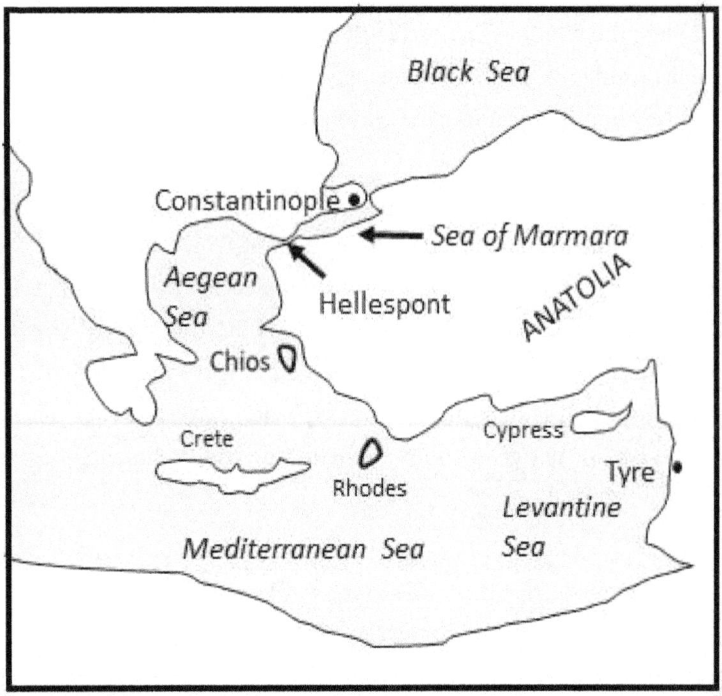
Black Sea
Constantinople
Sea of Marmara
Aegean
Sea
Hellespont
ANATOLIA
Chios
Crete
Cypress
Tyre
Rhodes
Levantine
Sea
Mediterranean Sea

## CHAPTER VI   CORSAIRS

He jerked the crossbow from Amilcare, who snarled, "It was a mistake!"

Bastone rammed the stirrup end of the weapon into Amilcare's midsection, buckling him. He raised the crossbow. Eudoxia gasped.

Captain Zaccaria whispered, "Bastone, no!"

Bastone lowered the weapon. He clenched his teeth and peered at Amilcare. "You are confined to quarters."

The captain glanced over the rail. "Is that the fishmonger—uh, the girl . . .?

Eudoxia and Bastone both answered, "Yes."

Esmeray stood shaking her fist. A cross bolt was impaled in the boat's deck at her feet. She shouted in Genoese, *"Che bruto, w*hat a jerk! *Che stronzo,* what an asshole!"

"Thank God she was not hit," said Eudoxia. "She *does* speak Genoese! What does she want?"

Esmeray had heard. "Passage on your nave . . . to wherever you are sailing."

The captain answered, "But . . ."

"Benedetto, I am without a maid," said Eudoxia. "And Bastone vouched for her."

The captain did not appear convinced. Sailors began hooting and whistling at Esmeray.

"She is creating discord in the crew . . ."

Esmeray shouted, "I will trade my trohantiras for passage."

It was too good of a trade for the shrewd captain to disregard. The captain threw up his hands. "Fine, fine, bring her aboard. Princess Eudoxia, please be certain she does not dally with the crew."

He turned to his first mate. "Secure the trohantiras at the stern. And add more oarlocks to the boat. He craned his neck to peer at the harbor tender, a small rowboat, stored on the top of the stern castle. "It will make a better tender than that little *canottino*. A ship as proud as the *Paradisio* deserves a robust tender, with four sets of oars."

A crew member threw a line with a loop on the end. Esmeray pulled it over her head and placed it around her waist. She leaned back, using her legs to ascend the hull as several sailors pulled her up to the deck. Benedetto opened the door for Eudoxia, who entered her quarters. Esmeray followed, gaping at the trappings of the luxurious cabin.

At her cottage, she had a thin mattress and pillow made of sailcloth stuffed with straw. She had considered her linen blanket a luxury, never having seen the room of a wealthy person.

Ornate carved wood adorned the walls. The bed curtains were open, showing the sculpted headboard of a grandiose bed. Beneath a porthole was a daybed, with carved wooden armrests and pillowed backrests. The furniture included a chest made of the same exquisite wood. Recessed into the top of the chest was a ceramic bowl full of water. Bolted to the floor was a table and bench.

"The wood is elegant!"

"Well, yes . . . it is walnut. But first, you need a proper dress. The captain may invite me to dinner and my maid is always with me."

Eudoxia opened the chest and removed a woad blue dress. "You are close to the same size as my . . . previous maid . . . maybe you are a little shorter. You can turn up the hem of this dress."

They sat together on the daybed as Esmeray shortened the floor length tunica of the blue cloth, the color she adored. She fashioned a headband of the same cloth. She washed her night tunic and hung it to dry.

Although distanced by social class, the two women were about the same age. They laid in Eudoxia's bed well into the night, comparing their diverse lives. After their long chat, Esmeray retired to the daybed, lying awake for a few minutes, not having talked so much since the days she had worked with the women cleaning mastica in Pyrgi. But Esmeray did not miss that tedious work. Now she regretted offering her boat for passage. It was a rash mistake. The captain could have let her on the ship anyway because Eudoxia wanted her as a companion. Esmeray had built the *Aspasia*, her father naming the trohantiras after her mother. It bothered her that she might never sail the family treasure again.

At sunrise, sailors rowed the *Aspasia,* towing the *Paradisio* out of the harbor. Esmeray looked on with interest from the top of the stern castle. The crew raised the three sails, bringing the nave underway.

Eudoxia provided Esmeray with a simple work dress, apron, and headpiece for her duties. Esmeray washed clothes, brought food cooked at the communal outdoor galley to their quarters, emptied and cleaned the chamber pots. She did not complain, no matter how uncomfortable the task.

After several days into their voyage, she threw scraps to the ship's mouser as she left the galley. The barber surgeon, an old graying sailor, grabbed her sleeve, startling her. "No, never feed *Fumotina*. It will spoil her appetite. The cat is not a pet; she works on this ship as do the rest of us. She is the best mouser I have ever seen and although small, she's plucky."

Esmeray kneeled to pet the little black cat, but she scampered away.

"Ha, ha! Like a little puff of smoke, she is gone!" said the sailor. "You know, in my day they never allowed women on ships—we considered it bad luck."

Esmeray frowned.

He added, "People think black cats are bad luck, too. How can that be? Fumotina has given our ship good fortune! She is getting on in years—like me.

"But times have changed, and it is refreshing to see a pretty face among these brutes! Let me know if any of them give you a problem. My razor is often at their throats. They are at my mercy!"

He laughed and gently released her arm.

Esmeray smiled, as she said, "*Grazie*, sailor!"

Esmeray's first thoughts each morning upon awakening were of her father. She was tormented with guilt that he might not have had a proper burial or a priest to bless him. Mercifully, she was occupied, busy learning to work as a sailor. If she had a break, she studied the mariners' routine from weighing anchor to getting under sail. The bustle on the ship distracted her from the trauma of her father's death. She watched a pair of sailors raise the heavy iron anchor, cranking wooden handles as they coiled rope onto a windlass. Others adjusted, furled, and unfurled the sails, according to the change in wind direction or ship's course. She memorized each man's role. Esmeray was familiar with the knots the sailors were using and the way the captain used the wind, both which gave her a feeling of comradeship. She looked up at the tall sails and though she had not studied math, proportions appeared in her mind. She knew the *Paradisio* was four or five times longer than the *Aspasia*, reckoning the sails were a hundred feet high. Over fifty sailors were needed to handle the sheets.

Every so often she glimpsed the Aspasia being towed in the *Paradisio's* wake. If she allowed herself more than a glance, the longing for her boat grew into an ache.

Their progress was slow the first few days across the open sea, tacking against the nor'westerly Etesian winds. At sunrise on the third day, the *Paradisio* sailed along the west coast of the island of Lesbos, the rising sun shielded by the isle's hills.

Esmeray poured the night soil over the taffrail, then lowered a bucket to catch sea water for rinsing out the chamber pot.

The moment they cleared the island, the direct glare of sunlight was blinding. A sailor high on the masthead crow's nest squinted as he visored with his hand against the sun. "*Ehi della nave!* Ship ahoy!"

Bastone, not finished with his morning pasta, tossed his bowl, "*Pronto arbalesti!* Crossbowmen ready!"

Esmeray tried to make out the approaching ship in the glare of the sun.

"She flies the cross of Saint George!" yelled the lookout.

The red cross on white meant another Genoese ship—Bastone's countrymen. Her anxiety eased. Calming after the false alarm, Esmeray hoisted the bucket full of sea water. The watch shouted, "*Pirati!* Pirates coming alongside in c*anottini!* Rowboats! They are going to board us! Pirati!"

The canottini had hid behind the cape, intercepting the *Paradisio* as the attacking ship, flying the Genoese banner, closed in. The pirate captain had timed his attack when the sun was behind his ship and when the winds were favorable.

Crossbowmen armed themselves and sailors mustered at their stations, waiting for Captain Zaccaria's command. The cries of the lookout distracted her. "Canottini to steerboard, watch for swimmers!"

Esmeray's attention shifted back to the bucket. "A pirate! Over here! A pirate is climbing aboard the ship!" She swung the bucket a few feet sideways, dropping it on the brigand who clung to the hull.

Bastone arrived to see the laden bucket smash on the pirate's head, who fell into the sea. Bastone took aim with his crossbow, the man dove under, the bolt finding its mark under the water with a fatal zip. Another swimmer began scaling the hull. Bastone reloaded, swung his bow over the rail, aiming. The enemy sailor, halfway up, pushed himself off the hull to escape into the sea. Before he hit the water, Bastone impaled him in midair with a bolt.

"Bravo, Esmeray! Go inside, at once!"

She watched through the porthole as Bastone organized the defense of the ship. As cross bolts flew through the air and skittered across the deck, Zaccaria bellowed orders from the top of the stern castle alongside the helmsman. Bastone organized sailors to watch for other swimmers that might board, directing his arbalesters to return fire.

He heard Zaccaria from atop the stern castle. "I see it is Giovanni Cavo's ship. The Genoese bandit from Rhodes."

Esmeray watched the chaotic scene along the length of the deck. A score of swimmers had boarded. *Paradisio* crewmen grunted, falling to the deck, as enemy cross bolts from the attacking ship found their marks. Bastone's marines propped up their rectangular shields amidships in a defensive circle, loosing cross bolts in all directions. The onslaught felled many of the enemy, though several raiders reached the arbalesters before they could restring their bows, resulting in hand-to-hand combat. Bastone led his marines in a counterattack, fighting with daggers and driving their shields into the attackers. His men killed those who didn't retreat overboard.

The captain yelled something unintelligible. Esmeray felt the ship turn. She was shocked, realizing the *Paradisio* was going to collide head on with the enemy ship. Her mind reeled on to how to escape, deciding she would swim to the *Aspasia*. She opened the door. Eudoxia screamed for her to stop. Esmeray observed the captain and the helmsman atop the stern castle. Together they leaned hard on the tiller. The ship shuddered, veering to steerboard. Bastone led his men to port, crouched behind the sidewale, loosing a hail of cross bolts as the enemy ship and the *Paradisio* sailed past one another in opposite directions.

"Beat to north. To north!" bellowed the captain. "Strike the jib and hoist the *genoa!*"

The crew, shorthanded because of casualties, struggled to adjust the sails. With the enemy ship now hundreds of feet aft, Bastone and his arbalesters dropped their weapons and joined the crew's efforts. The ship's barber surgeon surveyed the wounded, helping those that had the best chance to survive. Esmeray rushed across the deck. Although hindered by her dress, she jumped over debris and the bodies of dead and injured men, grabbing a lanyard along with others at the aft sail on the mizzen mast. Her experience sailing the trohantiras and the hours watching the sailors gave her the skill and confidence to join them.

Esmeray, next to Bastone, matched his eyes as she hauled on the lanyard along with the sailors to increase the aft sail to full. The first mate pulled her and a sailor off the line. "Go hoist the genoa!"

*Genoa?* Confused by the term, she followed the sailor as he hurried to the bow where they hoisted a large second jib that skirted the foresail, doubling the surface area. The ship surged ahead as the added sailcloth caught wind.

Zaccaria gave the helmsman full control of the tiller, turning his attention to the pirate ship. "They are coming about, but they'll never catch us. I will send my grievances of this attack to the Moresco brothers, the rulers of Rhodes. Preying on fellow Genoese!" Benedetto punched his fist up in an uppercut as he slapped his hand on his bicep. *"Che stronzi!"*

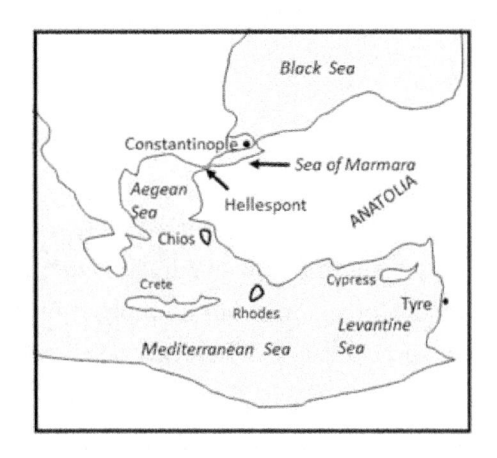

## CONSTANTINOPLE 1277 AD

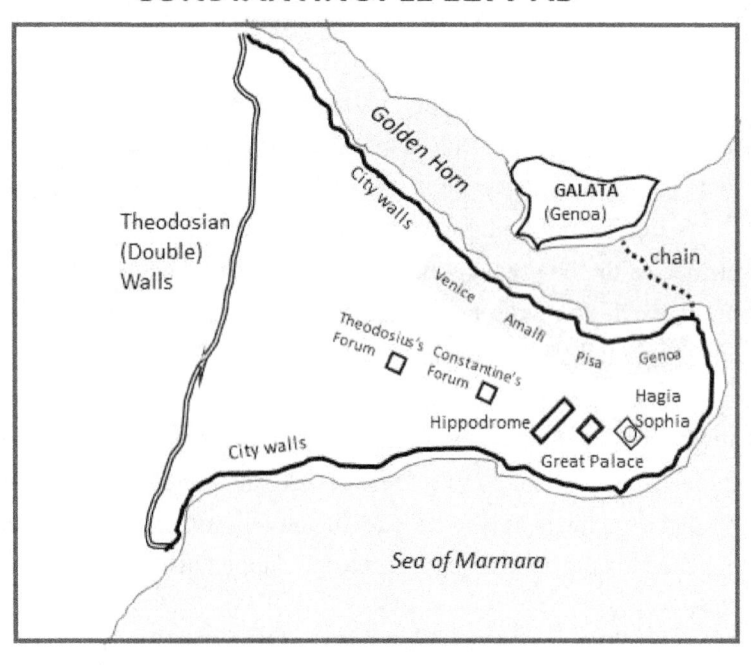

Maritime Republic Quarters | Amalfi |

## CHAPTER VII  CONSTANTINOPLE 1277 AD

The *Paradisio* approached Constantinople, the capital of the eastern Roman Empire. Over the previous two days they had traversed the narrows connecting the Aegean Sea to the smaller Sea of Marmara, whose waters lapped the waterfront of Constantinople. To Esmeray, the city had been the faraway center of the world. The *Romaioi,* the Roman citizens of her Anatolian village, had referred to Constantinople simply as *i Polis*: "the City." It was also known as the Queen of Cities. And her mother's Seljuk relatives had referred to the city just as reverently, borrowing from the Arabs the term Great City of the Romans.

The *Paradisio* sailed along the south shoreline of the city, past walls almost a hundred feet high. The ship glided by one tower after another, taking the *Paradisio* an hour to sail the entire length of the sea walls. Esmeray grew weary counting the barbicans. Beyond the walls, the upper tiers of the chariot stadium were visible above the buildings; however, the enormous dome of the Hagia Sophia, the Greek Christian church, dominated the skyline.

The grandeur she observed from this ship would soon fade when she walked among the quarters of the city still in ruin. Decades after the Christian crusade of 1204, there were still abandoned parts of the city after the Venetians had led the only sack of Constantinople during the city's long history. They had pillaged and carted off art and treasures that had taken centuries to accumulate. Most of the 400,000 citizens of the city had perished or fled to exile, leaving only a tenth of the population. The Venetians had then established a Latin regime. Only recently, during Esmeray's birth year, Emperor Michael VIII had expelled this western government, restoring Constantinople to its *Romaioi* Greek-Roman heritage. The Genoese had provided warships to the exiled Romans to recover the city, receiving many additional trading privileges, including sole rights to the Black Sea market.

The *Paradisio* sailed by several fortified harbors that were used by the fishers and Roman merchants of Constantinople. After rounding the southeast point of the peninsular city, they sailed over a submerged chain, raised in times of war to block enemy ships, and entered the main harbor. The citizens called the harbor the Golden Horn because of the immense wealth the trade brought to the city. Near the shore of the harbor was the trading colony of Galata, granted to the Genoese by the Romans. After the crew of the *Paradisio* furled the sails, oarsmen on the *Aspasia* towed the larger ship to dock under Galata's stone fortifications.

Once Bastone had finished the inventory of mastica, he went ashore with Eudoxia and Esmeray. He and the captain escorted them to a decorated carriage. Benedetto helped the women into the coach.

As Bastone approached the carriage, the captain said, "Bastone, I will leave Princess Eudoxia in your care. I must search the waterfront to find sailors to replace those lost during that disastrous fight with Cavo."

The cobbled streets were narrow and hilly, and their progress was further slowed by Genoese pedestrians who took their time moving out of the way. Bastone rode next to the driver as the women rode inside. Two of Bastone's men followed on foot.

As they made their way, Esmeray observed cats sleeping unmolested on many of the doorsteps to the shops. Customers stepped over them and the napping felines hardly noticed.

As they approached the Chapel of Saint Paul, a Latin Christian church, Eudoxia called out the coach window, "Bastone, please stop. I want to pray and give thanks for our safe voyage." Eudoxia had grown up Greek Orthodox, but her husband was a Roman Catholic, and she endorsed both churches.

Esmeray accompanied her as Bastone escorted them and watched from the back of the church as they kneeled at the altar rail. When they had finished, the priest raised a conversation with Eudoxia, who excused Esmeray.

The young woman joined Bastone to wait. "Officer, you did not want to join us in prayer?" said Esmeray.

"Um . . . well, Signorina, I must be vigilant . . . and safeguard Princess Eudoxia and . . . you. Were your prayers fulfilling?"

Esmeray knitted her brow because she had usually went through the motions of prayer, but was rarely moved by the ritual. She decided Bastone was not as barbaric as his comrades. He kept his beard trimmed. She loved the color of his eyes, and his breath was fresh as if he had chewed mastic. She touched her mouth and worried if her breath was as fresh as his. Then she reminded herself not to become attracted to him because all the Genoese were pirates.

"Or maybe since this is a Latin church, you do not feel as comfortable?" added Bastone.

Esmeray replied, "I have not been attending Mass in Chios. I accompanied the princess because it is my duty."

Eudoxia joined them and they returned to the carriage.

That evening they were guests of the Podesta of Galata, who governed the Genoese quarter. In the morning they returned to the Galata quay. Bastone and several of his men rowed the women across the harbor in the *Aspasia*. A pair of Bastone's men in front and a pair behind the party strolled through the waterfront agora and streets, Eudoxia paying attention to the wares.

"It's always invigorating to return to *i Polis*," said Eudoxia. "The people, the crowds! Besides, walking is more enjoyable here than in Galata. Romaioi build smoother streets."

They eventually left the agora where merchants displayed open containers of ginger, sugar, sandalwood, cinnamon, and other spices. As they moved up the street, they passed by a row of perfumers' shops. "The scents!" said Eudoxia.

They resumed walking, now toward Eudoxia's childhood home, where her mother lived in Constantinople. They passed one house cat after another, claiming their respective doormats, and stopped at a *thermopolia*, a shop that served warm food.

"There is fresh *boukellaton* nearby!" squealed Eudoxia. "We must have some!"

Bastone paid for two of the ringed-shaped breads. Eudoxia took a bite. "Yes, just like I remember. It has anise and . . ." She looked at Esmeray. "Tell me what else . . . you will know."

Esmeray tasted the warm bread, and her eyes grew wide. "Mastica!"

"From your home, Chios," said Bastone.

Eudoxia tilted her head toward the escorts. "Bastone, please get bread for yourself and your men, too."

Bastone didn't appear to heed Eudoxia, his neck craned toward the shop next to the bakery. She repeated in Genoese, instead of Greek.

"Oh, yes!" He handed a silver penny to one of his men. "Please excuse me, Princess Eudoxia, I was fixated on that shop. I need ink. And I believe cloth parchment is less expensive in Constantinople. It costs more than vellum in Genoa."

"Of course, we will enjoy boukellaton while you shop," said Eudoxia between nibbles.

Just as the group finished their snack, Bastone returned, appearing pleased.

Eudoxia raised her eyebrows, "Did you find any papyrus?"

Bastone took on a puzzled look. "Papyrus? As a scribe, I have heard of papyrus, what the ancients wrote on." He patted his leather shoulder bag. "I bought four quires." He removed a bundle of four sheets each folded in half. "Papyrus was made of reeds. This is cloth parchment, made from . . . I believe rags."

She smiled. "Let us continue."

The party entered a residential area of courtyard homes, a neighborhood of wealthy citizens. Esmeray could not help but notice, a few hundred feet distant, a stone bridge of multiple arches stretching from one hilltop to the next.

"Mistress," said Esmeray, "that bridge over there—it doesn't cross a river or stream."

"That is the aqueduct the ancient Romans built. It used to bring water from the mountains, but it wasn't repaired after the Venetians ruined our city."

"So, where do you get your water . . . now?"

"Rainwater collects in underground cisterns. The huge caverns hold all the fresh water we need."

They arrived at the entrance to a large compound and villa, the home of Eudoxia's mother, the widowed sister of Emperor Michael VIII Palaiologos.

The enormous villa and the tapestries, murals, statues, and ornate furnishings astounded Esmeray. The sumptuousness overwhelmed her senses. The lavishness almost made Esmeray feel sick.

She had a short time alone in her chamber, part of Eudoxia's suite, as they waited for Benedetto Zaccaria to arrive at the villa. The emperor had invited Eudoxia to the palace for dinner.

Eudoxia wanted to freshen up before dinner and asked Esmeray to bring some water to her chambers. A house servant gave her a bucket and guided her to a well connected to an underground cistern. There, she attached the bucket to a rope and lowered it into the well, then used a wooden hand crank to retrieve the bucket. She returned to Eudoxia's suite and added water to a large ceramic bowl for her mistress's sponge bath.

In her adjacent chamber, Esmeray put on the woad blue dress that Eudoxia had given her on the ship. The dress made her feel attractive, and the woad calmed her.

She then joined Eudoxia in the adjacent room and helped her dress. The hairdresser entered Eudoxia's quarters. "Esmeray, dear, please watch the stylist closely, so you can learn. Once you acquire the skill, it will be your task to arrange my hair."

Esmeray tried to appear interested as she observed. She did not look forward to this as part of her future and ached to be sailing instead.

Within an hour, a messenger from the *Paradisio* brought news that Captain Zaccaria had business with the emperor before the dinner and would meet them at the palace. Eudoxia's mother and handmaiden rode a two-wheeled carriage, and Eudoxia and Esmeray followed in a second carriage to the emperor's palace. Bastone rode with the driver. A squad of Bastone's men followed on foot. The emperor's wife, Theodora, greeted them at the atrium and escorted them through the palace to a large dining hall.

Emperor Michael and Empress Theodora were seated at the head of an immense table, the nobles sitting along the sides as servants delivered food and drink. Esmeray stood near the wall, several feet behind Eudoxia, ready to do her bidding. Other handmaidens and a few men also stood ready behind their respective masters or matrons. The dinner was extravagant, and the repartee was light. Michael refrained from discussing politics or business, which he and Benedetto had covered before the dinner. But religion, intertwined in the culture, was a common subject.

Empress Theodora beamed as she said, "I am very optimistic about the unification of the Catholic Church of Rome and the Eastern Orthodox churches." She glanced at Michael. "My husband successfully negotiated the union between the Latin and Greek churches three years ago, at the Council of Lyons in 1274. History will remember him as a saint!"

"It has been a great challenge, dear," said the emperor. "Initially, the Archbishop of the Orthodox Church had opposed the union, but since I replaced him with an . . . um . . . more agreeable archbishop, opposition has decreased."

Theodora's smile faded, and she glanced from her husband to her sister-in-law, Eudoxia, "It's a shame your sister Eulogia opposes the unification."

Michael quickly added, "But I have my lovely wife's support." He raised his wine glass to his wife and then Eudoxia, "and my loyal sister's endorsement. *Ya mas!* Health!" He downed his spiced wine.

There were seven dinner courses, including fish caught that morning, and freshly picked vegetables grown inside the city, broad beans, lentils, and chickpeas. Offered in bowls for the guests was a choice of simple sauce of olive oil or *garos,* the popular sauce made with fish offal, blood, salt, and pepper imported from India, and aged wine.

When dessert was served, Esmeray and the other attendants were directed into an adjoining room by a man servant with a high-pitched voice. He told them to quickly eat before the nobles finished their last course.

Esmeray was hungry after standing at attention, the aromas enticing her, and watching the dinner guests eat. With the short time to eat, however, she only sampled the food of the main courses, and went straight to the dessert, enjoying the pastry filled with chopped nuts and dripping with honey. Returning to the dining hall, Esmeray and the other attendants waited as the nobles finished their desserts.

Theodora accompanied the guests as they departed through the anteroom of the dining hall and down a long corridor. The emperor clasped Bastone's shoulder and called to Benedetto as they departed, "Captain, I will have a few words with Bastone. He will join you shortly."

The party reached the circular atrium, a spacious chamber with a domed ceiling. Leafy plants in huge terracotta vases lined the walls. The floor was a mosaic of miniature tiles, fashioned into the images of deer, large cats, and other wild animals loping through swirls of brightly colored forestry. The gentle trickle from a fountain in the center of the room added to the ambience. Marble benches surrounded the water feature. The carriage was summoned. Theodora nodded to a servant who in turn raised her hand, and a young woman appeared with a tray filled with small glasses of an aromatic digestif, made of wine flavored with cloves, black pepper, and mastica. The guests lifted their glasses, along with the empress as she said, "You will like this after dinner drink."

Eudoxia sipped her digestif, then patted her shoulder, glancing around as if she had lost something. "Esmeray, dear, I left my cloak in the dining room, or the anteroom. The night air is chilling."

A servant turned to go, and Esmeray said, "I will get it." Esmeray hurried off with the servant trailing.

"Please!" said the young woman, trying to stay in step with Esmeray, "I will get her cloak."

Esmeray, suffocated by the city, not looking forward to riding the carriage again, wanted to move and kept up her fast stride.

Esmeray entered the cloakroom, glimpsing the emperor and Bastone in discussion as she passed by the entrance to the dining hall. Neither of them noticed her. She retrieved Eudoxia's cloak and overheard the emperor speaking. Esmeray froze, suddenly realizing she should not be there. Also out of the men's sight was the servant girl, standing in the doorway to the hall. Their eyes met, wide with fright.

The emperor's voice was barely more than a whisper. "Giovanni Procida will meet you in Isola Vulcano."

"He has agreed to organize the Sicilian nobles?" asked Bastone, in a conspiratorial tone.

"Yes, and I will deliver the gold that I promised, part of my pledge to support the uprising. Pope Nicholas now approves our plan for Sicily, the requirement demanded by Peter, King of Argon, before he joins us. The Pope, however, will not publicly admit his support. Procida will embark on the *Paradisio* at Vulcano, then sail to Aragon, personally delivering the Pope's oath to Peter."

"And Procida's motivation?"

The emperor hesitated, his lips pressed together, with a glare intimating that Bastone should not question him. But he exhaled, he calmed and said, "Charles Anjou sent his knights to terrorize Procida's family. They raped his daughter and wife and killed one of his sons."

A shadow passed over Bastone's face as he clenched his jaw. Michael noticed. "So you understand. Your determination to stop Charles and avenge your own personal loss is a more powerful driving force than wealth—which makes you my most trustworthy *speculatore*. I should not have to remind you that no one, *not one soul* other than the trusted contacts, can know of the Sicilian plan. Tell no one else. It would be unfortunate if you had a slip of tongue and then had to silence an unlucky wretch."

"Yes, Emperor," said Bastone.

"To make certain you are trading intelligence with trusted speculatores, each interaction must begin with a hint, followed by the correct response."

Bastone leaned forward.

Michael said, "The initiator will say, *Animus Tuus Dominus.*

Bastone tilted his head sideways: "Courage is your Lord."

"And what would be your answer?" asked the emperor.

"My answer?" said Bastone. "I know it is Latin. Would I say—*si*, yes, or *certe*, certainly?"

"The response must be *Antudo*," said Michael.

Bastone's eyebrows knitted, and his forehead wrinkled. He threw his hands up, "Oh! Antudo. Formed by using the first two letters of each word of the motto, Animus Tuus Dominus. Most appropriate. Yes, from what little I know of Sicilian it is similar to Latin."

The emperor lowered his voice again, but Esmeray couldn't resist listening, holding her breath, straining to hear. "The date for the uprising is next spring, on Ascension Day at the Hour of Vespers, on Thursday forty days after Easter Sunday. Sicilians in every town will rise and expel the Angevin interlopers. You will notify your contacts in Catania and Messina. Use the same code word. They will spread the word throughout Sicily. Procida will alert the patriots in the capital of Palermo. It is extremely important this date is kept secret. If the revolt is premature, before we make all the preparations, it will surely fail."

Esmeray knew it was extremely dangerous to remain. She exited the cloak room, slipping into the hallway, unnoticed. Esmeray grabbed the servant's hand, to make her follow, but the girl resisted.

The emperor raised his voice, "What was that?"

Esmeray realized the emperor had heard them. The servant was unmoving. Esmeray dropped the girl's hand and rushed to the end of the long hallway.

Bastone was first out of the dining hall and confronted the servant. A flash of blue fabric diverted his attention at the end of the hallway as it disappeared around the corner. A few steps behind Bastone, the emperor gestured angrily at the servant, shouting, "What are you doing here?"

She was mute with fear.

"What did you hear?" demanded the emperor.

A pair of guards hurried from the opposite way Esmeray had fled. The emperor ordered them to stay in the hall, grabbed the servant girl's wrist, yanking her into the cloakroom. He looked back at Bastone.

"You have your orders," the emperor commanded.

Esmeray rushed down the corridor, chased by shrill cries of agony, suddenly replaced by silence, the abruptness distressing. She stopped, listened, but heard nothing more, wondering if she had imagined it.

Lantern Across the Sea

## CHAPTER VIII    THE ASSASSIN

When they returned from the dinner, Esmeray had taken off her blue tunica and carefully hung it to avoid wrinkles. She picked up her night tunic, chilly, in her bare skin. Eudoxia entered her chamber, her gaze dwelling on Esmeray's figure. There was an awkward pause as she stared. "Esmeray, are you cold? You don't want to sleep alone, do you?"

Esmeray stumbled back, covering herself with her tunic. "Mistress, I . . . um, I am sick from eating too fast."

Eudoxia, appearing disappointed, retreated to her own chamber. Esmeray had avoided Eudoxia's advance but had trouble sleeping. She couldn't rid her mind of the conversation she had overheard between the emperor and Bastone at the palace, and she questioned whether she had really heard the servant girl scream. Esmeray suddenly had a flash of anxiety. *Mother Mary!* She realized Empress Theodora knew she had gone with the servant girl to get Eudoxia's cloak. Esmeray broke into a sweat, now believing the shrieks had been real.

Despite her racing mind, she fell to sleep. But her slumber was interrupted by the cool night air. Esmeray opened her eyes and could see the night sky lit by a crescent moon, though she recalled closing the louvered doors to the balcony. A hand suddenly covered her mouth. She recognized Bastone's voice as he whispered, "Do not cry out."

The conversation between the emperor and Bastone flashed into Esmeray's mind. Anyone who overheard the covert plans would be silenced. She tried to control her anxiety, thinking of alternatives. If she screamed for help, would Bastone kill her?

Bastone whispered, "Come with me—your life is in danger!"

He grasped her wrist, but she resisted.

If she went with him, he would kill her. Her only hope was to shout for help. Esmeray took a deep breath, preparing to scream and fight.

Suddenly there was loud knocking in the next chamber. Eudoxia said, "Who's there?"

There was a loud crack as Eudoxia's door was forced open. She shouted, "Help! Watchman, guard, come at once!"

A male voice bellowed, "Where is your maid? She is wanted for treason!"

Bastone whispered loudly, "It's the emperor's henchmen. They will kill you!" He steered Esmeray to the balcony, the faint light of the moon revealing his black clothes, which were soaking wet. Bastone threaded a rope between the balcony shutters and closed them on the rope to anchor it. Esmeray lowered herself two stories to the ground, dashing away as Bastone was still rappelling. Halfway down the rope, he dropped to the ground, overtook her, catching her by the wrist. She tried to pull free, "I won't tell anyone!"

With a measured, tight voice, he said, "Come on! They murdered the servant girl!"

Believing him, Esmeray ceased struggling.

He released her wrist. "*Andiamo!* Let's go!" He rushed to the edge of the stone well.

Above, the shutters burst open, releasing the rope, which fell to the ground. A man yelled from the balcony above in the darkness, "Near the well!"

The night watchman bolted out of the dark, hardly visible in the light of the crescent moon, then abruptly halted, threatening Bastone with his spear point. Bastone's dark silhouette obscured the guard's view of the hand crank on the well hoist. Reaching behind, Bastone detached the crank, hiding it behind him.

The watchman glanced up and said, "I've caught an intruder!"

A voice from above, "Find the girl! I'm sending another guard."

The watchman peered at Bastone. "Where is the girl?"

Esmeray stepped out of the shadows. "Over here!" The watchman took his eyes off Bastone.

The ring of wood on steel echoed across the dark courtyard as Bastone deflected the watchman's spearpoint with the hand crank the same instant a second guard charged in, thrusting his lance. Bastone leaned out of the way, grabbing the shaft. As they struggled for control of the weapon, he spun the crank against the watchman's temple, who fell unconscious to the ground. Bastone slid the crank along the spear shaft, stripping the guard's hands from his weapon. The spear fell to the ground. Bastone spun behind the guard and hooked the hand crank on his neck. Forming a vise with his forearm and the crank, he applied pressure and the guard struggled, then blacked out.

Bastone jumped to the top of the stone wall surrounding the mouth of the well. "Feet first, arms close in—straight down the middle." He disappeared; a faint splash followed.

Esmeray heard more guards approaching. She vaulted to the top of the wall, briefly caught her balance, then jumped into the well. The dark plunge terrified her, not knowing how far the fall would be before she hit the water. Falling, falling, falling, then . . . *splash!*

The water was biting cold. She surfaced trying to catch her breath from the deep immersion as well as the chilling water. It was pitch black, except for a flame that cast a shimmer across the water. Bastone swam to a rocky shelf, pulling himself out of the water next to the source of light; half of his body unseen, half illuminated. The reverberations of her splash and the feeble light suggested the vastness of the underground chamber, the main cistern for the city.

Trying to fight her chill, Esmeray's rapid breaststrokes echoed across the manmade cavern as she raced to get out of the cold water. Hundreds of marble columns held up the cistern's ceiling, their capitals ornamented like those of a Roman temple.

She accepted Bastone's hand onto the ledge. For a moment they both stood, dripping, wordlessly facing each other. Mesmerized, she ignored her shivering.

Bastone's gaze dropped to her wet tunic clinging to her breasts and hips. Esmeray glanced down and crossed her arms over her chest. He shook his head, looked away, and turned, fumbling through a pile of clothes. She noticed the small oil lamp he had left burning.

Bastone offered some dry clothes. "Put these on."

He handed her a pair of linen *braies,* undershorts, and sailor's cutoff pants. Then he also gave her a tunic. He turned away to retrieve more clothes and said, "It was a gamble that I jumped first, leaving you, but we had to get out immediately, with more guards coming."

Bastone kept his back to Esmeray, as they both undressed. She lingered a moment, then turned her back. "Brrrr," she murmured as her teeth chattered.

He turned slightly, pulling his tunic over his head. "Is there something wrong?" said Bastone.

"No, no . . . even with the dry clothes, I am just still f-freezing." Her arms were wrapped around her chest.

Bastone embraced her, Esmeray's folded arms squeezed against him, and he briskly rubbed her back to warm her, "We will soon be on the streets where it will be warmer,"

She had appreciated the hug, accepting it as platonic, and said, "Thank you, Bastone."

"Er . . . yes . . ."

"Um . . . I mean, for convincing me to leave," said Esmeray.

"Uh, yes, *prego.* And you will be happy that we are going to the *Aspasia.*"

## CHAPTER IX  THE SEA OF MARMARA

After shoving off from its mooring at Galata, the *Paradisio* sailed southeast into the Sea of Marmara. Aboard the *Aspasia* being towed by the larger ship, Esmeray peeked out from under the canvas, watching the sunrise. When they had fled the city the night before, Bastone had left Esmeray hidden on the *Aspasia* with food and water. Captain Zaccaria would not allow an unescorted woman on board the *Paradisio*. To steal her out of the city unnoticed, Bastone hid her on the Aspasia in tow. Bastone told her to stay out of sight until he came for her. She slept most of the day under the canvas, hot, stifled, and bored.

Near sunset, the *Paradisio* anchored off a large island. Moored nearby was a two-masted ship, a little more than half the length of the *Paradisio*, flying a red banner emblazoned with a double-headed gold eagle.

After dark, Esmeray freed herself from her confinement and sat in her former fishing boat with only the light of the stars, eating bread, cheese, olives, and chasing the food with water. Perhaps Bastone hid her on the boat, planning to take her where she couldn't reveal the secrets she had overheard. Enslavement or worse, death could await her. She glanced up at the *Paradisio,* noticing a glow from the outdoor galley. There was also a dim light from an oil lamp in the porthole of an officer's cabin. No one was watching her, so this was her time to cut the *Aspasia* free and leave. Before she could act, the boat lurched, then again. The *Aspasia* was being pulled toward the *Paradisio*. Within moments she saw Bastone on the stern drawing in the line. It was too late for her to flee.

Using the same line, he rappelled down the ship's hull to the smaller craft and untied the *Aspasia*. "I am sorry you had to wait here so long," he loudly whispered, "now I will marry you."

"Marry?" Esmeray didn't believe him. The women she used to work with warned her of men's tricks. "What . . . what are you talking about?"

"It will be a marriage that will benefit both of us," said Bastone. "You need to get far away from the emperor, no?"

"Y-yes."

"I need to watch you closely," said Bastone. "I can't let you repeat what you heard in the palace."

Perhaps Bastone wasn't a pirate, like most of the Genoese. Esmeray recalled their embrace the night before. Was he showing affection? It didn't matter. She was a very fortunate woman. And she was aware that it was common for arranged marriages to benefit both parties, not only between nobles to accumulate power and influence, but among the chorikos as well. And although Esmeray always believed her parents loved one another, did her father, a Romaioi citizen of the empire, marry her mother, a Seljuk Turk, for diplomatic reasons? The marriage had contributed to decades of peace between their two villages.

"And if you come with me—it would please you to be sailing on the *Paradisio*, yes?" added Bastone. "But Captain Zaccaria will not allow unmarried or unescorted women to take passage on his ship—the same as any other captain."

"Oh . . . I see." Esmeray felt foolish to think he might care for her.

Bastone rowed to the ship anchored next to the *Paradisio*. As they passed the stern castle, engraved in Greek letters on the hull, was the ship's name: ΕΥΞΕΙΝΟΣ ΠΟΝΤΟΣ, *Euxinos Pontos*.

Members of the crew let a knotted rope down the side of the hull. A man and woman watched expectantly from the ship's deck, attended by a pair of sailors holding torches. Bastone gestured for Esmeray to ascend. She easily scaled the hull and he followed.

Reaching the deck, he nodded and said, "Captain Doukas? I am Ponzio Bastone, Officer of the Arbalesters."

"My pleasure, Signore Ponzio!" The men embraced and Doukas added, "And this is my wife, Lady Sasa."

"*Buona sera!*" Bastone leaned forward as she offered her left cheek first. Bastone hesitated.

"Oh, I am sorry, Signore Ponzio. I am Catalan. In greeting I remember now, the Genoese offer the right cheek first."

Bastone touched his right cheek to hers, then they joined left cheeks, she kissing the air. Sasa laughed as she said, "Signore, being a captain's wife, it is rare for me to greet gentlemen."

Bastone looked to the captain then to Sasa and said, "Please, call me Bastone."

The captain and lady both eyed Esmeray during an awkward silence. "Oh! And, of course, meet Esmeray, er . . . Signorina Esmeray."

They moved to the stern, entered the captain's quarters, and sat on cushioned benches which were securely fixed to the bulkhead. As the captain poured wine for them, he said, "When you arrived, I thought you were Captain Zaccaria and his wife."

Sasa glanced at Doukas, then shifted her eyes to Esmeray. The captain gently cleared his throat.

"You represent the *Paradisio* owners?" added Doukas.

"Yes, there are two owners." Bastone removed a parchment from his tunic and laid it on the small table in front of Doukas to review, but the captain hesitated to look at it and sipped his wine.

"Benedetto Zaccaria and my uncle, Ponzio Riccio, own the *Paradisio*," said Bastone. "I am the ship's scribe."

"Ah!" sighed Doukas, "then you can confirm that Zaccaria will pay me half the value of the Trebizond alum, the finest in the world . . . before we join your expedition."

"Yes, tomorrow morning, before we sail west," said Bastone.

"And Sasa, our ship's scribe, will help you go over our inventory and record the transaction."

"We will pay you the other half when we return," said Bastone.

"I am certain of that," said Doukas. "My Sasa is very sharp, unrelenting, and always makes sure we receive the total payment for our goods. And how did your captain's negotiations go with Michael?"

"The emperor has assured Captain Zaccaria that he has banned all vessels transporting alum from the Black Sea. Until you return from the voyage, your nave, the *Pontos Euxinos,* will be the last to bring Trebizond alum into the Mediterranean."

Doukas added, "Very good!" He raised his cup, and the others copied, "*Ya mas!*"

Sasa and Bastone went below deck into the hold to inspect and count the sacks of alum from Trebizond.

"Sasa, I saw you peering at Esmeray," said Bastone. "It is a complicated story, but do you think your husband, as captain at sea, would perform the marriage vows for us?"

"Ah, a romance? Tell me!" said Sasa.

Bastone concocted a story about how his family, being Catholic, would not let him marry a Greek Orthodox woman so they had to marry in secret. It enthralled Sasa.

"My husband will do it! And I am qualified to prepare the marriage contract—the Roman laws in Trebizond are identical to those in Constantinople."

In the captain's quarters, Sasa offered Esmeray a choice of several dresses to wear for the brief marriage ritual. She chose a woad blue tunica, though a more humble weave than the others, which Sasa gifted to her as a memento. Sasa also provided basics for the ritual. Bastone and Esmeray held lighted candles at the top of the stern castle. Under the stars, they recited their vows. Bastone produced simple wedding rings he had fashioned from his chain mail shirt. Doukas and Sasa spit three times over the side wale into the sea for luck.

Bastone gave profuse thank yous and rowed the *Aspasia* back to the *Paradisio*. He tied the trohantiras to the stern of the larger ship. "At this hour it's best for us to sleep on the *Aspasia*. In the morning, I will negotiate with the captain for your passage on the *Paradisio*."

Esmeray wanted to overcome her anxiety about her matrimonial obligation and pulled her tunica over her head, her figure alluring in the shadows of the dim light from the ship's lantern.

Bastone also shed his clothes, already aroused. He raised the edge of the canvas to invite Esmeray to their conjugal shelter. They moved to the stern, past the last rowers' bench. There was barely room for them to lie side by side. His intimacy and gentleness soothed Esmeray. Amid his passionate kisses, she had to know something. "Bastone . . . Bastone—wait! Now that we're married, is all of this—secreting me out of the city, hiding me, marrying me—just to keep me from revealing your plans?"

"Esmeray, I realized, just last night, I could not bear to let you be harmed. I have respect for you—your courage after you lost your father and your actions during the pirates' assault."

She wanted to believe him.

"Esmeray, during one of my early sea voyages years ago, I was on night watch in the crow's nest of the *Paradisio*. I was mesmerized as the nave sailed smoothly across the sea, the full moon reflecting across the waves—*perfetto!* But I realized something was missing. Yes, a partner to share all this. You—you were the one missing. And you love the sea so much—as do I, also a lover of the sea."

Esmeray sensed he was genuine. The romantic depiction melted away her distrust. She kissed him with full lips, her tears invisible in the dark, and took his hand, placing it between her legs. She recalled the women she had worked with told her it would be painful. "Please, not too fast."

Bastone showed a gentleman's control, as he warmed her and began with slow, even motions. After an initial brief pang, Esmeray felt pleasure build, then suddenly Bastone withdrew. She wondered if that was all there was. Bastone, however, promptly returned to Esmeray, and her pleasure intensified until her teeth tingled.

At sunrise, Bastone and Esmeray used the rope connecting the *Aspasia* to the *Paradisio* to ascend to the larger ship's deck. They joined the sailors for breakfast at the galley, amid their curious glances. The sailors knew better than to question their superior, and mercifully, Amilcare was not on deck. The crew shared breakfast with them. Most of the sailors remembered Esmeray but their glances betrayed their surprise that she had returned. The newly married couple finished eating and went to the stern castle. Bastone knocked on the captain's door as he said, "Capitano, it is Bastone."

"Enter!"

Benedetto was drinking diluted wine. The captain held up his cup as he welcomed him, "Bastone, have some . . . what! What is she doing on board?

"You should be with my sister-in-law . . ." The captain guffawed. "Oh, she failed to seduce another maid . . .and got rid of you!" He laughed again. "I am not surprised, but what is she doing here, Bastone?"

Bastone put his arm around Esmeray's shoulders and handed the captain their marriage contract. "We are married."

"No!" He took another drink, then paused in thought. "Hmm. Captains and officers," said Benedetto, "under special circumstances, can bring their wife on expeditions . . .but women are not permitted on the ship, so as to not distract the crew," continued the captain, "and they will be demoralized when they imagine you sleeping with your sweet bride." His gaze was lustful, but he regained composure.

"Sir, I *am* an officer, and this *is* a special circumstance," said Bastone. "Esmeray has lost her entire family. Her father died because of his service to us. We owe her. I am asking for your permission."

"Hmm." The captain stroked his bearded chin in thought. "She cannot stay in your quarters."

Benedetto Zaccaria grew up embracing the maxim: *A Genoese, therefore a merchant*. And a merchant must profit. He finished pondering. "Very well, Bastone, she . . . Esmeray can stay. She must quarter in one of the two guest staterooms at the stern castle. You will sleep at the fore castle in your own quarters," said Benedetto. "We have no passengers, so it will conveniently add to the ship's profits."

Esmeray smiled and looked at Bastone, but he did not seem to share her joy, "Sir, I cannot afford to pay for those luxury quarters!"

"But of course, Bastone, you have a concession because your uncle is part owner of the nave. How about half price?" said Benedetto.

The captain's eyebrows raised when Esmeray interposed, "Captain Zaccaria, do you remember that I helped the crew during the pirate attack?"

He appeared curious, rather than angry, that a woman would speak. "Yes?"

"I know you have not replaced all your lost crew and sailors are working extra shifts—I will do a sailor's work, with the wages going to help pay for my quarters."

The captain was silent and paused in thought, then said, "Bastone, your Uncle Riccio is my partner and friend and I want to give you a wedding gift—so Esmeray will have the suite for one-fourth the full price . . ."

Bastone and Esmeray both exhaled, "*Grazie mille!*"

"But Esmeray, you must dress as a sailor . . . as a man and do your duties. Bastone, it seems you married a woman both beautiful, *and* shrewd.

Michael A. Ponzio

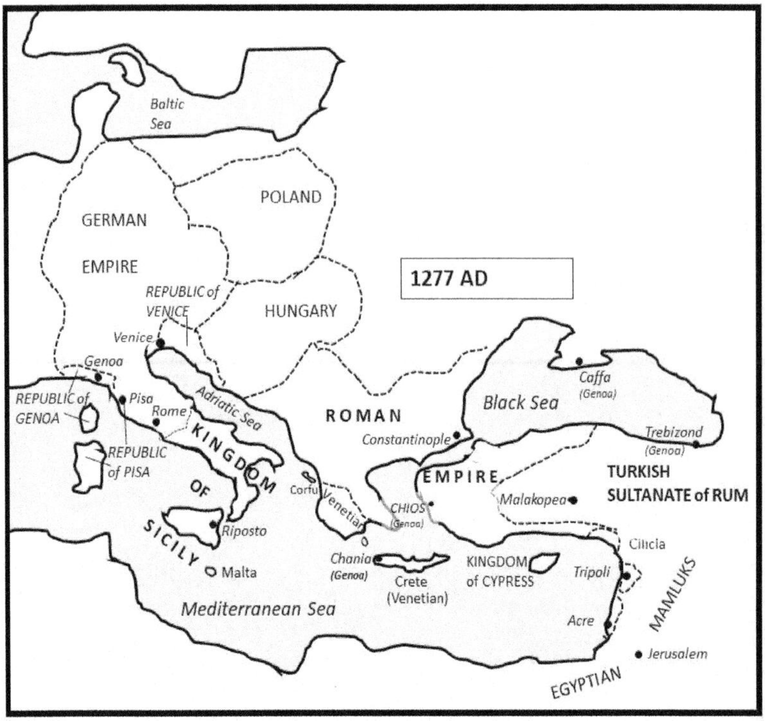

1277 AD
Baltic Sea
POLAND
GERMAN EMPIRE
HUNGARY
REPUBLIC of VENICE
Venice
Genoa
REPUBLIC of GENOA
Pisa
REPUBLIC of PISA
Rome
Adriatic Sea
KINGDOM OF SICILY
Riposto
Malta
Corfu
Venetian
ROMAN EMPIRE
Constantinople
CHIOS
(Genoa)
Chania
(Genoa)
Crete
(Venetian)
KINGDOM of CYPRESS
Black Sea
Caffa
(Genoa)
Trebizond
(Genoa)
TURKISH SULTANATE of RUM
Malakopea
Cilicia
Tripoli
Acre
MAMLUKS
Jerusalem
EGYPTIAN
Mediterranean Sea

## CHAPTER X     CRETE

The *Pontos Euxinos* and the *Paradisio* docked at Chania, the major seaport on the west coast of the island of Crete. Decades before, the Venetians had taken the island, which they called Candia, from the Romans and expelled the Genoese merchants. In 1263, however, the Genoese Captain Enrico Pescatore, with local support, had recovered the city and nearby environs. Now held by the Cretan Romans, Genoese ships could safely use Chania as a port of call.

As sailors and marines disembarked to the town's waterfront from the two ships for shore leave, the deck of the *Paradisio* was mostly vacant. Esmeray and Bastone leaned on the side wale looking out to sea. She said, "The crew will go ashore to get . . . uh . . . amusement?"

"Yes, and the ship will resupply with water and fresh vegetables—to go with our pasta," said Bastone.

"Macaroni, pasta—do the Genoese eat anything else?"

"We eat more than just pasta. Don't you remember eating the fish filet, the thin strips marinated and preserved in olive oil?"

"Yes, it was . . . er . . . *musciamm*?"

Bastone nodded. "And if we are lucky to get eggs, we make *capponada*: anchovies, black olives, capers, hard boiled eggs with olive oil. Of course, pasta is a Genoese sailor's favorite food. Each

Ligurian town, each village, each family, they have their favorite kind."

"Liguria?" asked Esmeray.

"It is the region, the land around Genoa. As you are from Anatolia, from the village of . . . what was its name again?"

"Malakopea," said Esmeray, "and what is your favorite macaroni?"

"Rigatoni—it has ridges like the smaller penne rigate that we bring with us on the ship."

"Hmm." Esmeray wandered over to the double cranks that hoisted the anchor. She tugged on the handle.

"What are you doing, Esme?"

"I wanted you to show me how you spun the crank the other night fighting the guard. The handle at the well came off so easily."

"Like most courtyard villas, they have a wine press, a grain mill, a well hoist—mechanisms that require handles," said Bastone. "Those handles are interchangeable among the devices in case one breaks or is misplaced. But here the crank arm is firmly attached by a pin to the anchor hoist."

Bastone went to the crank and removed a metal pin, grasped the handle, and whirled the crank arm in circular patterns. "Here, try it."

After a few attempts, Esmeray was spinning the crank arm smoothly through the air. "Hm . . . I like this!"

"I will show you a much more accessible weapon to use on the ship." Bastone replaced the crank and held his arm out toward the side wale.

"What? Oh, the belaying pins. Of course!" said Esmeray.

Along the side rail of the ship, scores of belaying pins, wooden rods, varying from one to two feet long, were inserted into round holes. The ends of the rods had been fashioned to the thickness of a man's thumb, to fit into the holes. The opposite ends were larger and rounded, giving the belaying pins the appearance of wooden clubs.

"You handle these all the time, tying the lanyards onto them, moving them to apply tension to the lines," said Bastone.

He handed Esmeray a pin. "What could you do with this to defend yourself?"

She smiled, "I'd hit you on the head." She playfully raised the rod.

"He grabbed her wrist, breaking her grip by pressing the rod down on her hand.

"Hey! That hurt! But how would this help against, say, pirates with swords?"

He handed her one of the longer pins and brandished two others. "Slash at me with your sword."

She hesitated.

"Don't worry, we will go slowly, and I won't hurt you."

Esmeray swung the rod downward and Bastone stepped to the side, parrying her weapon with one belaying pin and gently tapping the knuckles of her hand with the other.

"Now you try it."

They repeated, changing roles. Esmeray cracked down hard on his knuckles. Bastone grimaced, but he erupted into laughter, joining Esmeray's outburst. She sensed he enjoyed the play and she delighted in how his blue eyes sparkled and smiled by themselves. After days of fear and stress, she had forgotten how it felt to be happy. They dropped the pins to the deck and Bastone took Esmeray's hand and led her to the guest suite.

Esmeray woke refreshed to see Bastone sponging off from the wash bowl at the dresser. He glanced at her as he toweled his face. "Your quarters are comfortable!"

Footsteps resounded on the deck accompanied by loud banter. Sailors were returning from the waterfront. "Get dressed—wear your sailor's clothes. We're going on an excursion in Chania."

"We? — I am going with you?"

"Yes," said Bastone with a broad smile, "I cannot leave you out of my sight—remember, that's why I married you." Esmeray, still in a state of bliss, accepted his comment as sarcasm.

Esmeray's modesty made her hesitate to get out of bed.

"You are shy. Well, yes, don't move," said Bastone, "if you drop that blanket, I will never leave this room!"

He finished dressing and as he left said, "Hurry, I have a surprise."

They headed down the waterfront, busy with townspeople and sailors. The late afternoon sun was still above the horizon, but torches had already been lit along the street. Bastone steered Esmeray into a small shop. There, a gray-haired man worked pieces of metal with a small hammer. Bastone said in Greek, "Do you have any wedding rings?"

"Yes." The man led them to a counter. "Like these iron rings?"

Esmeray frowned. "Those are peasant wedding rings. I would rather keep the ring you gave me when we were married."

Bastone placed his hands on her shoulders, matching eyes, "Esme, those simple bands are an ancient heritage passed down from the first Romans. Even the nobles wore them.

"We'll still keep our marriage rings, but I never gave you an engagement ring."

The goldsmith said, "Here are some with gems." He pulled out several gold rings.

Bastone placed a hand around Esmeray's waist, "Do you like any of those?"

Her eyes grew wide, and her mouth dropped open. "That one! There, the blue stone—the color of the sea."

The smith handed her a gold ring with a blue stone speckled with flakes of gold. "This stone is the *lapis lazuli*. A blue stone from Persia, far to the east." The goldsmith peered at Bastone. "Like the blue eyes of your husband. An excellent choice."

"And young lady, the lapis lazuli will ward off the spirits of darkness and draw in the spirits of light and wisdom."

The goldsmith fixed the ring so it would fit Esmeray, and as the couple left the shop, she could not take her eyes off the beautiful gemstone. "It will go perfectly with my woad blue dress, and it's even more pleasing that the ring is the color of your eyes.

"At the goldsmith's you said something about ancient Romans. I am a Romaioi, a Roman, you are Genoese."

"Yes, the Romaioi of Constantinople inherited the empire from Rome, many, many years ago. There are ruins of their great cities all over Italy. Does that make sense?"

"Yes."

"I am descended from the ancient Romans," said Bastone.

"How do you know?"

"Latin, their language, the language of Romans in the west, has many words that are the same as Genoese . . . and my name."

"Your name—Ponzio Bastone—you are addressed as Signore Ponzio. Then your captain, Benedetto Zaccaria—his family name is second."

Bastone answered, "My father and his forebears have preserved the ancient Roman way. "For example, have you heard of Julius Caesar? His family name was Julius."

"I heard my father refer to the emperor as 'Caesar of the Romans,' but I have never heard the name Julius," said Esmeray.

"Hmm, well you have recited the Nicene Creed at Mass, right?" said Bastone.

Esmeray nodded and said, "I haven't been to Mass for years."

"Remember this part? '*Stavrothenta te ypér imon epi Pontíou Pilatou*, He was crucified for us under Pontius Pilate.'"

"Yes," answered Esmeray.

"He was the Roman governor of Judea. Pontius was his family or clan name. Pilatus was his familiar name. Pontius Pilatus, Ponzio Bastone."

"Oh . . . I see."

She cast her eyes toward the ground. "You know so much. I feel ignorant in comparison. I can't even read, you had to sign my name on our marriage contract."

"Please, no, Esmeray! You are . . . um . . . you are competent sailing a boat . . . you know all the sailors' knots, and . . . you even built a trohantiras with your father. I can't do that. And only you can be my Esmeray . . . the woman I dreamed about years ago."

She raised her head, "You will teach me to read?"

"Yes, of course. You are bright, it will be easy for you, but . . . only if you teach me to sail. I've been on ships most of my life, as a marine. Only rarely in a crisis do I help the sailors."

Her smile returned. "And Bastone, thank you for the beautiful ring."

In the twilight, they made their way up a small hill and arrived at the Greek Orthodox monastery of Agios Nikolaos. "Esmeray, as an envoy of Emperor Michael, I will have a meeting tonight with Enrico Pescatore, who is leading the resistance against the Venetians on Crete. However, he is essentially a pirate whom I barely trust."

Outside the entrance to the monastery courtyard, they hid in the shadows behind an opened gate. Bastone offered her a wooden comb.

"What?"

He slid off one end revealing a scribe's quill knife. "If there is trouble, run and tell Captain Zaccaria."

Esmeray's gaiety quickly evaporated and was replaced with concern.

"Use the knife, only if you are in danger, but keep it concealed, like this . . ." He held the handle in a reverse grip so the sharpened edge of the blade was along the outside of his wrist, "then slash like this. They will not detect your attack until it's too late." He demonstrated, cutting the air. "Keep the dull back of the blade against your arm, so it will not harm you, but it will cut them if they grab for the knife.

"Wait for me here and listen."

Bastone entered the courtyard and soon a man arrived, armed like Bastone with a dagger at his belt. The man shoved his palm against Bastone's left shoulder, knocking the marine off balance. Esmeray unsheathed the penknife. She took a step toward the stranger, his back toward her, but froze when the men laughed as Bastone clapped the other man's shoulder just as hard. Satisfied the meeting might continue without violence, Esmeray returned to the shadows.

Both men gestured with their hands as they talked. Esmeray was close enough to hear most of their conversation. Bastone promised Pescatore that the emperor would deliver weapons for the insurgents at the monastery of St. John Theologos on the nearby Souda Bay. The man referred to Bastone as a *speculatore*. Esmeray recalled the emperor had also used that word.

The collaborators completed their discussion. Esmeray and Bastone returned to the *Paradisio* to their respective quarters, and the ship, now resupplied, would be ready to cast off at sunrise the next morning.

The *Pontos Euxinos* and the *Paradisio* sailed west from Chania, the ships tacking to port using the Etesian winds that alternated between nor'westerly and northerly. The variable winds kept the sailors busy day after day, and the novelty of observing Esmeray performing a seaman's tasks had worn off. One morning, as Esmeray was working closely with a team of sailors hoisting the mizzen sail, the man behind her bumped her with his crotch. She turned and called out in Genoese, "Oh, I thought you were Bastone! No, you are too soft." She grabbed a nearby belaying pin, punched it into his stomach, knocking the air from him, and then shoved the rod down his pants. "Here is a hard *bastone!*"

The sailors nearby bent over with laughter. Even the sailor who got the end of her payback joined them. Bastone chuckled as he watched from across the deck. The captain, at first concerned with similar incidents, saw them disappear with her ability to join in the antics as well as laugh at herself.

A week after leaving Crete, Esmeray woke just before sunrise and carried her chamber pot to the bow of the ship. She poured the contents through the lattice of timbers, the crew's head, and the waste quickly mixed with the seawater from the turbulence of the bow wash.

In the dim light as she made her way back to her quarters, she heard Bastone talking to one of his men. Out of their sight, she stopped to listen as a man's voice rose in anger.

"What are you doing bringing that little whore on the ship! You are betrothed to my sister."

She recognized Amilcare's voice, the arbalester who shot the thief, leading to the death of her father.

"She isn't a whore—watch what you say, Amilcare," said Bastone. "You should remember," said Bastone. "I am your commanding officer, be careful!"

Michael A. Ponzio

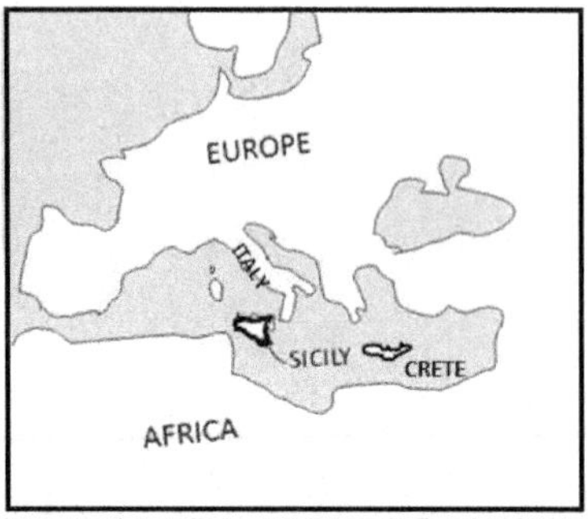
EUROPE
ITALY
SICILY
CRETE
AFRICA

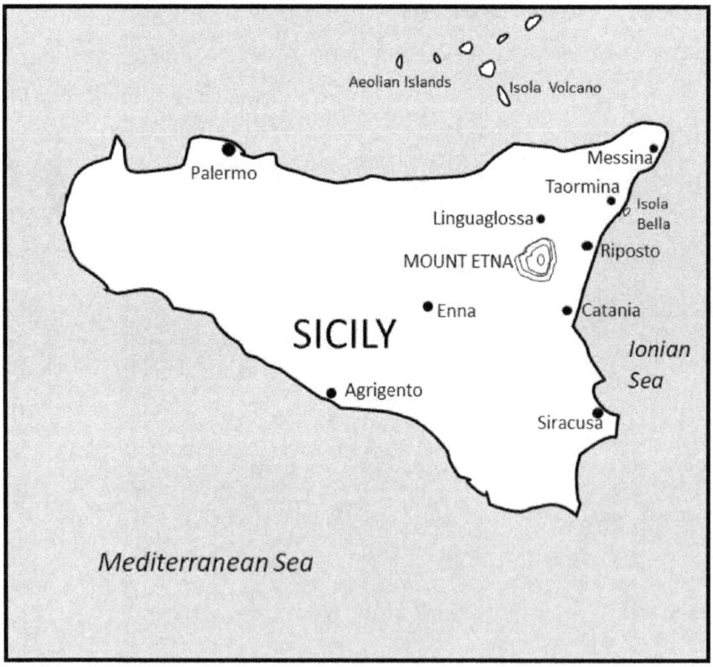
Aeolian Islands
Isola Volcano
Palermo
Messina
Taormina
Isola Bella
Linguaglossa
Riposto
MOUNT ETNA
Enna
Catania
SICILY
Ionian Sea
Agrigento
Siracusa
Mediterranean Sea

## CHAPTER XI    CATANIA, SICILY

Tacking to port in the late afternoon, the two ships approached Catania on the east coast of Sicily, much of the landscape displaying the flax color of the perennial dry summers. But on the slopes of the towering Mount Etna, which dominated the backdrop, the land became greener with altitude. Forests and green valleys alternated with large swaths of black volcanic rock, cooled lava, which eventually degraded to become fertile soils rich in nutrients.

It had been a somber day for the crew of the *Paradisio* with the death of their barber surgeon and mouser. A crewman had found the body of the aged barber below deck. Enfolded in his arms on his chest was lifeless Fumotina, the ship's mascot. The cat had served the ship for over fifteen years. Both had been honored with burial at sea.

 The summer sky was cloudless, the breeze was comfortable, bringing only moderate humidity. Bastone shared the extraordinary panorama with Esmeray as they watched from the taffrail. "I will never tire of Etna's magnificence," said Bastone.

Esmeray did not comment. Bastone glanced at her, expecting her usual smile, but she kept her gaze across the water. He was concerned about her lack of conversation over the last few days.

"It is typical for Etna to be smoking," he said. "We are lucky there are no eruptions of lava or ash."

As planned, the ship from Trebizond, sailing parallel to the *Paradisio*, veered north as Captain Doukas headed toward the Straits of Messina and would continue to the Island of Vulcano. There he would anchor alongside a Genoese ship, being loaded with alum. The mines on the island produced a lower quality alum than either Trebizond or Foca, but the Zaccaria brothers had found customers for the less expensive product. In a couple of days, the *Paradisio* would also sail north to join the ships at Vulcano.. Then the flotilla would proceed to Mallorca, the chief port of the Balearic Islands in the western Mediterranean Sea.

Catania had been a populous and busy port since Greek times, rivaling Messina and Syracuse. Near the waterfront at the south end of the city walls, looming above the terracotta rooftops, were the barbicans of Castello Ursino. It had been a royal dwelling of the former King Frederick, but was now occupied by the Baron of Catania, appointed by King Charles. Rising above the city was the bell tower of Saint Agatha's Cathedral.

"You will enjoy Catania. The people are welcoming, and the food is the best." Bastone glanced sideways at Esmeray, but she continued her stoic mien.

"Do you want on shore with me? I will be purchasing silk to trade on our voyage."

She nodded without looking at him.

"You can see our destination." He pointed. "See the castle—on the left, with the round towers. Only a short walk from the waterfront. You should wear your woad tunica. On the way back, we'll go by the *pescheria*, the biggest fish market you will ever see. With delicious street food!"

Bastone tried to pull Esmeray out of her gloominess.

"They sell cloth at the market, too. Perhaps you can find material for a new tunica?"

He didn't think anything would brighten her.

Within an hour the *Paradisio* was docked, and the captain awarded the crew shore leave in alternating shifts. Bastone and his marine escort waited for Esmeray to join them at the end of the gangplank. Zaccaria and a pair of marines disembarked, the captain paying a city official the docking fee and purchasing two merchant permits. He gave Bastone one permit and left with his escorts to purchase silk.

Bastone waited for Esmeray, wondering if she had changed her mind about joining him. There were numerous soldiers patrolling the waterfront, as if King Charles had the city on a war footing, expecting an attack. The city had not been militarized during Bastone's last visit several years ago.

His wife arrived. "Esme, glad you are coming. Good, let's go."

Bastone was not surprised that the nearest pair of Angevin soldiers swaggered toward them when he stepped onto the wharf. Without a word, he produced his merchant's permit, handed it to one of the Angevins, and held both arms out, glancing back at his marine escort who did the same, indicating they were not armed, other than permissible daggers.

Bastone reached to retrieve the permit, but the guard yanked it back and held out his palm. "*La taxe!*"

"The captain paid the tax," said Bastone, "er . . . la taxe. . . uh, *la fin*, finished!"

The guard held the permit up as if he would rip it in two. The second guard gripped his sword handle. "No, fin! La taxe!"

Bastone surrendered to the fact he would have to bribe the Angevins. His face reddened as he placed a bronze coin in each of the soldiers' palms. The guard did not release his permit. After he put another coin in their hands, the guard didn't resist when Bastone snatched the permit from him. As Bastone walked on, Esmeray followed, the Genoese marine trailing behind. As she passed the Angevin soldiers, one of them grabbed her rear. She turned, snatched the marine's dagger from his sheath, and faced the molester.

Esmeray had fire in her eyes. "Try that again!"

A handful of sailors on the *Paradisio* had been watching and started down the gangplank.

Bastone raised his hands for the sailors to wait and said, "No, Esmeray. Just go back to the ship. Now!"

Esmeray flipped the dagger to the Genoese marine, who caught the handle. She moved up the plank. When she reached the deck of the *Paradisio*, she turned, shouting to the Angevin guards. "Stronzi!"

The Genoese sailors burst out laughing.

Bastone and his escort entered the city, working their way through the narrow streets, crowded with pedestrians. There had always been beggars in Catania, but Bastone did not remember seeing scores upon scores of them as today, sitting against the walls along the cobbled ways, laying near fountains and market stalls in the plazas. Pedestrians deftly moved out of the way of the Angevin soldiers, who on more than one occasion, shouldered Bastone against the wall of a narrow street. The soldiers kicked the pauper's legs out of the way as they passed, swiping fruit off vendors' stalls as they walked by. The city was not the vibrant Catania Bastone remembered. He was sure it was King Charles's doing.

They arrived at Castello Ursino and Bastone presented his merchant's permit to an Angevin soldier manning the open gates. He tried his limited French, "*Voir le scribe, Monsieur Vadala.*"

"*Iu parru sicilianu.*" Although the guard's Sicilian was thick with a French accent, Bastone understood him, relieved the guard knew Sicilian.

He continued with a mix of Genoese and the little Sicilian he knew, "I am here to buy silk from the scribe Vadala."

He was led into the courtyard. After the incident on the wharf and the stress of the crowded streets, he welcomed the calm of the verdant garden setting. He noted the patches of vegetables and an orchard of mulberry trees. The trees provided the silkworms their food and habitat. The cloth was also woven at the location, providing enormous profits for the local baron.

The soldier gestured toward a short, stocky man pruning a tree. The Angevin soldier then beckoned Bastone's escort, "*Veni*, come," and gestured as if holding a cup and drinking, smiled and added, "*Vinu*, wine!"

The pair left and Bastone approached the man he assumed was Vadala. The man's back was to him. "Signore Vadala? I am Ponzio Bastone."

As he turned and said, "Yes, I am Vadala." He grabbed a walking stick propped against a tree, abruptly swinging the cane. Bastone ducked under a diagonal sweeping arc, moved forward to disarm, but the man was too quick. He whipped the stick away and continued a diagonal strike from the opposite direction. Bastone, still in close, struck the man's hands upward with his palms, deflecting the stick, and avoided being hit.

The shorter man stepped back, tossed the cane to Bastone, and thrust his paring knife forward. Bastone caught the stick just in time to deflect the blade, and when the man twisted his wrist to slice Bastone's fingers, the Genoese barely parried the blade again. Bastone tried to move sideways and backwards to take advantage of the stick's longer range, but the Sicilian remained close as he kept pressing him, rotating his knife. Finally, Bastone used the stick and his free hand to cross lock the man's wrist and stop the attack.

Vadala said, "I have a free hand. If I had a second knife . . ."

"But you don't," said Bastone.

Bastone released his lock and the men both stepped back at ease, the friendly match over, both catching their breath.

The shorter man laughed. "How did you learn the skills that have earned your name, Bastone?"

"When I was a youth, on the streets of Genoa."

"And you, Signore Vadala?"

"I grew up a shepherd. Sicilian sheepherders must know how to defend the flocks with the bastone. On your next visit, perhaps you and I can 'walk the circle' together and have a stick match.

"But now we have business, no?" said Vadala. He added in a soft voice, "*Animus tuus dominus.*"

Bastone glanced around and replied in the same covert tone, "*Antudo.*"

Vadala laughed, then said, "We are in Sicily, Signore Ponzio."

Bastone tried again, "*Antudu.*"

"Bonu, you have a message for me?" said Vadala.

"It will be next spring on Ascension Day, at the Hour of Vespers," said Bastone.

Vadala acquiesced with a slow blink. "How symbolic. Jesus rising into Heaven—Sicilians rising against tyranny! The Sicilian people will have the support of Genoa?"

Bastone nodded. He embraced the man, whispering, "A Genoese ship will be arriving in days delivering weapons that will be hidden in wine amphora."

"And the Romans of the east?" said Vadala.

"The same ship will have the gold that Emperor Michael promised," whispered Bastone.

"And the name of the ship?"

"The *Cicero.*"

Vadala slapped Bastone on the back and released his clinch. "How appropriate!"

Bastone tilted his head. "Signore? Cicero, the ancient Roman statesman?"

"Yes, he defended the Sicilians in court against a despotic governor, freeing the island from his tyranny," said Vadala.

Vadala took on a concerned look. "The people of Catania are very fearful of the repercussions of one more failed revolt. Who else will you convince to help us?"

"Giovanni Procida is negotiating with Peter, King of Aragon and his wife, Constanza, to help in the revolt. The queen's father was killed fighting King Charles, and she inherited the Sicilian throne."

"Yes, yes, I knew this. She was born in Sicily," said Vadala. "But what of Procida? Is he a mercenary? How dependable is he?"

"Charles's knights attacked Procida's home while he was gone, killed his son, and violated his daughter and wife."

"Then I am convinced," said Vadala.

"The emperor said you are to pass on the date and time to the patriots' leader of Val Noto," said Bastone.

"That will be Gualtiero Caltagirone, of course," said Vadala. "You are testing me, I see. He is governing his fief from Giarratana and will ensure the patriots of Noto will be ready."

"By the way," he added as he led Bastone to a private space in the orchard. "What port will your nave call on next?"

"Riposto."

"You certainly noticed how abusive the baron treats the people of Catania. Riposto is also in his fief. Because of King Charles's tax exemptions for the Angevin colonists, the Sicilians pay more. The baron also requisitions goods and some Catanese must lodge soldiers in their homes. Sicilians can't even make salt for trade anymore, Charles declared it a royal monopoly. And watch out for Angevin soldiers looking for bribes. My cousin, Samuel, is mayor of Riposto. Although he struggles under the baron of Catania, if you run into problems, mention my name, and tell him you are my *mbare*."

Bastone held both palms up. His forehead wrinkled.

"*Mbare* means, close friend, a *very* trusted friend."

They came to a small wooden table. Vadala motioned toward a stool. "Please sit. I was just about to have some tea."

They sipped from small ceramic cups. Bastone relaxed, finding the setting, the tea very calming. Too calming. Suddenly he feared that his escort must have been purposefully lured away, and he was drinking . . . tea, which had sedative effects.

Was this a trap? After his attack with the shepherd's staff failed, perhaps this was Vadala's second try to kill Bastone? Vadala was Bastone's designated contact, but . . . he was also the baron's scribe. The tea was affecting Bastone's perception.

Bastone sensed Vadala saw his unease. The man smiled. "The tea is good, no? It is from these white mulberry trees. They provide a place for the worms who make the silk, *and* a relaxing beverage."

Vadala knew the proper code words. Bastone eased as he realized the fear was in his imagination.

"So, what is your mission in Riposto," said Vadala. "My cousin there is certainly a patriot, but not a conspirator."

Bastone nodded. "To ensure a supply of resin for Michael."

"And will you make a circuit of Sicily and spread the word?" asked Vadala.

"In Messina, I will meet my contact."

"Alaimo?"

"Yes, then my ship will sail to England to trade alum."

Vadala's eyebrows raised. "Sail all the way to England?"

Bastone nodded.

"Did you know the English merchants in Messina are also supporting the cause?" said Vadala.

"There is an English trading colony in Messina?"

"Yes, I am acquainted with one of the merchants, by the name of Ciccio Inglese. He detests King Charles because of his high taxes and Inglese contributed funds for the revolt. During his last port of call at Catania, he jested with me that if Edmund Crouchback had become King of Sicily, conditions would be much better for the people."

Bastone tilted his head briefly. "Crouchback? Yes, now I recall that before Charles was awarded Sicily by the Pope, Edmund, the brother of King Edward of England, was offered the crown but couldn't raise an army." He touched an index finger to his temple as his eyes widened. "On our journey to England I could spread falsehoods that Edmund is going to reclaim Sicily." He slapped his knees. "And, after we return, the fact that we opened the seaway from England could deceive Charles into thinking Edmund's fleet could be next."

"Yes, every small bit of deception to divert Charles will help," said Vadala.

Vadala gave Bastone a tour of the orchard and the spinners' hall, where scores of women unraveled silk thread from cocoons floating in large pans of hot water. "They are using the latest method—spinning wheels," said Vadala.

Next they observed the weavers using draw looms, requiring two people to operate. "These looms produce the largest bolts of fabric. I am sure you will be pleased with your purchase," said Vadala.

They returned to the secluded table in the orchard, where Vadala poured wine into small, handleless cups. "When you return to your ship, I will send a cart along with your bolts of silk, the finest in Sicily!" He raised his cup and then sipped.

"Thank you, er, Signore Vadala. That is your surname?" said Bastone.

"Yes, my given name is Guiseppe, or just Pepe." Vadala laughed, then asked, "And was your father Ponzio? Your given name, Bastone—stick, would be *Vastuni*, in Sicilian! And who were you fighting in the alleys of Genoa?"

"The nobles' sons would try to claim the streets for themselves," said Bastone. "They were armed with daggers."

"And your surname. It is incredibly famous!" said Vadala.

"Signore?"

"At Mass, we recite the Nicene creed," said Vadala. "'*crucified under Pontius Pilatus.*' Pontius Pilatus is Ponziu Pilatu in Sicilian. Do you think you could be related to Ponziu Pilatu?"

"I have not thought about it," said Bastone.

"We could have something in common," said Vadala. "My surname may also have a curious origin."

He drank as Bastone's eyebrows raised. "Yes?"

Vadala swallowed, then said, "My father told me that the Alcantara Valley, north of Etna, was considered so magnificent, that the Arabs called it the Valley of Allah. In Sicilian you would say, va da allah–vadala. So, were my ancestors Muslim, Saracen, Arab?"

Bastone took a swig of wine, not sure how to respond.

Vadala cracked a smile and laughed. "Who cares? We are who we are. I am comfortable with being part Greek, ancient Roman, Arab, Norman, and every other conqueror of Sicily!"

Bastone returned the smile and toasted, "*Salute,* health!" as they clinked their cups.

## CHAPTER XII   RIPOSTO, SICILY

Zaccaria and Bastone had collected large swaths of silk in Catania to trade on their voyage to the North Sea. The *Paradisio* sailed to Riposto, the port founded to export surplus wine from the vineyards on the slopes of Etna. Sicilians, using investments from the Genoese, had built an artificial jetty with boulders of volcanic rock, forming a harbor for ships of trade. The town included many warehouses for the naval stores industry of Linguaglossa.

When the *Paradisio* docked at Riposto, the captain sent a messenger to Linguaglossa, notifying Concettu, the naval works foreman, to expect them the next morning.

Just after sunrise, the mayor, Samuel Vadala, the local representative of the Baron of Catania, a vassal of King Charles, met Captain Zaccaria as he disembarked. He collected the dock fee and briefly questioned Zaccaria of his intentions. He gave his approval for the visiting merchants to bring a small guard detail. King Charles welcomed trade but ensured the baron and other nobles of Sicily strictly monitored foreigners. Riposto had a small Angevin garrison, the soldiers patrolling the docks, keeping close watch on activities. Bastone did not observe open harassment as he had seen in Catania; however, he did find many paupers roaming the waterfront in ragged and torn clothes. They were more numerous than typical for a small town.

Samuel escorted them to a stable where they leased mules for the ride to Linguaglossa. Esmeray had changed from sailor's clothes into a simple linen tunica and rode side-saddle. Two guards were on mules behind her. At the front was Bastone riding beside Zaccaria, who said, "My primary goal is to check on the volume of resin and pitch production. Emperor Michael has placed a large order to waterproof new ships."

"Yes, I had heard that Michael is rebuilding the imperial fleet," said Bastone. He did not tell Zaccaria that the emperor also bought resin as an ingredient for Greek Fire. The identity of the specific components added to the resin to liquefy the mixture was a closely guarded secret of the Romaioi. They ignited the liquid and sprayed it onto enemy ships. Water could not douse the flames.

Early in the afternoon the group arrived in Linguaglossa at the blacksmith's stables. The barn was empty except for a couple of horses in stalls. The smith, Ponziu Lucianu, entered through the back door. Zaccaria introduced himself and Lucianu welcomed them. "Oh! *Benvenutu*, welcome *Capitanu! Amunninni a pranzu*. Let's eat lunch." He paused. "*Scusa.*" He repeated slower in Genoese. "*Benvenuto! Andiamo a pranza.* My grandson speaks Sicilian *and* Genoese and will help me when I can't find the right word." He shouted toward the back door. "Lucianu!"

The blacksmith gestured for Zaccaria to follow, "Captain, come, please. We will talk over *pranzu*—*veni*, come, or the food will get cold."

The grandson arrived and secured their mounts, while the Genoese followed the elder Lucianu out the back door to a courtyard enclosed by a stone house, a vegetable garden, and an orchard of fruit trees. Lattices threaded with grape vines lined the south side of the stone cottage, along with several fig trees. A dark-haired woman smiled as she carried bowls of pasta and placed them along a row of tables in the shade provided by a pair of large chestnut trees. An enticing aroma steamed from plates of meatballs. Women brought jugs of wine and baskets of bread.

Lucianu guided the Genoese party to benches lining the tables. Captain Zaccaria said, "What a feast!"

The blacksmith frowned, then his grandson whispered to his grandfather. The elder smiled. "Oh. Yes, thank you."

His grandson continued, "His daughters-in-law have been preparing the food since early this morning. But today's meal is not much larger than our family dinners on the Sabbath."

"And your family—you have siblings?" Zaccaria asked the elder Lucianu.

"Yes—we are nine—two sisters, seven brothers. They are coming now."

"You must have many children and grandchildren?" said Zaccaria.

"Yes . . . the grandchildren are with their *nonnas*."

Several adult couples entered the courtyard. Lucianu stood and gave one man a body crushing hug, who joined in with gusto. He released his grip. Lucianu turned to the visitors, his arm around the man's shoulder. "My brother Marianu," said Lucianu, "who is the best butcher. His meatballs are delicious!

"Marianu, our honored visitors are Captain Benedetto Zaccaria and Officer Ponziu Bastone."

Both stood, each nodding in acknowledgment. Marianu embraced Bastone, who noticed his surname had been pronounced with a Sicilian accent. In addition, the surname was stated first, followed by his familiar name, which was the same way his own family did, although most Genoese reversed the order.

Marianu had an enormous smile. "I made the meatballs special for our visitors, and not just with pork. I added some beef for our guests." He waved. "*Ciao. Mangia,* please . . . eat!"

"It is all very delicious," said Bastone. "I have never had eggplant with pasta. And my favorite pasta—rigatoni!"

Bastone found it all very pleasant, the people, the food, but thought it unusual for them to have such bounty, even meat. Most of the island's inhabitants were poor, some starving, from the excessive taxes imposed by King Charles.

Lucianu raised his cup. "Yes, rigatoni, also my favorite! Now I know we will get along."

"And what kind of cheese is this?" asked Bastone.

The blacksmith's grandson answered, "It is ricotta. We use two kinds of cheese, which makes the dish even better. Grated—see the white crumbles. We then melt cheese and pour it on top of the rigatoni and eggplant. And of course, we add olive oil, then basil leaves." He gestured, pulling with the forefinger and thumb across the front of his chest. "Perfetto!"

"You've heard of King Frederick? The former king of Sicily?" asked the younger Lucianu.

"Um . . . yes," said Bastone.

"The king loved to pour hot ricotta and whey on top of his bread," Lucianu said as his hands mimicked his narrative. "His famous saying was *cu non mancia ccu so cucchiaru lassa o zammataru,* those who don't eat with a spoon will leave ricotta behind."

Bastone said, "Zammataru—this is Sicilian for ricotta*?*"

Lucianu nodded, "A word borrowed from the Arabs."

"I agree, it is unbelievably delicious," said Bastone. "You are fluent in several languages and well educated. What is your work?"

Lucianu glanced across the table at his father Egidiu, and said, "I am an apprentice barber surgeon, being trained by my father."

"A dignified profession. Does it suit you?"

"Cutting hair and shaving customers is fine, but . . ."

"Your heart is somewhere else?"

"I have a fire inside me to be a musician," said Lucianu. "And I believe a soft melody with my lute would heal a patient better than a bloodletting."

"Hmm. Do you have any other creative remedies?"

Lucianu took on an earnest bearing and leaned closer. "Yes, but my father doesn't agree with my ideas."

Bastone's head tilted to the side and his eyebrows raised.

"Instead of pulling a rotten tooth—knock it out with a punch to the jaw. And no more enemas—just a shoe up their behind!"

Lucianu kept a straight face. Bastone hesitated, then laughed, slapping the younger man's shoulder, believing that Lucianu would be an excellent replacement for the late barber surgeon on the *Paradisio*. His wit and humor would complement the healing skills.

Bastone spooned in another bite. "Mmm . . . *e delizioso* . . . or in Sicilianu . . . *diliziusu*!" said Bastone.

Lucianu said, "You are used to the hard pasta cooked al dente, firm to the teeth. No, my mother, she makes all her pasta fresh."

"I can't remember the last time I had fresh pasta," said Bastone. "It is smooth to the tongue."

After the meal, which usually was the largest of the day for Sicilians, Lucianu and Concettu led the Genoese visitors on a promenade to help their digestion and to observe the resin works. Captain Zaccaria's family was heavily invested in the operation, and he wanted to look over the books and accounts. At Concettu's residence near the works, he examined the production and shipping records as the others waited outside. Bastone and the younger Lucianu gazed at the peak of Mount Etna, smoking lazily, and releasing white patches across the blue sky. "Etna is quiet today," said Bastone.

"Yes," Lucianu said, "*A Mungibeddu* is sleeping."

"You speak fluent Genoese," said Bastone, "but I am not familiar with, um, that name."

"Etna is the Latin name for the mountain and is used by Genoese, Pisans—the traders from Italy. But the name Etna derives from the word the ancient Greek colonists used for the volcano, 'I burn,' which of course she does every few years, now and then lighting the night sky with tongues of fire. Now Sicilians call the volcano Mungibeddu, beautiful mountain. In Genoese, it would be *Mongibello*?"

Wrinkles formed between Bastone's eyebrows.

"No, no," said Lucianu. "In Genoese it would be *Montebello*. Excuse me."

The two men shared genial smiles.

"No apology needed, Lucianu. You have an excellent talent with languages. Linguaglossa is isolated. Perhaps you learned from foreign traders on the docks of Riposto?"

"I lived in Messina for a few years at the monastery of San Salvatore and was tutored by the Basilian monks in reading and mathematics. The monks spoke Greek, as do many *Messinesi,* so I learned the language. Much of the literature I read was in Latin, not difficult to learn, being the source of the Sicilian language. I acquired your dialect in the Genoese quarter of Messina. You have stopped there during your trading ventures?"

Bastone nodded.

"And I can speak a little English."

"English?" Bastone's eyes widened.

"Yes, there are a few English traders in Messina."

Bastone considered Lucianu's talents. The ship needed a barber, and his language skills would also be invaluable on the voyage. A guard interrupted his musing. "Bastone, the captain wants you."

Bastone entered the house and joined Zaccaria who sat at a writing table with an account ledger opened. The foreman stood a respectful distance across the room so as not to disturb the captain, but ready to answer questions if they arose. "The production volumes have increased, and I am very satisfied with the numbers," said Zaccaria. "Bastone, did you bring the receipts to verify the numbers?"

Bastone nodded and patted his shoulder bag.

"Good, I am going to get some fresh air while you check them." The foreman's wife handed Zaccaria a cup of wine as he went outside.

Bastone totaled the amount of resin in his receipts and wrote it on a piece of scrap rag paper. Then he summed the amounts listed in the ledger. He asked the foreman to bring a chair and sit next to him. He pointed to his receipt total then the total in the ledger. "Concettu, are both of these sums correct?"

Concettu totaled Bastone's receipts, answering with a blank face, "Si."

When Bastone repeated his calculations, he ended with the same numbers. Also, he noted that the baron had paid taxes to King Charles based on the totals in the ledger. So the baron was under-reporting production, thus, paying less tax. Bastone asked Captain Zaccaria to return inside to look over the ledger with him.

Concettu's wife brought out two more cups and poured wine for her husband and Bastone, refilling Zaccaria's.

Bastone showed the captain his receipt totals, also pointing to the ledger total.

"Yes, exports have increased. It is good, no?" said Zaccaria. He raised his cup, Concettu joined, and Bastone followed. They drank together. They exchanged knowing glances in silence. Bastone sensed the captain and foreman were not surprised at the figures.

As they returned to the Ponzio family's house, Bastone asked young Lucianu to drop behind the others, so they could talk privately. When he explained the ledger's discrepancies, Lucianu did not act surprised. "You are the *Paradisio's* scribe and accountant, so you easily discovered the baron's methods," said Lucianu, "but it is not what you might think. The baron is not hoarding the money for himself. Baron Geoffroi uses the unreported profits to pay the excessive taxes imposed on the citizens, levied by King Charles. Hence the people of his barony, free of overburdening taxes, are not as destitute as the common folk in most parts of Sicily."

Recalling Baron Geoffroi's furtive intent to help the people, Bastone smiled and peered at Zaccaria as they walked, knowing the captain was enjoying tax-free profits, and only risked losing his investment if King Charles found out. Baron Geoffroi, however, was risking everything, including his life if caught.

When they reached Lucianu's home and stables, Bastone suggested Zaccaria offer the young Lucianu the barber post on the *Paradisio*. His language skills would be a bonus. The captain agreed.

Linguaglossa was a small hamlet with no accommodations for visitors. Zaccaria and his men bedded down in Lucianu's stable for the night. Esmeray, staying in the blacksmith's cottage at the invitation of Lucianu's wife, briefly said goodnight to Bastone.

Zaccaria shifted on the layer of straw thrown down as he pulled up his blanket, "The books showed we will have enough resin to meet our orders, and . . . more." He rolled toward Bastone and whispered, "It exceeds my expectations. I noticed that most of the resin is being shipped to Messina. King Charles is expanding his fleet, just as Emperor Michael is doing in Constantinople. Satisfy both customers and more profits for us! Tomorrow we'll discuss production of the roof tiles. *Buona notte, paisan.*"

In the morning, the Genoese visitors had oranges and hard bread for breakfast and drank diluted wine. Esmeray sat among the women at the far end of the long table without greeting Bastone, but otherwise she appeared talkative.

The blacksmith and his grandson Lucianu joined Bastone and Zaccaria. "These oranges are . . . tart, but delicious," said Bastone. "We never see them in Genoa."

"We owe the Saracens for them," said Lucianu. "Centuries ago they were the first to plant orange trees in Sicily."

"Do they quickly spoil?" asked Zaccaria. "I wonder if Genoese would take to the taste?"

"They may last a few weeks," said Lucianu.

Zaccaria looked up and said, as if talking to himself, "Hmm. Directly shipping to Genoa would make it in time."

The elder Lucianu said, "Captain Zaccaria, I understand Baron Geoffroi will arrive from Taormina this evening to discuss the production of clay roof tiles. Today, my family asks for your help. The Church of Sant'Egidiu in our village needs repairs because of the damage from a recent earthquake. Cistercian monks from the Abbey of Santa Maria La Novara have arrived to help in the restorations. With your men's aid, we could complete it today."

Zaccaria collected his men and joined the villagers to repair the church. It was a typical summer day, warm, cloudless, with moderate humidity. They finished the repairs by early afternoon. Murals had covered the walls of the chapel, but sadly, the earthquake had damaged several of the paintings. The monks of La Novara promised to stay until they restored the chapel's frescoes.

The townspeople provided a simple pranzu of fresh bread, olives, cheese, and hazelnuts, along with wine. As they sat in the shade of a few lemon trees in the church courtyard, enjoying lunch, the priest told the story of Linguaglossa's patron saint.

"The people named this church after Abbot Egidius, Egidiu in Sicilian." The priest glanced and smiled at the barber Egidiu sitting with them. "Sant'Egidiu saved the hamlet from the lava pouring out of Mount Etna."

"When did this happen, Father?" asked Bastone.

"It's *anno domini* 1277, so . . . just over a hundred years ago, the brave cleric stood right here in the lava path streaming toward the hamlet. Saint Egidiu held up a cross and prayed to God, who parted the molten rock into seven tongues. They built the Church of Sant'Egidiu at the place where the miracle occurred."

"And the name Linguaglossa," said Bastone, "it is unusual—repetitive?"

The priest's raised his eyebrows, "Officer Ponzio, you must know this from your Greek. I heard you speaking in Greek with the monks."

"I am the captain's bodyguard, but also the scribe, and being fluent in Greek helps in my trade."

The priest continued, "So you know that many of the inhabitants of Sicily speak Greek, descendants of colonists who arrived a thousand years ago."

Bastone nodded.

"*Linguagrossa* was the original name of the hamlet, from *grossa lingua di lava,* meaning 'an enormous tongue of lava.' Over time, the local people substituted the Greek word for tongue, *glossa* for *grossa,* and you are correct saying the name is unusual; it is quite amusing, but the name of our village is now *lingua glossa*—literally: tongue tongue."

After they ate, the Catholic priest held Mass, then they returned to Lucianu's house. Baron Geoffroi arrived from Taormina to hear Zaccaria's proposal on the manufacturing of roof tiles. Lucianu's late father had willed the land where the clay deposits were located, as well as the business, to his nine children, of whom Lucianu the blacksmith was one. The nine siblings sat in Lucianu's courtyard among other villagers waiting for Zaccaria to speak.

People mingled and shared wine. Bastone told Esmeray about the church repairs, asking how her day had gone. Her response was curt, as she remained taciturn and frosty. Bastone was confused with her behavior.

Instead, he turned to the young Lucianu. "King Charles awarded this fief to the baron, so why is he holding this meeting in public? I would think he would just decide himself."

"The people of Linguaglossa are very stubborn," said Lucianu, as he tapped his fist into his palm, "especially the Ponzios, who are *testa dura*, hard-headed. Perhaps the baron is fooling us, giving us the illusion that we influence decisions. He is very shrewd, and so he receives our cooperation. But also, he thinks we are related."

"Related?" Bastone's eyes widened.

"The Baron's name is Geoffroi Pons. When written, it is Pontius. The same as my name and yours as recorded in legal documents."

"Your grandfather introduced me as Ponziu Bastone, I assume because Sicilians place the surname before the common name, like the ancient Romans. By coincidence, my family prefers this order, although most Genoese place the surname second."

Lucianu laughed, "But Sicilian, my language, is more like Latin. Marianus in Latin—Marianu in Sicilian—Mariano in Genoese. So, I am more Roman than you!"

"Ha! Really?" said Bastone. "When I heard your father pronounce my name, he said Ponz*iu*. Was it due to his Sicilian accent, or do you spell your name with a 'u'?"

"Yes, we do spell it with a 'u.' And we can write our names in Sicilian, instead of Latin. The former King of Sicily and Holy Roman Emperor Frederick formed a school of poetry, and the sonnets are spoken *and* written in Sicilian," added Lucianu. "Since Frederick's reign, the Sicilian courts have written documents in Sicilian instead of Latin."

"You should be proud, Lucianu," said Bastone.

The mention of writing made Bastone recall the pages of the ledger at the resin works, written on cloth parchment.

"Lucianu . . . where does your uncle get the parchment for his record books?"

"From Catania, where it is made."

"The cost is low enough for documents in Sicily to be written on the cloth parchment?" asked Bastone.

"Not all documents," said Lucianu.

Bastone cocked his head.

Lucianu said, "The Pope found out the monks of La Novara made a copy of the Bible on the cloth parchment and then banned its use because he declared animal parchment was the only thing holy enough to carry the Sacred Word."

Bastone snorted in derision. Then he said, "I wish I had known they made the parchment in Catania. I would have bought some while I was there."

Captain Zaccaria stood. After gaining the townspeople's attention, he described his business proposal. Lucianu whispered to Bastone, "Let's see what *cousin* Pons's decision will be."

After Zaccaria finished, the villagers discussed his plan for production of roof tiles. It was proposed to use carts for local deliveries. The tiles could be stored in warehouses at Riposto, then shipped by boat to Messina, Catania, and Syracuse. Lucianu's brother would build pallets and erect a small hoist to load the product onto the ships. Geoffroi appeared receptive to the commoners voicing their opinions.

Agreeing with the consensus from the village, Geoffroi endorsed the project, elating the villagers, who began celebrating. During the festivities, Bastone discovered another connection between Geoffroi and the people of Linguaglossa. The baron had been a troubadour in the court of King Charles before retiring. For his services, the king had awarded the fief of Taormina to him. Knowing this, they persuaded him to sing, and young Lucianu accompanied the baron by playing a stringed lute.

Learning that the Genoese would stay in Linguaglossa another night before returning to the *Paradisio,* the baron and his wife Anastasia welcomed Zaccaria, Bastone, and Esmeray to spend the night at their Linguaglossa villa. In turn, the captain gifted them a package of mastica gum.

The hosts and guests gathered for a light dinner. Anastasia then invited Esmeray to explore the villa as the men talked over wine.

"Captain, I assume Concettu showed you both account books?" said Geoffroi.

Zaccaria glanced at Bastone with a deliberate blink, and then nodded to the baron, who said, "I was King Charles's personal troubadour. He appreciated my services and rewarded me with this beautiful fief, along with its hardworking and deserving people. I believe God put me in this world to be an entertainer and to give people joy and happiness. And to allow the citizens of Taormina, Castiglione, and Linguaglossa to have a good life, I share the profits from their labors with them."

"That is very generous, Baron Pons." Zaccaria raised his glass. "*Cent'anni!*"

Geoffroi and Bastone joined him, "*Salute per cent'anni*, may you live for a hundred years!"

The house grew quiet after the guests were shown their rooms and the oil lamps were extinguished. Bastone and Esmeray in their own bedroom were alone together for the first time in weeks.

"You have been very subdued with me, Esme, but I look around the courtyard and see you carry on lively conversations with others."

She sat on the edge of the bed with her arms crossed. "You were busy. It was my first time in a while to talk . . . with other women, that's all."

He joined her on the bed and put his arm around her shoulders. She peered straight ahead.

"There is something else," he said.

Esmeray abruptly spun and faced him. "No, it is *someone* else. You are betrothed to a Spinola woman!"

"No. I am married to you!"

"I heard Amilcare. He told me on the ship." She bit the edge of her hand, then made a chopping gesture in the air. "I want the truth!"

He barely stifled a laugh as he said, "The truth is I love *you*, Esme!"

"You are laughing?"

"No, I mean, I am pleased—you will make a real Genoese yet! You are picking up the hand gestures!"

He sobered. "That was an arrangement between the families. I will not abide by their wishes."

Esmeray did not look convinced.

Bastone smiled faintly, narrowed his eyes seductively, and tilted his head, "My brother was betrothed to Amilcare's sister, not me."

"Why should I believe you?"

Esmeray shoved both hands against his shoulders. He willingly fell back, and she landed on top of him on the bed. "Instead, you will return to Genoa so your family can pour scorn on me!"

Their eyes locked. Eyes to eyes, body to body, their desire for each other, fueled by stress and anger, drowned their quarrel in raging passion.

## CHAPTER XIII   ISLAND of VULCANO

Lucianu ran along the wharf, a wicker basket swinging from his hand. He rushed up the gangplank, boarding the *Paradisio*, out of breath.

Bastone had watched his flight. "You are here just in time, we'll shove off right away." He left to survey the ship as the crew readied to leave port. A howl came from the basket, charging Esmeray with curiosity. "You have a cat!"

"Yes, I remember you mentioning the ship's mouser had died. Mizar will take care of the rats *and* guide us on our journey."

"Guide us? Mizar? What kind of name is that?"

The sailors pulled in the gangplank, preparing to get underway. Lucianu placed the basket on the deck, removing the top. The cat gazed up at them, content to remain in the bin.

Esmeray squatted down to peer at the scrawny cat, black and gray stripes along his body and a large white patch on his chest. "Here is your new home, Mizar."

"Where did you get him? He's not much bigger than the rats in the hold!" Esmeray's brow wrinkled. "And you said he would *guide* us?"

"I got him from a Saracen merchant at the docks, who told me Mizar is the Arabic word for the northern star that guides sailors."

Lucianu picked up the cat and set him on the deck. The feline assumed a sitting position; his chin was level with a calm gaze, his front legs straight and haunches on the deck, and his tail curled neatly around his lower parts, as if posing for a sculpture. "I also thought he looked feeble, but when rats infest a ship, a seaman would say, 'a lame cat is better than the brawniest sailor.'"

"I must get to work," said Esmeray. She joined sailors on steerboard to push the ship from the dock.

"Well, Mizar, you must also do *your* work." Lucianu picked him up and took him below.

A handful of men climbed into the *Aspasia*, and secured a bow line from the *Paradisio* to tow the ship out of the harbor.

After exiting the harbor, the captain guided the *Paradisio* to tack steerboard off the nor'westerly mistral wind. They sailed along the coast, with Etna still dominating the landscape to port. The tidal currents through the Strait of Messina, the narrows between Sicily and the mainland Italian peninsula, were moving from south to north, boosting the *Paradisio* to over five knots. Two hours after their departure from Riposto, Bastone pointed out a town perched on cliffs above a small island. "Esme, that is Taormina, where Baron Geoffroi lives."

Esmeray peered at the town's buildings, the stone walls bright in the morning sunlight. "A majestic location! And that little island we passed is beautiful."

"That is the island's name."

"What?"

"*Isola Bella!*"

She laughed.

"So . . . Esme . . . are we . . . better?"

She continued gazing toward the seashore. "I will live for the day . . . or day by day . . . until . . ."

"We won't have to cope with my family, if that's what you're thinking, for at least a year."

Esmeray looked expectantly at her husband, eyes widening, her mouth opening.

Bastone checked to make sure no one was watching, then discreetly placed his hand gently on hers on the taffrail. He affectionately squeezed her hand and asked, "You lost your blue ring?"

"No, it is tucked away, safe in my cabin, but I still take it out at times to peer at the lovely color. I wore it while we were ashore in Sicily but took it off to do sailors' work."

"I understand. I remember how excited you were when you first saw the ring." Then he spoke in a conspiratorial tone. "The captain is taking us to Flanders and England to trade the alum."

She scrunched up her face. "Hmm?"

"They are lands in the far north," said Bastone. "There the weavers use the alum in the dyeing of the wool. Don't tell anyone we are going to England. The captain is keeping it from his crew until we reach Mallorca."

"Why?" asked Esmeray.

"Zaccaria wants to be the first to sail from the Mediterranean to the North Sea. It will be more profitable than carrying the alum overland and he will have an advantage over his competitors. Also, many sailors would be alarmed if they knew we were headed for the Ocean Sea. It's best if he reveals the destination later."

She still looked confused. "I have never heard of Mallorca."

"It is an island about two weeks sailing to the west, near Spain."

Esmeray's eyes widened. "A new place to explore!"

Within an hour the wind died and the sails grew slack. The tidal flow, however, moved them ahead at a few knots, even with the lack of wind. Then suddenly there were gusts from the southeast which rapidly grew in intensity. The strong winds carried fine sand. The captain barked commands as the sailors hurried to adjust the sails to avoid running straight downwind with such a strong wind. They soon gained control by tacking to port.

Esmeray went to the stern with another crewman to measure the vessel's speed. He loosely coiled a long, thin rope on the deck that was attached to a wooden plank a couple of feet long. Knots had been tied along the rope at equal intervals. The sailor glanced at Esmeray and said, "Ready?"

She nodded.

"Now," he said, as he turned over a sand glass that measured thirty seconds.

Esmeray threw the board into the water behind the ship. As the rope unwound, she counted the knots that bounced over the stern into the water. "Uno, due, tre, quattro, . . . otto."

The sand finished in the glass, the sailor said, "Stop!"

They traded huge grins. "Eight knots." said Esmeray.

The sailor agreed. "*Rapido!* It is because the sirocco winds from Africa added to the ocean current boosts our speed."

They made it to Messina harbor and anchored for the night. A sharp ridge of mountains formed a backdrop to the city, with only a scattering of trees showing on the peaks. Over the centuries, the inhabitants had cut down the forests.

Bastone and Esmeray sat on a coil of rope near the galley eating with the crew. The sun had just set. Bastone glanced across the harbor and scrutinized King Charles's fleet of war galleys and transport vessels anchored near the shore. More ships were being constructed. Bastone's lips moved as he tallied the fleet.

"You are counting?" asked Esmeray.

"Um, . . . yes . . . er . . . the more ships, the more resin needed, the more profits. My uncle not only owns a quarter of the *Paradisio* but is invested in Linguaglossa's naval works as well.

"Esme, there are churches of the Basilian Order in Messina. I thought you might be interested in taking an Orthodox Mass, more familiar to you than the Latin Mass in Linguaglossa."

"No, I am fine, ready for the open sea after we pass through the straits."

"The winds are erratic in the narrows and the seas are usually choppy," said Bastone. "But the currents in the straits are predictable; they change about every six hours. After sunrise, the current will again be favorable, although the sirocco winds from the southeast have disappeared and the nor-westerly mistral has returned."

They gazed in silence across the harbor as the lights on the waterfront sparkled in the twilight.

"Bastone, I believe you."

"What?" He peered at Esmeray.

"I believe it is your brother, not you, who will marry the Spinola woman. Amilcare is just trying to torment me," said Esmeray. "I love you."

Bastone ached to hold Esmeray but dared not even touch her hand. Esmeray stood to leave and said, "Goodnight. I will see you in the morning." Her eyes darted behind Bastone's shoulder. "What is that light? Up in the tower?"

"It is a faro. The light at the top warns sailors who have not made it to port by dark. Basilian monks keep a fire burning each night in the tower. It has saved many sailors' lives. And there is an immense light tower, high as the length of three ships in Genoa's harbor . . ."

Esmeray stiffened.

"I am sorry, of course. The thought of Genoa alarms you."

"Buona notte, *mi dolcezza*, my sweetheart."

Bastone waited for Esmeray to enter her cabin, then knocked on the captain's door, suggesting they sell mastica to the waterfront merchant who had bought some during their last call. The captain gave him leave to take the harbor tender. Bastone retrieved a few small bags of mastica from the hold. Sailors lowered the tender over the side. He rowed alone to a galley, a ship of King Charles's Sicilian fleet, moored two hundred feet across the harbor. On board for less than an hour, he rowed to the waterfront, disembarked, strode a few blocks from the harbor, knocking on the door of a shuttered merchant's shop. It was overshadowed by the Palazzo of the Census Minister of Sicily. Appointed by King Charles, the minister, a Sicilian noble, was in charge of levying the royal taxes.

Shortly the view hatch opened. In the dim light, Bastone held up a sack. "I have the savory mastic the minister requested."

"Wait." The hatch closed, then snapped open, "I am the Minister's captain of the guard," he said in Sicilian. "What is the code word?"

"I am here to see the Minister; he is expecting me," said Bastone.

"Wait." The hatch closed.

The guard returned, let Bastone into the shop and led him through the back door which was connected by a tunnel to the palazzo. There, Bastone was challenged by the minister, Baron Alaimo, with the appropriate phrase, and he replied, after which he informed Alaimo of the date for the revolt. Bastone also told the baron of his guard's suspicious request for the code word. Alaimo began surveillance of the guard.

An hour past sunrise, the helmsman piloted the *Paradisio* out of Messina's harbor and sailed north. Currents, as predicted, were northerly and were increasing, but they would reverse direction in five hours. The crew adjusted the sails to a port tack on the mistral winds. After the sirocco abated, the sky was again dry and clear and a pod of dolphins amused themselves, playing in the bow wash of the ship.

Esmeray measured the *Paradisio's* speed. She reported to the captain and helmsman at the starboard tiller.

"Captain Zaccaria, we are making five knots."

"Grazie, sailor."

As Esmeray left, she heard the captain. "Good, we will pass through the narrows in about two hours, time to spare, before the currents reverse."

The going was steady. An hour later, she went to retrieve her chamber pot, which she had not disposed of while they were still in harbor. When she reached the bow, the winds suddenly died. The sails flapped, but the currents continued to move the vessel ahead. As she was about to pour the waste through the latticework at the head, the ship rolled and creaked.

Bastone rushed out of his cabin and looked up to the sterncastle. The captain stood calmly beside the helmsman pointing toward the bow. The first mate was wide eyed with excitement. The helmsman shouted. "It's bigger than any whirlpool I've ever seen!"

Sailors rushed to the bow as a whirlpool appeared wider than the ship's beam. The sailor next to Esmeray said, "This is the sea monster that swallowed the ancient Odysseus!" He held up his palm and closed and opened his fingers as if he were signaling "give me money," but the gesture meant, "you are scared."

Esmeray waved her hand along her hip, meaning "Get lost!" The sailor laughed.

The ship was caught by the vortex, shuddered, and rotated, as timbers groaned. Hoots erupted from the sailors. Bastone was amused by Esmeray's reaction. She thought the crew had lost their senses, glancing at Bastone who appeared unruffled. She soon joined the sailors at the rail, hanging on during the thrilling ride.

There were a few moments of stomach churning, then the *Paradisio* broke free continuing on a new course. Sailors laughed and hoorayed. Just as suddenly as the wind died, it returned, and the ship passed the northeast promontory of Sicily, entering the Tyrrhenian Sea, headed for the Island of Vulcano.

The sun set as they sailed north, then they turned west, tacking with the mistral winds. Esmeray's shift was over and she retired, dozing off. She woke to shouting and hurried from her quarters.

Fiery veins glowing yellow, orange, and red were spewing into the night sky on the far horizon. The spectacular show of light was from a distant volcano. The helmsman said, "Trustworthy Stromboli! The oldest faro in the world."

Esmeray asked him, "Stromboli? I thought we were going to Vulcano?"

"Yes, we are. But I have sailed here before and at this distance I can measure . . ." Extending his arm, he pointed his fist at the horizon, peering along his arm as if taking aim. "The direction to Isola Vulcano is the width of my fist to the left of Stromboli's fire. That's how to use nature's faro to steer to Vulcano. No worry."

Within an hour the *Paradisio* anchored on the southeast coast of Vulcano near the *Euxinos Pontos* and another cargo ship. The reflection of the half moon was bright on the calm sea. Most of the crew was getting ready for a night's sleep. Esmeray saw Bastone at the taffrail scanning the harbor, peering toward the lone dock of the village on shore.

"Notte!" she called to him, reaching to open the door to her quarters.

"Esmeray!" Bastone said in a hushed tone, then whispered. "Wait! I am expecting a visitor, a new passenger for the *Paradisio*, and would like to . . . uh, have a conversation with him."

Esmeray smiled. "Another secret meeting?"

Bastone looked about, touched his index finger to his nose and whispered, "*Zitto.*"

Her eyes blazed. He glanced around and pecked her quickly on the cheek. "I am sorry I told you to shut up, Esme," he said.

"It's not unusual for an officer to have confidential discussions, which can't be done in my cabin that I share with Ottolino. This is important. And please I need your help. Keep watch. I don't want anyone overhearing us."

Esmeray's eyes narrowed, and she responded in a low and calm tone, "You are using me. And you are keeping secrets from me. In Constantinople, I overheard the emperor call you a speculatore. What does it mean?"

"I will tell you later. You are my wife *and* confidante. I will tell you everything after my meeting."

Her expression softened.

Bastone gently clasped her shoulders, gazing into her eyes, paused, and then said, "Grazie, mi dolcezza."

"You call me sweetheart. Your blue eyes are alluring, but . . ."

"You are thinking—can I trust this man?" said Bastone. "Give me time." Bastone tenderly released her and went to the taffrail to continue his vigil. Within a few minutes a cannotino arrived, rowed by a local fisherman. Aboard was a lone man with a small duffel bag.

Bastone dropped a rope. He helped the man onto the deck. The visitor was tall and lean, with sharp features. His long nose was matched by a jutting chin. As he drew closer, Esmeray saw he was in his sixties or seventies, and she was impressed by his agility scaling the hull on a knotted rope. Bastone embraced him, turning unexpectedly to Esmeray. "Signore Procida, please meet my wife and confidante, Esmeray."

"Esme, Doctor Giovanni Procida."

Procida bowed slightly and took her hand. "Signora."

Even in the dim light, Bastone noticed her face blush. She said, "It is my . . . pleasure, *Dottore*."

The doctor glanced at her clothes. "I see you are an adventurous lady—a sailor; as Bastone's trusted confidante, I am sure you are capable of using such a disguise.

"I am inspired that women take strong roles. You have my utmost respect. Indeed, the textbook of women's medicine I studied at the

University of Salerno was written by *le Mulieres Salernitanae,* the Women of Salerno, doctors who taught medicine generations ago."

Bastone gestured and the men entered the vacant guest suite as she remained on the deck. They sat at a tiny table bolted to the floor, sharing cups of wine.

"I hope these accommodations are adequate, Doctor Procida."

"More than enough, and a good respite." He motioned with his cup at the elegant quarters. "Ha! I willingly suffer for the cause."

Bastone showed a half smile and held that the doctor had a sense of humor.

Did you notify Gualtiero Caltagirone to prepare the patriots of Val di Noto?" said Procida.

"Through the intermediary, Vadala, in Catania."

Procida pursed his lips as he touched his chin with an index finger. "Vadala? Oh, yes, I remember him. His cousin Samuel is one of us. And Alaimo?"

Bastone nodded. "In Messina."

"That takes care of Val Demone," said Procida. "At Favignana, I will meet with Palmiero Abate, the Lord of Trapani, to organize the patriots of Val di Mazara. That will cover all three of the *valli* of Sicily. It's too risky for me to go to Palermo. I would be recognized, and it would be disastrous for our plans. We will have the backing of the most influential Sicilian nobles of each of the three provinces and they will disseminate the plan to their loyal patriots."

An hour later, Bastone rejoined Esmeray. In silence, they gazed at the silhouette of Isola Vulcano in the half moon's light. Bastone placed his hand on Esmeray's and gave her a gentle squeeze. "*Domani,* tomorrow. I promise, I will tell you everything." Then he headed toward the bow to his cabin.

Esmeray said goodnight to his figure ebbing into the dark. "Buona notte."

Michael A. Ponzio

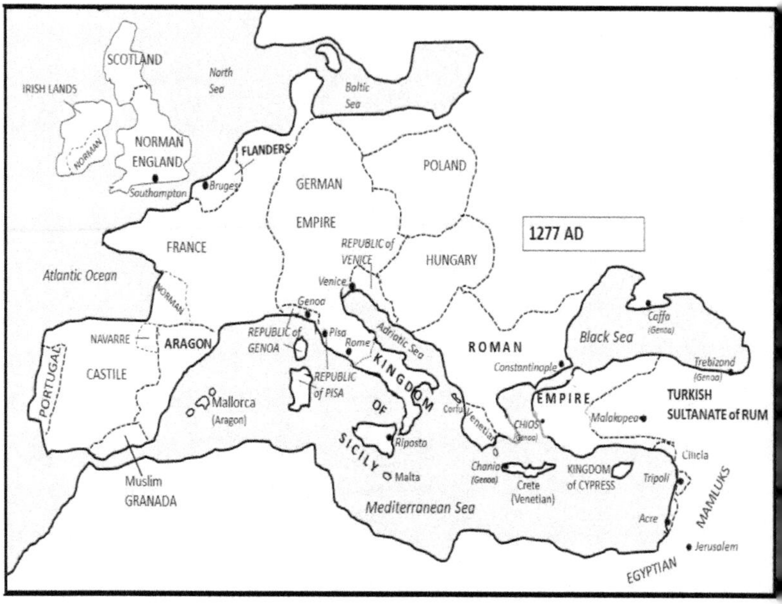
SCOTLAND
IRISH LANDS
NORMAN
North Sea
NORMAN ENGLAND
Southampton
FLANDERS
Bruges
Baltic Sea
POLAND
GERMAN EMPIRE
1277 AD
FRANCE
REPUBLIC of VENICE
HUNGARY
Atlantic Ocean
NORMAN
Venice
Genoa
Caffa
(Genoa)
NAVARRE
ARAGON
REPUBLIC of GENOA
Pisa
Rome
Adriatic Sea
ROMAN
Black Sea
PORTUGAL
CASTILE
REPUBLIC of PISA
KINGDOM OF SICILY
Constantinople
Trebizond
(Genoa)
Mallorca
(Aragon)
Corfu
Venetian
EMPIRE
TURKISH SULTANATE of RUM
CHIOS
(Genoa)
Malakopea
Riposto
Cilicia
Malta
Chania
(Genoa)
Crete
(Venetian)
KINGDOM of CYPRESS
Tripoli
Muslim GRANADA
Mediterranean Sea
Acre
MAMLUKS
Jerusalem
EGYPTIAN

## CHAPTER XIV   MALLORCA

Several days later, the *Paradisio* and the two ships in its company weighed anchors off the island of Vulcano. The lateen rigs bent to a port tack using the mistral winds and sailed toward Sardinia, the halfway stop to the Balearic Islands. Esmeray welcomed their departure because the sulfur odor from the Vulcano's fumaroles permeated everything when they were anchored in port. The ships were laden primarily with alum for markets in England and Flanders, where the cloth makers used the product as a mordant, adding it to the dyes to fix the colors to the fabrics. Zaccaria expected to make a profit from the large volumes he was transporting. These were the first ships in centuries, however, to undertake such a large and potentially hazardous trading venture. In addition to the primary cargo, the alum, each ship carried supplemental low volume, high profit, trade goods to barter during their voyage. The *Paradisio's* hold included mastica from Chios. Trebizond was the home port of the *Euxinos Pontos* and a terminus of the silk road. The ship carried bolts of the fabric to trade. The Genoese ship that had been loaded with alum at Vulcano, the *San Giorgio* brought velvet cloth, gold thread, and lace cloth, high-quality products made by the women of Genoa.

Without incident, they reached the port of Cagliari, Sardinia, in just over two days, the captain's dead-reckoning predicting their location and time of arrival accurately. After spending one night and refilling their water barrels, they sailed another several days to reach Mallorca.

They anchored in the harbor of Palma, the capital city of the island of Mallorca. The Cathedral of Palma was still in the early stages of construction but was already rising majestically above the waterfront. James II, King of Mallorca, with help from his brother, Peter III, King of Aragon, was building the church. At Palma, Zaccaria waited for more ships from Genoa to join their small fleet on the journey to the north. In the meantime, sailors were given leave.

The *Paradisio's* officers stood around a small table covered with maps in the captain's quarters just after sunrise. Bastone was next to First Mate Ottolino, the lead helmsman, and Lucianu, the new barber surgeon, stood opposite.

"Please sit. I will be brief," said the captain.

The helmsman and first mate glared at Lucianu, who was wearing a dull red tunic in contrast to the subdued grays and browns of the crew.

The captain said, "Lucianu is joining the *Paradisio* as the barber surgeon."

"Why the red shirt?" asked the helmsman.

"Treating wounded, shaving crewmembers, and the like . . . it hides the blood," said Lucianu.

"Every crew member may be called to battle," said Ottolino. He looked intently at Lucianu, "Do you have any fighting experience?"

Lucianu shook his head.

"Perhaps his shirt is to hide the blood when the pirates cut him!" said the helmsman, who was joined in laughter by the others.

"No, sir," said Lucianu. "My brown pants will suitably conceal my reaction in battle."

The captain was about to intervene and call for order, but instead laughed with the others.

Zaccaria said, "He will have other duties as a translator. He speaks English." The captain gestured to the cups of wine for the officers and held up his cup. "*A salute nostra!*"

The officers responded with "Salute!" and drank as well.

Zaccaria studied the maps on the table. "These portolan charts drawn by Genoese cartographers are the best I have ever seen. I trust them. The mapmakers sailed from port to port around the Mediterranean and reckoned distances accurately. But they will not cover our whole journey."

The officers peered expectantly at Captain Zaccaria.

Beaming a huge smile, the captain said, "Have more wine. We are going to sail to the alum markets of Bruges and Southampton on the North Sea."

Ottolino almost spit out his wine. "What!"

The helmsman said, "Genoese ships have been sailing through the Pillars of Hercules, as far as Seville and North Africa, for many years, but not to the North Sea. I, for one, look forward to the challenge of navigating through the Ocean Sea."

"The English wool is more valuable per weight than the alum," said the captain, "so if we can pack at least 1,500 *cantaria* into the *Paradisio's* hold, we'll make a profit—a much higher profit than the overland shipments." Bastone recalled the first time he had picked up Esmeray. She weighed about one *cantarium*. His attention returned to the captain's discussion. "In addition, we will sell mastica at the ports on the way to Bruges."

Lucianu's eyes grew wide. He scrutinized a map. "I see this portolan is written in Latin and Arabic."

Zaccaria said, "Yes, it is the best map of the world. A Saracen geographer drew it for King Roger of Sicily years ago. In addition," he pointed to a book on the table, "this codex is a guide of ports and distances recorded by an ancient Greek named Pytheas, who sailed to Britain in ancient times. It has details listing the ports and coastal landmarks, and distances. I am sure we will be the first ships to sail from the Mediterranean to the North Sea since the ancient Romans."

"Sir, may I look at the codex?" asked Lucianu.

The captain nodded. "Do you read Greek?"

"Yes, one of my tutors in Messina was an Orthodox monk."

"Belissimo! That will be extremely helpful. I was able to figure out a few of the port names, but the narrative was too complicated a task."

Lucianu, already immersed in the book, nodded without looking up.

Zaccaria said, "We will have more than maps. A Mallorcan captain will guide us through the straits to the Ocean Sea. He knows the currents and winds. The Mallorcan sailors, who are mostly Catalan, sail into the Ocean Sea and trade along the west coast of Spain. They are just as excited as we are to go further north. Bastone, tomorrow you will ride to the north coast of Mallorca to the monastery at Miramar and consult the Mallorcan captain as well as a man named Raimundo Lullio, the seneschal to King James's royal household. Take Lucianu and our documents to plan with them."

The captain turned to the other officers. "Meanwhile, we will go to shore with the luxury goods and merchandise to sell among the nobles of Mallorca."

Giovanni Procida disembarked the *Paradisio* and went into Palma to call on James, the King of Mallorca. Within the hour, he returned to the *Paradisio*, paid for his passage from Vulcano, collected his possessions, and said farewell to Bastone. In a few days, he would accompany James on an Aragonese galley to Barcelona. There he intended to inform King Peter that the Pope had endorsed the plan for the Sicilian revolt, thus gaining military support from the Aragonese.

On the trip to the monastery, Bastone was pleased that Esmeray had worn her plain tunica, rather than her sailor's clothes. They had found a stable in Palma where they leased mules. The proprietor and his daughter, Terra, guided them to Miramar. The party included

Bastone, Lucianu, Esmeray, and two of his marines as escorts. He was surprised the stablemaster brought his daughter along as well, but her role was soon evident. Terra spoke Catalan and Genoese, as the Balearic Islands had formed a close trade relationship with Genoa. Lucianu frequently questioned her on the semantics of Catalan as they rode north from Palma, soaking up the language.

Esmeray rode next to Bastone as they traversed across a flatland, entering low hills, which closed in to form a valley. She commented, "I think Lucianu likes Terra . . . of course he is inquisitive, but he has not stopped talking with her since we left the city."

"She is attractive . . . and confident . . . like you, Esme. I understand the allure."

They passed a farm where donkeys supplied the power to mill grain and draw water from a well, to irrigate the fields. Lucianu pointed and said, "*Il asino*."

Terra answered with "*Si, ase o ruc*" in Catalan.

Lucianu patted his steed. "*Mulo?*"

Terra said, "*Mula*."

They laughed together.

Esmeray glanced at Bastone. "They get along very well."

After four hours, they reached the monastery on the north coast of the island. Esmeray kept Terra company, enjoying the sunny day, comparing their lives and watching over the mules as the men met with Raimundo Lullio, a Christian mystic.

He led them across the cloister to join the Catalan captain and his officers waiting to discuss the voyage. Raimundo was talkative as they passed bubbling fountains surrounded by raised beds of herbs as well as lemon, orange, and carob trees. Birds chirped and sang as they flitted among the garden.

"I have studied both Greek and Arabic philosophy and I have concluded that with logic and prayer we will convince the Muslims to turn to Christianity. It makes perfect sense. There are twelve

Franciscan monks here, like the twelve disciples of Christ, studying Arabic, so they can go to Africa as missionaries. Please read my works. I have written them in Catalan, Latin, and Arabic so that others will find truth through contemplation," said Raimundo.

The group followed Raimundo as he exited the cloister, pausing in front of a stone building, the entrance covered by a portico supported by two columns. "Here we are, gentlemen, the library, where your associates are waiting."

They entered a large room with one wall lined with windows, the shutters opened allowing the room to be fully lighted. The opposite wall was covered with shelves containing thousands of scrolls and books. Bastone thought the most extensive archives of maps were in Genoa, but this collection rivaled it. He learned the mapmakers were a compendium of the descendants of Catalan colonists who now called Mallorca their homeland, Jewish merchants, and a few Muslims, former sailors now slaves, but devoted to passing on their knowledge.

As Lucianu assisted a group interpreting the Greek documents, Bastone returned to the cloister. There he met the captain of the Mallorcan ship who would guide Zaccaria's flotilla bound for the north, gathering within a few days in the Bay of Palma. The Genoese rode back to Palma and arrived just before sunset.

When they returned to the *Paradisio*, Lucianu could not contain himself and revealed to Esmeray and Bastone, "What have I done to deserve this? I am going on the greatest voyage in many generations, but today I have been struck by the Sicilian thunderbolt, *colpo di fulmine*. Love has struck me like lightning. Nothing can prevent me from returning to my Terra!"

Bastone, ignoring the captain's rules on showing affection in sight of the crew, put his arm around Esmeray's shoulders and said, "My friend, *fortunato in amore*, we are both lucky in love!"

After the *Paradisio's* arrival in Mallorca, it took almost a week to assemble the flotilla that was to sail to the North Sea. Shore leave was granted to the *Paradisio* crew during the wait. Lucianu took the opportunity to visit Terra, taking his lute with him. The first ship to arrive was the Mallorcan nave, *Santa Ponsa,* whose captain would guide Zaccaria's flotilla through the Pillars of Hercules, the straits that led to the ocean. Over the next several days, ships from Genoa arrived to join the flotilla, including a large galley owned by Benedetto Zaccaria, the *Divitia*, manned by 140 oarsmen, free citizens of Genoa, who were paid for their service. During their journey, the oarsmen would spend the nights ashore.

A few days later two more galleys, the *Allegranza* and the *Sant'Antonio*, captained by the Genoese brothers Vandino and Ugolino Vivaldi, dropped anchor in the harbor.

Esmeray woke to the harbor full of ships. Famished and sleepy, she left her quarters heading toward the galley. She turned around, having forgotten her chamber pot, which she meticulously emptied first thing each morning before breakfast. She almost bumped into Amilcare, a menacing smile on his face.

"Buon giorno, little concubine."

Esmeray took a step back, and moved further, repelled by his foul breath, then held her ground. She patted her back pocket and made sure the penknife Bastone had given her was there. "You brute! We are *married*. Bastone's brother will wed your sister."

Amilcare's laugh was edged with cruelty. "Bastone doesn't have a brother." He walked around her, continuing to smirk.

In his cramped quarters, Bastone lowered his hinged desktop from the wall to study the items sold to the nobility of Mallorca and to update the account on the *Paradisio*. He decided he would keep his promise and tell Esmeray his role as a speculatore. Bastone exited his cabin and intercepted Esmeray, carrying her chamber pot to the bow.

"Esme!"

She stopped and looked at Bastone but seemed to talk to herself. "Because we are at anchor, there is no bow wash to disperse the waste." She poured the contents through the lattice at the fore of the ship. "But the current will help."

She continued to stare at the water.

"Esme, you are quiet. Are you sad?"

"No, no . . . um . . . the ride yesterday was tiring."

"I did not forget my promise," said Bastone, "to tell you *everything*. Let's get some breakfast."

The cook at the midship galley filled their bowls with pasta mixed with chickpeas. With a little olive oil sprinkled on them and a piece of freshly baked bread, it was a comforting meal. They sat atop the luxury quarters at the stern, now empty because most of the crew was on shore.

"Dolcezza," said Bastone in a hushed tone. "You must understand I am revealing this knowledge to show how much I trust you. Yet the more you know, the greater the danger to you."

"Go ahead."

"King Charles of Anjou announced he will lead a new crusade to the Holy Land, but the Venetians, who will supply most of the transports, are instead advocating he divert his fleet and attack Constantinople. Those bastards from Venice did the same thing several generations ago. Another sacking could weaken the city and open up Europe to the Muslims."

"In Crete, at your secret meeting, you were helping the Romans of Constantinople against the Venetians. And what did you do in Linguaglossa?" asked Esmeray.

"I guaranteed a resin supply to Emperor Michael."

"And Vulcano?"

"There, I told Giovanni Procida of Michael's pledge to make an alliance with Aragon. Procida, in turn, is on his way to Barcelona to report the emperor's promise to gain King Peter's partnership."

"Now I understand why the servant of the emperor was murdered. Are you a special messenger? Is that what a speculatore does?"

"Among other things. And yes, I am an agent of Michael. I lived in Galata for about two years. Genoa and Constantinople have been allies for centuries and the Genoese not only supplied ships for the emperor and fought in their armies, but men who were willing to take risks did services for them."

"Services?" asked Esmeray.

Bastone glanced around, although the few sentries were not within hearing distance. "Speculatore means spy in Latin. I infiltrated Venetian colonies and reported fleet locations and strengths. I caught Michael's attention when one of his squadrons on which he was a passenger, although greatly outnumbered, defeated a Venetian fleet because of the intelligence I provided. Since then, I have been one of his most trusted speculatores."

"Oh."

"As a speculatore, I agreed not to marry. It would interfere with my missions and . . . make me vulnerable. I am telling you this to show how much I love you." Bastone pondered on the significant risk he was taking with her life by telling her his secrets. He felt he could trust her but hoped he could earn her confidence.

"Why were you *really* counting ships in Messina?" said Esmeray.

"Helping to find the truth about King Charles's crusade," said Bastone. "Those ships are not horse transports to convey a crusader army to the Levante as he announced to the Pope. Instead, Charles is building a fleet to assault Constantinople, as Emperor Michael fears. And while you slept, I met with the admiral of King Charles's fleet and promised to supply the Angevins with Genoese ships. After that I went to shore, contacting a Sicilian patriot in Messina."

Esme's eyes grew wide. "What! Help the Angevins?"

"Esme, it is a ruse. The Republic of Genoa will not supply ships to Charles. The Genoese merchants control the fleets. They own more ships than the government, and although they are traders at heart, sometimes profiteers, and even pirates, the merchants will not weaken the Christian world like the despicable Venetians. It would threaten our own city's security. For a thousand years, Constantinople has been the bulwark against enemies wanting to invade Europe, and now the city holds back the Seljuk Turks."

"So you make agreements with some, but deceive others? And you broke your oath by marrying me. Is that why you lie to me so easily? A master at deceit?"

"Lie to you? What lie?"

"What is your brother's name?"

"My . . . brother? It's hard to . . . um . . ."

She flung her bowl at him, rushing off without looking back.

## CHAPTER XV   THE SILK MERCHANT

The coolness of early morning was lifting as the sun rose across the harbor of Palma. Esmeray had finished breakfast and was on the stern castle gazing toward the waterfront, enjoying the daybreak. Next to her on the taffrail, his front paws tucked under his body, was Mizar. He had completed his nocturnal duties below deck. With calm seas in port, he would take his morning nap, soaking in the sun's warmth.

Esmeray gently petted the feline. The cat was sleeping on the narrow beam without a care, now barely fitting after gaining weight since he had come aboard. Like all cats, he was comfortable with heights, confident he would not fall. Mizar was an effective mouser. Esmeray smiled to herself. Only once did he have to be disciplined after he joined the crew of the *Paradisio,* chasing him away from the sand which covered the mess area at midship. She had then taken him to the lowest deck to a box of sand for his use.

She glanced below, where the captains of the Genoese fleet had assembled on the main deck of the *Paradisio*. Kegs and planks had been used to arrange seating in a half circle facing the stern castle.

Esmeray longed to be out at sea now. A day in port was one day too many for her, let alone the weeklong stay at Palma. Now she observed Bastone, pen and parchment ready, attending the meeting, along with scribes from each ship. At first she believed he had been careful when they were together, for her benefit, aware that if she became pregnant, it would spoil her freedom at sea, but then as always, cynicism crept into her mind. Yes, he didn't want me pregnant, but it was for his own convenience.

Esmeray observed Bastone scribbling notes. She was attracted to him, but was wary of his stories and was determined to keep up her guard.

Captain Zaccaria stood as he addressed the mariners, at times pointing to a map drawn on heavy parchment nailed to the bulkhead of the stern castle. "The galleys will need to stop each night, so the fleet will sail from port to port along the Spanish coast until we pass though the straits. Our first stop will be the island of Ibiza, here—then we'll anchor on the mainland coast at Dania the following night, then Alicante, these latter two ports are now under Aragonese control. The next day's sail will bring us to Cartagena—Castilian territory. The following two nights we will anchor off Almeria, then Malaga, both ports of the Muslim Emirate of Granada. They are Genoese trading partners so there will not be a problem. The greatest threat to us is from the Berber corsairs. They sail from the African coast, always on the prowl to intercept shipping in the straits. They use small, fast boats, surround a cargo ship, then swarm aboard. We will make our passage in the daylight, which will discourage them."

"They certainly will not be a threat with three galleys escorting us," said one captain.

Murmurs amidst the group expressed agreement.

Zaccaria gestured and nodded toward a man seated next to the Vivaldi brothers. "Signore Doria is the primary investor of the two galleys captained by the Vivaldis. He will describe their special undertaking."

Doria stood. "Captain Zaccaria will open up the trade routes to the north . . ." He glanced at one Vivaldi brother, then the other, "and we also have a grand vision. After the fleet passes through the Pillars and sails north on the Ocean Sea, our galleys will instead turn south."

A buzz rose among the men . . . "to the west African coast?" . . . "to the port of Sale' or to Safi?" The men exchanged glances, curious, but not astounded. Genoese ships had been trading with these ports along the Atlantic coast of Africa for decades.

Doria spoke above the murmurs. "Yes, we will call on the African ports for resupply. You will achieve greatness by resuming the sailing routes of the ancient Romans, and we will retrace the journeys of the Phoenicians, but go even further—we will sail around Africa to India. Proving that Genoese are the best sailors in the world!"

The flotilla departed Mallorca and the winds were cooperative as they sailed from port to port toward the coast of Spain. The galleys had nominal sails and could not keep up with the fleet without the help of the oarsmen. The rowers sculled to the timing of the high-pitched whistles blown by the *celeustes,* captains' assistants who maintained a steady pace.

Several days out of Mallorca, as night approached, they anchored off the mainland port of Dania, held by Aragon. Next was Malaga, a Muslim-held port, the local authorities allowing the galley oarsmen to sleep on a sandy beach a distance from town. Late afternoon on the following day, the fleet anchored just outside the harbor of Almeria, the port controlled by the Muslim Emirate of Granada. Captain Zaccaria gave approval for traders to go ashore.

Bastone sought Esmeray. "Come with me. I will be trading for silk."

"Silk?" Esmeray appeared interested.

"The Muslims make silk of the highest quality, which is understandable; they are the ones who brought sericulture to Almeria. I know where to purchase the finest bolts of silk, then we will sell it for large profits in the north."

Esmeray changed from sailor's garb to her simple work tunica. In Almeria, women had to wear a face covering in public. She retrieved a red band of cloth from her meager wardrobe, draped it over her head, and threw the ends over her shoulders, forming a wimple. Then she pulled the cloth up to cover her mouth, revealing only her eyes. She remembered her knife hidden within a comb and strapped it on her leg. Several of Bastone's marines rowed the *Aspasia* to the busy wharf and tied up, where one of his men stayed with the boat. Bastone walked beside Esmeray along the narrow streets as Amilcare and another marine followed. There was barely space for the couple to walk abreast.

Bastone glanced at Esmeray. "These narrow streets remind me of the *vicoli,* the alleyways of Genoa I prowled in my youth. There are alleys so narrow, a man can touch both sides at once. Does this make you feel confined, Esme?"

"No, in fact, when I was a girl, I explored tunnels and caves."

"Caves? Tunnels?"

"When the Turks raided, we escaped and hid in tunnels that had been dug under our village. They protected us for years until . . ." her voice caught.

"Esme?"

"I lost my mother and brother in the last raid and never saw them again."

"I'm sorry, Esme. Your father and you escaped to Chios?"

"Yes."

Her face clouded. She became silent, Bastone respecting her inability to share more.

Near the center of Almeria, the narrow street suddenly opened up into a wide plaza, across which spread a large *suq,* a market, teeming with merchants and customers at stalls where food and products were sold. Delicious aromas of cooked food pervaded the marketplace. Bastone stopped at a vendor, and they enjoyed the delicious smell of cooked meat and vegetables as they watched the vendor prepare and fry triangular shaped pastries, called *sanbūsak*. "Esmeray, would you like to try one?" asked Bastone.

He held up four fingers to the vendor, who handed him the pastries, and Bastone passed two to his guards. Esmeray and he moved away from the guards and the stall to enjoy theirs. Between bites Bastone asked, "Esme, did you see the ingredients he was adding?"

"Yes, and I am tasting them—the pastry is filled with salty pounded meat, with vinegar or something like it. The herbs and spices I recognize are mint, and pepper, but there are other tastes I am not familiar with, except . . . yes, it is mastica. I thought I saw a bowl of it at the vendor's stall, but wasn't sure."

"What was it like living in Anatolia?" asked Bastone.

She hesitated.

"I'm sorry, Esme. Is it too painful to remember?" said Bastone.

"No. I still have loving memories of our family. My father married the daughter of the *beg*, the leader of a nearby nomadic clan of Seljuk Turks. The inhabitants of our village were Christian Romaioi, citizens of the Roman Empire. Father had built a comfortable house of mud bricks, and like the rest of the village, it was connected to a vast underground of rooms and passages. We kept goats and grew millet, flax, and cotton. There was peace between our communities during most of my life. There were minor raids by other tribes of Turks, but we always retreated to the safety of the subterranean hideouts when we were threatened, and I felt protected. But then there was an overwhelming attack."

Esmeray recounted the event that had changed her life six years earlier in the village of Malakopea in Anatolia.

Her mother leaned out the open door of their home, "Esmeray! Get down from that tree. You are going to break your neck!"

Esmeray was expected to spend all of her free time spinning flax, wool, or cotton. A creative girl, she had made a spindle twice the length of her old one, to whirl the cotton into longer threads. With her invention, she climbed onto a tree branch to make the longest threads possible.

Her brother was racing across the stubble-strewn fields, the crops already harvested after the Romaioi peasants had dry-farmed the land. He screamed, "Seljuks are coming! Raiders!" She parted the leaves, which concealed her in one of the few trees in the village. Rushing alongside her brother were his goats and sheep, open mouths gasping and eyes bulging with fright. A cloud of dust loomed behind them, staining the clear blue sky.

A hundred paces away and approaching fast, the thunder of the Seljuks' horses became louder. Mothers herded their children into the houses and further into tunnels as the men in the village grabbed their bows and spears and ran toward the attack to delay the raiders.

Ten years old, Esmeray had hidden in the underground several times during previous raids. There had always been early warning, affording the family time to make it to safety. She recalled one of the events and having to live in the chambers for over a week, eating stored food. They had cooked, the priest had held Mass, children had played, and Esmeray had been disciplined for wandering and exploring the tunnels by herself.

Esmeray froze on the tree limb as villagers fled and screamed below her. Horsemen emerged from the approaching dust storm. A flight of arrows was loosed from the galloping mass, and Esmeray's brother stumbled forward, an arrow in his back, the horse archers' mounts trampling him.

"Mary, mother of Jesus!" cried Esmeray. She closed her eyes as tears flowed but couldn't rid the image of her brother. "God, why have you allowed this!" She lost control of her bladder.

Her mother leaned out of the front door of the house. "Come down! Hurry! They are almost here!"

During the few moments Esmeray hesitated she locked eyes with her mother. The village defenders had lost their battle to stop the enemy and the pounding of the horses' hooves grew louder. "Esmeray! Now!"

Her mother looked away beyond the tree as the Seljuk horse archers reined to a stop, jumped from their mounts, and began storming the village buildings. Esmeray's mother disappeared within the house as an enemy warrior chased her. He passed under Esmeray, her tunic dripping with urine. She pushed her spindle covered with yarn between her legs. The Turk bolted into the house.

The Seljuk returned from inside the house and stood in the shade under the tree. He looked about for more quarry, grunting in surprise as Esmeray's mother again appeared at the doorway. He motioned with his sword for her to come outside.

"No!" Esmeray screamed, the warrior looked up, and the girl thrashed the soldier on the head with her spindle, the stone weight clanging on his helmet and urine splashing in his eyes. He wiped his face, his cursing replaced by a grunt as Esmeray's mother thrust a spear into his chest, the blade hardly piercing his leather armor. As she leaned on the weapon, the man grabbed the spear head and raised his sword. The woman leaned into him, found traction on the edge of the doorstep and drove forward with her legs. The man stumbled back into the tree. The spear point had pierced his heart.

Esmeray climbed from the tree. Her mother grabbed her hand, and they rushed to the back of the house, descended into an opening in the floor, and hurried down a sloping tunnel to the first of eight levels of underground chambers. "Brother is dead!" cried Esmeray. "Where is Father?"

"Quiet!" her mother whispered. "They could be following." She pushed her daughter ahead, "Hurry!" The shorter girl passed easily through the shaft, but her mother had to bend over, lagging behind. Esmeray glanced back, the scolding whispers from her mother driving her on, "Go, go, go!"

Lengths of the tunnel were left narrow by the builders to force invaders to slow and turn sideways to negotiate the passage. Above these sections were small chambers where villagers could hide and thrust spears down at enemy invaders as they squeezed through. With her narrow body, Esmeray hurried through these sections, hardly impeded. She glanced up, hoping to see villagers armed and ready to protect the underground, but was disappointed the chambers were empty.

Esmeray came to where the tunnel split into three and stopped. She could no longer hear her mother breathing and could not see her in the dim light which streamed through the vent shafts. The villagers had been taught that the left tunnel and center tunnels led to dead ends. Esmeray continued on the right leg of the split. She pulled off the roll of thread from her spindle and discarded it, retaining the spinning stick, the thicker end weighted with a ring of stone.

She arrived at a large, excavated chamber, the ceiling the height of three men and twice as wide. A vent supplied faint light. Where she had just exited the tunnel into the chamber, a solid stone wheel stood next to the wall. The wheel's diameter was barely larger than the tunnel opening and as thick as two or three hands, designed so it would roll with gravity to seal the tunnel.

Esmeray heard someone approaching, her mother speaking in Turkish. The girl heard a bowstring snap and instantly lunged sideways, barely avoiding being hit by an arrow. Instead, it clattered across the chamber, creating a spray of dust motes in the shaft of the vent light. Her mother's screams echoed from far along the tunnel, "Esmeray, close the door!"

A fist-sized rock was wedged under the stone wheel, holding it in place. But to reach it, Esmeray would have to cross the opening.

Avoiding exposing herself, she used her spindle, reaching across the tunnel opening to try to dislodge the rock. Tears rolled down Esmeray's cheeks as she stabbed the rock over and over but could not move it.

Her mother appeared at the tunnel opening, her arms pinned behind her by a Seljuk raider and said, "Close it now!" Instead of stabbing, Esmeray hooked the tip of the spindle behind the lodged rock and tugged. It broke free and the huge stone disc thundered across the tunnel entrance. Esmeray's last view of her mother was her face showing triumph. The heavy disc wedged into a groove carved in the floor and locked in place.

Over the next few days, Esmeray was in shock, stumbling through the tunnels and chambers, eventually finding other villagers, women and children, who had escaped the Seljuk attack. They shared the stored food and remained hidden for several days. Esmeray wanted to go to the surface to find her mother and father, but the adults made her stay. They waited.

She had lost track of time, but a few days later Esmeray's father, and other men from the village, arrived and led them to the surface. The village had been plundered, and the livestock stolen. Esmeray and her father found her brother's remains. Neither spoke as they buried him. The fate of her mother was unknown. Although a great risk, her father left Esmeray with friends at the village and traveled east hoping his Seljuk father-in-law would help find his wife. Their Seljuk relations and friends had apparently fallen to the same fate as their village. Her father found only a few scattered survivors and no word about his wife. Because of the local Seljuks' tolerance to Christians, they had been targeted by rival Turks.

Esmeray and her father gave up hope in the ruins of the village, journeying west to the fortified town of Manisa, still garrisoned by Romaioi troops of the Greek-speaking Roman Empire. The empire had lost the ability to protect its citizens on the eastern frontier from the Turks. Esmeray and her father continued west to the island of Chios, their home now for six years.

Esmeray finished her story.

"Esme, I am sorry. So incredibly sorry," said Bastone. "You were resourceful as a girl, as you are now."

The guards had finished their food. As they moved on, Bastone said, "I have one more stop before the silk trader's shop." He found a luthier's shop where artisans made and repaired Spanish lutes, Arabic *ouds*, and other stringed instruments. Almeria was renowned for the quality of their instruments, and Lucianu, not able to get shore leave, asked Bastone to purchase a five stringed lute for him. Selecting one, they resumed to the silk merchant's shop.

They continued, squeezing by local pedestrians in the alleys, Esmeray received stares from men and women. After several minutes, Bastone found the shop he sought, owned by a Jewish merchant who specialized in the silk trade. Bastone and the trader withdrew to a backroom to discuss business, as Amilcare, the other marine, and Esmeray waited in the shop. Esmeray stared out the door to avoid Amilcare's glare, willingly studying the cracks in the stone wall outside rather than look at his face.

Several residents casually glanced in the door as they passed. A trio of men went by, returning to peer into the shop. The way they looked at her brought back memories of the disgusting way the Genoese sailors in Chios had gawked. In her peripheral vision, Esmeray saw Amilcare whisper into the other marine's ear. When the strangers entered the shop, their crowding forced Esmeray to step back, bumping into Amilcare. He suddenly gagged her with her own veil, tightening the cloth and muffling her cries for help. The strangers tied her hands together. She struggled violently as they dragged her down the alley.

Michael A. Ponzio

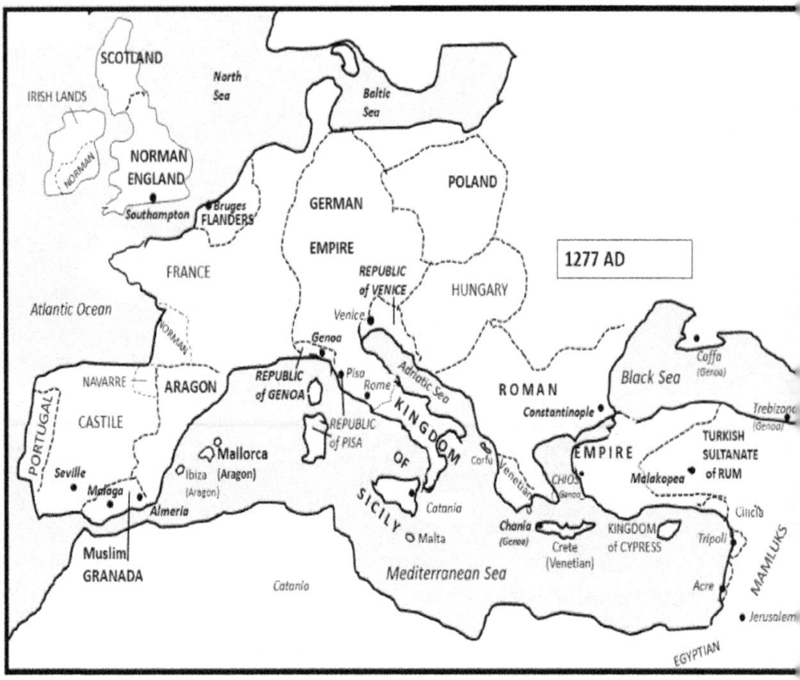
1277 AD
SCOTLAND
IRISH LANDS
NORMAN
North Sea
Baltic Sea
NORMAN ENGLAND
Southampton
Bruges
FLANDERS
GERMAN EMPIRE
POLAND
FRANCE
REPUBLIC of VENICE
HUNGARY
Atlantic Ocean
Venice
NORMAN
Genoa
Caffa (Genoa)
Black Sea
NAVARRE
ARAGON
REPUBLIC of GENOA
Pisa
Rome
Adriatic Sea
ROMAN
Constantinople
EMPIRE
PORTUGAL
CASTILE
REPUBLIC of PISA
KINGDOM OF SICILY
TURKISH SULTANATE of RUM
Mallorca (Aragon)
Ibiza (Aragon)
Seville
Malaga
Almeria
Corfu
Venetian
CHIOS Genoa
Malakopea
Catania
Cilicia
Chania (Genoa)
Crete (Venetian)
KINGDOM of CYPRESS
Tripoli
Malta
Muslim GRANADA
Catania
Mediterranean Sea
Acre
MAMLUKS
Jerusalem
EGYPTIAN

## CHAPTER XVI   ALMERIA

Bastone finished negotiations, returning from his meeting in the back room of the Jewish merchant's shop. A lone marine was strumming the lute Bastone had obtained. He looked up and stopped playing discordant tones.

"Where is . . ." Bastone snapped his head around, searching. "Where is Esmeray?"

"Amilcare said you had authorized . . ."

"Authorized? Authorized what!"

"To sell your concubine."

"God's bones! You idiot! We are *married!*"

"But the rumors were . . ."

"What happened?"

"Three men—they spoke Arabic—muffled her and took her. Amilcare went with them."

"Which direction?"

"Toward the waterfront."

Bastone threw his bolts of silk at the marine, "Deliver these to the captain and tell him not to wait for me!"

He ran out of the shop down the narrow street. The Muslims and Christians enslaved each other during war, but even in peace an ongoing slave trade spanned the Mediterranean. The unfortunate victims would be taken to foreign lands to work. Bastone feared that Esmeray would be smuggled to nearby Africa. The fastest way to chase her down would be with the *Aspasia*.

Bastone arrived at the harbor and found a pair of marines and Amilcare waiting on the *Aspasia*, as if nothing were out of the ordinary. He grabbed Amilcare's collar with both hands and shoved his face close. "What the hell have you done!"

"I have made a good profit . . . you will appreciate your share . . . and you are relieved of your burden."

Bastone shoved Amilcare back, releasing his grip. "I should kill you right now! Where is Esmeray?"

"On a Berber dhow headed to Africa."

Numerous dhows, distinguishable by their single lateen sails, were leaving the harbor.

Bastone pointed, "Which one?"

Amilcare shook his head. "Um . . . I don't know."

"Go ashore, now!"

Amilcare hesitated.

"Get off this boat!" said Bastone as he ground his teeth. Amilcare jumped to the wharf. Bastone shouted to the other marines, "Push off and ready the oars!" He manned the remaining pair of oars.

"Row, ROW! I'll find her boat if I have to search every dhow!"

When they reached the harbor mouth, Bastone prepared the sails. The mainsail and jib quickly caught the easterly, and Bastone steered to ride a fast beam south. The dhows had one sail, no oars, and Bastone was sure he could overtake the Berber vessel but finding the right one was the problem.

They raced into the open sea, sailing past a handful of boats. Bastone craned his neck to see if they had hidden Esmeray in the dhow's open holds, receiving suspicious looks from the crews. But the dhows were fishing boats, with only nets piled on the bottom boards. The Muslim crews of the boats, although wary, did not appear overly concerned. Bastone dreaded the thought that he would not find Esmeray. He shook his head, removing thoughts of vengeance to concentrate only on finding Esmeray.

On board one of the many Berber dhows off the shore of Almeria, Esmeray sat with her hands tied securely behind her back, although they had loosened the wimple, removing the gag.

Esmeray's worst nightmare came to reality. She was certain Bastone was behind her abduction, even making a profit. There was no one to help her now. She was determined to get free, or she would die fighting before being taken to an Arab's harem.

The Berber sailors, her captors, suddenly became excited. She twisted around and with disbelief saw the *Aspasia*. Esmeray shook and rolled her head, loosening her wimple. A gust of wind unfurled the red cloth, now whipping around conspicuously. One of her captors noticed and shoved her to the floor of the boat. Her head painfully found a rib on the hull. Esmeray wondered if the crew on the *Aspasia* had seen her signal.

Bastone saw the bright flash of red and piloted the *Aspasia* toward the dhow. Esmeray was still laying on her side in the bottom of the Berber vessel. Her hands tied together, she pulled up the back of her tunica, finding the quill knife. After cutting her bonds, she stood to dive overboard. A slave trader grabbed her wrist, closing his fingers on her blade, and screamed as he pulled back his bloody hand. He seized her other wrist with his uninjured hand, Esmeray drawing more blood with a swipe of her blade. She dove into the sea as the dhow continued south.

"There she is!" Bastone shouted.

Esmeray swam toward the *Aspasia* as he steered to intercept her. She pulled herself aboard, refusing Bastone's hand. The wind shifted, Bastone overcompensating as he yanked the mainsheet. The *Aspasia* heeled, the Genoese marines instinctively shifted to port and avoided capsizing. The sails luffed, causing the boat to flounder. The dhow came about and was running fast toward them with the favorable wind direction.

"Esme, how are they armed?"

"Swords."

Esmeray shouted, "Oarsmen, come about!"

Bastone yanked an oar from a rowlock. "Here they come! We will fight after all. Get ready!"

The Genoese marines manning the oars couldn't turn the trohantiras before the dhow, assisted by the tail wind overtook the *Aspasia*. A Berber stood at the bow with his sword held high.

Wood versus steel. Like his street battles as a youth. That is how he had gotten his nickname, *il Bastone, the Stick*, not because he was thin, but because he was adept at fighting off dagger attacks with a mere stick. Time after time, he had frustrated the sons of the nobles who despised him as low class.

The boats collided, the Berber slashing at Bastone, who used the oar to parry the sword cut. He redirected the oar, the crunch of bone resounding as he smashed the man's hands with the edge of the oar blade. The Berber dropped his weapon into the sea, but tough and resilient, he tried to seize the oar. Bastone avoided the man's grasp by pulling the oar away, reversing the end and thrusting the handle into the attacker's sternum. The Berber grunted as he doubled over, dropping to the deck.

Esmeray took command of the mainsheet and tiller. Another Berber pushed forward and slashed down at Bastone with his sword, but before the weapon reached its target, the *Aspasia* swiftly came about and darted away from the enemy dhow.

Her chestnut hair whipping free behind, Esmeray shouted, "Now they will see how the *Aspasia* can fly!"

Esmeray outsailed the Berbers, pulling steadily away from the dhow, fleeing toward Almeria. Finally, the *Aspasia* neared the harbor entrance, the slave traders giving up their pursuit. She guided the boat toward the wharfs. The *Paradisio* and the fleet of alum laden ships had departed. "Sail through the straits. We'll catch up to the *Paradisio* in Seville," said Bastone.

Esmeray had been focused on escaping during flight, but now as she navigated along the coast, heading west, she brooded over the abduction and was puzzled why Bastone had changed his mind and come after her. She refused to talk with him, her emotions in conflict, whether to despise him for trying to get rid of her or to thank him for freeing her. Grateful that she now had the sea to calm her, Esmeray let herself meld with the environment. She ignored Bastone's attempts to make eye contact, sensing he knew better than to initiate conversation.

As they approached the Atlantic Ocean, rising out of the sea was a monolithic promontory, a mountain topped by a sharp crest. The ancients called these narrows the Pillars of Hercules. To their right was Mount Jabal Ṭariq, the mountains to the left in Africa were the imagined second pillar. Muslims had controlled the sea traffic through the straits for centuries and simply called it "The Passage" in Arabic.

Suddenly the wind funneling through the strait increased in velocity, blowing westwards, gaining in intensity. The moist winds carried from the eastern side of the strait created distinctive cloud formations on the ridges of Mount Tariq. In Mallorca, Esmeray had overheard a Catalan helmsman describe how those unusual clouds were formed when the winds blew from the east. The helmsman said the presence of those unique clouds signaled the conditions were ideal to sail through the straits.

They sailed steadily ahead for a half hour, then slowed as they neared the massif, the water churning because of the opposing current from the Atlantic Ocean. As they departed the Mediterranean Sea, the wind picked up, allowing the *Aspasia* to overcome the current.

They continued along the coast. Bastone said, "Look for the mouth of a large river. We'll sail upriver and join the fleet in Seville. There is a large Genoese trading colony in the city."

Bastone's break in the silence left Esmeray free to think. As much as she loved sailing the *Aspasia*, she would welcome getting back on the *Paradisio*. Her duties would give her distance from Bastone, enabling her to devise a plan on what to do to free herself of him.

They caught up to the fleet, still anchored near the mouth of the Guadalquivir River, the ship captains waiting for a favorable tide. After boarding the *Paradisio,* Esmeray secured the *Aspasia* on its tow line. Because of the changing tides and difficulty catching wind, it took two days to progress upriver to Seville, where the sailors and marines were allowed to take shore leave in the city. The alum ships were resupplied and readied for the sail north. The Vivaldi brothers prepared their galleys to venture south, intending to find a route around Africa to the spice islands of the east. The *Divitia,* Zaccaria's war galley escorting the fleet, would return to Genoa with trade goods loaded in Almeria and Seville. The anticipated pirate attacks had not materialized in the passage to the Atlantic.

Once all ships were resupplied, shore leave was over and the cargo ships departed Seville. The Mallorcan nave, *Santa Ponsa,* led, followed by the *San Giorgio* loaded with a cargo of alum from the island of Vulcano, then the Roman ship from Trebizond, the *Euxinos Pontos.* The *Aspasia* was again in tow behind the *Paradisio,* which sailed in the rear. After leaving Seville, the flotilla sailed along the coast, veered north, and continued along the coastline of the Kingdom of Portugal.

It had been two weeks since Esmeray had escaped from her captors in Almeria. She had not exchanged one word with Bastone during that time. Esmeray leaned on the side rail of the *Paradisio* watching the coast go by as the sun was setting to port. Bastone joined her vigil in silence, but at a distance so she might remain comfortable. It was the first time since Almeria they had been alone. Bastone had left her be, but decided he had waited long enough, now compelled to talk, hoping she had healed a bit.

"I am sorry," he said. "I am sorry about leaving you alone while I was with the Jewish merchant. It allowed that bastardo Amilcare to his evil doings. I had to keep the encounter covert but should have just kept you with me."

He paused, but she did not reply.

"The shopkeeper represents the Jewish community in Almeria. Their trade with Sicily was stifled by King Charles's excessive taxes. It was important that I negotiated their promise for financial support to help expel Charles."

Without looking at him, she flicked the back of her hand from under her chin and outwards. A Genoese gesture meaning she didn't care.

Abruptly she leaned towards him, her eyes widening, chin tilted down, "You, Amilcare, and Zaccaria all tried to get rid of me!"

"No!" Bastone's jaw dropped. "Amilcare, yes . . . not me!"

She wasn't moved, fuming. "Amilcare wants me gone so his sister will marry you, and the captain must be furious that you took the risk to come after me."

He shifted closer to her, "Because I love you. I won't take you ashore on my next mission. I promise."

"Why should I believe you? How can I trust you? And why hasn't Amilcare been punished for trying to *enslave* me?" said Esmeray.

"The captain does not know the whole story. Zaccaria admitted Amilcare is a stronzo and even his own cousins hate him. But when he questioned the marines, they would not betray Amilcare, so Zaccaria assumed it was entirely an Arab undertaking." Bastone reddened and whispered through clenched teeth. "Do not worry—I will take care of Amilcare—after this voyage is done."

They locked eyes, faces serious. A pit formed in his stomach. Certainly she still believed he was part of her abduction.

A melody floated above the wind. Lucianu was playing his new five string lute Bastone had bought in Almeria, singing in the forecastle cabin. They could hear the Genoese words above the breeze. It was a love song about Terra, the woman he had met in Mallorca.

"After the Almeria incident," said Bastone, "the captain ranted about how disruptive your presence is on the *Paradisio*. He would never have you enslaved. He suggested leaving you in Seville and picking you up on our way back to Genoa. I convinced him to allow you to continue on the ship. The abduction was all Amilcare's doing."

He tried to touch her hand, but she pulled it back. Lucianu's soothing music, however, cooled Esmeray and she said, "Give me time to consider all of this."

"Thank you, Dolcezza," said Bastone. He was certain she still did not trust him and would have felt the same in her place.

They were quiet for a few minutes gazing across the water. "We have been following the coast for weeks," said Esmeray, as she viewed the rocky shoreline. "I thought we were to sail across the Ocean Sea?"

"The maps show that soon we'll pass the Roman faro, the Tower of Hercules," said Bastone, "then we will not see land for weeks."

"The Pillars of Hercules, the Tower of Hercules. Who was Hercules?"

"That is a good question, Esme. Hercules possessed immense strength and defended the weak. He was an ancient . . . um . . . Roman god, or part god . . . his father was a god."

"You mean like Jesus?"

"Esme!" Bastone glanced around to see if anyone was within earshot. "Shhh! That's blasphemous!"

"Is there a god? What god would allow my family to be murdered?"

Their eyes remained locked in silence. Bastone did not answer. He was not surprised she was taking her anger out on God. And because he didn't condemn her, he questioned his own faith.

When the ship rounded a small promontory an immense tower drew their attention. Taller than the faro in Messina, but not as lofty as the *La Lanterna* of Genoa, it had been built by the Romans a thousand years earlier to assist in their sea trade with Britain. Until Zaccaria's fleet, Romans had been the last seafarers to trade between the Mediterranean and Britain.

After sailing past the lighthouse, the Mallorcans, piloting the lead ship, veered north into the Atlantic Ocean. The fleet tracked in their wake on a route straight toward Brittany, the northwest coast of France. Up to this point they had followed the port-to-port description by Pytheas, an ancient Greek navigator writing of his coastal voyage to Britain. But eschewing this coastal route where the westerlies pushed ships toward the shore, they now set a beam reach, using these same winds to tack north, reducing the crossing by two weeks.

During the idle periods of the journey, Esmeray accepted Bastone's offer to teach her to read and write. She still had not forgiven him, agreeing only if they focused on the lessons. He taught her Latin, not too difficult for her, because many words were the same or similar to the Genoese she had acquired. She learned fast, but she did not show any intimacy during the lessons. Bastone, however, longed to restore their warm relationship, jesting with each other, moments of physical playfulness and affection. Once or twice during the lessons, when he was looking over her shoulder checking her writing, he had to restrain himself from embracing her.

## CHAPTER XVII   HAMPSHIRE, ENGLAND

When the Genoese trading fleet reached the English Channel, half of their trading flotilla continued to Bruges to trade alum in Flanders. Along with other Flemish cities, Bruges had highly skilled weavers, spinners, and fullers making the finest cloth in Europe. The *San Giorgio* and the *Paradisio* headed toward England. After their trading was completed, the fleet would assemble before sailing back to the Mediterranean.

The *Paradisio* docked in Southampton, England, to unload 1,500 sacks of alum it had transported almost 3,000 miles across the seas. The *San Giorgio,* from Trebizond, mooring at the next slip, held 1,000 sacks. Each cloth sack of alum weighed one Genoese cantarium, about one hundred English pounds. To hoist the heavy sacks, the crew used the masts' horizontal spars as booms, functioning as make-shift cranes. The sailor below deck in the hold tied two ropes to a sack. One of the ropes was threaded through a block and tackle, a double pulley system, which hung overhead from the boom, the second rope hung free. One or two sailors on deck easily hoisted the sacks from the hold, due to the four to one lift advantage from the block and tackle. As they swung the sack toward dockside, another crewman grabbed the loose rope hanging from the sack and guided the container to the dock, directly onto wagons and two wheeled carts. The unloading operation took over a day using the multiple hatches in the deck and the three sail booms as cranes. The product was then taken to a warehouse for storage, where Zaccaria made transactions with dyers and weavers.

To eliminate the middlemen and purchase wool at lower prices, Bastone and Lucianu visited a waterfront tavern frequented by sheep farmers. Bastone mingled with the customers, buying drinks for those who welcomed the novelty of speaking with foreigners. The wealthy merchants complained about the taxes imposed by King Edward. The customs duties they called the *maltolt*, "the bad tax" charged to traders per exported sack of wool, were ruining exports. As Lucianu translated, Bastone learned that most of the farmers were not happy with the amount of money they had received for their wool. Lucianu overheard a tall, blond-haired drover say to his partner, "Well, William, let's finish our ale and head to the woolhouse."

The man he had called William, who was even blonder and just as tall, swigged the rest of his drink. Lucianu elbowed Bastone to follow, moving toward the pair. They eyed Bastone and Lucianu as they approached.

"Gentlemen, may we buy you another round?" said Lucianu.

The drover flicked his head, tossing away the mop hanging in front of his eyes, and laughed. "You called us gentlemen? We're merely hedge-born."

Bastone looked at Lucianu, who shrugged.

The man added, "You know. We are churls—peasants." He glanced at his partner. "Isn't that right, William?"

"Peasants, ah . . . *il paesani!*" Lucianu explained to Bastone.

"Richard, maybe these are the foreigners that we heard about, that pay us higher prices than the wool house. Do not make fun of them."

He turned to Lucianu and raised his voice. "We are not peasants. We are wool farmers and want to sell you fleece. Do you understand?"

"Yes, our ship is docked nearby," said Lucianu. "How many woolsacks can you sell us?"

"Two wagons full, sixty-four sacks," said Richard.

Lucianu talked with Bastone in Genoese, who held up three fingers.

William's mouth hung open, and his eyes grew wide. "That's three pence a sack?"

Lucianu nodded.

"God's nails! That's a lot more than the wool house pays," said Richard. "Show us the way to your ship."

William was all smiles, and not totally from the ale, though that certainly contributed. He raised his chin and puffed out his chest. "My good man, Richard, we are successful gentlemen merchants, don't be such a muckspout!"

"You say I have a foul mouth. We *are* talking with sailors. I am sure they aren't uppishmen who can't take a little banter."

The men laughed at their own joke, leaving Bastone and Lucianu befuddled. Lucianu held his palms up as he raised his shoulders.

"And one more condition for the purchase," said Lucianu. "Lead us to other wool farmers who will sell to us, but do not tell them we gave you an inflated price."

Richard looked at William. "We could take them to the mills. It's on our way home."

"There are risks. That's a gathering place where sheep farmers sell to middlemen," said William. His face became serious as he addressed Lucianu. "The middlemen hire thugs to discourage any competition. You also must keep secret our dealings with you."

Lucianu translated. William showed four digits and Bastone nodded.

William and Richard delivered their woolsacks to the *Paradisio*, then drove their horse-drawn wagons across Southampton. Lucianu and Bastone followed on ponies they had leased; their saddlebags contained a small amount of mastica and silk bolts they hoped to sell. They crossed a recently built bridge over the River Test at Redbridge, about six miles west of the port. Two miles along the river they came to a small estuary off the river, spanned by a wooden causeway, where a grist mill was located, its paddles turning with the incoming tide.

A few tents and awnings had been erected by the wool buyers to conduct transactions with the farmers. Scores of wagons had assembled and were piled high with woolsacks, the containers shaped in rough cubes, to some extent standardized in weight.

Richard tapped his draught horse with his goad stick to encourage the steed to move. "Good luck and watch out for trouble!"

William followed and waved farewell. "If you return next year, come straight away to our farm at Roundtree to buy our wool. We are just north of the village of New Sarum."

Bastone and Lucianu wandered among the crowd, trying to get a feel for the system of transactions. Lucianu was distracted by the operation of the mill. A worker exited a shed next to the grist mill.

Luciano greeted him. "Hail, good fellow!"

The worker hesitated, then said, "Er . . . Hello, sir."

Lucianu continued, his hands innately moving with his speech. For a few moments, the Englishman's head bobbed, following Lucianu's gestures. "It is fascinating that this mill is driven by the ocean currents." said Lucianu. "Does it operate twice a day when the current recedes and when it rises?"

The man blinked a few times, recovering, as if he did not comprehend, "I am sorry. I was stumped by your accent, your gesturing, and choice of words, but I think I understand. The channel current, yes . . . you mean high and low tides?"

"Tides? This is a new word for me," said Luciano. "These ocean currents are called tides?"

The man nodded, then said, "And we are truly fortunate. The Lord has provided us with double tides here. We are blessed with two high tides and two low tides a day, and the grist mill operates on the incoming and the ebb tides. It's the most productive gristmill in Hampshire County!" He tipped his hat and moved on.

Lucianu translated for Bastone, and they were both impressed, but perplexed. The Englishman's description didn't match what they had learned of the tidal frequency in Seville and the Straits of Messina, only two tides per day.

Mingling with the crowd waiting to sell their wool, Bastone learned that the farmers negotiated on a price with the middlemen buyers. The farmers received a written voucher which they presented at the wool houses, receiving payment when they delivered their fleece at Southampton. Lucianu and Bastone approached several wool farmers waiting at the back of a line of wagons. But the farmers were startled, uncomfortable with the foreigners' presence, refusing to talk with them. After more attempts Bastone succeeded in making agreements, offering higher prices than the middlemen. He issued vouchers. One by one, more wool farmers agreed to sell to Bastone.

"That's ten wagons of wool for the *Paradisio*," said Lucianu.

Bastone smiled from their accomplishment. "Belissimo!"

A group of burly men rapidly approached, body language and expressions seething with aggression.

"They aren't hiding their intentions," said Bastone. His street fights as a youth flashed in his mind, recalling the craftiest thugs had approached in a friendly manner before they attacked. "Are these the hoodlums that William warned us about?"

"No daggers!" said Bastone. "We'd never make it out alive if we killed one of them!"

The lead man pulled a knife and shouted, "You stole those ponies!"

Bastone retreated and pulled Lucianu along. "Run!"

They jumped on their mounts and escaped, following the road toward the village of New Sarum. The pair agreed they might be arrested for horse theft and hoping for a place to hide, headed for the farm that Richard had mentioned.

They slept in the woods near the hamlet of New Sarum and found the Roundtree farm in the morning. Richard offered to hide them at his farm, after hearing their story. He met William at the tavern in New Sarum, where he learned that Bastone and Lucianu were wanted for theft of livestock. Richard suggested they try to take on the appearance of English folk. Bastone and Lucianu shaved their beards, bought two carts and sacks of wool from Richard, who advised Lucianu to only speak when necessary, and Bastone not to talk around strangers, acting the part of a deaf and speechless person.

Two days after their escape from the mill, they drove the carts full of woolsacks toward Southampton. Bastone, guiding the lead cart, tapped his draught horse with his goad stick, pausing at a creek. He dipped a leather bucket to collect water for the horses.

A sudden shout from behind, "Hail fellow! Watch out!"

Startled, Bastone lost balance and tumbled into the water.

"God's bones! Lucianu, what are you up to?"

"Just practicing my English."

He let the younger man help him up as he dripped on the bank.

"And . . . um . . ." Lucianu laughed, "testing your reactions. Remember, in your disguise, you cannot hear nor speak at all. You must always act as if you are deaf and dumb. It will be easy. Mute people and Genoese have much in common."

Bastone looked puzzled.

"They both talk with their hands."

"I *will* talk with my hands!" Bastone held up a fist and slapped the crook of his raised elbow. He then shoved Lucianu into the creek.

Lucianu sat in the shallow water as they laughed. "Well, you better wash your hands. Those were dirty words!"

They arrived in Southampton, pleased to find that most of the wool farmers they had given vouchers had arrived and sold directly to Zaccaria.

## CHAPTER XVIII    RETURN TO MALLORCA

The *Paradisio* and *San Giorgio,* fully laden with woolsacks, cast off with the second ebb tide of the day. They reached the channel and eventually joined the two ships of their flotilla that had traded alum in Flanders for finished cloth and wool.

Lucianu strummed his lute and sang as he sat on the roof of his cabin he shared with the helmsman. The beat of snapping lanyards, the call of seagulls, and the pounding of the waves provided accompaniments.

*"I think of Sicily and the memory brings pain to my heart.*
*A place of youthful folly, now desolate.*
*Enlivened once by the flower of noble minds.*
*If I am expelled from paradise, how do I tell of it?*
*If my tears were not bitter,*
*I would believe them to be the rivers of that paradise."*

Bastone had ducked out of his quarters to listen. As Lucianu finished, he let the resonance of the strings fade to silence. Bastone asked, "Did you write that song of your native land?"

Lucianu smiled. "I fashioned the melody, but the poetry is by Ibn Hamdis, a Saracen, born in Sicily. He was forced to leave when the Normans invaded."

"*Bella*, nice! or in Sicilian, *Beddu,*" said Bastone. "And tell me about the love ballad you sang at the wharf. I was throwing kisses at Esme as she watched from the *Paradisio*, although she ignored me. I imagine onlookers thought the song was for Esme and me, but you sang it for Terra, back in Mallorca."

Lucianu pointed. Mizar and a second cat, a long-haired calico with orange, white, and black patches, her fluffy tail whirling above her gracefully, were making their rounds for vermin.

"I thought Mizar was sick. And where did the other cat come from?" said Bastone.

"During our wool buying adventure, Esmeray got a female cat from an old sailor on the wharf. He said that type of cat lives in the forests of Norway, its ancestors brought to England by the Norsemen long ago. Mizar is well again. Esmeray claims that Cassiopeia, that's the female cat's name, healed Mizar with love." Lucianu added, "And that love ballad was for the cats, not Terra."

Bastone groaned, moving his hands, up and down in front of his abdomen, "Ha! *Que forbu!* What a character! You lured me into that one!"

A few months before, when the Genoese trading fleet had sailed from the Mediterranean, the heavy sacks of alum had served as ballast to steady the ships. Now as the fleet returned south heading toward the Atlantic, ballast in the form of river cobbles had been added to the ships' holds. Lacking sharp edges that could cut into the wooden hulls, the smooth stones were ideal. With all the remaining space below deck packed with woolsacks, some sailors had to sleep on deck.

During the voyage, Esmeray was busy with her duties as a sailor, keeping her conversations with Bastone crisp. He wanted to prepare her to meet his family in Genoa. When he tried to engage her, she would make an excuse that she had a duty on the ship.

One day as the fleet sailed toward Spain on the prevailing westerlies, Lucianu asked Bastone if he wanted to hear his new ballad. He invited Bastone into his empty cabin, his roommate at the helm. Closing the door, Lucianu put down his lute and handed Bastone a cup of wine, raised his own, and drank.

Bastone glanced back at the door, confused, and said, "So, you have a new song? Perhaps a musical proposal of marriage for Terra?"

"No, not a love ballad. It's the song I wrote from the poetry of the Saracen. I can't get the words out of my mind. '*I think of Sicily and the memory brings pain to my heart, A place of youthful folly, now desolate,*'" said Lucianu.

"But the Saracen was speaking of times long ago," said Bastone.

"I overheard you talking with Esmeray on our way north." Lucianu paused, waiting. Bastone kept a straight face, hoping Lucianu had not heard too much, trying to bluff his way out of telling his friend the details.

"I am greatly concerned," said Lucianu, "about my family's safety in the homeland. Is there going to be an invasion of the island?"

Bastone swallowed some wine, avoiding the question. "This Burgundian wine we got in port is as good as the Sicilian. But the cost of buying imported wine in England! We must stock up more on the home vintage the next voyage."

Lucianu drank as he kept his eyes on Bastone, maintaining a steady gaze. The long, silent pause that followed was awkward. "You are lucky you are governed by the Baron of Taormina," said Bastone. "When I visited Linguaglossa, your family and friends had a good life; however, most of Sicily is oppressed by King Charles's iron-handed rule."

"I know of this tyranny, experiencing it when I was tutored in Messina," said Lucianu.

Bastone weighed his options. It was dangerous to have yet another know of the plan. But he decided Lucianu might also be helpful for the cause. He said, "King Charles's much heralded plan to launch a crusade to recover Jerusalem is a massive charade," said Bastone. "Venice, supplying many of the ships for Charles's fleet, supports his plan to attack Constantinople instead. They will loot and kill as they did decades ago. Constantinople, just recently recovering from that sacking, guards the eastern gate to Europe from the Muslims. The independence of Europe will be at risk. My mission is to carry information and promises of alliance and gold to defeat Charles. The revolt will start in your homeland."

Lucianu's mouth hung open. He stared into space for a moment. "This makes it difficult with Terra. But I *must* return to Sicily—my family . . . my friends."

Within a few weeks, they navigated through the straits to the Mediterranean Sea; because of more favorable currents and winds, they found the passage less difficult than when they had sailed west. A week later they arrived at the harbor of Palma on the Isle of Mallorca to resupply. The Mallorcan nave, the *Santa Ponsa*, would remain in its home port. The following day, the other three vessels would continue east. The ship from Trebizond had the longest voyage home to the eastern Mediterranean, then to the Black Sea. After a short stop in Corsica, the *Paradisio* and the *San Giorgio* would sail to Genoa.

Night fell as Bastone gazed across the Palma harbor. Troubled by their upcoming arrival at Genoa, he envisioned a dozen ways to introduce Esmeray to his family. Now, concerned he had waited too long to warn her of his family's likely assault on their marriage, he knocked on the door to Esmeray's quarters. There was no answer. He entered the room and found it empty, including any sign of her meager belongings.

Bastone searched out the night watch. "Have you seen Esmeray?"

"No, sir."

"Who went ashore?"

"Sailors, marines—a few officers disembarked. Ottolino, and, yes, the barber surgeon departed about an hour ago."

"Lucianu?"

The watchman nodded.

Bastone headed down the gangplank. "And, sir," added the night watch, "I heard a woman talking to Lucianu on the dock. Hmmm? Yes ... it could have been Esmeray."

The waterfront of Palma was quiet except for a couple of taverns. Part of the crew was taking their turn in the drinkeries. It must have been Esmeray the watch saw talking with Lucianu. Bastone was puzzled that she had disembarked with Lucianu. He had a fleeting thought they might have a dalliance, but quickly ridded that idea. Lucianu was enamored with Terra and besides he was a friend and a gentleman.

Bastone went to the nearest tavern to ask crew members if any of them had seen Esmeray. When he entered, heads turned and the natter of the crowded place quieted. Esmeray, wearing her sailor's clothes, a duffle bag at her feet, was talking to sailors from the *Paradisio*. Normally, women of the night were the only females that frequented sailors' taverns, but most of the patrons this evening were crewmen Esmeray worked with, so she was safe there. Esmeray saw Bastone and stomped out the door without looking at him.

Bastone hesitated, all eyes on him. Then he turned to follow Esmeray, chased by a flurry of hoots and ribbing. "You're in deep water, Bastone!" "No warm bed for you tonight!"

An old sailor next to the door grabbed his sleeve. "She was looking for Lucianu."

Coming out of the tavern, Bastone saw her running down the waterfront. She was quick, but hindered by her bag, Bastone overtook her and grabbed her wrist. He released his grip. As their breathing returned to normal, their eyes remained locked.

"Why did you jump ship?" said Bastone.

Esmeray turned her face sideways to Bastone, her bag dropping to the ground, tethered to her wrist, glaring at him. "When we get to Genoa, your family will convince you to abandon me. And you will. They will say our marriage was not real!"

"No! I will defend you!"

She folded her arms. "I doubt it, blood is thicker than water."

Esmeray picked up her bag. "Even if you support me, I could not face the hatred and rejection. It's terrifying! I am going to ask Lucianu and Terra if I can stay with them."

"The watchman said he heard a woman's voice when Lucianu disembarked. Was that you?"

"Yes, Lucianu refused to take me with him. He said I was making a mistake leaving you."

"You are."

"Well, I am not going with you."

Bastone tried to embrace her, but Esmeray shrugged him away.

She stepped backwards several paces, holding her bag against her chest.

Bastone followed, reaching toward her. "Esme, wait! When you told me about the loss of your brother in Anatolia, I understood your feelings. I also am haunted by painful thoughts of my brother's death."

Esmeray eyes grew moist. "You have . . . no . . . you *had* a brother?"

"Yes. Francesco, my oldest sibling, was to marry into the Spinola family. He was among the Genoese who joined the Milanese to fight King Charles. My brother was captured in the battle by the Angevins. Charles demanded a ransom for his release along with several nobles.

My family made the payment, but Charles had him executed anyway. I will make my brother's sacrifice meaningful, doing everything I can to end Charles's ambitions."

Esmeray sobbed. She turned away as if to leave, then faced him again. He hoped she had changed her mind.

She shook her head. "I am sorry about your brother, but I must leave!" She sprinted from the dim light of the wharf into the dark.

Bastone's heart sinking, head down, he boarded the *Paradisio* and went to his cabin in disbelief. He lay sleepless in his bunk, staring in the darkness. Bastone knew he loved her, struggling to think of ways to convince her to come to Genoa. He got out of bed, lowered a hinged desk on the wall and lit an oil lamp. His cabin mate, Ottolino, stirred and said, "Blow out the lamp!" then rolled over and went back to sleep.

After Bastone finished writing a message to the captain, he read the letter. Dissatisfied with his note, he tossed the document away, watching the parchment flip over as it glided to the bed. On the back of his note to the captain were practice sentences written by Esmeray, her studies cut short by their discord. The thought of her inspired Bastone, certain she was worth any effort.

He left the letter to the captain on his bunk. Dousing the light, he stuffed his helmet and *usbergo*, mail shirt, and other possessions into a cloth bag, and picked up his crossbow. He left his bulky shield and cracked open the cabin door.

Amilcare was the night watch making his rounds. As was typical for the night guards, he was armed with a crossbow. Bastone waited until Amilcare moved toward the bow. The previous watchman had pulled the gangplank in for the night. The last sailors to return from the taverns were scattered prone across the deck, sound asleep. He softly padded to the stern where the tow rope was connected to the *Aspasia*. Suddenly he heard Amilcare shout behind him. Bastone was certain if Amilcare recognized him, he would relish the opportunity to shoot, claiming it was a mistake because of the dark. Without looking back, Bastone jumped over the taffrail, just as he heard the clack of a crossbow trigger. Gripping the rope tied to the *Aspasia*, he spun around, landing with his feet against the *Paradisio's* hull, still hanging on the line, peering over the edge of the deck. Amilcare was talking to someone, his silhouette blocking the other person. A few groggy sailors woke and crowded around Amilcare, pointing toward the wharf. The crossbow shot was not for Bastone. Amilcare's intended target was on the dock.

Bastone lowered himself to the *Aspasia* and heard the gangplank being moved to connect up to the dock. He untied the line from the *Paradisio*, rowed the *Aspasia* about a mile along the shore, finding a small inlet, where he moored the trohantiras, hidden from view of the *Paradisio*. An hour before dawn, he disembarked the *Aspasia,* and headed toward Terra's home. He overtly approached the house, not wanting to alarm the occupants. Within fifty paces of the front door, the mules in the stable brayed in alarm.

There was a shout out of the dark, "*Atura,* Halt!"

Bastone didn't understand Catalan but froze in his steps.

A woman's voice. "*Es l'amic de Lucianu*, he is Lucianu's friend!"

Terra lit an oil lamp at the front door of the house. Her father stood next to her, lowering a pitchfork. Lucianu came out of the stables, looking sleepy.

Terra spoke in Genoese. "Bastone, what are you doing here!"

"Isn't Esmeray with you?"

She glared at Lucianu. "No! Lucianu said she returned to the ship."

"I told her to go to the ship and make peace with you, Bastone. You didn't see her?"

Bastone looked up, lifting his palms. "Christ's teeth! I shouldn't have let her go! She said she was coming here." His chin dropped to his chest, sure he had lost Esmeray for good.

Terra waved her hand beside her head. "Mother Mary! Are you both useless? Action is what we need! Father, help me saddle the mules. We'll search on the way to the waterfront."

Lantern Across the Sea

## CHAPTER XIX    LA LANTERNA

Esmeray returned to the *Paradisio*, but the crew had removed the gangway to the ship for the night. Clouds reduced the light of the half moon, and it was too dark for her to identify the night watch pacing the deck. Standing on the wharf, Esmeray waved her arms and got the watch's attention. His face was unrecognizable in the shadows, but he waved in acknowledgment. He crouched down, briefly out of sight behind the side wale to lift the gangplank, sliding it to the wharf. But when he straightened up, he was coolly aiming a crossbow at her. Clouds drifted from the face of the half-moon revealing the arbalester's identity. As he pulled the trigger, a crewmember shoved his weapon to the side. The cross bolt missed Esmeray by an arm's length, skittering across the wooden dock. Her knees buckled from the near miss. Bastone had spoken the truth. Amilcare was solely behind the abduction. She took a deep breath and tried to regain her confidence.

Crewmen wrenched the crossbow from Amilcare as a shouting match ensued. The ruckus halted when Esmeray crossed onto the ship. She raised her chin, glaring at Amilcare, making a biting motion on the edge of her hand. The sailors and marines showed their respect, remaining silent.

Across the wharf, the sun was rising above the Cathedral of Palma. Esmeray reached Bastone's cabin just as Ottolino opened the door. The *Paradisio* was preparing to weigh anchor, obliging the officers, including Ottolino, as first mate, to be ready on deck.

Zaccaria's voice suddenly boomed from atop the stern castle. "Where is the *Aspasia*? Both night watches are to report to me. Now!"

As Ottolino exited his cabin, he handed Esmeray the letter Bastone had left for the captain. Seeing the cabin was empty, she said, "Where's Bastone?"

Ottolino declined to answer and hurried away to supervise the crew. She tried to read the document but with her nominal literacy, only recognized her name, a phrase or two, and the word *love*. Esmeray was puzzled.

Sailors lifted the captain's tender, a canottino, from the stern castle, lowered it to the water, then connected it with a towline to the *Paradisio's* bow. The sailors rowed the canottino, towing the *Paradisio* toward the harbor mouth. Esmeray found Zaccaria atop the stern castle with the helmsman.

"You are still here?" said the captain. "I thought you jumped ship. Lucianu told me weeks ago he was leaving, but Bastone . . . he left saying nothing. He left you here, too?"

She gave him the letter, waiting. The captain glanced at the letter, looked up and said, "It is addressed to me, um . . . sailor . . ." he waved her away and returned to reading.

But Esmeray remained. "My name is in the message, I wanted to know . . ."

His jaw muscles clenched as he spoke between his teeth, "What are you doing reading a captain's correspondence?" He scanned the document, eyes sweeping rapidly back and forth, then looked up and calmed. Clearing his throat, he tilted his head for Esmeray to follow him out of hearing distance of the helmsman.

"Of course . . . um . . . So, you could not read . . . all of it?"

Esmeray shook her head. The captain read the letter to her.

> "Captain Zaccaria, I have the Aspasia and in return give you more than adequate compensation, which is this month's salary plus my share of the expedition's wool profits. And I will remind you of my generous payments for Esmeray's otherwise empty quarters, money you would not have received. But I expect nothing less from the shrewdest of traders. As they say, 'Genoese therefore merchants.'"

Zaccaria laughed, then read on.

> "I do not anticipate any references from you for employment in the future, but I hope you were satisfied with my performance over the last several years."

Zaccaria paused, smiled at Esmeray as he continued reading,

> "I must leave the Paradisio for Esmeray. My grandmother often quoted a proverb, which I am taking to heart: 'When love knocks on the door, don't leave it in the street.' With respect, Ponzio Bastone."

Zaccaria had appeared reassured by the letter, but then suddenly shook the letter in exasperation. "What the hell is going on? Where is Bastone and why are you here? Hmmm . . . I did notice the coldness between you and Bastone on the return from England. But you are a hard-working sailor. I will make it . . . um . . . worth your while to stay as a crew member," said the captain. "It's lonely in my quarters."

She had ignored the captain's suggestive remarks in the past, but this time did not hide her look of disapproval.

Zaccaria noticed. "Uh . . . I apologize. You can stay in the present quarters . . . as my guest."

Esmeray ran to the edge of the ship and dove off the upper deck.

Bastone arrived at the waterfront just as a figure plunged off the stern castle of the *Paradisio* as it approached the exit of the harbor. He jumped from his mule and ran to the edge of the dock.

"Esmeray!" yelled Bastone.

Terra and Lucianu joined him dockside to watch Esmeray's even strokes propel her toward shore. Esmeray reached the wharf, climbed the ladder, and as she reached the top, Bastone grabbed her. He pulled her into a tight embrace, her clothes soaking him. He held her close and followed with a deep kiss, disregarding norms against displaying affection. Bastone did not see her tears of joy nor detect the weeks of tension drain from her.

Lucianu and Terra watched, looking both relieved and pleased. Esmeray shivered as she nestled against Bastone, his arms encircling her. Terra handed the reins of a mule to Bastone and interrupted, "Let's get Esmeray dry clothes."

The four mounted and began the ride to Terra's home. Esmeray sat behind Bastone, sharing a mule. She embraced him, enjoying the intimacy and warmth, then asked one question after another before he could answer the previous one. "You quit your officer's position? Will your family be enraged? What about your uncle's investment? Where is the *Aspasia*?"

"We'll talk later. Isn't it more important that we are together, mi dolcezza?"

"Yes . . . yes . . ." she squeezed him.

Two weeks later, with reflections of the half-moon dancing on the swells of the Tyrrhenian Sea, the *Aspasia* ran with the westerlies toward Genoa. Bastone and Esmeray had sailed nonstop, alternating between sleeping and navigating, from Mallorca to Corsica. After a two-day break in Corsica at the port of Ajaccio, they continued to Genoa. Esmeray was thrilled as the tailwinds propelled the *Aspasia* across the sea. A light blazed on the horizon. She knew it was not a star. "Bastone! Bastone, wake up!"

Her husband tossed off his blanket and sat up. "What?"

"Is that the light tower, the faro, of Genoa?"

He rubbed the sleep from his eyes and looked east. "La Lanterna! Yes! It is the lantern across the sea, the most welcome sight for homesick Genoese sailors. The first sight of La Lanterna means we are twenty miles from Genoa." He glanced at the wake alongside the trohantiras. "We're going at least ten knots and should reach Genoa in two hours."

"I can't meet your mother in these sailor's clothes!"

"Hmm. I think you are irresistible even in your . . . uh . . . pants."

Esmeray gave him a sly look and gestured for Bastone to move closer.

"Oh, sorry, mi dolcezza. I have upset you. You have had to endure enough lewd remarks. Go ahead and slap me, I deserve it."

Her hand swiftly went to his cheek, but she didn't strike, and instead pulled him closer. Her kiss was soft, warm, and breathless.

Bastone's voice was husky, "With one caress you can seduce me under this full moon." He drew away and glanced upwards. "But the halo around the moon suggests a thunderstorm is coming. We must keep sailing, and it will take all of our concentration.

"But as for your clothes, yes, yes. I have a plan."

Bastone took his turn at the tiller and Esmeray handed him a chunk of hard bread. They savored the crusty food and shared wine. After washing down the dry bread with a swallow from the skin, Bastone said, "My sister married into the De Mari di Luccoli clan, whose compound is near my family's. We'll stop there first; it will delight her to provide you with a bath and a proper tunica."

"Will your family be angry with you for giving up your share of the expedition's profits? And what about us?" said Esmeray.

"They will think I am crazy, but the family shares are still intact. Zaccaria and my uncle, the owners of the *Paradisio,* will collect the most profit. But there are other investors, many shares bought by the rich nobles and worth thousands of Genoese liras as well as shares purchased by common folk who invested smaller amounts. That is the Genoese way.

"And if my family doesn't approve of our marriage, fine, we will still have each other."

"Will you be applying for a marine's position on another nave?"

"No, up until now, hiding my covert tasks using the guise of a marine traveling from port to port, worked well. But the time is too short. When we get to Genoa, I must prepare for my next mission."

"Where will that be?"

"I don't know yet, but I will find out in Genoa. I will need to use the *Aspasia*, mi dolcezza."

"And I will be your helmsman . . ."

Esmeray waited for him to reject her idea. When he didn't comment, she was relieved. Grateful they had the *Aspasia,* the trohantiras being especially dear to her, having been named after her mother. The boat had taken care of her, as her mother always did, until the end. And she cherished the memory of the long hours building the boat with her father, sawing and planing the timbers, and hammering the pitch rope between the plank joints. Esmeray broke off another piece of bread and handed it to Bastone.

A second beacon appeared on the horizon. "What's that other light?" asked Esmeray.

"There is a light tower on each side of the harbor entrance. That is the light of the smaller faro, called the Greeks Tower, about a hundred feet tall. La Lanterna is at least twice as high. At night, sailors can see the light of the Greeks Tower ten miles from shore, so now we are less than an hour to Genoa."

Half an hour later, a sudden gust of humid wind shook the mainsail. Bastone glanced at the moon, now two hours from setting. "The halo is faint, which means the storm should not be too fierce. We should ride it out, but we must heave to."

"No, we should keep running down wind," said Esmeray.

Bastone shouted above the sudden downpour and roaring wind, "I am not challenging your ability as a sailor. I am only telling you that once I was on a ship during a storm and the helmsman and captain didn't run from a storm because they were near the coast. We can no longer see the lights from the faros, and we would risk crashing onto the rocky shore."

"I've outrun storms. The *Aspasia* won't be able to take on the water it will bring!" yelled Esmeray.

"*Va bene*, fine, you decide, but consider, we have been running at ten knots and the storm caught up to us—it's moving faster than us. We should ride it out."

Esmeray paused, then gave in to Bastone's argument, shouting, "You make sense. This one time, I'll follow your sailing advice. Heave to!"

Bastone quickly reefed the mainsail, reducing the sheet area. "All I can tell you is they tacked the boat into the wind!"

She kept the bow pointed close to the wind to prevent capsizing, but still preventing the boat from being pushed backwards.

"You're doing it! We are tacking but not moving forward," said Bastone.

Bastone attached a line to the hull, securing it around Esmeray's waist and his own. The bow pointed skyward on every wind driven upsurge, obstructing their view. With low visibility through the rainstorm, they were prevented from anticipating and bracing for the next wave. Without the tie offs, they would certainly have been thrown overboard.

With determination, Esmeray maintained her grip on the tiller, keeping the beam in line with the wind and surges. Bastone tightened his grip on his wife's lifeline to keep her aboard and held onto the hull with the other. It was hard to keep their eyes open as rain pelted them sideways. Waves broke across the deck and their mouths filled with salt water.

Minutes felt like hours to Esmeray as she struggled to keep the bow windward. Muscles fatigued. Fear crept in. The Aspasia was taking on water. She was tiring. Holding the boat abeam was the priority because capsizing would be a worse fate than foundering. Sudden anxiety flashed through her mind. Should we have run? Is this the end of us—of our lives?

Bastone stayed tied off, stretched to retrieve his helmet, and bailed. Another sideways wave hit the Aspasia. Bastone shifted his body to compensate as Esmeray steadied the trohantiras. She knew they couldn't defeat the sea; they must adapt to the sea's rhythm. A sailor must embrace the sea, become part of the sea. With renewed confidence, Esmeray merged with the storm.

Michael A. Ponzio

## Harbor of Genoa

*La Lanterna*

*The Greeks Tower*

## CHAPTER XX   GENOA

The full moon had shed its halo, a brilliant orb to the west, floating just above the sea. To the east, an arc of mountains urged Genoa toward the sea. Docks and warehouses packed the limited flat land available along the port's semicircular harbor, which teemed with ships. Behind the harbor front the walled enclaves and towers of the noble families ascended the hills steplike, giving the impression of an amphitheater filled with houses and churches attending the grand performance of the Tyrrhenian Sea.

The *derecho*, the fast-moving thunderstorm, had quickly drenched the city and sped on toward the east. The storm had not broken Esmeray and Bastone but had strengthened their bond.

Bastone slowly guided the *Aspasia,* its mainsail furled, between scores of trading vessels and war galleys anchored outside the moles, seawalls created in phases over the millennium Genoa had been a port. He entered the harbor between the promontories of two moles that protected Genoa harbor. They passed the right mole under the light of the Greeks Tower, the smaller lighthouse, where the ships from the eastern Roman empire anchored waiting their turn at the busy docks. The lighthouse's name stemmed from the slang the Genoese used for the Romans of Constantinople—*Greeks*, because their empire was oriented towards Greek rather than Latin culture, including Eastern Orthodox Christianity.  On the left mole, over twice as high as the

*Torre dei Greci*, the Greeks Tower, was the impressive La Lanterna, adding its illumination, warning the sailors returning home.

*Aspasia's* jib was taut from the westerly breeze, the boat gliding into the harbor. Bastone steered to the right, past several cargo ships, and headed toward a vacant mooring post under the Greeks Tower. He nodded at Esmeray. She furled the jib, placed a hand on the wooden post, and guided the boat, which gently bumped to a stop. Esmeray made a bowline knot, securing the trohantiras to the mooring post several feet from the jetty. Bastone dropped their stone anchor at the stern.

"You will be a sailor yet!" Esmeray said, beaming. "A perfect landing." She glanced across the harbor at the wharfs in the middle of the city. "Why are we tying up here?"

"I am to meet an agent of the emperor on one of these ships from the east," said Bastone.

Esmeray's smile faded.

"Suddenly, I feel exhausted. Are you?" said Bastone. The moon was about an hour from setting. "The full moon always departs for the sun. It is an hour to sunrise."

Fortunately, they had avoided losing the spare main sail during the storm, although they had lost all the oars. Bastone had also lost his crossbow to the storm.

"I continued bailing after the storm passed," said Bastone. "It's dry enough to sleep. Look, it will be comfortable here." He doubled-over the spare sail and made a snug nest along the bottom of the hull, then draped the rest over a line to make a canopy for privacy. They lay embraced in the confined space, but exhaustion overcame their longing for affection, and both were soon asleep.

They had slept through the day, waking an hour before sunset. Bastone pulled back the sailcloth to look out. As they lay side by side, he kissed Esmeray gently but fully. Her eyes remaining closed, she opened her mouth, just as enthusiastic. She reached down, Bastone groaned, but she released her grasp and said, "Oh, what am I doing, people might see us!"

"We can . . . no, you are right, mi dolcezza. Instead we'll go into town and get a tunica for you—perhaps a woad one? There was a pause between them as they gazed into each other's eyes. Bastone wondered what she was thinking.

She abruptly shattered his contemplation as she pulled the sailcloth back on top of them and kissed him over and over on his lips, his neck, his face, continuing down his bare chest. Quickly, but ardently, her caresses persisted until he was spent. Astounded, but eager, Bastone tugged off her tunic, removed her sailor's pants, barely taming his desire, and explored. The salty residue of the storm gave way to her sweetness. Because there were other boats moored nearby, she stifled herself, reminding Bastone of their first time together.

They slept. An hour later a solid thunk sounded on the deck, waking Bastone from the deep slumber which followed carnal leisure. He pushed through the end flap of the tarp. A crossbow bolt had impaled the deck. There was a piece of parchment tightly rolled around it. He unrolled the parchment and read the penned message. *Fire the beacon when a quarter is half of the moon's life.* The message was a riddle from the emperor's courier. Bastone looked up at the Greeks Tower, knowing "the beacon" signified the faro. He had easily deciphered the simplest part of the message, but the rest of the riddle took longer to decode. Pondering ideas and rejecting them, he remembered it had been a full moon the previous night when they had arrived, reckoning the meeting with the courier would be in eight days. He crumbled the flimsy piece of paper, a rare commodity in Europe, chewed it into a pulp and swallowed, its fragility confirming why most documents were written on parchment or rag-cloth paper.

The small water barrel in the boat had survived the storm and was full. They welcomed a sponge bath. Now relaxed, but rejuvenated, the couple prepared to go into the city.

"The citizens will be on their *passeggiata*, the daily promenade in the plazas and neighborhoods," said Bastone.

Esmeray draped a scarf to cover her hair, yanked it off, tried several more times and still appeared displeased. She glanced down to smooth the wrinkles in her tunic and pants, then shook her head. "The ladies will be wearing their finest clothes. I look like a pauper!" She wrapped her arms around herself and chewed on her lip.

Bastone's kiss was warm but brief. "We can wait until the passeggiata is over. The streets will be mostly empty, people will be preparing their evening meals. When you meet my older sister, she will approve of you. I know you will love her. We are close."

"I am sorry about your brother," said Esmeray.

"Yes, I think of him all the time. He was very generous and although he teased us when we were younger, he was a protective older brother."

"It's painful to recall lost ones. Try to remember the better times."

They were both silent for a time. Then she gave him a cheerful kiss, patted her scarf, once more smoothing her tunic. "It's the best I can do. I lost all my clothes in Mallorca, but at least I have sandals. Let's go."

They had moored next to a jetty which had been built centuries earlier by enlarging a natural strip of land, using quarried boulders as well as debris from the ruins of ancient buildings. Upon the jetty, dwellings and small storehouses were spaced along a walkway paved with flat stones that led from the narrow peninsula to the heart of the city. To disembark the *Aspasia,* Bastone placed a foot on the mooring pole, clasped it with both hands, then swung around the pole as he leaned back toward the breakwater. Using the momentum and a boost from a leg, he leaped to the jetty.

He stood on the embankment, holding out his arms to catch her.

"You can do it, Esmeray."

"Yes, I can, but get out of the way. I don't need help!"

She vaulted to the jetty alone but accepted her husband's hand to scale the side of the steep jetty to the walkway. As he helped her over the loose boulders, Bastone said, "Esme, you wouldn't accept my help jumping from the boat, but you let me help you up the jetty?"

"I wanted to hold hands for a second," said Esmeray. She tipped her head to his shoulder. "Our time together was special . . . different!"

"Yes, mi dolcezza," he threw a kiss to the air, *"Belissimo!"*

"Are you sure the passeggiata is over?" said Esmeray, "I don't want anyone to see me like this!"

He waved his arm toward the city. "Yes, it is done. My sister will be at home."

Esmeray squeezed his hand as they headed toward the center of Genoa. A group of monks carrying bundles of erica and juniper wood for the signal fire went by, headed in the other direction.

After they passed, Esmeray looked over her shoulder, then upwards to the top of the Greeks Tower. "It must be hard work, climbing the tower with the wood on their backs. The monks here keep the tower fire burning at night, as in Messina?"

"Yes, they are from the Monastery of Santo Stefano," said Bastone, pointing up on the hill. "Next to that highest tower, which is part of the Embriaci family compound."

They moved along the waterfront, passing large wharfs occupied by trading vessels. Bastone pointed left and said, "See, the *Paradisio* is berthed at that dock." Then he gestured to the right, "That wall and tower is the Zaccaria family compound."

Behind the warehouses along the harbor front were open plazas, surrounded by shops and houses with balconies, porticoes, and arcades, which encouraged mingling and socializing, useful in the art of trade. There was significant foot traffic, but with the passeggiata over, they were mostly men.

"Where is . . . the Spinola family enclave?" asked Esmeray.

"There are two branches. One compound is straight ahead near the harbor front and the other . . . I assume you want to know where the family of Amilcare lives?"

Her smile changed to a grimace as she nodded.

"It's up the hill near the De Mari di Luccoli and the Ponzio compounds."

"Are the Spinolas and Luccolis very rich?" asked Esmeray.

"Yes. The wealthiest families vie for leadership of Genoa. They are the Spinola clan, the Grimaldis, the Fieschii, and the Dorias. Genoa is a republic, and the people elect two *Captains of the People*, the co-leaders of the city, usually from one of these four families. Currently, the captains are of Spinola and Doria families, but they have weakened the republic since they arranged to be elected for 22 years. Further along the harbor front are the enclaves of the Grimaldi and the Vivaldi . . . the family of the two brothers who sailed with us to the Ocean Sea, then went on to Africa. You can see their clans' towers—the tallest ones ahead. Now we'll leave the waterfront and head uphill before we reach their districts."

"Where is the Ponzio tower?" Esmeray asked.

"The Ponzios do not have a tower," said Bastone. "They are status symbols of prominent families, who build conspicuous towers to show their wealth."

Esmeray said, "The people elect their leaders—that's odd. And you said we passed the Zaccaria enclave. Are they Captains of the People?"

"Perhaps the Zaccarias *are* the wealthiest family. But they don't desire to lead in politics. They are traders and military leaders."

They turned right, climbing away from the harbor. High walls and stone buildings without windows lined the narrow streets.

Occasionally they passed intersections with narrow alleys. The way was steep, and they frequently had to climb lengthy flights of stairs.

"The side streets are very narrow," said Bastone. "A tall man could stretch his arms out and touch both walls. "I explored all of them as a youth. One should only venture into these narrow alleys in your *own* neighborhood . . . unless you are looking for trouble."

Esmeray laughed, "As you were when you were a wild young man! The view of the city from the sea is impressive. But here, I feel confined." She glanced over her back. "The sea isn't visible now, and the buildings look dreary," said Esmeray.

"Yes, but behind many of these walls are beautiful gardens, courtyards, and large villas. Perhaps we will have time in the next few days to visit the Cathedral of Saint Lorenzo, and the Palace of the Sea, as well as other magnificent buildings. They have plazas open to the sky."

They arrived at the compound of the De Mari di Luccoli family. Bastone knocked on the gate. The viewing hatch opened and quickly snapped shut, then a man opened the door.

"Bastone! I heard the *Paradisio* had returned." He looked over Esmeray. "A trophy from your pirating? A gift for your brother-in-law?" Leering at Esmeray, he arched one eyebrow with a lascivious grin and bumped the inside of his fists together, index fingers extended.

Bastone snarled, "*Stai zitto*, shut up! *Mi moglie*, my wife."

"*Scusi!* Scusi signora!" He bowed profusely and waved his arm to enter, saying to Bastone. "Your sister is here."

The walled compound encompassed multiple residences and buildings of the Luccoli family. The guard pointed to a balcony on one of the houses along the enclosed courtyard. Light glowed through the open shutters of a second-story room. "She is in her residence."

Bastone took Esmeray's hand, guiding her gently through the entrance, and stared at the man. "You are lucky you are my brother-in-law's cousin," growled Bastone. "Next time!" He made a cutting gesture across his own throat.

Oil lamps cast a warm glow across the courtyard and the twilight illuminated strip gardens of flowers, climbing vegetables, and fig trees growing next to the south-facing walls. In the center of the courtyard, stone benches rested under palm trees encircling a raised cistern.

"How pleasant," said Esmeray. "Compared to the streets, this is a sanctuary!"

"Bastonino! Uncle Calvo!" A woman leaned on the rail of a second-floor balcony.

Esmeray looked up and saw an attractive woman, Bastone's sister, with the same hue of blue eyes and similar features. "*Who* is Uncle Calvo?" asked Esmeray.

Bastone's face reddened. "That was my sister's pet name for me, since I was bald when I was born, and it took a long time for me to grow hair."

Bastone's sister called out, "The domestic will show you into the house. I'll be right down!"

As they entered the anteroom, his sister's eyes widened when she saw Esmeray entering the room alongside her brother. She quickly dismissed the servant. Bastone's sister kissed her brother's cheeks, then warmly embraced him. She turned toward Esmeray and forced a tight smile, waiting for Bastone to explain.

"Maria Grazia, we are married. My wife, Esmeray."

"Well . . . I thought . . . the light was dim . . . from the balcony—I thought you had a young sailor with you." She awkwardly took Esmeray's hand with both of hers, released her grasp and hugged Esmeray, kissing the air at her right then left cheek. "It is a pleasure to meet you!"

A servant placed a tray on an end table and departed. Maria Grazia gestured towards the sofa. She sat opposite on an upholstered chair and raised her cup. "Salute and congratulations!"

They drank together. Maria smiled, her eyes sparkling, almost closing, with crinkles around them.

"You must tell me everything about how you met Esmeray," said Maria. "How did you return to Genoa? I was concerned when you did not return with the *Paradisio*."

Bastone described their story, leaving out his role as a speculatore, ending with Esmeray's need to find a tunica to prepare to meet the family.

"I have a large wardrobe and I am delighted to help Esmeray with her clothes. She's a little taller than me, but we'll find her a good fit."

A servant entered and whispered to Maria Grazia, who looked at Bastone as if he should leave, then said, "Esmeray will be my guest here tonight. I sent a message to Father that you are here. You should go see him—he'll be at the *Factoria de Balistrai.*"

Bastone's eyes grew wider.

"He is working late hours supervising the crossbow factory. King Charles is in Pisa gathering a fleet to attack Genoa."

Lantern Across the Sea

## CHAPTER XXI   PALACE OF THE SEA

Maria Grazia promised Bastone she would not tell their parents about Esmeray, allowing him to do so on his own time. It was after sunset, so for safety a pair of her husband's cousins escorted Bastone on his trek across Genoa. Genoese families were competitive and suspicious of outsiders, not just of sailors and travelers coming and going because it was a port city, but anyone not in their *consorterie*, their family union of nobles, or their trade guild. When a common enemy threatened the city, however, the Genoese swiftly banded together.

They made it without incident to the enclave of the Pallavicini clan, where the Balistrai Corporation was located, manufacturing crossbows for Genoese marines. Like the investments the Genoese citizens had made in sponsoring trading ships by buying shares in the ventures, the factory was a communally held enterprise, funded by the outlays of ordinary people as well as nobles.

Bastone found his father, Ponzio Trocone, standing at a workbench in the factory, inspecting a newly assembled crossbow. He supervised scores of craftsmen, carpenters, and metalsmiths, working on various stages of the weapon. During a crisis, however, he made crossbows himself. The scents of wood resin, metal, and sawdust filled the air. He looked up and rushed to greet his son, pounding him on the back with joy. Trocone returned to his work, continuing to check the trigger and mechanisms as Bastone brought him up to date on his travels. Bastone did not tell him about Esmeray. He planned to introduce her to both his father and mother the following day.

He recounted his life over the past year as he watched his father work, and marveled at his dexterity. The senior Ponzio was wearing leather gloves that he had made to replace the loss of several of his digits.

"Son, it is unusual to be working at night under the oil lamps, but Genoa may soon be under attack. We haven't fought a major sea battle with the Pisans for many years. I remember—it was in 1240 or 41. Yes, near Isola de Giglio south of Livorno, the Pisans attacked our fleet. Frederick, the German emperor and King of Sicily, was the instigator. The Pope had denounced him as a heretic, so Frederick employed the Pisans to stop us from delivering Catholic prelates to attend a council. My bolts ended many sailors' lives that day, but the filthy scoundrels captured our ship and we lost most of our squadron. Our crossbowmen had killed so many of Frederick's personal guard that he cut the fingers off the captured Genoese arbalesters."

Bastone had heard the story many times and could recall it by heart, but respectfully listened to his father's tale again.

"Ha! Ha-ha! I showed them!" He recalled his father's unique laugh when he told this story—the cackling was both crazy and vengeful.

Trocone pulled off his gloves, revealing that both hands were missing the index and smallest fingers. He still had the two middle fingers and a thumb on each hand. A huge grin spread across his face. "They missed! Ha-ha! As they forced my hands onto the chopping block, I pinched my thumb and middle fingers together, making the *sign of the horn* to ward off bad luck, and it worked! The stronzi were in a hurry to dismember the next man in line, and with all the blood, they didn't notice!"

A smiling image of Lucianu's father, Egidiu, the Sicilian barber-surgeon, flashed in Bastone's mind. Both Lucianu's and Bastone's fathers had a space between their two front teeth. When he was a boy, Bastone had asked his father about the gap, and he had said they were his "lucky happiness teeth."

He slipped his gloves back on and returned to work. "And I showed them seven years later at the Siege of Parma. Yes, we Genoese arbalesters led the sortie that broke the siege and beat Frederick that time." He made two fists and pumped them in the air. "Ha! Ha! And with these hands!"

His father strung the new crossbow as he continued. "And history repeats. As in 1241, the Pisans are again mercenaries for another King of Sicily. They really don't need any urging; they are always waiting for a chance to take Corsica back from us. So King Charles is hiring them to attack Genoa." Tacone gave his son a knowing look. "If Charles has the balls to enter the fight, I want you to avenge Francesco for the family!"

He handed Bastone a crossbow. "What do you think of this beauty?"

Bastone hefted the weapon as if to check its weight. Raising the crossbow to his shoulder, he sighted along the stock. "I see you made the stock of . . . are these *layers* of wood?"

"Yes, an improved construction. I glued olive wood, yew wood, and horn together to make the stock. The bow itself is made of high-quality steel. The stock is not as rigid as those made of a single piece of wood, so there is less chance for it to crack from the tremendous compression when strung. Also, the bolts will shoot farther. This model will hit a target at 250 paces."

"I'll need one to fight the Pisans. I lost mine in the storm."

"It's yours, son. What else do you need?"

"I saved my *usbergo*, shirt of mail, but I do not have a *pavise*."

"I have a shield for you. Before we got busy preparing for war, I rescued a family treasure passed down through the generations. Now, I must get back to work. Go home and get some rest. Tomorrow, at the second hour, Zaccaria and Doria are requiring the fleet's officers to meet at the Palace of the Sea."

Bastone embraced his father. As he departed, Tacone said, "The Pisans have beat us in the last few sea battles. Remember your brother. It is our time for vendetta!"

Esmeray immersed herself in a much-welcomed bath, then joined Maria Grazia and her two children for the evening meal. Maria Grazia's husband was in the city recruiting oarsmen for his galley, contributing to the war effort.

After Maria Grazia kissed her children goodnight and the nanny led them to their bedrooms, she helped Esmeray try on one tunica after the other from her full closet.

"I have never seen this many beautiful clothes in my life!" said Esmeray.

"I am enjoying this as much as you," said Maria Grazia. "I don't need so many dresses and they fit you so nicely. Especially this purple linen. The tunica clings just right to your slim figure, but still appropriately."

"It fits well, and the purple is beautiful," said Esmeray. "The color reminds me of the sunset. Yet I am not a princess or even a noble. Can anyone wear purple? In the east, commoners aren't allowed to wear the color."

Maria Grazia said, "Here you can wear purple if you can afford it."

The servant removed another item of clothing from the closet. Esmeray's mouth opened, and her eyes grew wide. "*Madonna!* That's *my* color!"

Maria Grazia displayed a knowing smile. "Am I right that my brother's eyes have seduced you?"

The domestic offered the woad garment to the women. Esmeray's cheer withered. "Oh, it's not a tunica."

"No, no, sweetheart, it is a light cloak. To compliment your purple tunica, here, wear the cloak over it. See, the colors look attractive together."

"Yes! I can wear both? Indoors? To meet your mother?"

"Of course. It will be perfect!" said Maria Grazia.

"Grazie, Grazie!" Esmeray kissed her sister-in-law.

Bastone ascended the steep incline to his family's enclave, wondering how Esmeray was faring. He had complete trust in his sister that she would not tell their parents about Esmeray until he was ready. His mother greeted him at the Ponzio home a block uphill from his sister's house in the Luccoli compound. There he took a needed bath. His father arrived in time for a late dinner, four hours after sunset. Exhausted, Bastone hardly stayed awake during the meal. After his father retired to bed, Bastone answered his mother's questions about his voyages during his absence.

In the morning he hiked down to the Palace of the Sea, so named because it overlooked the docks, the harbor waters splashing its foundations. He remembered they had constructed the building when he was a youth. Originally built as the administration center for the Republic, it was currently used as a customs house. The Captains of the People now governed from their own enclaves.

Hundreds of men conversed and milled about the area outside the front doors. Bastone caught sight of his Uncle Riccio, who was talking with Benedetto Zaccaria. He was uncertain at first if he wanted to approach Zaccaria, having jumped ship, but he hadn't seen his uncle in a year and went to join them.

"*Zio* Riccio! Buon giorno!" He slapped his paternal uncle on the shoulder, then embraced him.

"Bastone!" His uncle shot a glance at Zaccaria. "How did you arrive in Genoa? Your captain told me the *thunderbolt* hit you and that you threw away everything for a woman!"

Bastone hesitated. Zaccaria and his uncle waited expectantly for him to answer.

"We sailed the *Aspasia* from Mallorca to Genoa," said Bastone.

"Impressive!" said Zaccaria. "Bastone, you are the most skilled arbalester officer, but your abilities as a sailor are . . . mediocre. Sailing a trohantiras across the open sea . . . and through a thunderstorm is rather daring. You are lucky that Esmeray is a *skilled* sailor."

"Zaccaria told me you are married. What about the Spinola woman?" said Riccio. "Our family has been trying to join a noble consorterie for generations. It's hard to believe your parents will approve."

"Well, uh . . . we have met everyone's . . . uh, requirements."

A merchant among the crowd signaled to Riccio. "I will see you later, nephew. A customer needs me. War may be terrible, but I need to lease all my ships before the fleet sails tomorrow."

Zaccaria clasped Bastone's shoulder, "I bid that you return as the officer of the arbalesters for the *Paradisio*. The nave will be the flagship, supplying material for the war galleys. I need you, Genoa needs you!"

As Zaccaria spoke, Bastone nodded, but kept his eye on his uncle moving from one person to the other, making deals. Then Riccio found his sons and departed. Bastone became anxious, realizing he had to reach Esmeray and introduce her to his parents before Uncle Riccio told them about the marriage. Bastone cut off Zaccaria, "Yes, sir. I will serve you on the *Paradisio* if Amilcare is not one of the crew."

Zaccaria hesitated as if in thought, then nodded.

"I'll be there before you shove off tomorrow." Bastone turned to leave.

Zaccaria grasped his shoulder. "But you must organize the new arbalesters and instruct them. There is no time to lose!"

Hours later, Bastone ran up the hill to his sister's house. He entered the courtyard, paused to catch his breath, and asked the doorman, "Is my mother, um, is Signora Luccoli's mother, here?"

"Si signore."

Bastone was too late. He was about to utter a curse, but the unrestrained laughter of women erupted from his sister's house. When he entered the atrium, Esmeray, Maria Grazia, her mother-in-law, and his mother, were enjoying antipasto and wine, carrying on a merry conversation. Esmeray's glance at him conveyed she was genuinely comfortable and in good spirits. Bastone was pleased. She was very attractive, wearing a violet tunica and a cloak of woad, her favorite color.

Later in the day, the Luccoli and Ponzio families shared in the passeggiata. Bastone had a few private moments with Esmeray as they strolled arm-in-arm.

"Tell me why Mother is so cooperative," said Bastone. "I am pleased but shocked, mi dolcezza."

"Your sister is kind. She gave me these clothes! And I think your mother was impressed with me."

He was very happy for Esmeray, but growing more suspicious about his mother. Now over the shock that she had accepted Esmeray, his mind was sharper. Her behavior was not as he would have predicted.

"Yes, of course, you look exquisite, but . . ."

"Your mother said she will gladly welcome me into the family, if I convert to the Catholic Church and a Roman Catholic priest marries us."

"Was that all?"

"First, I must give personal testimony to a priest. I'll study Catholic beliefs, sacraments, and prayer. A Catholic priest must baptize me, then I can have communion."

"Esme, you will go through with the . . . the indoctrination? I didn't think you took religion seriously."

"I will do it for us." She looked around to make sure no one could overhear. "It's *nothing*, really."

Given the religious commitment Esmeray was making, Bastone softened his judgment of his mother. He believed there was a way his family would accept his wife.

Bastone squeezed her hand a little too hard.

"Ouch!"

But Esmeray was smiling.

## CHAPTER XXII   THE BLOCKADE

The Genoese fleet was to sail the next morning and Bastone was confident his sister would take good care of Esmeray. He hurried to the crossbow factory where he practiced shooting the new crossbow, familiarizing himself with any peculiarities the weapon might possess. His father also had a shield for him.

"This is a unique pavise," said Bastone. "It is more curved than my last shield, better to deflect enemy bolts. And what made you choose these emblems? Bright red, with images of an eagle's wings and yellow lightning bolts. Did you build this yourself?"

"I restored an ancient Roman shield."

"*Non credo*, I can't believe it! The wood would have rotted."

"Yes, you are right. I found splinters stuck to the bronze boss and rims. Had the metal parts been iron, they would have rusted away."

Bastone hefted the shield. "The boss will be useful to thrust into the enemy in hand-to-hand combat. Thank you, Father. Where did you find this relic?"

Trocone had a straight face. "Passed down through generations. Maybe a Pontius used it in battle?"

His son laughed and pressed the heel of his palms and his fingertips together, moving his hands up and down. "I can't believe I'm hearing this!"

It was an hour from sunset when Bastone collected his weapons, taking them to the *Paradisio*. He visited Esmeray before sailing the next morning. She was outside in the courtyard twisting thread.

"I thought you hated spinning because you always had to do it as a child?"

"I am bored here, but it is a good way to spend time and it gives me calming thoughts of my mother. Of course, sailing the *Aspasia* kept my father *and* mother in my thoughts. She teared up. "After you return, we will sail together again."

Bastone put his arm around her shoulders. "I'll return, I promise."

She handed Bastone a parchment.

He began reading, "'On February 4, 1279, in the inventory of Ponzio Bastone, soldier, I find *bariscella una plena de macaronis*, a barrel full of macaroni and' . . . yes, this is my will."

Esmeray's voice shook. "So, your own sister must think you aren't coming back. Maria Grazia had a notary bring two copies of the will today so I would sign them as inheritor. You must sign them to complete it. A copy will be kept in the city archives at the Palace of the Sea."

"Yes, I remember the notary, Ugolino Scarpa, who drafted the will. But look at the original date. I had the notary prepare it last February. It's not for my departure. My sister cares about you—it's just a formality—I *am* returning."

Esmeray calmed. "But a barrel of pasta?"

"Now you see how much we Genoese value our pasta!"

She laughed. "You expect me to believe that is your most valuable possession?"

"No, see the other items. A bolt of lightweight silk, special silk I traded for in Trebizond. And a silk pillowcase woven a special way, called satin. The silk and satin pillows are from China and treasured for their sheen."

"And this item, a *white* knife?" Esmeray looked puzzled.

"If you sell this knife, don't take less than fifty Genoese lira. The white blade is *woost* steel, known as Damascus steel by crusaders. The other two knives are valuable because the handles are ivory."

"You got all these trading?"

"Yes, they are souvenirs, but they are investments. You are better?" said Bastone.

"Yes." She placed her hand on his. "When you get back, let's share the satin pillow."

Bastone embarked the *Paradisio* that evening to be aboard for castoff at sunrise. Ottolino and he talked as they lay in their cabin berths.

"How does Esmeray feel about you leaving?" said Ottolino.

"She fears the worst, but my sister will take care of her, if I don't return."

Bastone forced himself to focus on the coming battle as he fell to sleep.

Before daybreak the ships teemed with sailors preparing for cast off. Bastone did last minute checks on the crossbow and bolt inventory and mustered his marines to ensure all were aboard. Zaccaria, responsible for supplies and support, shared the command of the fleet with Oberto Doria, who would lead the war galleys rowed by paid soldiers, free citizens of Genoa.

King Charles had imposed his hegemony over Italy, coercing the Pisans to attack Genoa, once again willing to renew the century long feud for dominance of the Tyyrhenian Sea. Charles's spies had learned that Genoa had discovered his plans to attack Constantinople instead of Jerusalem. He wanted to eliminate the maritime republic's fleet as a threat while he was absent in the east.

The Genoese, smarting with the memory of their earlier defeats in the sea battles with the Pisans, were eager for revenge. With a victory here, the Genoese could deal a double blow to their enemies, defeating their arch enemy, Pisa, and weakening Charles's forces that would go east. They planned to blockade the harbors of Pisa and Livorno to keep King Charles's northern squadron from joining the fleets he had assembled in Naples and Messina. Zaccaria's cargo ships would provide the oarsmen and sailors with food and supplies.

The evening of the second day from Genoa, the fleet arrived at the island of Gorgona. It was close enough to Pisa to serve as an overnight rest stop for the galley crews as they patrolled the blockade of the city. The only inhabitants of the island, the Benedictine monks of Gorgona Monastery who lived inland, were not disturbed.

The crew of the *Paradisio* organized a supply camp on the island, then departed with a score of galleys, establishing a blockade off the port of Pisa. For the next few days, no Pisan ships ventured from port. At daybreak on the third day, two rows of Pisan war galleys, intentionally sailing with the glare of the rising sun behind them, rowed out of the port. The celeustes on the Pisan galleys blew their high-pitched whistles to keep the rowers in time.

Genoese galleys intercepted the Pisan sortie resulting in ship-to-ship skirmishes. When a pair of the Pisan galleys broke through the blockade, the Genoese galleys in reserve and the *Paradisio* entered the melee.

Experienced arbalesters needed fifteen to twenty seconds to string a bolt and shoot. To keep up a steady rate of fire, Bastone had trained his arbalesters to time reloading while the adjacent marine was shooting. As he loosed bolts from his weapon and reloaded behind the cover of his Roman shield, he focused on the "crack-crack-crack" staccato of the crossbow triggers and was assured that his men were following the rotation tactic. They outvolleyed the Pisans, and the vicious onslaught of crossbow fire decimated the enemy rowing crews, picking off their helmsmen and putting a handful of their ships out of action. Several Pisan galleys, however, came alongside the *Paradisio,* the enemy crews impaling the ship with grappling hooks. Angevin troops boarded the *Paradisio*, shouting their battle cry, "King Charles! King Charles!"

Bastone scanned the enemy boarding party, unable to locate the Angevin king. He exhorted his arbalesters to maintain their continuous fire, but several panicked, dropping bolts and slowing their reload. The Genoese retreated to midship, some losing their shields. A shout pierced the din. "Charles is leading them!"

An imposing figure, wearing highly wrought officer's armor, with a sword held high and brandishing an oval shield, charged across the deck at the front of the Angevin soldiers. At this close range, his shield, covered with an array of *fleurs-de-lis',* the symbol of Angevins, would not be enough to save him from an expert arbalester. Bastone pulled a bolt from his belt. He knew if he took the seconds to cock his crossbow and shoot, he would be cut down.

But the bolt that might have saved Constantinople and avenged his brother, Francesco, was not released. Instead, Bastone scrambled back to his men, barely escaping. His arbalesters loosed their bolts, drew their daggers, and counterattacked. Joining them, Bastone entered the fight. After the Genoese succeeded in repelling the Pisan boarding detachment, they did not find King Charles's body among the dead.

The Genoese fleet had captured half the Pisan force and the remaining enemy galleys withdrew to their home port. Officers disciplined the vengeful crew, stopping them from tossing the Pisan dead overboard. They led the men in prayers for both the Genoese and Pisan dead and buried them at sea. The *Paradisio* sailed for Gorgona.

Bastone stared at the floor in a daze as his commanding officer berated him. "You coward! Why didn't you take the shot? Charles would be dead!" yelled Zaccaria. "Genoa would have unrestricted trading rights throughout the Mediterranean!"

Bastone didn't care if the man *was* King Charles, he had no qualms about his decision to live, to see Esmeray again.

On the same day the Genoese fleet had left the harbor to battle the Pisans, Bastone's mother and the Abbess of Santo Stefano Abbey had arrived at Maria Grazia's house. The abbess was the head of the nunnery of a double monastery, where separate communities of monks and nuns alternated using a church and rectory but had separate dormitories. After interviewing Esmeray, the abbess approved her for Catholic education. The classes were at the nunnery and the next morning a pair of monks escorted Esmeray to the nuns' section of the abbey. When she arrived, the abbess told Esmeray that two guards would return in the afternoon to escort her back to Maria Grazia's house.

Shortly after Esmeray arrived at the monastery, they cut her hair, declared her a holy sister, then placed her in solitary confinement because of her violent objections. Bastone's sister, concerned when Esmeray did not return that evening, sent a messenger to the abbey but the monks sent him away without explanation. The next morning, when Maria Grazia went to the abbey, she was also turned away without any information about Esmeray. Maria Grazia questioned her mother and was told Esmeray had chosen to become a nun and was not allowed any visitors.

The Genoese had averted the invasion by Charles and continued to blockade Pisa's harbor. They had also prevented the northern fleet of

Charles from joining his forces in Messina and Naples, which were being readied to assault Constantinople. The *Paradisio* returned to Genoa for more supplies as the galleys patrolled outside the Pisan harbor. Bastone jumped off the ship as it reached the wharf and hurried up the steep hill to his sister's house.

Maria Grazia's eyes welled with tears as she told Bastone what had happened. "I am sorry my dear brother, she went to the abbey a few days ago for her catechism, but never returned and they won't let me see her! Mother has certainly made up a story about Esmeray becoming a nun. Father won't talk about it."

The monks also turned Bastone away from the abbey. He considered forcing his way in but knew that would end any chance to free her. He returned to his home and confronted his parents.

"Mother, I know Esmeray would not choose to join an abbey."

"Maybe she had a religious elation or mystical experience," said his mother.

"She is not . . . um, interested in, um, she is not highly religious."

"So the truth comes out!" said his mother. "I should have known, her being brought up under that heretical Orthodox Church. It's a good thing she will learn true Christianity as a holy sister. You will *never* marry that woman!"

"Father," said Bastone, "are you going to help? The family pledge was for Francesco to marry, not me."

"But, as a family," said Tacone, "to gain the prestige and power of the Spinola consorterie, we promised to marry their daughter into our family. You are now our only son."

"Why did I bother to come home!" said Bastone. "Just to be tricked by such . . . *testa dura*, hardheaded, parents. You are despicable! I will remove her from that . . . prison, and you'll never see us again!"

"Bastone!" His father was red-faced. "You are leaving? You haven't changed. You are a quitter! As a boy, you often ran in the streets, instead of attending monastery school. You didn't want to work with me so you quit the factoria, then you went to sea instead of helping Riccio. Now you are quitting the family?"

Clenching his jaws, heat rose within Bastone, but he steadied his voice. "I will never forget my brother. I will honor his loss in greater ways. You are my parents, I still love both of you . . . but . . . this is beyond pardonable."

He turned abruptly to leave and paused to look over his shoulder. "And Mother, I am already married to her!"

He left the house and crossed the courtyard to the storehouse. There he found his possessions and gathered the bolt of silk, his Damascus knife, and satin pillow. He had already collected his military gear from the *Paradisio* and had stored them on the *Aspasia*, which Uncle Riccio had moved to his private docks.

Riccio was inspecting his vessels and approached the trohantiras, calling out, "Captain Ponzio, permission to board!" His uncle's curly hair bounced as he spoke. Although Bastone would have preferred to be alone, he calmed, encountering his Uncle Riccio's high spirits.

"Permission granted, *Zio* Riccio."

Bastone produced a wine skin, and they took turns.

"You look miserable, nephew. It's not about that shot you didn't make, is it?"

"You heard about that?"

"I just came from the *Paradisio*. And the man you didn't skewer wasn't King Charles anyway."

Bastone's eyebrows raised.

"I talked to one of my ship's captains who arrived from Naples. Charles wasn't in Pisa; he was in Naples holding a grand celebration as he knighted his two sons along with a hundred Italian and French noblemen. The Angevins were merely shouting their liege's name as a battle cry—which is not unusual." Riccio swallowed, "So what are you doing with all that plunder? Running away from home?"

"I . . . Uncle, do you know what happened to Esmeray?"

"Not directly, but I believe the adage, *Tra moglie e marito non mettere il dito,* never interfere between a husband and wife."

"You will help me release her?"

Riccio nodded, his curls agreeing.

"We *will* be together again," said Bastone. "And when she returns, our boat must be ready. I need lira to make improvements. Do you know any merchants that want a bolt of Chinese silk? I will price it at half its value."

"Nephew, what happened to 'Genoese, therefore a merchant'? I'll give you the full amount, or the deal is off," said his uncle with a broad smile. "Then of course I will sell it for a large profit!"

Bastone handed Riccio the skin, "Drink on it, Zio!"

Bastone purchased lumber, rope, and a large jib to function as a genoa sail, a foresail that overlapped the mainsail and would increase the boat's top speed. The trohantiras gave Bastone a place to sort out his thoughts. He abandoned the idea he could free Esmeray by proving they were married. Their marriage document was not witnessed by a Catholic priest, but by followers of the Greek Orthodoxy, who were despised by the Roman Church. And Bastone was certain that the abbess had collaborated with his mother on detaining Esmeray at the nunnery, or his wife would be with him now. He needed time to think of a strategy to free her. Bastone occupied himself for the next few days working on the *Aspasia*, his mind rambling, devising plans to rescue Esmeray. He built a small cabin of wood at midship. The berth was scarcely high enough for two people to crawl in and stretch out to sleep, with a tiny space for storage. He strung new lanyards so they could use all three sails at once, the mainsail, jib, and genoa. They had lost all four sets of oars in the storm and Bastone replaced only one pair, to return the boat's arrangement as it was before Zaccaria had used it as a harbor tender. He decided he should find a small rowboat, a canottino, as a lifeboat and possibly use it for the mission.

With an hour of daylight left, he strode along the mole where the Greeks Tower was located. Perhaps a fisherman might have an old canottino he could renovate. Overhead was a half moon. He recalled the message he had found a week earlier. *Meet at the beacon on the first quarter which is the first half.* The first quarter moon is . . . a half moon! He had almost forgotten the coming evening was the meeting with the emperor's courier.

Ahead of him the monks of Santo Stefano were carrying wood to the lighthouse for the night. He followed the line of monks; each hauling a bundle of firewood on his back. The first few entered the Greeks Tower and began the 200 steps climb to the top. The last monk in the line stumbled and his bundle fell to the ground. He looked over his shoulder at Bastone, "I'm getting old. Signore, can you help me?"

Bastone crouched down as if to lift the wood.

"Listen!" said the monk. "*Animus Tuus Dominus.*"

"*Antudo*," whispered Bastone.

"It is still forty days after Easter, on Ascension Thursday at Vespers," said the stranger. "But Procida cannot alert the patriots in Palermo. That is your duty, now. *Capisce*?"

Bastone said, "*Si.*"

"*In bocca al lupo, g*ood luck!" said the monk. "Take the wood."

Bastone said, "*Crepi il lupo*, may the wolf drop dead." He paused, "And leave the habit."

The courier looked around, then removed the monk's robe, pulling it over his head. "It's yours." He left wearing his tunic and leggings.

Bastone took the firewood and habit, returning to the *Aspasia* to devise his plans for the following evening.

## CHAPTER XXIII   THE ENCOUNTER

Bastone slept in the cabin he had added to the *Aspasia*. In the morning he considered using the sharp Damascus blade to shave his beard but thought better of it and found the shop of a barber-surgeon with its white and red striped pole. The barber liked to talk. He was proud he had graduated from the medical college in Genoa. Bastone thought of having his hair trimmed in a tonsure to perfect his impersonation as a monk, but decided it wasn't necessary. He was glad to finally leave, after learning more than he cared for about barbering.

In the evening he donned the habit over his tunic, hefted the bundle of wood, and hid behind a warehouse along the mole. As expected, at the twelfth hour, a group of monks bringing wood from Santo Stefano marched down the narrow spit of land toward the Greeks Tower. He fell in step after the last one passed, delivering his wood as the others did at the top of the lighthouse. The twilight was fading when he departed along with the monks returning to the monastery. Freed of their loads, the brothers chatted. One monk slowed and walked beside Bastone. "I don't recognize you, Brother."

Bastone said, "I am new . . ."

"Are you on pilgrimage?" asked the monk.

"Oh, yes, yes, I am, Brother."

"Going to Rome?"

Bastone nodded and let the monk do the talking.

"Where are you cloistered now?"

"Um . . . Nizza."

"Yes, the Abbey of Santo Ponzio di Cimella is there. A large and influential monastery. The abbots of Santo Ponzio have established many new churches, a few just down the coast from Genoa, *Saint-Pierre de l'Escarene* and *Notre-Dame sous Gattieres* . . . oh, I am sorry, I didn't introduce myself. . . I am Guglielmo, the abbey historian. Who is the current abbot at Santo Ponzio? No, wait . . . I can almost remember . . . just give me a clue . . ."

"Um . . . Guglielmo . . . do you mean the abbot . . .?"

"That's it! Guglielmo in Genoese, the abbot is Guillaume de Berre. You are correct, Brother!"

A second monk dropped back and inserted himself between the men, giving them both a friendly squeeze around the shoulders. "Brother, I see you have met our historian. He is just stretching his voice, because when we reach the abbey, it will be time for Vespers, when we must follow our vow of silence."

They entered the church, comprised of a central hall flanked by columns and aisles along each side. Bastone was thankful the monastery was large, with over fifty monks. During the service, as he awkwardly imitated the monks' chants and mouthed the words while they sang, none of the brothers noticed him. The prayers over, the monks filed out of the church. He was last in the queue to leave the sanctuary as the nuns entered from the opposite side for Vespers. Instead of leaving the sanctuary, he hurried down an aisle and hid behind a column, putting him in a good position to see the nuns' faces as they headed toward the altar. Bastone had a sinking feeling when he did not see Esmeray among them.

The nuns gathered in front of the altar and Bastone realized this was his chance to search for Esmeray, because the women's section of the monastery should now be empty. He stole from one column to the next until he was near the door where the nuns had entered the church. He slipped through the doorway into the nuns' section of the monastery.

Bastone rushed from room to room, searching through the nuns' spartan quarters, but he could not find Esmeray. He wondered if they had locked her in confinement. He went outside, finding a tiny outbuilding past the nuns' cloister. The door, with only a small window, was locked from the outside with a heavy latch. The hut was empty except for a cup, a bowl, and scraps of cloth. He entered and discovered the cloth was soaked with fresh blood, then swore, "Mother Mary!" Bastone became angry, then frustrated. He wanted to fight someone, something, fearing it was Esmeray's blood.

Bastone refrained from slamming the door and returned to the building where he found the abbess's office. He sat in one of the high-backed chairs facing her desk, struggling to contain his anger and trying to calm himself. He refused to believe she was dead and planned what to say to the abbess upon her return.

Within half an hour, the abbess entered, went to her desk, and gasped. She went pale, then quickly composed herself. "Who are you?"

"Do not call for help. I have a proposal," said Bastone.

She sat down and said, "Go ahead."

"I know Signora Ponzio is paying you to hold a young woman against her will, under the deception she has volunteered to enter the nunnery. Enslaving a Christian, even an Orthodox Christian, is against Church and Genoese laws. You may wish to continue receiving those, um, donations. If so, the signora can assume Esmeray is still under your, er . . . direction, if you tell me the truth." He slid her Bible across the desk. "Place your hand on the Bible to swear the truth."

"*You* make *me* swear on the Holy Book? Ugh, a merchant, not much better than a pirate."

She was stock-still, but Bastone sensed her internal struggle. Then the abbess abruptly slapped her hand on the Bible. She locked eyes with Bastone, and her chin rose slightly.

"Was Esmeray here?"

She nodded.

"Was she harmed?"

"Not intentionally," said the abbess. "She struggled."

"Is Esmeray in the monastery?"

She shook her head.

"Did you sell her?"

Another shake of the head.

"Do you know where she is?

"No."

Bastone departed through the cloister. Discarding the habit and scaling the courtyard wall, he dropped to a shadowy vicoli, and headed toward the *Aspasia*. Wracked by his inability to find Esmeray, he strode down one alley after another obsessed with trying to make sense of what had happened. Was the blood Esmeray's? The abbess could be a liar. If Bastone's mother had declared Esmeray a heretic, what would the abbess have thought of her? Then Bastone recalled a dreadful rumor, the Church sold heretics into slavery . . . or worse.

He shouted into the darkness, his voice echoing along the alley. "Are any thieves lurking out there? You want a fight?" He pounded on closed doors set in the walls. "Now is the time! Come on!" He kicked at loose pavement stones as he stormed down the hill toward the harbor. A vicoli intersected the street and the three-way junction formed a small plaza. It was a poorer neighborhood with no courtyards and the residences had taken advantage of the openness of the plaza by planting fruit and fig trees along the sides, the vines and limbs climbing the walls.

Then Bastone heard someone yell from the side alley. "I've been waiting for this fight!"

Shutters opened on the upper levels of several houses. "Shut up out there!"

Amilcare moved from the shadows into the faint illumination of the moon and halted ten paces from Bastone. Three other men fanned out behind him. Glints of metal from the sheaths on their left hips confirmed they were all right-handed, armed with daggers. Bastone was about to sprint toward the harbor, but Amilcare's men had blocked the three escape routes.

"I know everywhere you have been," said Amilcare. "You can't find your little whore because we caught her fleeing the abbey. We took good care of her before we dumped her body in the harbor, right, men?"

Amilcare's escorts snickered. Waves of fire poured through Bastone. He said to himself, *"God's death, it can't be true!"*

"Bastone, *stickman*, let's fight knife versus stick, like we did years ago on these same streets," said Amilcare. He drew his dagger with his right hand. "But where is your stick? It looks like it must be dagger against dagger?"

Bastone was completely surrounded, all escape routes were blocked, and he didn't believe Amilcare would fight him alone. In the unlikely event that the fight was single combat, Amilcare's men would certainly kill Bastone. And even if Bastone killed Amilcare and escaped, the Spinolas would hunt him down and destroy his family. Bastone had few alternatives

Keeping his eyes on his adversaries, Bastone stepped back to the wall, reached behind him, and pulled on a small tree branch growing up the wall, but it would not break. He found another, yanked, but it didn't snap.

"Ha-ha." Amilcare crouched and edged toward Bastone, holding his dagger close, his free hand out, ready to grasp or parry. "I'm going to stick the stickman!"

Amilcare had cautiously advanced within five paces and Bastone again reached over his shoulder for a narrow branch as he drew his dagger with his other hand. Amilcare reversed his guard to lead with his dagger and lunged. Bastone cracked a branch off the tree, twisted his body sideways, and parried Amilcare's knife with the stick. He feinted a thrust with his dagger and Amilcare retreated out of range, yelling to one of his escorts. "Your dagger!"

A dagger flew in the air, Bastone sprang forward when Amilcare glanced to catch the knife. In rapid succession Bastone used his stick to deflect Amilcare's thrust, slicing his enemy's wrist with his own blade, following with a smash to his opponent's temple with the butt end of the stick. Amilcare slumped to the ground, stunned, but breathing.

Discordant clattering from the fallen daggers reverberated from the cobblestone street, echoing across the plaza. The ringing of metal stopped. Amilcare's escorts looked at each other without expression. Bastone marched toward the one blocking his way to the harbor, both weapons ready. The man backed away and Bastone ran, glancing over his shoulder. The escorts repeatedly stabbed Amilcare, yelling across the dimly lit plaza so the residents would hear: "Ponzio Bastone has killed Amilcare! Bastone killed Amilcare Spinola!"

Bastone knew the Spinolas would be after him. He rushed to the *Aspasia*, refusing to believe Amilcare's claim that he had killed Esmeray. It was too horrible for him to accept, but he knew it was blood he had seen in the cell. He sat on the deck of the *Aspasia*, angry, confused, speculating, planning. An hour passed. A babble of voices drew near as lights bobbed at the end of the wharf. Bastone readied himself to fight the Spinolas. They came closer and Bastone made certain his dagger was in its sheath, brandished an oar, and decided if he fought from the *Aspasia*, it would give him some advantage.

In the light of the oil lamps, he recognized his father and uncle amid his cousins. From the dock, they faced Bastone on the *Aspasia*. "Son, you must leave Genoa. There is word that you killed Amilcare!"

"I didn't do it! I only stunned him, then his own men killed him!"

There was a pause, then his father said, "I believe you. If you go now, we may avoid bloodshed. Think of your family."

"I can't leave without Esmeray!"

"Uncle!" one of Ricco's sons shouted. "Someone's coming, look!"

Torch lights winked as a group of strangers descended the slope toward the harbor, passing between buildings.

"It's too late. The Spinolas are coming!"

"No, don't fight! I am leaving!" Bastone untied the ropes from the dock bollards, cast off, and readied the oars.

Rapid, light footfalls moved along the dock. Then suddenly there was a flash as Esmeray jumped aboard the moving boat.

"Esme?"

Bastone pulled on the oars. "Ciao Father, Uncle, Cousins! I regret that I . . ."

A cacophony of shouts from his cousins interrupted him. "Eh Bastone, forget about it! We don't want that kind of talk! Get out of here, *cugino!* Shut up and get going!"

"Ciao, son!" His father raised his hand in farewell then turned to Riccio. "Here they come, get ready." He drew his dagger.

Bastone heaved on the oars and propelled the *Aspasia* from the dock. Esmeray raised the jib. In the light of the waxing gibbous moon, they anxiously watched as the younger men formed a defensive line in front of the senior Ponzios and the crowd of strangers approached them. The *Aspasia* was fifty paces from the dock when the groups clashed.

Instead of the screams of violence and the groans of pain, shouts of joy broke out. The men embraced rather than fought. Across the harbor surface they heard, "Welcome, brothers! The Luccoli and Pallavicini are here!"

Relieved, Esmeray and Bastone sailed toward the night, beyond the two lighthouses and out of Genoa's harbor, using the westerlies to tack south.

In the morning's light, Bastone regarded how the nuns had butchered Esmeray's hair. Her long, wavy locks had been alluring, but now shortened, her chestnut hair took on a new flair, with waves and curls in all directions.

"Esme, those sensual curls! Should I call you *Riccia?*"

She lowered her chin and rolled her eyes. "Curly? Like your uncle?" She lightly kissed him. "I miss the tickle of your beard." She caressed his chin. "Mmm, so smooth! Should I call you *Liscio?*"

"Mi dolcezza, I'm so sorry the nuns abused you. Did they hurt you?"

"No, other than the bruises I got as they tried to hold me down to cut my hair. The confinement bothered me the most. The nuns couldn't hold me and needed help from the monks. They threatened to kill me if I resisted any longer."

"But the blood in the cell?"

"My monthlies, that's all."

"You don't seem very upset," said Bastone. "The clergy are such hypocrites—the violence, the bribes, the lying . . ."

Esmeray shrugged. "They think they are doing God's work—I pity them—they are slaves with no minds of their own. They justify violence with their religion. It is not a surprise to me."

"How did you escape?" said Bastone. "And" . . . he scratched his head, "My uncle moved the *Aspasia*. How did you find her?"

"The nuns took my clothes, gave me a coarse tunic to wear, and left me in solitary confinement with only a cup of water and a chamber pot. I used my sailor's knots."

"What? The nuns left you with a rope belt?"

"No, I tore strips off the bottom of the old tunic they gave me, tied the pieces into a bowline knot, looped it around the bar, and pulled it up, unlocking the door. It was difficult through the tiny window.

"When I found that someone had moved the *Aspasia* from the mooring near the Greeks Tower, I went to the *Paradisio,* but I wasn't allowed to board. Ottolino saw me and threw me a pair of trousers and told me the *Aspasia's* location. I fell asleep under a pile of sails on your Uncle Riccio's dock—it was too dangerous to be on the *Aspasia*—then I woke hearing shouting."

Bastone gave her a quick but ardent kiss. "Just in time!" He held her close a few moments, as he said, "I was so worried you'd been harmed, but I believed in you. What a relief you're safe!"

Esmeray insisted on taking the tiller first to let Bastone sleep. He agreed since she would have been somewhat rested from her nap beneath the sails. But he couldn't sleep, his mind racing with anxious thoughts of the last several days. He longed for peace, to escape to a hidden place with Esmeray. His father's last words plagued him: "You are a quitter! You quit everything!" Bastone wished his father could know of his mission and his role as a speculatore. He was certain his father would think of his son in a better light.

Bastone finally slept a few hours, then suddenly woke in a sweat. He didn't know where he was or if he was awake or dreaming, thinking that Amilcare had murdered Esme. He crawled out of the cabin, feeling wobbly. The cool air revived him and Esmeray was at the tiller. "Esme!"

"Yes, Bastonino—mi dolcezzo! Va bene, all's well on board."

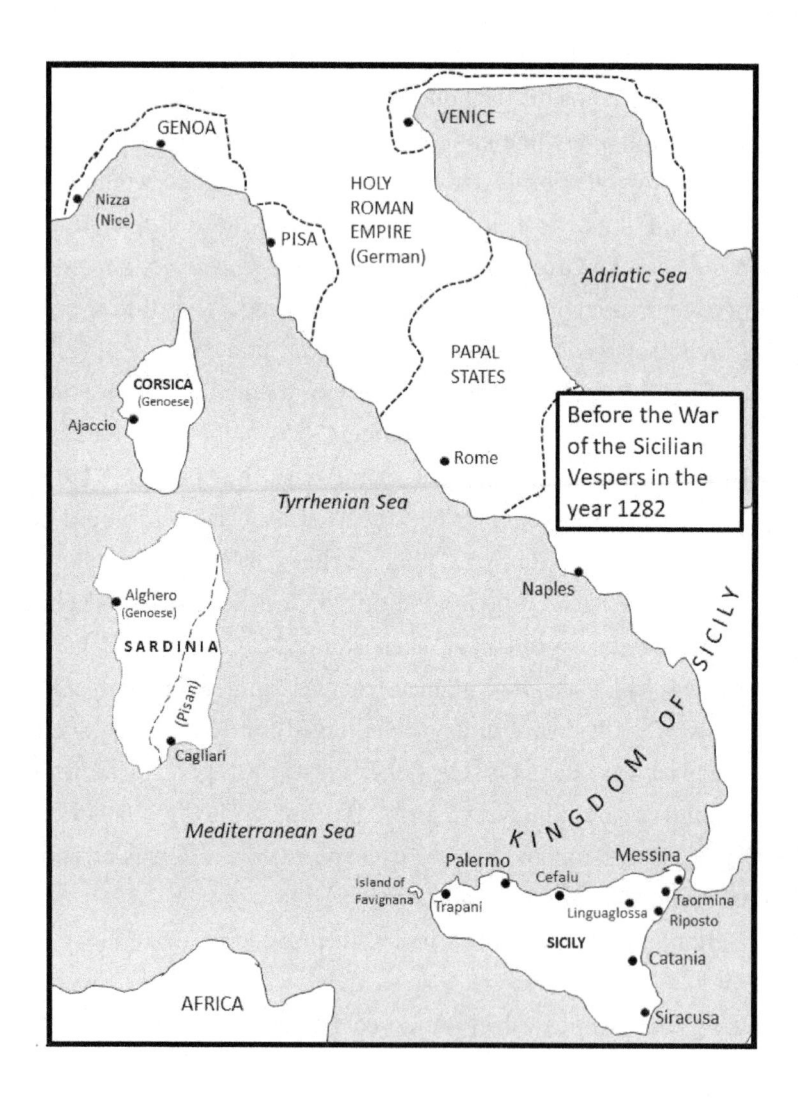

Before the War of the Sicilian Vespers in the year 1282

## CHAPTER XXIV    FAVIGNANA

Avoiding the coast of Italy south of Genoa where King Charles was in control, they sailed instead across the Tyrrhenian Sea, from one island to the next. Ports of call included Ajaccio in Corsica, and Alghero, Sardinia, after which they traveled off the west coast of Sardinia. The northwesterly mistral winds boosted them across the open sea to Favignana, a small island west of Sicily. Esmeray was navigating the *Aspasia* as the island came into view. The west side of Favignana was dominated by hills; the east side was flat. The island was only a couple of miles across and twice as long. They approached a fishing village sheltered along a bay on the north shore of the island.

"I thought you were to alert the people of Palermo. Why are we in Favignana?" said Esmeray.

"Remember my meeting with Procida at Vulcano? I must visit Palermo, the most important city and capital of Sicily. It is also the most heavily garrisoned with the greatest number of Sicilians loyal to King Charles. Procida intended to stay here, on Favignana, until he was ready to notify his contacts in Palermo."

"He told you the names of the contacts?" asked Esmeray.

Bastone nodded.

"Do you think Charles has soldiers here?" She pointed. "There is a castle on that mountain top and anyone up there has a perfect view of us right now."

"All I see are fishing boats now, but we need to remain cautious," said Bastone.

Under a warm but gentle October sun, they furled the mainsail and reefed the jib, slowing to glide above the incredibly clear, turquoise water toward the shore. To their starboard, the village of Favignana was perched on a rocky shoreline which enclosed the harbor. Overlooking the village was a treeless mountain topped by a stone castle. Ahead of them was a sandy beach, the strand curving around their portside, the shore turning rocky again. They beached the trohantiras and were ignored by fishermen who continued mending nets along the strip of sandy beach. Esmeray covered her shorn hair with a kerchief. They jumped from the grounded bow to the sand. A score of men, either sitting on their heels or cross-legged, were repairing a large net which stretched out hundreds of paces. Bastone asked one of the men, "Can you tell me where Signore Ponziu lives?"

The fisherman continued to weave cords and tie knots on the net, as he said, "Ponziu? There are many with that name on the island. Which one?"

"Um, Petru. Ponziu Petru."

"Hmm. Which one?" said the man.

*"Signore?"*

The nearby fishermen laughed.

"Petru *nannu* or Pitruzzu?" said the fisherman.

Bastone smiled along with them. He scratched his head. "Did you say: '*nannu*', uh, in Genoese . . . *nonno*. Yes, I would like to see Grandfather Petru."

The fisherman paused his handiwork and stood. "Bonu, Good! I am pleased! You are at least . . . trying to speak Sicilian." He shook Bastone's hand. "The person you are looking for is Petru nannu. Pitruzzu, little Petru, his grandson, is only a few years old. Come, I'll take you to Petru."

A ripple of genial laughter passed among the fishermen as they continued their work.

Esmeray and Bastone followed the man along the beach, where several boats had been pulled out of the water and mounted on driftwood logs bleached white in the sun. A brawny man with muscular arms and dark hair down to his shoulders was waterproofing the hull of a fishing boat with pitch.

"Petru! These, um, sailors, are here to see you." He departed.

"*Addiu!*" Bastone acknowledged with a static wave and a quick upward tip of his chin.

He nodded to Petru. "Signore Ponziu, I was told to ask for you when I arrived."

Petru pursed his lips and glanced at Esmeray. He said, "She is your . . . wife?"

"Yes."

"She is in your full confidence?"

Bastone nodded.

"Yes, yes, a good wife makes a good husband," said Petru. He enunciated carefully, "*Animus Tuus Dominus.*"

"*Antudu,*" said Bastone.

"*Va bene*, fine," said Petru as he smiled.

"Giovanni Procida sent me," said Bastone.

"And you speak Sicilian, but with an accent not much different from Procida's," said Petru. "But I thought *he* would return."

"He has been delayed and has sent me as his agent," said Bastone.

"Here, sit with me in the shade of my boat." Petru handed Bastone a wine skin.

"*Grazie.*" Bastone swallowed and passed the skin to Esmeray.

Petru accepted the skin from Esmeray after she had sipped, and said, "What's your name, *paesanu*?"

"Ponzio Bastone—and my wife Esmeray."

"Hmm . . . Ponzio. Not Sicilian, but perhaps a distant cousin?"

Bastone smiled with a nod.

Petru focused on Esmeray as he said, "A woman in sailor's garb?"

She glanced down at her clothes, then she raised her chin and stared at him with unblinking eyes.

"No, no, mi scusi, signora . . . your clothes are fine . . . I watched as you skillfully guided your boat to shore. Signora, your husband is a lucky man. And Bastone, you have my respect for trying Sicilian. Esmeray, do you also have the gift of language?"

She had found opportunities to improve her Sicilian, with Lucianu's help during their long sea voyage. She said, "*Cu avi lingua passa u mari.* Those who have language cross the sea."

"And you have learned Sicilian proverbs, too. Ha! Bonu! You sailed from . . . ?"

"Genoa," said Esmeray.

"That far! I am even more impressed." said Petru. He offered Esmeray the wine skin and looked at Bastone. "Procida said he would have a message."

"The date for the uprising is next spring, on Ascension Day, at the Hour of Vespers. I am to go to Palermo and notify the patriots next spring, but early enough so they can prepare."

"Hmm. Why are you here so early? You're not sailing back to Genoa now, are you? It's risky during this season," said Petru.

"No, we're looking . . . um, for a place to live."

"So, you will stay for the winter?" said Petru. "I know of a vacant fisherman's cottage just north of the village."

"That will suffice, grazie." said Bastone.

Bastone asked about the Angevin garrison, and laughed when Petru told them the soldiers stayed in their castle atop the mountain and only came down when they ran out of wine. "That is the Castle of Saint Catherine, owned by Lord Abate, the Baron of Trapani, which includes Favignana. The baron supplies the Angevins with plenty of food and wine and forbids harassment of our village. Perhaps it is not so bad in Trapani, but I have heard many stories of the Angevins' cruelty to the people of Palermo.

For several weeks, Petru helped them make traps woven with fine rushes and strips of cane, showing them the best places to locate the cone-shaped baskets. Esmeray taught Bastone how to use the traps, which caught a variety of sea life, including octopus, cuttlefish, eel, and white fish. Petru told them, however, the most bountiful catch was in June, when the bluefin tuna were migrating past Favignana, and the entire village worked together to trap schools of the tuna in the centuries old ritual called the *mattanza*.

Without the stress of the outside world, the winter was a pleasant time. Esmeray and Bastone savored each day together. The fish were plentiful, and spending hours at sea to manage the traps, with Esmeray's tutelage Bastone improved his sailing skills. Bastone taught Esmeray how to shoot his crossbow. With leg strength, she could string and cock the steel bow using the belted hook. Typical of most crossbow novices, after several weeks of steady practice, she could shoot with accuracy.

One morning, as spring neared, Esmeray and Bastone relaxed outside the cottage, mesmerized by the play of light on the sea. For most of the winter, the *favonio*, a balmy wind from the west, had kept the weather mild, but today the surface of the water seemed to shiver in the cold *mistral* wind. Esmeray trembled as chill covered her arms and legs, breaking her contemplation, reminding her that soon their paradise would end. She laid her head on Bastone's shoulder, her arms encircling him, and gave him an affectionate squeeze.

"When must we sail to Palermo?"

"I should notify my contact there early enough so he can inform the patriots and give them time to prepare. We will visit during the Easter festivities, plenty of time before Ascension Day. Then we can return to Favignana."

# 13th Century Palermo

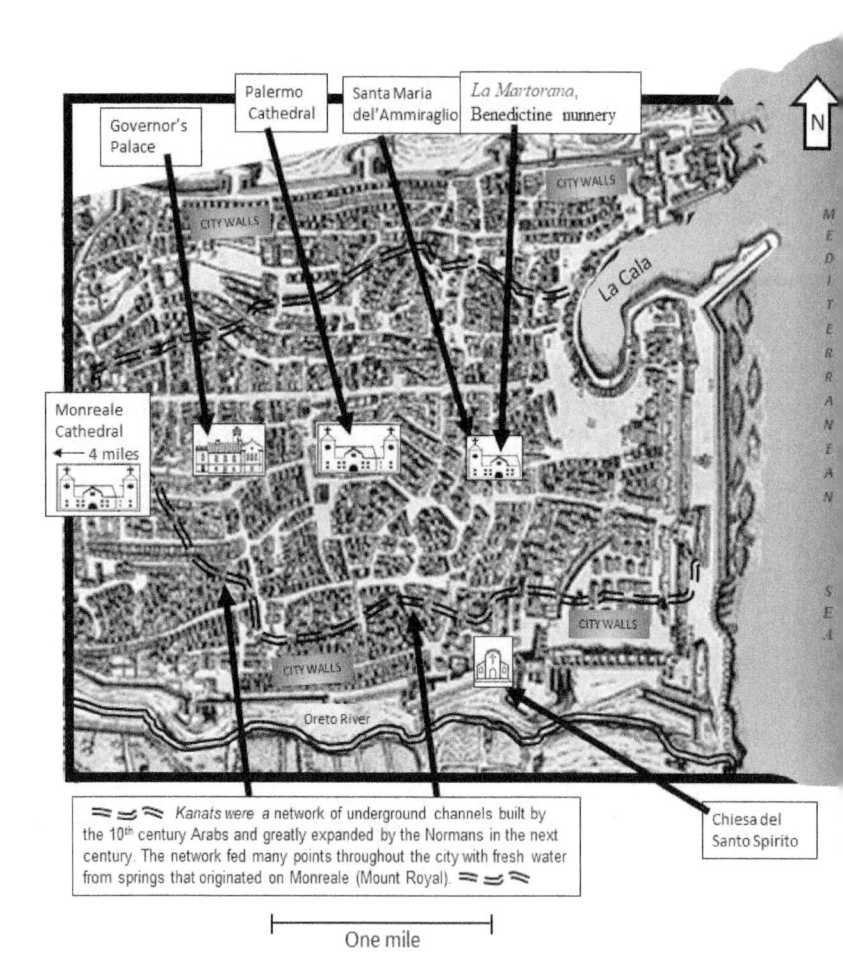

Governor's Palace

Palermo Cathedral

Santa Maria del'Ammiraglio

*La Martorana,* Benedictine nunnery

CITY WALLS

CITY WALLS

La Cala

Monreale Cathedral
← 4 miles

CITY WALLS

CITY WALLS

Oreto River

Chiesa del Santo Spirito

≋ ≋ ≋ *Kanats* were a network of underground channels built by the 10th century Arabs and greatly expanded by the Normans in the next century. The network fed many points throughout the city with fresh water from springs that originated on Monreale (Mount Royal). ≋ ≋ ≋

|—————— One mile ——————|

MEDITERRANEAN SEA

N

## CHAPTER XXV  PALERMO

At sunrise on the day before Good Friday, Esmeray and Bastone sailed east to Sicily then followed the north coast, arriving just before sunset at *La Cala*, Palermo's inner harbor. They slept late after the long day at sea and missed Good Friday Mass, which was at dawn, but by early afternoon they had joined thousands of citizens and visitors for the processions and celebrations. The presence of Angevin soldiers was noticeable on the waterfront, and thousands of them patrolled the streets, but their numbers were small compared to the vast crowds. With the large number of pilgrims from the countryside, the soldiers were kept busy in surveillance of the crowds, and most did not take time to carry on petty harassment of citizens.

Esmeray wore a simple tunica she had made herself. She had draped a woad scarf over her shoulders and hair, which had partially grown back during the winter months. When they had disembarked and Bastone had paid his mooring fee, the harbor master informed him the governor, an Angevin appointed by King Charles, did not allow citizens or foreigners to carry any weapons, so he was without his dagger. Esmeray's quill knife hung on a necklace hidden down her tunic. Bastone gave the official an extra coin to protect his boat and promised him more if it was not disturbed. In addition, they removed the tiller handle and hid it under extra sails in the cabin.

Bastone and Esmeray entered the city gate, intercepting a solemn procession slowly winding down the streets, making its way through all quarters of the city. The procession, which had begun at the Palermo Cathedral, consisted of eight *vares*, platforms decorated with flowers, candles, and wooden statues, carried on the shoulders of male citizens. The statues depicted the characters of the eight events of *The Passion*, as written in the Gospels, beginning with Jesus's arrest through his crucifixion. The pace of the procession was reminiscent of a funeral march. Pall bearers carried the vares in chronological order according to the Passion as they passed silent spectators along the street.

Following the last vare was a troop of men beating a slow rhythm on drums accompanied by others playing a dirge on their flutes. Following the musicians were scores of women holding Paschal candles, symbolizing the light of Christ. All the participants were dressed in black, moving in a pattern called the *annacata*, as they stepped forward and back, side to side, making the statues sway with them.

Two miles west of Palermo another procession marched along, in the same fashion, originating at the Cathedral at Monreale. To accommodate the enormous Easter crowds, the citizens had organized additional smaller processions that started and finished, respectively, at the churches of *Santa Maria dell'Ammiraglio*, Saint Francis of Assisi, and the *Chiesa del Santo Spirito*, Church of the Holy Spirit. The pall bearers went on as long as they could, enduring the sweat and pain holding the *vares*, until relieved by others. As the marchers passed, citizens provided them with water. The processions would go on for twenty-four hours until Saturday afternoon.

The faithful also would continue to celebrate the entire week following Easter Friday. King Charles ruled with an iron hand and the long religious holiday was a God-given respite for the people. Since Charles had conquered Sicily, Palermo and the other communes on the island had suffered under his avaricious fiscal policy. His tax collectors forced both the commoners and Sicilian nobles to pay heavy taxes. The nobles had to provide ships to him, as well. Palermo's economy had been further devastated when Charles relocated the capital of Sicily to Naples.

After the procession passed, Esmeray said, "So depressing. But I respect the people's passion. Can we go somewhere . . . brighter?"

Palermo had been the capital under the Arabs and the Normans, and their traditions were present in the multicultural characteristics of the citizens, architecture, and food. Bastone and Esmeray navigated through the crowds in the streets and open-air markets. There were no food vendors, because the Catholics and the Greek Orthodox congregations practiced the black fast on Good Friday, abstaining from all food except water until after dark, when they would have one meal but without wine, dairy, or meat. Then three hours after noon on Saturday, the black fast ended, and the vendors could sell food, except meat. Esmeray and Bastone arrived outside the Church of *Santa Maria dell'Ammiraglio*, next to *La Martorana*, a Benedictine nunnery.

"What are those red domes on top of the church?" asked Esmeray.

"They are from the Arab occupation when they converted the church into a mosque. Now it is a church again."

"Palermo is the first place I have seen people with red hair. It is striking!" Her stomach groaned. "And I am getting hungry. But there is nothing to eat."

"There is a little bread left on the boat—later." Bastone added in a quiet voice, "This is where I am to meet my contact."

At the entrance to the church *of Santa Maria dell'Ammiraglio*, a pair of Angevin soldiers examined the worshipers, stopping those with handbags or shoulder bags for inspection. They were looking for weapons. In front of them, a soldier returned a woman's bag, pressing it into her chest, his hands lingering as if to feel through her tunica. She glared at him. The man accompanying her, likely her husband, stared at the guard, but then quickly pulled the woman into the church. One guard made a comment to the other in French, and they both laughed. As Esmeray and Bastone passed the guards, one kissed the air toward Esmeray, but they entered without incident.

Inside, the stained-glass windows provided moderate lighting. Many people were making their annual prayer confession so they could attend Easter Mass, and the couple had to wait their turn to kneel before the altar. A priest stood beyond the alter railing with his hands in the *oran* position, palms held upward, wide and raised, to lift the worshipers' prayers to heaven. Esmeray and Bastone moved to the second row, crossed themselves, then kneeled on the marble floor. Bastone touched his forehead, chest, left shoulder, then the right shoulder. Esmeray also touched her forehead but ended by touching her right shoulder before her left.

For prayer, Esmeray held her hands as a steeple, palms pressed together, fingers pointed up to God, and the right thumb over the left forming a cross. Bastone noticed it differed from his hands, in which his fingers were intertwined and folded with his thumbs also forming a cross.

Their supplication lasted almost half an hour as nearby worshipers came and went. Unexpectedly, the priest at the altar approached them. He gestured for them to follow him where the other worshipers would not hear. "Palmiero Abate has not arrived. Come back tomorrow." He returned to the altar to pray.

They left the church entering the rush of pedestrians and the bright sunlight. Returning to the *Aspasia* they ate a meager meal of bread and wine.

The couple slept late on Saturday morning and after waking, enjoyed their intimacy. Esmeray's stomach growled and she said, "Let's go find something to eat."

Bastone looked at the sky through the open door of the cabin. "The sun appears to be in the seventh hour, only an hour or so past noon. I don't think the vendors will sell food until the ninth hour."

"In Chios, they broke black fast at noon." said Esmeray.

Bastone agreed they could try. They dressed and entered Palermo. At the first piazza, Esmeray pointed to a nearby vendor. The food on display looked like oranges, but half their size. A pleasant scent of cooked food engulfed them as they perused the fare.

"Those smell wonderful," said Esmeray.

"They're *arancini*, little oranges," said Bastone. "Balls of rice stuffed with meat, peas, and cheese, covered with breadcrumbs. But there can't be meat. It is still Lent."

"*Si!*" the vendor said. "These are my special arancini, made for Lent! No meat. Instead, calamari."

"May I try just one arancini, first?" said Esmeray.

"Si" He handed her one, to sample. "*Uno arancinu.*" Then gave Bastone one, "*Due arancini!*" He flashed a big smile and laughed. Then suddenly the vendor appeared irritated. Two soldiers approached from the side. They didn't break stride, however, and bumped Bastone away from the stall.

Bastone grumbled.

A guard touched his sword handle. Bastone knew he should have remained silent.

"*Excusez-moi monsieur.*" Bastone controlled his anger and appeared apologetic, then took Esmeray's hand and they stepped away.

The soldiers each grabbed a handful of the arancini and left without paying. Once the guards left, Bastone purchased their food. After savoring the arancini, the bright colors of an adjacent stall caught Esmeray's attention. The nuns of La Martorana Abbey had crafted food to sell, the proceeds going to their convent.

"Are these fruits? They look like fruit, but too perfect ... they are shiny," said Esmeray. "I recognize the figs, lemons, and the oranges from Linguaglossa. But these two?"

"It's a peach," said Bastone. "And that is a perfect rendition of a slice of watermelon."

"Oh, now I see they are not real fruits," said Esmeray.

A nun overheard her. "They are *frutta martorana*. You will like them. Very sweet. Made from a paste of almonds and sugar called *marzapane*."

"They are works of art!" said Esmeray. "Marzapane, that's an unfamiliar word to me—it sounds like 'march bread,' but what is sugar?"

"Sugar is what makes the marzapane so sweet. A spice made from a cane grown near Trapani," said the nun.

Bastone purchased several of the confections. Between bites, Esmeray said, "This is sweeter than honey!"

They were about to leave when Esmeray showed interest in another confection, tubes of fried pastry dough filled with a white, creamy filling. "Sister, what is this called?"

"In Palermo, it is a *cannolu*. The filling is ricotta cheese with sugar."

"Yes, sugar. Please I would like two *cannolu*."

She cleared her throat. "Of course, young lady."

"I am learning Sicilian, sister. Are two of these—*cannoli*?"

The nun smiled and said, "Si, signora. And the recipe is from the sisters of the nunnery in Caltanissetta."

They paid a second visit to the church to meet the conspirator Abate, but the priest again told them to come back the following day.

After a restful night in the cabin of the *Aspasia*, they returned to the church on Easter Sunday. The priest reported Abate had not arrived and speculated the governor had the church under surveillance. He gave Bastone directions to *La Chiesa del Santo Spirito* where he should find Abate there on the following day.

---

It was March 30, 1282, and Bastone and Esmeray woke to a sunny *Pasquetta*, Easter Monday. They grabbed chunks of bread they had bought the evening before and hurried to the meeting with Abate, eating as they walked. The Church of the Holy Spirit was a mile from the harbor and a few hundred paces outside the southeast walls of Palermo, surrounded by lush greenery and ageless cypress trees overlooking the Oreto River. The church also served as the chapel for Cistercian monks, who had established an adjacent monastery.

As the couple crossed the city, they were greeted several times by bright faced pilgrims exclaiming, "Christ is risen!"

Easter Monday was also known as Monday of the Angel, because in the Bible when the women had found Jesus's tomb empty, they had been met by an angel.

Bastone answered the passionate believers with the traditional response, "He is risen indeed!"

As they approached the city gate, the streets became more congested. "I had expected there would be fewer people here," said Bastone.

"They are carrying baskets of food," said Esmeray. "Perhaps after Mass, they will have an outing in the countryside."

Stationed at the city gate were two Angevin soldiers. Each wore a steel helmet with a conical top, a chainmail *gorget* which covered his neck and collar bone, and at the belt was an *armer l'épée*, a one-handed sword. The pair of guards casually nattered as they allowed pedestrians free ingress and egress. A hundred paces outside the gate, near the church, squads of soldiers patrolled among the throngs of people. Entry to the Church of the Holy Spirit was slowed, due to soldiers searching the parishioners for weapons. There were scattered comments from the crowd, expressing concern that they would miss the service. Some had given up waiting and were resting on a carpet of pine needles under cypress trees, enjoying their lunch.

Bastone and Esmeray paused before joining the mass of people trying to enter the church. "God's bones!" said Bastone. "How will I find my contact in these conditions?"

A man wearing a worn tunic, trousers, and the wide-brimmed hat of a farmer approached them with intent. He stopped to face them, leaned on his walking stick, nodded to Bastone, casually tipping his straw hat to Esmeray. "I thought we'd never meet. Please come and eat with us, but before, I must ask—she is intimate with your, um . . . mission?"

"*Si.*" Bastone nodded.

"*Animus Tuus Dominus,*" whispered Abate.

"*Antudu,*" said Bastone under his breath.

He smiled and held his arm out in the direction of a group of men and women sitting nearby in the shade. Bastone and Esmeray joined the group. One woman offered Esmeray a *cannolu.*

"Grazie!" said Esmeray.

Bastone addressed Abate, "Procida could not come."

"He informed me and revealed your identity," said Abate. "I have watched you the last few days going back and forth to your boat. I wanted to make sure you were indeed his envoy."

"It will be on Ascension Day, at the Hour of Vespers," said Bastone.

"Thirty-nine days. We'll have plenty of time to prepare. If enacted too soon, our effort will fail."

Abate broke off a chunk of bread and handed the loaf to Bastone. "So now we can relax and celebrate the Eastertide." He drank some wine from a skin. "The disguise is good, no? The men accompanying me, dressed as peasants, are my guards, but the ladies, they aren't really *ladies* . . . I hired them. They rarely wear head coverings, walking the streets of Palermo to attract their . . . um, clients." He laughed, but when the couple didn't appear amused, he sobered.

Abate cleared his throat, then said, "I trust you are involved because, as they say, you are Genoese, therefore, a merchant. The Genoese who have settled here formed small colonies to trade, not to conquer. That is acceptable. It will leave us Sicilians free to govern ourselves."

It was no surprise that Abate assumed Bastone's motivation was the same as most Genoese, for profit. Freeing Sicily would open more trading opportunities for Genoa. Bastone's primary inspiration, however, was to avenge his brother's death and provide some meaning to his loss.

Abate drank and gestured with the skin toward a handful of Angevin soldiers pushing their way through the crowd toward the church. "It's better we meet away from the crowd. The Angevin, Sergeant Drouet, is widely known and reviled for terrorizing Palermo."

There were shouts near the church. A commotion rippled across the mass of people, swelled at the periphery, then burst forth as Angevin soldiers shoved people aside to exit the crowd. Following the soldiers was the hated sergeant, dragging a young woman, and more guards holding back a man struggling to reach her. "She is my wife. Let her go! Help us paesani! He molested her! She had no weapon."

The high shrieks of women and groans of men resounded. "The poor woman, what will happen to her?" asked Esmeray.

People scattered as Drouet and his squad of Angevin soldiers exited the crowd with the woman, her husband still frantically trying to reach her. Now free of the confines of the crowd, the determined husband evaded the soldiers, lunged, and snatched Drouet's dagger from its sheath. The Angevin let go of the woman and grasped his sword, but before he could complete his draw the husband thrust the dagger into Drouet's heart.

The soldiers unsheathed their swords to take revenge. "Kill both of them!" shouted a guard. A throng of male citizens had gathered around, and through sheer numbers they overwhelmed the guards, disarmed them, and killed them with their own weapons.

A stampede began in all directions. The bells of the Church of the Holy Spirit began tolling as pockets of fighting between citizens and Angevin soldiers erupted. Abate ran to the nearest group, then another, shouting, trying to stop the carnage. "It's too soon! Stop, the French will massacre us!"

He returned without success and shouted above the loud ringing as the church bells continued. "The people have gone mad! It is a horror! They even killed a Sicilian woman who had married an Angevin. When I tried to interfere, the patriots threatened to kill me!"

The deafening resonance of the church bells, the tolling extended by the priest to announce the crisis, finally ended, replaced by the distant pealing from churches across the city. In less than a quarter hour, the fighting in front of the Church of the Holy Spirit was over. With shouts of "*Moranu li Francisi,* Death to the French!" a mob of Sicilian men swept toward the city gate, armed with the soldiers' swords and a variety of tools, sticks, and improvised weapons. Scores of slain Angevins lay on the ground. Years of cruelty had erupted in acts borne of extreme hatred. Hundreds of women and children, having observed the slaughter, were dumbstruck with shock, some on their knees crying.

"It happened so fast!" cried Abate. "There was no stopping it. Bastone, it will not be safe for any foreigner in the city. Behind the church is a small Cistercian abbey, where the monks will keep you out of sight. I will be back soon and escort you to your boat, so you can sail to Messina and notify the patriots."

He nodded to his men. "Let's go join the battle." He glanced at his walking stick that Bastone still held. "Does your skill reflect your name?"

Bastone offered it to Abate. "You'll need it to fight."

"No, keep it. We came prepared. Ladies?" The women removed daggers from their tunicas and passed them to Abate and his men. The armed troop moved toward the city gate.

One of the women stood. "I'm going to help the wounded."

The other women joined her to assist the monks from the Cistercian monastery, who were assessing the injured. The abbey's barber surgeon rushed from one fallen person to another, pointing out the wounded that might survive. Esmeray and Bastone helped move those he selected into the church. Citizens became enraged at the impartial attention as the surgeon examined both Sicilian patriots and Angevin soldiers. The prior, leader of the small abbey, fearing continued violence, directed his monks to administer only to the Sicilians.

Inside the chapel, a few of the French-speaking monks, Angevins and Provencals, were discussing treatment of the wounded. The brothers hushed when suddenly, a group of Sicilian men burst into the church. They confronted a monk who was giving a bandaged man water. One showed the monk a handful of chickpeas. "What are these? Say the word."

The wide-eyed monk said, "*Ciciri.*"

They left him and confronted another monk and when he answered, his French accent gave him away. He did not roll the *r* as a Sicilian would. One man said, "Moranu li Francisi, he is one of them." The vigilantes pulled him to his feet and began dragging him to the door.

The prior rushed to them. "Stop, he is a good man. He is helping the wounded patriots!"

The lead vigilante addressed the prior, "There are Angevins hiding all over the city. Abate has told us to force the Angevins to say ciciri. Those who pronounce ciciri with a French accent are to be executed!"

They exited the church taking the unfortunate monk. Returning shortly, they continued interrogating other monks.

A vigilante called out, "Which one of you is Bastone!"

Esmeray's intense look caught Bastone's eyes, and she shook her head. Bastone was about to answer. She shouted, "No!"

Bastone, however, had recognized that the man was among the guards who had escorted Abate earlier and said, "Here!"

The inquisitor drew close. "Abate wanted me to tell you that he has killed the Angevin governor and taken control of the revolt. You must notify your contacts in Messina and Catania to revolt and kill all the French. He will be here as soon as he is able to escort you to your boat."

The vigilantes dragged another monk outside. "Those poor men. Do they have to kill them? They are not like the heartless soldiers," said Esmeray. "Can't they just send them back to France?"

A patriot whose abdomen was being sutured overheard her. He squeezed out words amid pain from the surgeon's needle, "Angevins raped . . . argh . . . my wife. I say . . . k-kill, th-them all!"

The surgeon finished stitching and mumbled. "I'm out of silk thread." He shouted to the women and monks attending to the hurt. "Do any of you have a silk scarf? I need the thread for sutures."

"I respect these monks' courage," said Esmeray. "The patriots will surely execute them, but they remain, helping others."

Patriots wanting revenge entered again and challenged another monk, who was on his knees cleaning a man's wound with vinegar wine. "What are these?" One held his palm in the monk's face. The monk trembled as a chickpea rolled onto the floor. "Answer me!"

"Cic . . . ciciri."

"Say it again."

"Ciciri."

The patriot looked at the others, then grabbed the monk's cowl and pulled him to his feet. "Close, but not good enough!"

As the monk was shoved toward the front door, he shouted, "I am from Naples! My accent is different!"

The prior grabbed the unfortunate monk's sleeve to stop his arrest. A patriot struck him on the head with a sword pommel. On his knees, bleeding from the wound, the prior would still not let go. When the abductor threatened him with the blade, the prior shrank away and the mob dragged the monk outside.

The prior turned to Bastone. "You must leave. The only person between you and the mob is the messenger sent by Abate. If he isn't here to vouch for you, your accent might also fail the test. Don't wait until Abate returns. I will disclose a secret way to the harbor —but you must take several monks with you. They are French but have always done God's work for the community. It is insane that *all* the French must die. The people here have gone berserk! Will you save these brothers?"

Alternatives raced through Bastone's mind. He knew if they remained or tried to flee, the frenzied mobs would probably kill anyone with an accent. If the mob caught him with French monks the ending would be the same, but he was willing to take that risk. He glanced at Esmeray, and, with a slow blink, she concurred.

Bastone picked up the staff and said, "Show us the way."

The prior led the couple and three monks out the rear door, picked up a coil of rope, and continued to the back of the monastery. At the center of an outdoor cloister was a stone wall encompassing the top of a well. Bastone and Esmeray shared a knowing glance, understanding she was recalling their escape in Constantinople.

"Underground aqueducts beneath the city lead to the harbor," said the prior. "The well leads to the subterranean channels."

The Arabs had originally excavated the limestone caverns. When the Normans had governed Sicily, they expanded the system of channels. The subterranean aqueduct brought spring water from the heights at Monreale and distributed it across the city, excess water draining into the harbor.

The prior handed the rope to Bastone, who passed it to Esmeray. She fashioned a mooring knot around a post. "It hasn't rained lately, so the water in the channels will be shallow," said the prior. "From the bottom of the well, crawl along the tunnel to a larger passageway. There, you can walk. Follow the direction the water flows all the way to the harbor. It will take about an hour, so be patient."

Bastone grabbed the rope. He addressed the monks, "Have any of you been in the tunnels?" They shook their heads. "I will go first, then."

He began rappelling into the well. He reached the bottom where water was flowing into the well from one tunnel, discharging into a second tunnel on the opposite side. He pulled himself up into the tunnel where water flowed out and entered it headfirst. It was several inches deep as he crawled along on his hands and knees, frequently scraping his head. Esmeray descended next and crawled after Bastone into the tunnel. Two monks followed. As the last monk started to enter the small passage, he groaned, then said, "I can't, I can't do it! It's too cramped. I am deathly afraid of confined spaces! Prior, help me back up!" His voice faded, "I'm not coming . . ." then he shouted, "God be with you!"

They squeezed through the confined passageway into a larger channel, but still had to crouch as they moved downstream in ankle deep water. They could hear muted church bells still tolling above as they stooped, moving along the larger tunnel in the direction the water flowed. They passed more side channels, each providing a source of faint light. Slogging through the tunnel, wet, tired, and shivering, the group continued without complaint. Bastone and Esmeray had developed stamina from hardships at sea. The Cistercian monks' endurance had been forged during their lives of hard manual work and prayer.

After an hour of uncertainty, Bastone was relieved to see the light of day ahead at the outfall. But when he arrived, he let out a deep sigh, peering at the darkening sky between iron bars.

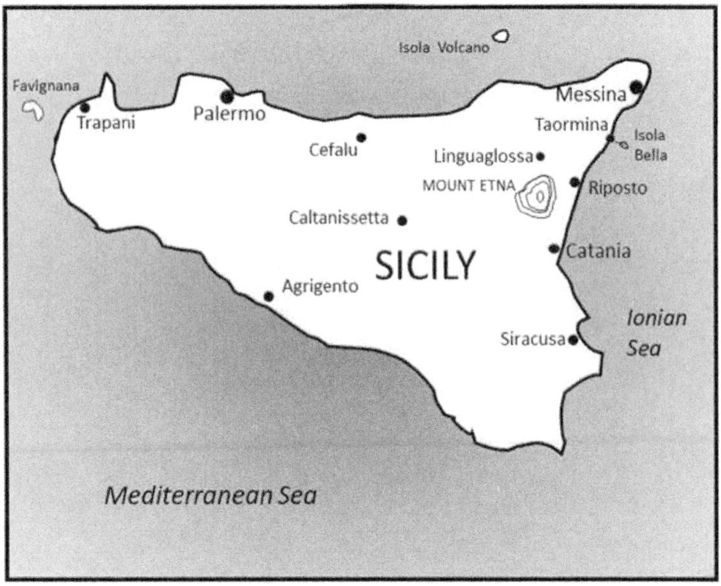

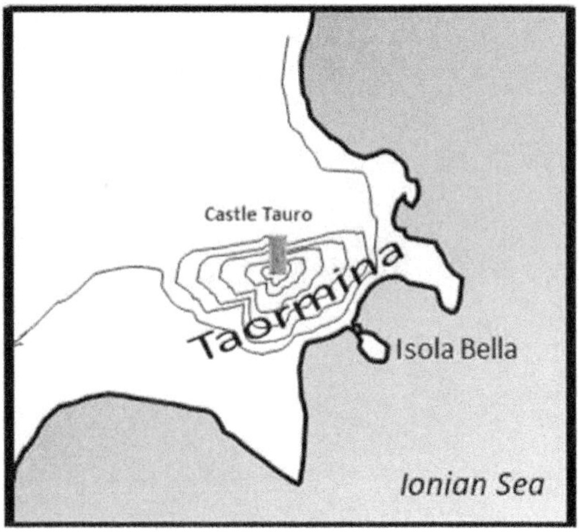

## CHAPTER XXVI    MESSINA

Bastone glanced at the monks' belts and said in Sicilian, "I need a rope to get through these bars." He added gestures, and a monk untied his rope belt, handing it to him.

Bastone looped the rope around two of the iron bars. "Esmeray, use your best sailor's knot and tie the ropes together."

She used a double half hitch. Bastone inserted the walking stick in the loop, rotating it, the rope squeezing on the iron bars. Grunting after a couple more turns, a monk took one end of the cane, Bastone the other. As the bars began to bend, grit fell from the stone wall where the metal rods were imbedded. Then suddenly the line snapped. "Mother Mary!" said Bastone

Esmeray examined the rope. "The knot held." She gestured to the other monk to untie his belt. "We'll try again."

Esmeray crouched, soaking the rope in the water. "A wet rope is stronger."

The wet rope didn't break and the bars bowed inwards. Bastone repeated the process on the adjacent bars. They bent enough for Bastone to squeeze through.

"Esmeray, we are about a mile south of the harbor. I have a better chance to make it to the *Aspasia* if I am alone. Stay out of sight inside the tunnel. I'll return with the boat."

In the light of the gibbous moon, Bastone headed toward the harbor. The relentless peal of church bells had ended, and the nocturnal background noise of the city had returned to occasional shouts, thuds, dog barks, and frogs croaking along the waterfront. He stole quietly in the deep shadow of the city wall close to his left. To his right, a series of warehouses blocked the view from the cargo ships moored along the wharf. He was gaining confidence he would get to the trohantiras without incident. Crossing an open area, he heard a shout.

"You! Stop!"

A group of men advanced at a fast stride. Bastone didn't forget the patriots had killed a monk at the church for having a Neapolitan accent. He broke into a run toward the harbor. Figuring he was halfway to the *Aspasia*, he was confident he could stay ahead of them, but they would likely catch up as he pushed off.

As he fled, cries of "Moranu li Francisi, Death to the French!" spewed from the mob of pursuers. After Bastone had run a few hundred paces, he had left most of the patriots behind, except for a couple of men keeping pace with him. He glanced over his shoulder, and the closest pursuer was well ahead of his compatriots. Bastone suddenly reversed his direction, running straight at the man. Glints of metal hinted that the man had a dagger in his hand. Bastone swerved, at the same instant parrying the knife with his staff, then redirected his weapon to crack the attacker's temple. The man crumpled to the ground. Bastone sprinted away, glancing behind to see another speeding toward him. Hundreds of paces behind, the rest of the mob advanced at a fast walk.

Bastone knew they would catch up to him when he boarded the *Aspasia*. He had to get rid of them one by one. He abruptly stopped and waited as his next adversary drew near. His pursuer slowed, looking over his shoulder. Also armed with a *bastone*, the stranger halted ten paces away, waiting for his comrades. Bastone held his staff in two hands like a sword. He moved toward his opponent. The man retreated. Bastone had to finish him quickly.

"*Senza palle*, you have no balls!" said Bastone, then added a derisive laugh.

The man abruptly halted, pounded his walking stick to the ground, then began circling Bastone, weaving an umbrella of loops with his staff over his head. Bastone kept his face to the man, stepping into the opponent's path. Still out of striking distance, his opponent changed his direction and began circling the other direction. Bastone had picked an experienced adversary who was "walking the circle," the fighting tactic of shepherds. Bastone feared this duel would not be over before the rest of the mob arrived.

Bastone turned and ran, but immediately halted. Two men had slipped by while he was distracted by the shepherd and were now blocking his way. He cursed himself for falling into the trap. One had a sword likely stripped from a dead Angevin, the other held a dagger. Bastone slowed, and the shepherd closed in from behind.

In his youth, Bastone had fought against multiple opponents armed with daggers and had survived those street fights. As the three men closed in on him, he steadied his breathing, reminding himself not to anticipate. He shifted his two-handed hold to grip the middle of the staff with one hand.

They attacked at once. He simultaneously deflected the sword thrust with his staff, ducked the arc of the shepherd's bastone, and seized the wrist of the assailant wielding the dagger, redirecting the blade from his torso. Bastone stamped on one man's knee, vaulting over the crumpled body, breaking through the encirclement, and ran.

As he sprinted away, he saw torch light on the docks. He didn't look back until he had jumped aboard the *Aspasia*. A ship was being loaded nearby, an unusual activity for nighttime. His pursuers arrived, shouting to the workers on the dock, "Stop the Frenchman!"

Bastone slipped the bowline off the mooring pole, pulling the oars out of the cabin as the mob reached the *Aspasia*. He attempted to shove off by pushing against the dock with an oar. A patriot grabbed the oar, but Bastone jerked backward, and the man fell into the water. Another man held the bow, preventing Bastone from pushing away. Bastone smashed the man's hands with the oar. Now he pushed away, but the assailant jumped aboard. Before the intruder regained his balance, Bastone struck him with the oar, knocking him overboard. Suddenly newcomers, armed with swords and crossbows forced their way through the mob to the edge of the dock.

One of the mob, pointing at Bastone, said, "Shoot him!"

"No! Stop!" Abate was among the armed group. "He is one of us! He is helping the patriots' cause!"

Shouts erupted from the mob. "Why did you run? Say ciciri! Say it!" Some attempted to reach Bastone. Abate convinced the mob to leave, his men urging them away from the docks. Bastone returned to the dock, tying off.

He jumped onto the pier, spent, but relieved. "Grazie, Abate!"

"I sent men to escort you to your boat," said Abate, "They told me what happened at the church and why you fled. But where is your wife?"

"She is safe . . . hiding . . . waiting for me."

Abate appeared reassured. "There have been too many deaths today. Many undeserved. Bastone, I need you to sail to Messina immediately! Tell them the revolt has begun prematurely. Don't stop at Cefalu. Messina is the key. I have sent riders, but I do not know the status of the Angevin garrisons on the way to Messina. The messengers might not get through. Sail night and day without stopping."

"Of course, I am leaving tonight, but I need your help," said Bastone.

Abate shrugged, "My help? Ha! You were doing well against that horde."

"When I escaped from the church," said Bastone, "two monks, French monks, fled with me. They are hiding where the aqueduct flows into the sea, near the south end of the wharf. Will you help them? Their deaths, as you said, would be undeserved, yes?"

"Certainly. In fact, I am arranging for a ship to leave tonight to evacuate those Angevins that have treated the Sicilians fairly. I will make sure the monks are on board."

Bastone slapped Abate on the shoulder. "*Ciao!*"

As Bastone boarded, Abate threw him the bowline and said, "*Addiu! In boca al lupo!*"

"*Crepi!*" said Bastone.

Bastone rowed the *Aspasia* toward the mouth of the harbor, hoisted the jib to catch the breeze, and sailed to the aqueduct outfall, where Esmeray waited. He told the monks about Abate's promise to give them safe passage.

By the next morning Bastone and Esmeray had made good progress, now sailing off the coast of Cefalu. The banners of King Charles were absent from the fortifications and were not flying from the masts of any ships, suggesting Abate's messengers had already informed Cefalu of the revolt.

Esmeray and Bastone took turns sleeping and piloting, and a day later, they rounded the Cape of Peloro, the northeast headland of Sicily. About the second hour they arrived at the harbor mouth of Messina, reefing the sails, and surveying the city. The Angevin fleet remained in port, and the blue flag of King Charles, emblazoned with an array of fleurs de lis, still flew above the city from Castle Mategriffon. "We're ahead of the riders sent from Palermo," said Bastone. "I must warn Alaimo of the revolt."

A dark shadow seemed to pass over Esmeray's face. Bastone placed a gentle hand on her shoulder and kissed her forehead. She took a deep breath. "I knew there would be danger when I accompanied you from Genoa. We'll find a nearby cove, and I'll hide the *Aspasia* as you steal into the city."

Bastone gazed toward the harbor, stroking his chin with his thumb and forefinger. "We haven't seen any Angevin ships since we left Palermo. The activity in Messina's harbor appears normal, and the banner of Anjou is still prominent across the city. They know nothing of the revolt. I think we'll have time to sail in, notify Alaimo and then depart, hours before the rider arrives from Palermo. We will leave before the fighting in Messina starts. My duty is to be a messenger, not fight in the battles."

Esmeray brightened, but with a tight smile.

They sailed into the harbor and tied on a mooring post next to fishing vessels berthed side by side. To reach the wharf, they crossed from one deck to another. After a short walk, Bastone entered a shop which sold inks, quills, parchment, and rag paper. A lone clerk sat writing at the counter.

"*Buon giorno*," said Bastone. "I have the savory mastic the minister requested."

The clerk tilted his head, then said, "Just a moment." He left through a door in the back of the shop and returned shortly. The clerk lit an oil lamp, gave it to them, and held the door open.

Looking into the dark tunnel, Esmeray's eyebrows raised. She turned to her husband, "I feel like a *speculatore*."

When they reached the palazzo of the minister, a steward escorted them to Baron Alaimo's office. "Please sit," said the baron. He nodded to Bastone, who introduced Esmeray. The baron bowed slightly. He turned to his steward, "Bring wine."

"Lord Alaimo," said Bastone, who remained standing with Esmeray, "On Easter Monday, the citizens of Palermo revolted prematurely. Abate dispatched us to deliver the word to Messina. Next, I will alert Catania."

"A spontaneous revolt." The baron took a deep breath, his cheeks expanding as he blew out an enormous sigh. "Last year, after you took ship's leave to inform me of the date for the revolt, I consulted with Lord Paulo Riso, head of the most powerful family in the city. Circuitously, I hinted, probed, and tried to sense his inclinations. He showed he was still loyal to King Charles. Without his support we cannot free Messina."

Bastone described the frenzied outburst of rage from the citizens of Palermo, and how they surged through the city, killing soldiers and civilian Angevins, men and women, even monks. "We sailed here without stopping. Abate also sent riders to alert you. A messenger should arrive within a day."

Alaimo paused in thought. "If the messenger from Palermo carries the mob's feverish thirst for revenge, I fear he may urge the citizens to arms before he consults with me. But we are not ready to defeat the French. The governor, Vicar Herbert of Orleans, maintains a strong garrison. The Angevin fleet in Messina has over one hundred ships, protected by thousands of soldiers. And the Riso family supports King Charles's government. I must contact Lord Riso, informing him of the revolt without remark or bias, hiding my inclinations. If he proclaims support to drive out the French, we will revolt immediately, but if he asserts his loyalty to King Charles, I must delay our uprising and continue to prepare."

The steward brought a tray with three cups of wine. Alaimo saluted. They drank in concert.

"Bastone, you said you're going to Catania?" asked Alaimo.

Bastone nodded.

"My good friend Geoffroi Pons is the Baron of Taormina. I fear that when the messengers from Palermo deliver word of the revolt, he and his wife will be in mortal danger. Will you evacuate them on your ship?"

"We are sailing a trohantiras, but . . . yes, we will help them. I met Geoffroi in Linguaglossa last year. The people respect him. Is he a conspirator?"

"No, no . . . but he does not warrant the same fate as those French in Palermo."

After their short time with Alaimo, Bastone and Esmeray hurried to the *Aspasia*. Esmeray sailed out of the harbor, southeast with the nor'westerly mistral winds. By early afternoon, Bastone was at the tiller as they glided into the small cove next to Isola Bella, the tiny island below the heights of Taormina. A group of men, armed with an assortment of captured weapons, including swords, French helmets, and one with a crossbow, emerged from the scrubland on the main shore. They descended to the pebble beach, plodding across a narrow isthmus of stones, only inches above the sea water, toward Isola Bella. Their progress was laborious. With each step, their feet sunk among the loose pebbles, the clacking of the stones audible above the gentle wind.

"Bastone, they are patriots, but they could be dangerous," said Esmeray.

"Yes, they are certainly not French. The people in Taormina must have already rebelled and stolen the garrison's weapons. *Dolcezza*, take the tiller while I prepare."

Esmeray beached the trohantiras, the crunching of the pebbles underneath the bow joining the chorus of shifting and rolling stones under the men's feet. Bastone strung and cocked a bolt in the crossbow and set it out of sight on the bottom board behind the cabin. "Esme, be ready to use it."

Seeing the trohantiras beach, a handful of men split off from the band who continued to the island. They gathered near the bow of the *Aspasia*. Bastone stood at midship, in reach of the oars.

A man wearing a sock cap, its red knitting flopped over an ear, said in Sicilian, "What is your business?"

"We are sailing to Riposto and have stopped for a rest," said Bastone.

"Your *Sicilianu* is awful, but you are not French," said the man.

Another elbowed him and said, "Mariu, make him say the word."

Mariu hesitated. "Um . . . how? I don't have any peas. . ."

"You mean ciciri?" said Bastone.

"Yes, ciciri, you rolled the *r*—you are certainly not a Frenchman."

The others voiced at once. "We killed all the French in Taormina. Death to the French!"

"You killed them all?" asked Bastone.

"The baron and his wife are missing," said Mariu. He turned and looked up the steep hill toward Taormina and pointed to the fortifications on the highest point above the town. "About twenty of the Angevins have retreated to Castle Tauro."

The patriots raised their fists and looked past Bastone, who followed their gaze. The men shouted, "*Llibbirtà per la Sicilia!*" A flag had been raised at the highest point of Isola Bella, the banner was partitioned diagonally into two triangular halves, one brilliant yellow and the other bright red. On the bicolor field was the ancient symbol of Sicily, the three-legged *trinacria,* the legs representing the three coasts or headlands of Sicily.

Bastone was going to announce that the revolt had begun in Palermo, but it appeared the news had already arrived in Taormina. He wondered about the fate of Baron Geoffroi and his wife. They had taken great risk to provide their citizens a better life.

Mariu drew closer to talk under the shouts of the men celebrating the raising of the flag. As if he guessed Bastone's thoughts, he said, "Perhaps Baron Geoffroi and Anastasia fled to the castle. He was a fair governor for a Frenchman. Many people, however," he flicked his head back toward his comrades, "still want him dead."

Bastone squinted as he peered up the steep hill. The blue flag of Anjou flew from the town as well as Castle Tauro. "I thought you said you expelled the French from Taormina?"

"Yes, we slaughtered the local garrison, but then a brigade of Sicilian mercenaries loyal to the king arrived from Messina and the soldiers sortied from the castle. Fighting against two forces, we retreated, leaving the Angevins to recover the town. We are gathering patriots from the countryside and will soon counterattack. By raising the trinacria, we are showing the Angevins their time is short."

Mariu leaned into the bow and pushed the trohantiras off the beach. "Go! Tell the people of Riposto and Catania. Go, before a fanatical patriot attacks you because you are not Sicilian!"

Bastone manned the oars and Esmeray worked the tiller, turning the bow toward the sea, pulling the main sail into position. The *Aspasia* was a hundred paces from the beach. There was a distant clack, then instantly a thud on the stern. "The bolt came from shore!" said Esmeray.

Esmeray yanked on the mainsail and shouted, "Unfurl the jib!" She filled both sails, the boat gaining speed.

"Esme, lay flat against the bottom boards!"

Now prone, she could not steer and keep the sails from luffing. The *Aspasia* was floundering.

Bastone returned to the oars, aware the arbalester would be reloading. An expert could set a bolt, string, and cock the trigger in twenty counts. He furiously pulled on the oars and counted. At fifteen, he flattened to the deck. Within five counts there was the clack of a crossbow firing, then a thud. A bolt was impaled in the cabin door. He crawled into the cabin, retrieved his shield, strapped it on his back, and grabbed the tiller. "Esme, stay down!"

The *Aspasia* escaped the cove, the wind picking up, propelling the boat a hundred paces from shore. There was a remote clack, followed by another thunk. Bastone felt the impact on his back, relieved it hadn't penetrated, knowing the shield would have been pierced if they had been closer.

He steered the boat to the far side of the island to shield them from the crossbowman on the shore, then turned southeast out to sea, leaving behind the bright red and yellow flag rolling and snapping in the wind.

## The Three Provinces, *Valli*, of Sicily

Leading Sicilian nobles in conspiracy with Giovanni Procida:

Palmerio Abate in the Val di Mazara.
Alaimo of Lentini for the Val di Demone.
Gualtiero Caltagirone for the Val di Noto.

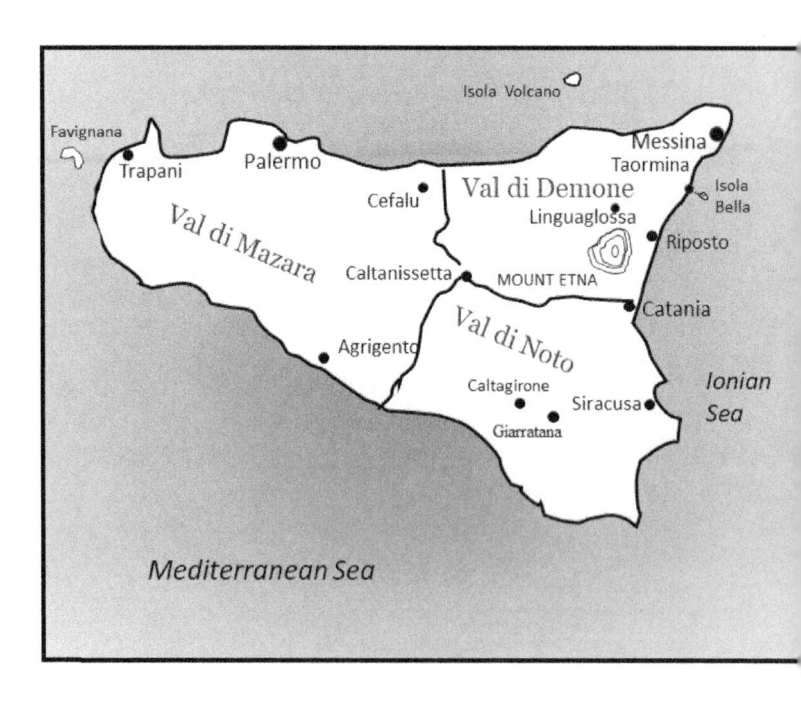

## CHAPTER XXVII    RIPOSTO

The *Aspasia* arrived off Riposto as the sun dropped behind Etna, leaving the breakwater barely visible. "I don't want to enter the port when it's this late," said Bastone. "I can't tell whether the patriots or the Angevins control the town. We can stay the night on a nearby beach."

They sailed north for a few miles and anchored a hundred paces offshore near the mouth of a small river. It was cooler with the night breeze. Esmeray and Bastone lay on the cabin roof, succumbing to a fiery session of lovemaking, releasing the stress which had built up over the last several days. Afterwards, they slept peacefully under the blankets, gently rocking with the *Aspasia* amid the mild seas.

They woke with the sunrise. Bastone tore off a chunk of bread from a loaf and handed it to Esmeray. "We'll go to Riposto and on to Linguaglossa. I am concerned about the fate of Lucianu's family." He pulled up the stone anchor, drank water from a skin, and turned to hand it to Esmeray. She sat at the helm, tears flowing.

"Esme? Dolcezza? What's wrong?"

"Nothing, everything. I have you, the sea, us, but it won't last forever."

He sat and put his arm around her. "We will always be together."

They enjoyed quiet moments as the breeze and gentle ripples of the sea held them. Bastone gave Esmeray a quick but fervent kiss. He manned the oars, rowed to shore, and jumped onto the beach. As he undressed, he shouted, "Esme, join me for a bath in the river! It's shallow, but it's fresh water." He ran into the briskly flowing stream, sat on his heels, and scooped handfuls of water, splashing himself. "It's fine. Come on in." Esmeray joined him, screaming in shock. "I thought it would be cold water, but this is freezing. You dog!"

After a quick bath, they returned to the *Aspasia* where Esmeray took the helm, Bastone hoisting the sails. Within half an hour they could see the breakwater at Riposto. Bastone squinted as he peered toward the port. "*Molto bene!* They are flying the red and yellow trinacria! Word of the revolt must have reached Riposto."

Esmeray guided the *Aspasia* into the tiny harbor and docked next to a war galley also flying the trinacria. Samuel Vadala met them as they disembarked. A pair of men, one armed with a crossbow, escorted him. He embraced Bastone. "We meet again. Another Ponziu from across the sea joins us!"

Bastone raised his eyebrows.

"Lucianu arrived from Mallorca before Easter and is in Linguaglossa," said Vadala.

Esmeray beamed. Bastone shared her excitement. "Belissimo! He made it from Mallorca safely!"

Vadala smiled and bowed his head to Esmeray. "Signora Ponziu."

He laughed as he said, "I will not ask either of you to repeat the word ciciri. I am still the mayor here, but now a mayor of the people, not for the Angevin governor. The patriots freed Riposto and Catania! But you must eat," said Vadala.

Bastone said, "No need, we can eat later. I am eager to see how Lucianu and his family are doing."

"I must first acquaint the townspeople with you. You are not Sicilian, but if they see you with me, they won't be suspicious."

Vadala glanced at the *Aspasia*. "She looks secure. Don't worry, I will make sure no one touches your boat." He took Bastone by the elbow and guided him down the wharf. Esmeray walked beside them, and Vadala's escorts followed. They moved along the waterfront, past warehouses and shops.

Vadala stopped and greeted people as they nodded or waved. He introduced Bastone as the Genoese cousin of the Ponziu family who frequented the port, delivering resin and pitch from Linguaglossa. They shared wine with other patrons at a tavern, and finally Vadala appeared satisfied that Bastone and Esmeray would be familiar to those at the harbor front. "I am sorry I cannot offer mounts for you. Weeks ago, King Charles's men arrived from Messina and seized all our horses and mules."

A shiver passed through Bastone, realizing it was fortunate the revolt was premature. The Angevins had been collecting mounts for the campaign against Constantinople, which meant Charles was very close to launching his fleet.

"There are donkeys I could loan you," said Vadala.

"No need, we will walk," said Bastone. He glanced at Esmeray.

She nodded in agreement and said, "We should get some extra clothes from the boat first."

"It's a five-hour walk, but you will arrive before dark," said Vadala. "I will send a pair of trusted men with you to Linguaglossa. These are dangerous times."

Esmeray and Bastone were elated to find Lucianu and his family safe. Lucianu's initial joy at their reunion soon turned to concern, and he talked privately with Bastone and Esmeray in the courtyard behind his uncle's stable, sharing wine.

"Do you believe all the Angevins deserve execution?" said Lucianu.

Bastone's head tilted slightly, "Was there fighting here? There were soldiers in Linguaglossa?"

"No, no," said Lucianu. "In Riposto. Initially, there was little resistance by the Angevins. Several of their soldiers were killed, and a score surrendered. The citizens were divided on what to do with the Angevins prisoners. Some had treated Sicilians with respect. While the patriots argued over the fate of the men, Angevin galleys arrived from Catania and a battle erupted at the docks. The people of Riposto repelled the invaders, even captured one ship, but the Angevins killed many citizens in the fight, erasing all sympathy any had felt for the prisoners. The people executed them."

Bastone's visage darkened. "We experienced the same horrors in Palermo, although Abate rescued most of the decent French, allowing them to sail to Provence."

"Yes, yes . . . decent. There are good people among the French," said Lucianu. He lowered his voice. "We have Geoffroi Pons and his wife Anastasia in hiding."

Both Esmeray and Bastone gasped as Lucianu continued, "They absolutely must leave Sicily. It would be too dangerous to arrange a ship from Riposto. The people of Linguaglossa are in danger for harboring them and cannot hide them much longer. Sicilians in nearby villages and towns know only that Geoffroi is an Angevin, and Anastasia is his wife. They did not have the benefit of Geoffroi's fair governance but were instead treated cruelly by the Baron of Catania, even with Vadala's efforts to help them."

Esmeray said, "If we can get them aboard the *Aspasia* . . ."

Lucianu interrupted, "Perhaps we could sneak them aboard at night? But it would be risky. How would you conceal them?"

"Bastone added a small cabin to the *Aspasia*," said Esmeray. "It is large enough for two, but it would be safer to sail the *Aspasia* to a secluded place."

"Yes, but how would we conceal them on the way to the *Aspasia*?" said Bastone. A rumble of hooves nearby caught his attention, and he paused.

They overheard Lucianu's uncle, Marianu, in the stable. Marianu raised his voice so he would be heard in the courtyard, "Lord Caltagirone, you are welcome to join us for wine and food. We will answer all your questions."

Marianu opened the rear door of the stables, escorting Caltagirone into the courtyard. Esmeray, Bastone, and Lucianu stood as the two men approached. Marianu's wife and family were watching from the house.

Marianu said, "Lord Caltagirone, Baron of Giarratana, has arrived from Catania. Lord, my nephew Lucianu, Signore Ponziu, and his wife." Each bowed their head as they were introduced. "I believe Signore Ponziu can answer your questions." Nodding to Caltagirone, he said, "I will take care of your horse, sir."

As Marianu was entering the stables he shouted, "Giuseppe, Vincenzo, *veni ca*, come!" Two boys bolted from the house and ran into the stables.

Caltagirone peered at Bastone. "You are not Sicilian. There is something about you . . . you are a knight?"

"I am Genoese. I have served as an officer of the arbalesters on the nave *Paradisio*."

Caltagirone raised his eyebrows. "Hmm. There are Genoese on both sides of the insurrection. You could be an Angevin spy. What are you doing in Linguaglossa?"

"I was sent from Palermo by Abate to report the revolt," said Bastone.

"What is the code word?" said Caltagirone. The baron was clever, trying to trick Bastone.

Bastone took a step toward the noble, planning to be discreet, "Lord . . ."

Caltagirone placed his hand on his sword and shouted. "Guards!"

A pair of soldiers hurried from the stables, with swords drawn. Bastone froze, holding out his hands. Lucianu stiffened. Esmeray gasped. A faint "No!" came from the nearby house.

"I will place my dagger on this table," said Bastone. "May I then approach you and give you the word in secret?"

Caltagirone nodded.

Unarmed, Bastone faced Caltagirone who told the soldiers to step back so they could not hear them.

"I respect your ploy, Lord Caltagirone, but may we begin again?"

With a knowing smile, the baron said, "*Animus Tuus Dominus*!"

Bastone answered, "*Antudu*."

Caltagirone slapped Bastone on the shoulder. He tilted his head toward his soldiers, who then sheathed their weapons, the tension dispersing.

The baron joined the group at the table as Marianu's wife hurried out of the house, serving wine, bread, and olives. Caltagirone accepted a cup of wine and sat with Lucianu, Bastone, and Esmeray. The lord's guards were taken to a nearby table and were also served.

Bastone addressed Caltagirone, "My primary duty is as a messenger for Emperor Michael. I have been helping Giovanni Procida to plan the revolt, delivering messages to the Sicilian nobles Abate and Alaimo, to further the cause. My contact in Catania notified you?"

Caltagirone nodded. "Yes, and only a speculatore would know that."

The baron peered at Esmeray. "Is she a speculatore, as well? Ha!"

Esmeray straightened her back. She locked eyes with the baron for a tense moment and looked away just short of insulting him.

"Esmeray is my wife, Baron," said Bastone.

Bastone sensed she had not found his sarcasm amusing, and he was relieved she contained her anger. It was not the right time to assert herself.

She stood abruptly. "Excuse me."

The baron said, "My apologies, Signora."

With a blank expression she bowed her head slightly, then went into the house.

Caltagirone asked, "You have expelled the French from Linguaglossa?"

Bastone looked to Lucianu, who said, "Well . . . yes."

"What is the status of the nearby communes?" said Caltagirone.

Bastone put down his cup, "The people of Taormina overpowered the garrison, but the surviving Angevins retreated to Castle Tauro. The Angevin governor sent troops from Messina, rallied his troops and reoccupied Taormina."

Lucianu added, "The Angevins from Catania also raided Riposto."

"Details?" asked Caltagirone.

"The citizens of Riposto defeated the Angevin garrison, then repelled a squadron sent as reinforcements, capturing a war galley," said Lucianu. "No prisoners were taken."

After a few moments of silence, Caltagirone drank, then said, "Yes, Sicilians are determined not to let this opportunity slip away to free themselves. I passed through Catania. It is now free of the Angevins, but I received word the Angevins sent galleys from Messina to blockade Palermo. Yes, Messina is the key. I will need to plan my tactics and obtain rations for my troops. They are following and will be here soon."

He drank and Lucianu poured the baron more wine. "When this area is under complete control, I will head to Messina. Bastone, what can you tell me that will help us free the city?"

"I just left Messina two days ago, notifying Alaimo of the uprising in Palermo," said Bastone. "But he was certain a citizens' revolt in Messina only would succeed if the Riso family abandoned their loyalty to King Charles. They still support the Angevins."

"Without the Risos' support, we can't recruit enough citizens," said Caltagirone. "I have a thousand men on their way from Catania. We need ten times that to breach the walls of Messina."

There was a pause, the men pondering. When Caltagirone did not continue, Bastone said, "Concentrate your men at the city gate, at the same time Alaimo leads the citizens to attack the governor at Castle Mategriffon." Bastone paused and the others leaned forward.

"Coordinate these attacks with a raid on King Charles's fleet," said Bastone. "A three-pronged assault."

Caltagirone leaned back and crossed his arms over his chest. "The first two assaults make sense, but we need ships and men to attack the fleet."

"Patriots from Riposto can crew the ship they captured," said Lucianu.

"One ship against a hundred?" said Caltagirone.

"I noticed in Messina," said Bastone, "the ships are moored close together and some are still under construction. Start one burning and the others will go up in flames."

Caltagirone said, "Perhaps, but only if we had the Greek Fire like the Romans of Constantinople."

"What is Greek Fire?" asked Lucianu.

"It is a liquid that readily burns. The Romans use siphons to spray the flaming liquid onto enemy ships," said Bastone. "They also use catapults to hurl terracotta pots containing the liquid. And—like magic—the liquid bursts into flames when the pots break on the ship's deck. Water does not put out the fire. The ingredients are a well-kept secret, but I know one element is resin."

"We produce pine resin and pitch here," said Lucianu,

"We can't just haul a barrel of resin or pitch onto an enemy ship and build a fire under it," said Caltagirone.

Bastone rubbed his scalp. "We don't know the secret ingredients that make the mixture into a liquid."

"Olive oil is a liquid, and we burn it in lamps," said Lucianu. "But we only have a few jugs in the whole village."

"Oil lamps need a wick to burn," said Caltagirone. "And a fire starter."

Bastone's eyes opened wide. "A wick—a fire arrow! To make a fire arrow, you soak the cord in pitch, attach it to an arrow or a crossbow bolt near the tip, and light it on fire."

"Who has a crossbow?" asked Caltagirone.

Bastone patted his waterproof case leaning on the table.

"Of course, you are an arbalester!" Caltagirone smiled. "By tomorrow we will have the plan ready, no?"

Bastone nodded.

Caltagirone glanced at Lucianu, "Is there a place where I can locate my headquarters?"

"There is an empty villa, where you and Bastone may board."

"Good, we can work on the details of the assault on Messina."

Lucianu guided the lord, with his brace of guards, Esmeray, and Bastone, to Anastasia's nearby villa. On the way Lucianu whispered to Bastone, "Our two friends are safe in my uncle's wine cellar."

Several of Anastasia's staff, residents, and caretakers of the villa prepared a simple meal of *alla cacciatora* for the guests. Lucianu joined them. In the kitchen, Caltagirone's guards enjoyed the hunter-style stew of onions, bell peppers, herbs, and chicken. After the meal, Esmeray retired to their bedchamber. The men discussed the attack on Messina.

Later, Esmeray woke when Bastone entered the room and lit an oil lamp. Bastone undressed. "Dolcezza, you didn't have to leave so early."

"No, it was best. You have become used to me being . . . your partner in your missions, and Lucianu respects me, but the baron, well . . . it was better I was not there."

Bastone lay next to Esmeray and lightly kissed her. "Ah. A real bed." He closed his eyes, tired from the day's activities, his drowsiness enhanced by the wine.

Esmeray raised herself up on an elbow. "What are the plans for Messina?"

"Now? Can't we talk tomorrow?"

"I won't be able to sleep, worrying that you are going on a dangerous mission."

"Hmm ... mm."

She shook him. "Bastone!"

He opened his eyes and sat up against the headboard and sighed. "Lucianu and I will make a quick raid to Messina's harbor and then withdraw. Caltagirone and Alaimo will lead the fighting. Don't worry."

"You are going to take the *Aspasia,* aren't you?"

"I must. It's the best way to steal into the harbor to reach the Angevin fleet. We will set their ships on fire."

"How?"

Bastone described how they would use pine resin and tar with flaming arrows to ignite the ships.

"I'm going with you!"

"No! Absolutely not! It's too dangerous."

"You don't trust me? You think I am not capable? I am the best pilot for the *Aspasia.* Remember when you floundered the boat after rescuing me from the Arabs at Almeria? And do you recall when I navigated us through the storms in the Tyrrhenian? I also escaped from those terrible nuns! And didn't I show a sailor's grit and strength as a crewmember on the *Paradisio*?"

"That's not it! Certainly, you are my capable, beautiful Dolcezza."

They lay facing each other in silence, Esmeray's intense stare possessing Bastone's senses. Then her expression softened, the light of the oil lamp bright in her tears. "I cannot bear to lose you. Without you, life is meaningless."

"But . . ."

"After Father was killed, I needed just the *Aspasia* and the sea. Now, with you, my Bastonino, and the *Aspasia* and the sea—I have everything."

"Va bene, Esme," he sighed, "Welcome aboard, Captain Esmeray!"

Lantern Across the Sea

## CHAPTER XXVIII   SICILIAN FIRE

On a moonless evening, Esmeray piloted the Aspasia into the harbor of Messina, gliding slowly using the jib sail to prevent the noise of oars. The mistral wind had calmed to a breeze with the night. Beyond the harbor mouth, Vadala and a hundred Sicilians waited expectantly on board the captured Angevin galley. A thousand patriots from Val di Noto, led by Caltagirone, hid outside the south gate of the city. Alaimo and thousands of Messinese scattered throughout the city were ready.

The Angevin soldiers were quartered in the city; the docked ships of King Charles's fleet were mostly empty of personnel. A few squads of arbalesters and Angevin sailors were scattered among the ships. Watchmen made rounds on the wharfs carrying oil lamps.

Days earlier in Linguaglossa, Bastone had soaked a short piece of thin rope in melted pitch and attached the infused strand to the tip of a cross bolt. At the workshop, Concettu made terracotta pots about the size of an egg, filled them with bits of resin suspended in olive oil, then sealed the tops. Lucianu shook one of the clay-fired balls, suspending the resin pieces in the oil, then threw it against a pile of wood, breaking apart the container and spattering the oil-resin mixture. Bastone lit the pitch-soaked cord and fired a flaming bolt toward the pile at a hundred paces. The fuse had changed the trajectory, and the shot missed. A second shot, however, landed within the resin splotch and the wood caught on fire. Bastone was certain he could light a target as large as a ship's hull on the first shot.

Two long rows of Angevin ships were moored alongside the sea wall of the harbor. Now, as the *Aspasia* approached the nearest, Bastone propped up his shield and placed a score of bolts covered with pitch upon the deck. A patriot from Riposto used an improvised shield made of scrap wood and strung a bolt in the crossbow he had recovered from a dead Angevin. Bastone brandished his crossbow, the bolt inserted and cocked. Lucianu struck firesteel on flint, the sparks kindled the char cloth, and he blew lightly on the embers, adding them to wood shavings to start a tiny fire in an iron pot. He lit a pitch torch in the flames and used it to ignite the rope on Bastone's cross bolt. The pitch in the rope sizzled and crackled, then flared.

Lucianu reached into a bag of resin-filled pots at his feet and hurled one at the nearest ship. The terra cotta pot shattered on the hull. Crack! He threw a second pot, then flung another at an adjacent ship. The fragile pots shattered and resin splattered and stuck to the hulls of the ships. Bastone loosed a flaming bolt from his crossbow. His aim was true, sinking into where the resin had splashed on the ship. The resin crackled and spit as it caught fire, then burst into larger flames which spread to the deck. The other crossbowman shot, but his bolt missed the incendiary target.

Shouts of alarm erupted from within the stationary fleet. Lucianu had been unable to hide the flames behind Bastone's shield while he was igniting the arrows and the enemy targeted them. The clack, clack, clack of Angevins firing crossbows sounded from the ships. The bolts were silent in flight. But then, thunk! An Angevin bolt stuck in Bastone's shield, and another hit the hull just beneath him.

Bastone reloaded, shot, and set another ship on fire. He cursed himself however, worried for Esmeray. She was wearing his chain mail shirt but was still vulnerable. He paused and glanced at her.

She shouted at him, "Don't worry! They are firing at the light from your fire arrows, not at me. Keep shooting!"

The *Aspasia* continued along the line of moored ships as Lucianu smashed pots on the hulls. More enemy bolts missed their marks, passing through the sail or deflecting off the mast and clattering upon the deck. Bastone shot again and put a third ship afire. His fellow crossbowman again missed. Bastone crouched behind his shield to string his crossbow as he peered at his inept comrade. "Take the tiller and give the crossbow to Esmeray."

The man hesitated, but Bastone's glare convinced him and he removed the belt and hook device used to cock the crossbow. He traded it with Esmeray for the mail shirt, then hunkered at the stern and assumed the tiller. She donned the tackle and strung a bolt. Lucianu held the torch and lit her fuse, then hurled another pot, and it shattered on a ship's hull. Esmeray hit the mark with a flaming bolt and a fourth ship was burning. The fire soon spread to other vessels, the blazing ships lighting up the sky.

"Bastone!" Esmeray was crouching next to Lucianu, who lay on the deck. "He's got a bolt in his leg!"

Bastone shouted, "Lucianu, can you stem the bleeding yourself?"

"Yes, yes—but Esmeray, I need a cloth to wrap my leg!"

In the light of the burning fleet, she used her knife to cut a strip of cloth from the bottom of her tunic. Lucianu crisscrossed the strips over the bolt protruding from his thigh, then tightened it around his leg.

"Hand me the knife and get behind the shield!" Lucianu cut more cloth from his own tunic, adding more bandage.

Suddenly the *Aspasia* veered toward the flaming ships, causing Esmeray to lose balance. Bastone whipped his head toward the stern and discovered the helmsman slumped over the tiller, a bolt projecting from his neck. With the *Aspasia* bearing down on a fiery ship, Bastone pulled the man away, yanked the tiller, barely avoiding the burning ship. He repositioned his shield to protect his wife and shouted, "Esme, take the tiller! Andiamo, let's go!"

Flames were licking the masts of several ships. He manned the oars, furiously rowing as Esmeray turned the boat toward their escape route from the harbor. Bastone pulled with all his strength on the oars, "We have accomplished our mission. The patriot commanders will see the blaze and begin the assault."

When the *Aspasia* cleared the burning fleet, Bastone secured the oars and went to Lucianu who lay on the bottom boards. "Tell me what to do."

"My leg is still bleeding, and the wound needs more pressure."

Bastone placed his palms on each side of the bolt. "Here?"

"ARRRGH! YES, that's it, just . . . don't m-move . . . the bolt." Lucianu groaned, "You are helping, but it's no use. I won't make it to Riposto. Please take my body back to my family . . . and tell Terra my last thoughts were of her."

"Zitto, shut up! You're going to live!" Bastone then talked slowly. "Now try to think clearly. Can we remove the bolt to stop the bleeding?"

"Your crossbow bolts don't have barbs, but if this bolt does, pulling it out will tear me apart and I'll certainly bleed to death."

Bastone looked about the deck. He found an Angevin bolt and held it up. It had two barbs at the point. Lucianu groaned. "Bad luck! I know how to remove the barbed points, but I cannot do it myself and it requires goose quills."

"Quills? I have several in the cabin, in my scribe's kit . . . how will they work? You must instruct me!"

"There is not enough light . . ."

Esmeray stood at the tiller. "Bastone! The galley from Riposto is approaching. They must have seen the fires."

Bastone grabbed the pitch torch still burning in the metal pot and held it above his head. "Stop! Paisani, patriots! A comrade is dying! We need a surgeon!"

As the galley passed, the faces of the men from Linguaglossa and Riposto glowed with concern, illuminated by the blazing fleet.

"They looked right at us!" said Esmeray. "Why don't they stop!"

"I am one man," said Lucianu. "The patriots must attack now, to free Messina. Bastone, promise me you'll tell Terra . . ." The galley slid by in the opposite direction, and the turbulence from the oars and wake caused Lucianu to groan in pain. He coughed, then was silent.

"Mother Mary!" Esmeray shouted. "Lucianu!"

"Look!" Bastone pointed to the galley's stern. A lone figure jumped from the deck into the water. Esmeray steered her boat to the man swimming toward them and helped him aboard. "It's Egidiu!"

"Your father's here. Lucianu!" Bastone hurried into the cabin and brought out his writing quills. "What else do we need?"

Egidiu climbed aboard, seemingly unfazed by the cold water, and said, "Sail closer to the fire, so we have more light." He examined his son's leg. "Bastone, give me two unused quills this long." He spread his index finger and thumb. Bastone cut two quills the proper length. "And bring a skin of wine and enough cloth to replace the bandage."

Esmeray guided the boat into the calmer water of the harbor and furled the sails. Half the fleet was in flames and the Angevins were in retreat. It was bright as daylight near the burning ships, but the heat was intense. Egidiu washed the puncture with wine, as Esmeray and Bastone worked to reduce the blood loss, all dripping with sweat. Lucianu groaned as his father wiggled the bolt to insert the two quills along the sides, then pushed the hollow quills to cover the points of the barbs. When he pulled the bolt out, the points, sheathed by the smooth quills, did not tear the inside of Lucianu's thigh. He poured more wine in the wound, drained it, then said, "Hand me the pitch torch."

Lucianu was wide awake now and screamed as Egidiu dripped hot pitch over the opening and bandaged the wound shut. Esmeray brought the *Aspasia* to full sail, soon catching the mistral wind outside the harbor. They would make for Riposto.

King Charles's soldiers were spread thin trying to deal with the ships aflame and multiple assaults by the patriots. Within hours, the Angevin survivors retreated to Castle Mategriffon with the governor and his family. By morning, Messina was in the hands of the people.

Now the patriots controlled all of Sicily. The Messinese elected Alaimo as captain of the people. He declared the city a free commune and allowed the governor, Herbert of Orleans, and his family safe conduct to Naples, upon his pledge never to return. The mercenaries holding Taormina and Castle Tauro for the Angevins surrendered without a fight and were given pardon. Alaimo sent word to Emperor Michael notifying him that the Sicilians had destroyed King Charles's fleet and sent ambassadors to Pope Martin requesting that he grant the cities of Sicily to be free communes under the protection of the Holy Church, similar to those of Genoa, Venice, and Pisa.

Luciano drove the cart stacked with boxes of pine tar sticks, as his father, uncle, Bastone, and Esmeray walked alongside. A few miles from Linguaglossa, he tapped the donkeys with a goad stick for them to halt. Esmeray petted one donkey, and the other nuzzled her, eager to receive the same affection. Bastone slid a box off the top of the stack. "Are you all right?"

Geoffroi and Anastasia sat in a space hidden among the stack of boxes. "We are fine," said the baron.

Lucianu said, "Bastone, two miles ahead, the road splits. Esmeray and you will take the road to the right to Riposto. We will head north with the cart to *Fiumefreddo*, Cold River, then follow the river to the beach." He glanced from Bastone to Esmeray. "You told me that you anchored where the Fiumefreddo flows into the sea."

They nodded.

"That's where we will meet."

By late afternoon, Geoffroi, Antasia, and Lucianu had joined Esmeray and Bastone aboard the *Aspasia,* sailing toward the Straits of Messina. Esmeray worked the helm. Anastasia kissed Bastone on the cheek. "Thank you, Signore Ponzio."

Geoffroi embraced him. "We are in your debt."

"The people of Linguaglossa speak highly of you, Baron Pons," said Bastone. "And . . . it's the least I can do for a distant cousin."

Geoffroi smiled, then cocked his head, "Where are we going?"

"Eventually we must go to Mallorca, so Lucianu can reunite with his beloved, but in our small trohantiras with five of us, we cannot cross such an expanse of sea. We will sail from island to island, to Vulcano, then Ustica, and, if the weather allows, to Sardinia. There you can find passage on a ship to Provence," said Bastone.

Just less than a week later the *Aspasia* entered the harbor of Cagliari on the southeast coast of Sardinia. The port was under the control of Pisa, an ally of King Charles where Geoffroi and Anastasia would have a good chance to find a ship. Within hours of their arrival, Geoffroi purchased passage on a vessel to Provence. The group had drawn close on their brief journey and the parting was solemn.

Lucianu, Bastone, and Esmeray sailed a few days along the coast of Sardinia and arrived at Alghero, a Genoese controlled port where trading vessels from Genoa called before sailing onto Mallorca. There they hoped to find a ship for Lucianu.

They beached the *Aspasia* close to the harbor. Bastone and Esmeray remained with the boat, Lucianu insisting he needed to walk to help his leg recover, trekking to a nearby tavern on the waterfront to inquire about the destinations of ships in port. He planned to return with water, bread, and pasta. Esmeray and Bastone collected driftwood along the beach to make a fire for their meal. Bastone whittled shavings from a dry stick to make a nest of tinder. Holding the char cloth on top of a piece of obsidian, he struck the sharp edge of the stone with his steel fire starter, producing sparks. "I picked up this obsidian in Vulcano, but it doesn't spark as well as the flint stone I lost." With patience, he created enough sparks to smolder the cloth. He blew carefully, coaxing the embers into tiny flames, which lit the tinder. Esmeray built a pyramid of sticks above the flames, adding larger pieces to boost the campfire, then sat on a remnant of a tree trunk that had washed ashore.

She held her hands toward the fire to warm them. "The fire is comforting. And Bastonino, you'll eat pasta this evening. How did you survive without your pasta!"

He joined her on the log. "You jest, Dolcezza, but you are right—no pasta since Linguaglossa."

Bastone gazed at her. Esmeray laughed. "Thank you for regarding me with respect—even the first time you saw me. Not like most men, whose stares are consumed with lust. It's the reason I was attracted to you. No, perhaps it's those blue eyes!" She laughed and leaned against him, then gave him a quick, joyful kiss.

"I thought all you needed was the sea and the *Aspasia*?" said Bastone.

"I liked our life in Favignana, away from stresses of the world, but then being with you on your quests is exciting, although dangerous."

"You perceived the missions as thrilling? Like the exhilaration of fighting storms at sea?"

She squeezed his arm. "Yes."

"Esmeray, when I was younger, discovering a passion for the sea initially fulfilled me, but I had a longing, a dream, to find a partner to share my love of the sea."

"I recall you saying that—it was on our wedding night, and we were under the sails on the *Aspasia*. I was still doubtful of your honesty, but since then you have proven your sincerity over and over."

After a long, uninterrupted kiss, Bastone took her hand and gently enticed her toward the boat. "Is there time?" said Esmeray.

"Just in time!" Lucianu called out from behind carrying skins of water, wine, and the bailing bucket crammed with food. "I see you have the fire ready. I bought fresh ciciri to cook with the pasta. We'll have *pasta chi ciciri*. I went to the wharves to find hard pasta but could only get penne. Sorry, Bastone, no rigatoni . . . Wait! We don't have a pot to cook the pasta!"

Bastone climbed onto the beached trohantiras, then promptly returned with his helmet half full of seawater. "Here is a suitable container to boil the water."

Lucianu chuckled. "You are getting better at jesting, Bastone."

"Oh, he is serious!" said Esmeray. "Nothing will stop him from his pasta! And I see he prefers the sailor's way, to cook with salt water."

The fire had produced excellent coals, where they balanced the helmet to cook the food. As they savored the pasta chi ciciri, Lucianu said, "I found a way to Mallorca! On the waterfront I met Lancelotto Malocello, a Genoese captain. He has stopped at Alghero for supplies on his way to Africa and will give me passage to Mallorca."

The fire crackled as they ate for a few moments in silence. Lucianu finished and sipped from the wine skin. "Do you remember, over a year ago, when the Vivaldi brothers sailed with us through the straits into the Ocean Sea?"

Bastone cocked his head for a moment. "They thought the Spice Islands could be reached by sailing around Africa, yes?"

Lucianu nodded. "But according to Lancelotto, there has been no word of what happened to the Vivaldis. Lancelotto is married to their sister, and they are sailing to Africa to find her brothers."

Bastone glanced at Esmeray, wondering what her reaction might be, noticing her gaze cast out to the sea.

"Lucianu, we will miss you," said Bastone. "And I just noticed, you got your beard trimmed. Terra will be pleased."

Esmeray's eyes were moist. "When does your ship cast off, Lucianu?"

"It sails the day after tomorrow. And I look forward to my reunion with Terra, but I will miss you both, *mi mbari*. And where are you going? To Genoa?" asked Lucianu.

"No, no," said Bastone. He shook his head, then glanced at Esmeray. "We, um . . . choose to be free of, um, family pressures."

Lucianu shrugged his shoulders.

"Eh, I understand—mother-in-law and daughter-in-law, storm and hail. Where will you go?"

"We will return to Favignana," said Esmeray, half-heartedly, "Where we had a quiet life."

Lucianu grew quiet, his eyes avoiding contact.

Bastone said, "Esme is undecided where she wants to go. She probably would rather explore with Captain Lancelotto, eh, Dolcezza?"

"It's all fine," Esmeray smiled, "We will have time to think in Favignana."

Lucianu's head was down.

"Don't worry, certainly we will see each other again!" said Bastone.

"There is something else," said Lucianu as he looked up, "I heard at the port that King Charles has landed an army in Sicily and has Messina under siege."

## After the revolt of the Sicilian Vespers

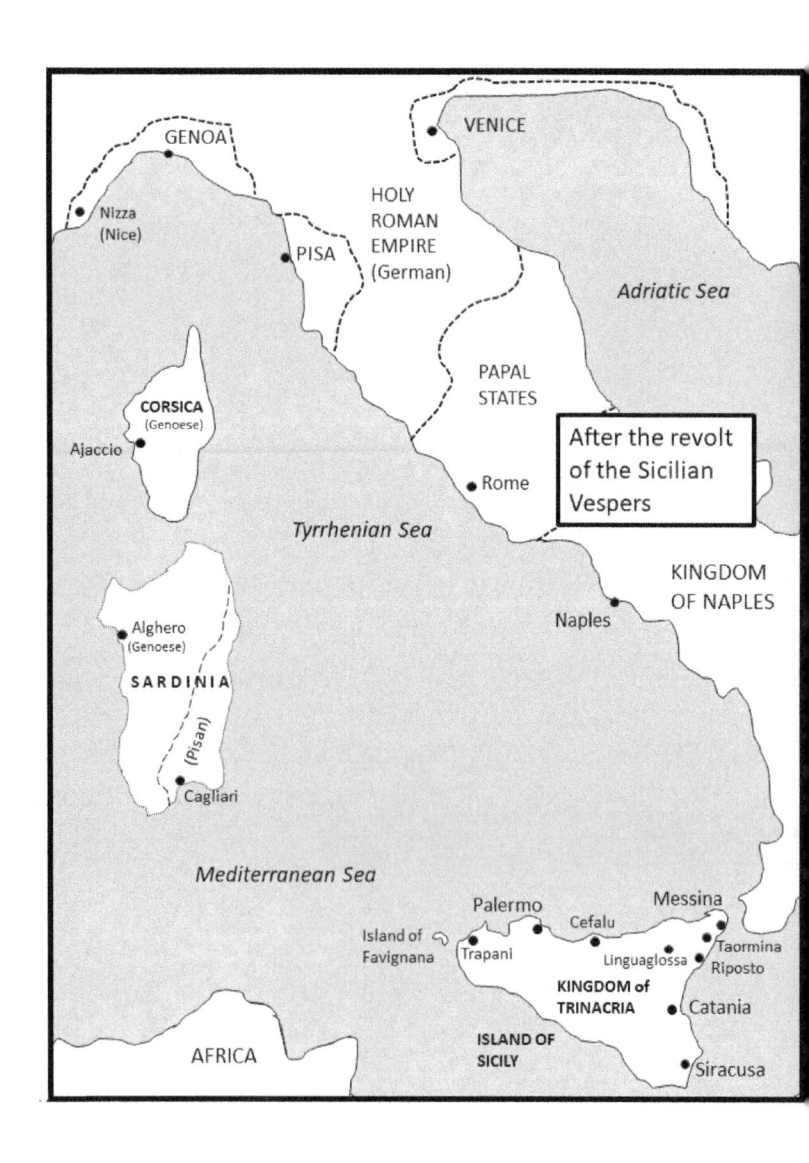

## CHAPTER XXIX     RETURN TO FAVIGNANA

Just before dawn, Esmeray and Bastone accompanied Lucianu to the wharf to see him off to Mallorca. They promised to meet again, although Esmeray was tearful when she and Bastone, who was also somber, returned to the *Aspasia*.

Within an hour, they were sailing south along the Sardinian coast, later stopping overnight at Cagliari to resupply before setting out across the open sea to Favignana. During the two-day crossing, they took turns, one napping while one was at the helm. On the second evening from Cagliari, Bastone slept fitfully, groaning and thrashing in the cabin. Esmeray could hear him through the open door, as he pleaded in Genoese, "We must go back! He will burn Messina! Don't abandon them!"

She shouted, "Bastone, Bastone, wake up!"

He quieted. Within a few minutes, he stuck his head out of the cabin. "What a nightmare!" Still groggy, he joined Esmeray and drank from the waterskin.

"The fresh air will help," said Esmeray. "You were talking in your sleep, your dreams revealing your fears. I know why you are troubled. The siege of Messina compels you to return to Sicily, as if your work has come undone."

He sighed as he tilted his head back and stared at the dark sky. Esmeray continued, one hand on the tiller, keeping tension on the mainline. "You were true and kept your word, succeeding in your role to stop Charles's invasion of Constantinople. His fleet is destroyed. I realize your family's prestige was diminished when you didn't marry the Spinola woman, but you did a greater good. You avenged your brother."

Bastone leaned over and kissed her.

He drank again. "It is up to the Sicilians. This is their chance to control their destiny and be free. Free of foreign control, foreign taxes, foreign domination."

They beached the *Aspasia* on the north shore of Favignana, near the house of Ponziu Petru. He confirmed Messina was under siege, but so far the patriots had repulsed the Angevin troops.

Petru and his family helped them clean the same abandoned cottage where they had lived a year earlier. As they talked while preparing the house, Petru told them they were just in time for the *tonnara*, the annual hunt for bluefin tuna. The schools of the large fish were migrating from the Atlantic to the warmer waters of the Mediterranean to spawn. Since the time of the Arab occupation, the people of Favignana had been conducting the mass fishing event. Knowing Esmeray was a fisher herself and an experienced sailor, he thought she should take part, being one of the few women who had the strength to do the strenuous work. Historically, the women of Favignana only took part in the tonnara by praying to the Madonna to protect their men at sea. Esmeray had been at the brunt of the men's ridicule when she had served on the *Paradisio*, but she had gained their respect and overcome their bias, and was willing to join the *tonnaroti*, the fishermen of the tonnara.

The next day, Petru took Esmeray and Bastone a few miles off the east coast of Favignana, where fishermen from all over the island were readying the huge trap. They had created a large underwater enclosure out of netting. The enclosure was roughly cubical, with a large net anchored to the seabed with heavy stones, nets on three sides extending from the seafloor to the surface, held up by floats, then fastened to the hulls of a flotilla of fishing boats that had gathered at the edges of the chamber. The top and fourth side of the chamber were open. More nets were tied together extending from the open side creating a corridor for a mile in the direction of the tunas' migration path, widening to a funnel shape where the fish entered.

They arrived in time to observe the leader of the tonnara, the *rais*, an Arabic word for chief, bless the event, praying to a statue of Saint Peter. Petru guided his boat to join the rest of the vessels surrounding the capture chamber, fastening the top of the net to his side wale.

The first few tuna had traversed the mile long funnel and arrived at the cubical underwater chamber, butting into the nets, jumping above the surface, trying to escape. Within half an hour, the *chamber of death* was full of the large fish. Divers closed off the open end the tuna had entered and unpinned the bottom net of the chamber from the seabed. Scores of tonnaroti began raising the net from the seabed. It tested the men's strength, requiring them to work in unison. To coordinate the men's efforts, the rais would sing "*Aimola! Aimola!* Oh, my Creator, help us!" A hundred *tonnaroti* answered, shouting "*Aimola, Aimola!*" simultaneously, raising the net, heavy with tuna. The chants were repeated, the men gaining their rhythm, slowly hoisting the tumultuous mass of tuna, packed together, jumping and splashing in frantic mayhem.

Bastone and Esmeray joined the communal struggle. There had been times as a sailor that Esmeray had pulled on lines until her muscles seared with pain, but pulling these heavy-laden nets challenged her stamina and grit. The effort tested Bastone as well. The rhythmic chanting in response to the rais plus the camaraderie of straining shoulder to shoulder drove the fishermen on. Esmeray recalled her work on the *Paradisio*, such as furling sails, that required the collective strength of teams of sailors. Most of the *tonnaroti* were too busy working to notice her, but a few nearby, after brief surprised looks, quickly returned to the hard work. Finally they had raised the mass of writhing tuna to the surface. Tonnaroti used gaffs to hook the tuna. Their bulk required teams of at least five or more fishermen to land the 300 pound fish into the boats. Esmeray clung to the net to hold it in place, her hands like claws, so stiff they would not open. At times, she grabbed the fins of a tuna to help pull the fish over the side wale after *tonnaroti* had raised the fish with gaffs.

Men shouting, fish thrashing—the surface of the pool was a turbulent mass of splashing seawater, blood, and entrails. One huge tuna after another was hooked with gaffs, the teams of men hauling the huge fish into the boats. Gaffs and clubs were used to subdue the tuna as they were pulled up to avoid men being severely injured by the huge flailing fish. The pool of floundering and splashing tuna turned even darker with blood. The frenzy ended when the last tuna had been hauled into the boats.

Carrying on an old tradition, some men jumped into the pool of seawater and blood. Petru, eyes wide, glanced at Esmeray, as if asking if she wanted to be *baptized*, which she declined. He, however, threw himself into the carnage.

With second thoughts, having experienced the rhythm and harmony of the hunt through the singing and hard work with the tonnaroti, Esmeray was compelled to complete her accord with the tonnara, and she plunged into the pool. Dressed as a sailor, no one would have noticed she was female except for the fishermen who had worked beside her. One of them shouted, "*La Madonna*. She has blessed our hunt!"

As she was climbing up the net back into the boat, others saw her, repeating, *"La Madonna e buona fortuna!"*

The tonnara, also called the *mattanza*, slaughter, now over, the flotilla sailed with the bounteous catch to Favignana. On the way back to the island, after the frenzy and adrenaline of the mattanza, Esmeray felt a period of calm, and an immense release from all tensions of the world.

She imagined that Favignana could easily become her new home with Bastone, living a quiet life, but still including the exhilaration of sailing as well as checking their small fish traps. And there would be the annual excitement of the tonnara, although once per year would be enough for Esmeray.

Lantern Across the Sea

## CHAPTER XXX    SIEGE OF MESSINA

The heat of the July afternoon passed as the sun sank behind the mountains to the west of Messina. Sicilian leaders filed into the meeting hall of Castle Mategriffon overlooking the city. Waiting for them to take seats around a large table were Giovanni Procida and Alaimo Lentini, who enjoyed wine together. Procida sipped and allowed the liquid to rest on his tongue for a moment, savoring the richness before he swallowed. His gaze moved beyond the city, across the natural harbor protected by a hook-shaped peninsula. The Greek colonists who had founded the city two thousand years before had named the place *Zancle*, scythe, referring to the shape of the natural breakwater. On the curved spit of land, a lighthouse towered above the adjacent Basilian monastery of San Salvatore. In a few hours, the monks would light the faro, but no ships would be arriving at port to require the beacon. It had been over three months since the people had freed Messina of the Angevins, but now King Charles had returned with a fleet raised in Naples, besieging the city by land and sea.

Patriot reinforcements had slipped into Messina. The Messinese had burst from the city gate with a fierce sortie against the king's land siege, driving the king's army to their ships, but the Angevins had counterattacked and chased the patriots back into the city.

The high-ranking attendees of the council sat around the table, the lesser nobles and populace standing behind them. Alaimo stood with Procida at the end of the table and toasted, "*Animus Tuus Dominus!*"

With raised cups, the crowd answered, "*Antudu!*" The secret passwords had become their rallying cry. Sprinkled among the group were shouts of "Moranu li Francisi!"

Alaimo, the noble who had led the uprising within the city and had been elected as captain of the people for Messina, gestured toward Procida. "You know Doctor Giovanni Procida. He has been fighting against King Charles for years, risking his life to free Sicily."

Murmurs of confirmation and nods were directed at the doctor. Procida remained standing and Alaimo took a seat. Next to him was Palmiero Abate, the Baron of Trapani, who had expelled the French from Palermo. On Procida's immediate left was Gualtiero Caltagirone, who had stormed Messina's walls leading a brigade of patriots. Other nobles were present, but Alaimo had also invited commoners and peasant fighters, considering their presence critical to their decisions today.

Procida surveyed the room. Ciccio Inglese had organized the few English merchants in Messina into a company of fighters. Ponziu Marianu, the butcher from Linguaglossa, displayed his usual smile as he waited for Procida to speak. He had accompanied Caltagirone in the assault but refused to carry a bladed weapon and instead fought with his shepherd's staff. And to the discomfort of a few of the men, the heroines of Messina, Dina and Clarenza, were present.

There was a representative of the Jewish community, whose commerce had been stymied by King Charles's policies. The Jewish merchants had helped finance the revolt. Even the Muslim community was represented. A troop of fighters, descendants of Muslims who had been expelled from Sicily a generation earlier, had slipped through the Angevin blockade. They fought alongside the Messinesi, hoping a change in government would allow them to return to their ancestors' homeland. Thus, the defenders of Messina embodied the culturally rich heritage of the island.

After the sortie from the city had failed to push the Angevins into the sea, Procida was determined to raise morale. "Paesani! King Charles has assaulted the walls thrice and we, the citizens, have repelled them each time! Has he broken us?"

The gathering shouted, "No!"

"Remember the night the French made a surprise attack?"

Nods and grunts scattered across the gathering.

"There!" He pointed to Dina and Clarenza. "They were among the women who guarded the ramparts so our soldiers could rest. They detected the Angevins, those filthy dogs who had not even spared old people, nor women, nor children. While Dina hurled rocks down on the enemy soldiers, Clarenza rushed to the cathedral and rang the bells in the campanile to wake the city, and we repelled the attack.

"The people of Messina will die fighting before submitting to Charles again. Courage is your Lord!"

"*Antudu!*" answered the group.

Procida unfolded the banner of the revolt. "Paesani, the lower field of dark red symbolizes the blood of Sicilian patriots—your blood and the blood of your families that has been shed for our freedom! The top is bright yellow denoting the sunlight that shines on our island to enhance fertility and to guide us."

Inspired by Procida's words, people stood, the Christians crossing themselves. Procida continued, "For all our strength, for all our effort, we need help from other powers." There were grumblings.

Gualtiero Caltagirone shouted, "Sicily's communes are free and must remain free!"

There were affirmations.

A second noble asked, "Will Emperor Michael send us aid?"

Procida gestured to a man standing with others behind the seated nobles. "The Genoese merchant, Alafranco Cassano, went to Constantinople and reported to the emperor that Charles's fleet at Messina has been destroyed. Alafranco, tell us what you learned during your visit."

"The emperor cannot provide any more help. He has already emptied the Roman treasury to finance our revolt. Michael has less than a hundred galleys to defend their empire. King Charles's force now besieging Messina has 75,000 soldiers and 200 ships."

Procida said, "I recommend we appeal to King Peter of Aragon to come to our aid." He had to raise his voice to be heard over the resulting grumbling, "I have thrown in my vote with the three commanders, Abate, Alaimo, and Caltagirone, and the result was three for sending a delegation to King Peter and one against."

During the uproar that followed, few noticed when Caltagirone, head down, barely able to control his anger and grimacing, subtly ground his fist on the table. The raucous grumbling continued. One man called out, "Keep Sicily free." Another shouted, "No foreigners, we'll be trading one oppressor for another!"

Procida held up his hands for quiet. "The Pope will not help us. We sent ambassadors to Rome requesting that the Pope grant us the protection of the Holy Church. It is our misfortune that Pope Martin is French, and instead he has directed us to recognize Charles as our rightful king."

There was angry shouting and Procida again held up his hands for quiet, without success. "Listen! Listen to me! The Pope has excommunicated all Sicilians!"

The hall grew quiet.

Procida held up a parchment. "We have drafted a contract which calls for Peter to guarantee that he will restore the benefits your parents and grandparents had during the rule of William the Good."

After a moment of silence, Alaimo said, looking back and forth to broadcast his voice, "I recall my father telling me, years ago, that he respected King William. The king reduced Messina's taxes, stimulating trade."

Nods and murmurs of acknowledgment came from the representatives of merchant families.

A comment erupted from the group standing: "No foreigners!"

"Remember that King Peter's wife is Constance," said Procida, "the daughter of Manfredi, the last legitimate Sicilian king. I fought in the battle against King Charles when Manfredi lost his life, fighting for Sicily. Constance was born in Catania. Your queen would be a Sicilian."

Abate caught Procida's eye, who nodded. Abate stood. "During William's rule, he continued the religious tolerance of the Norman kings. Christians, Jews, and Muslims co-existed, even shared, each other's cultures, keeping peace among Sicilians and permitting great prosperity. Thus, without overtaxing, Sicilians of different cultures worked freely side by side."

Procida let the people absorb the line of reasoning. A score of anxious conversations broke out, but there were no outbursts of protest. He said, "I will leave immediately for Tunis, where King Peter has already mustered a large fleet."

The council was over, the attendees carrying on lively conversations about what might happen when King Peter arrived.

Hardly anyone noticed when Caltagirone made a hasty exit, not hiding his fury.

Procida was seventy-two yet preparing to undertake another long voyage. He hoped instead to delegate someone for the mission, but there was only one speculatore he trusted enough. He gazed out the window at the Messina lighthouse and spoke to the sea.

"Where is Ponzio Bastone?"

## Lantern Across the Sea

Thank you for purchasing this book. I know you could have picked any number of books to read, but you picked this book and for that I am extremely grateful.

I hope that it added interest, knowledge, and entertainment to your everyday life. If so, it would be appreciated if you could share this book with your friends and family and post comments on Facebook and Twitter.

If you enjoyed this book and found some benefit in reading this, I'd like to hear from you and hope that you could take some time to post a review on Amazon. Your feedback and support will help this author to improve.

I want you, the reader, to know that your review is very important and if you'd like to *leave a review on Amazon, search the book on Amazon Books by its title or my name.*

### Amazon's Michael A. Ponzio Author Page
Amazon.com: Michael A. Ponzio: Books, Biography, Blog, Audiobooks, Kindle

### Michael A Ponzio Author Facebook:
https://www.facebook.com/AncestryNovels/?ref=bookmarks

### Author's Ancestry Novels website:
*History & Historical Fiction: Pontius, Ponzio, Pons, and Ponce*
https://mikemarianoponzio.wixsite.com/pontius-ponzio-pons

## ABOUT THE AUTHOR

Since childhood, Mike Ponzio has read about history, trading books with his father, Joseph E. Ponzio. Mike traveled across the Mediterranean, the locations inspiring him to write *Ancestry Novels*. The stories chronicle the lives of historical characters which the author imagines may have been his family's ancient ancestors.

Mike met his wife, Anne Davis, in 1975 at a University of Florida karate class. Since that time both continue to practice and teach Cuong Nhu Martial Arts. With John Burns, they wrote and published six instructional books on martial arts weapons. Mike retired in 2015, after working as an environmental engineer for thirty-seven years. Anne and Mike have raised four sons, who are also engineering graduates, following in the footsteps of their Davis and Ponzio grandfathers.

**Ancestry Novels by Michael A. Ponzio**
The Ancient Rome Series:
Pontius Aquila: Eagle of the Republic
Pontius Pilatus: Dark Passage to Heaven
Saint Pontianus: Bishop of Rome

The Warriors and Monks Series:
Ramon Pons: Count of Toulouse
1066 Sons of Pons: In the Wake of the Conqueror
Warriors and Monks: Pons, Abbot of Cluny

The Lover of the Sea Series:
Lantern Across the Sea: The Genoese Arbalester

Nonfiction Historical:
Brigadier General Daniel Davis and the War of 1812: The Destiny of the Two Swords

Printed in Great Britain
by Amazon